worship of the common heart

Also by Patricia Henley

Hummingbird House

Back Roads

The Secret of Cartwheels

Friday Night at Silver Star

Learning to Die

worship of the common heart

new and selected stories

PATRICIA HENLEY

MacMurray & Beck
Denver

Copyright © 2000 by Patricia Henley
Published by:
MacMurray & Beck
4101 East Louisiana Avenue, Suite 100
Denver, CO 80246

The short story collections *Friday Night at Silver Star* and
The Secret of Cartwheels were first published by Graywolf Press.

Some of these stories were originally published
in the following periodicals:
*American Fiction 1987, Sycamore Review, Mississippi Valley Review,
Ploughshares, The Atlantic, The Boston Globe Sunday Magazine,
Cropdust, Cross-Canada Writers Quarterly, Northwest Review,
Permafrost, Cutbank, The Missouri Review.*

Printed and bound in the United States of America

1   2   3   4   5   6   7   8   9   10

Library of Congress Cataloging-in-Publication Data
Henley, Patricia.
Worship of the common heart : new & selected stories /
by Patricia Henley.
p. cm.
ISBN 1-878448-02-01
1. West (U.S.)—Social life and customs—Fiction. I. Title.
PS3558.E49633 W6   2000
813'54—dc21   00-041817

MacMurray & Beck Fiction: General Editor, Greg Michalson
Worship of the Common Heart cover design by Laurie Dolphin.
The text was set in Janson by Pro Production, Mahwah, N.J.

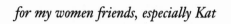

for my women friends, especially Kat

You who knelt on the frozen leaves,
You who know how dark it got under the ice;
You know how hard it was to live
With hatred, how long it took to convert
Death and sadness into beautiful singing.
                    —Gerald Stern, "Singing"

Contents

SUN DAMAGE   1

THE PLEASURE OF PEARS   31

WORSHIP OF THE COMMON HEART   41

THE SECRET OF CARTWHEELS   65

LESSONS IN JOY   85

ACES   105

HARD FEELINGS   123

THE LATE HUNT   145

SLINKERS   157

LABRADOR   173

LOVE YOU CAN'T IMAGINE   213

CARGO   245

SAME OLD BIG MAGIC   259

LET ME CALL YOU SWEETHEART   265

THE BIRTHING   273

VICTORY   293

PICKING TIME   311

FRIDAY NIGHT AT SILVER STAR   329

AS LUCK WOULD HAVE IT   339

Sun Damage

Jack Ransom died on the road.

That was to be expected. The day before Memorial Day, in Bloomington, he went into a coffee shop with another salesman. They ordered pecan pie and ice cream. Jack said he wasn't feeling well and went outside and sat down on the limestone steps and died. A heart attack.

His daughter Meg found out from her brother Vinnie who called her at Chico's in Santa Fe, right in the middle of the big summer sale. She'd tucked the phone between her shoulder and chin and kept on folding pale linen garments.

"Meg, please come. Help me round up Mother," he'd said. Among other things. Specifics about the funeral.

Meg was thirteen years older and she'd left home to live with Aunt Georgia when Vinnie was only three. Vinnie and Meg hardly knew each other. Their father had died and their mother needed rounding up. As though she were feral.

Meg wore dark glasses on the plane. She had not cried yet and expected to at any moment. She expected her eyes eventually to be puffy and tender to the touch. But the tears stalled. Vinnie had mentioned Terre Haute when Meg asked where he thought their mother, Hannah, might be. Terre Haute or the iris farm in Brookston with Jelly Cooke, her friend since high school. Hannah sometimes went out to Brookston for weeks on end and stayed with Jelly, her hands in the dirt during the day, helping out. At night, Vinnie said, she and Jelly went carousing. Meg was sure that was the word he used. That meant cards, no doubt. Hearts. A little gambling. A little gin. They probably dressed up in their clothes from God knows when—dresses from the fifties, with maddening pintucks, tough to iron.

If she were in Terre Haute she'd be harder to find. If people heard you'd come from there they'd say, "How long did it take you to get the smell out of your clothes?" Meg had seen Hannah's feelings get hurt by such remarks. It was a smell both organic and industrial, putrid, persistent, uniform in its delivery. No one in the Wabash Valley was spared. Hannah was born there and had grown up in town, with plenty of silverware and china and linens. Her father owned a watch and clock shop and half the city block on which he lived. Everyone thought Hannah and her brother Dennis would fare even better in the world than their parents, but they hadn't. Hannah married Jack and moved to Tippecanoe County early on and Meg's Uncle Dennis followed them. Dennis had been a mechanic at a meat packing plant and had a little plot of land nearby, close to the slatternly village of Webber, and on that plot of land he grew a truck garden and sold strawberries and cucumbers and watermelons on muggy summer nights at a stand beside the road. He did not have a wife. Though later

Meg had heard that he married a woman who raised sheep and sold the wool to local weavers. The wife had died young. In her fifties.

All of that happened while Meg was moving. She moved for twenty years, it seemed. She followed Neil Diamond on tour for a year, obsessed with him; she could certainly see that now, what a brainless period that was. She worked in a logging camp in the North Cascades. She waited tables in Santa Cruz. She'd thought of herself as unencumbered, spontaneous. She'd changed her first name twice, to Heather and then to Laverna, Roman goddess of thieves, wanting first to be earthy, then neo-pagan. Though now she liked the sound of Meg. Margaret Mae Ransom. In business it helped to have a solid name. Her family had always been business people and she'd come to it late, but she loved it. During that time of moving around, she'd lived in apartments and houses with other women and sometimes she would have a man, sometimes two men, she'd be seeing and sleeping with. In those days if she had a date, a night's worth of tips, a new dress or haircut, she was happy. It had not taken much. And the stories she heard about Uncle Dennis, and yes, even the stories she heard about her mother and father, from Vinnie and from letters Hannah wrote, those seemed like only stories, events in lives unconnected to hers.

When Aunt Georgia died and left Meg a very, very small fortune—that was the way she always told the story—she moved to Santa Fe and invested in Chico's. She was settled. She lived alone. Her life was about order now. Getting up at six o'clock to meditate. Making sure the books were meticulously kept. Friends you could count on for a walk or a dinner. She rarely drank. She did not own a television. That sort of life. Her vices, if you could call them that, were clothes and an abiding interest in sex. She'd grown up Catholic and still went to Mass on Christmas Eve, for the spectacle of it. But she and the Pope did not see eye to eye on birth control.

Jack had seldom written. Once in awhile, after Hannah and he were no longer living together, he'd send Meg a blank card, a generic card of a lace-and-roses still life, with a short message—*Happy Birthday, Baby,* or *Treat yourself*—and he'd send a check for twenty-five dollars or fifty dollars. Meg always let Jack know where she was and she always let Hannah know where she was. That was the best she could do.

She'd never been a good daughter.

"What'd you say?" The little woman next to her on the plane was speaking, an apple-shaped woman with opulent gray hair.

Meg said, "I beg your pardon?" She realized she must've said, out loud, "I've never been a good daughter."

"I thought you were speaking to me," the woman said. "Oh, look—"

Meg turned to the window.

"—we're almost down!"

There was Indy: neat, flat, easy. She picked out Speedway, a place she'd never been. And the White River, where she'd spent many an evening parked in this one's car or that. Panting. Giving an inch. The inch Hannah always warned her against.

She sighed at the thought of all she had to traverse: renting a car, the hour on the interstate, then the little back roads and one lane bridges. How much do you owe your blood relatives? This was a question that had burrowed into her like a tap root all day.

The woman in the next seat plucked a lipstick from her bag and applied it without a mirror. Lipstick as violet as vetch. Then she got out a pack of cigarettes and held them in one brown paw, done with Meg, done with the flight, eager for a smoke.

And Meg thought, Here we go. With a reluctant heart.

Vinnie let her into the house on Bicycle Bridge Road six miles out of Delphi. He still lived there, he and Jack. She had not seen Vinnie since he'd come to Santa Fe three years before. He was handsome, animated in a boyish way, with grins that would slip out as though he were shy. He wore baggy chinos and polo shirts in candy colors. He smelled the way young men smelled—like new clothes and some woodsy soap they used.

"It's kind of hard being here alone," he said. "I'm glad you're here."

He fed her couscous and broccoli and peppered feta cheese, the whole mound in a pasta dish, drizzled with olive oil. He gave her white wine to drink in a glass Meg knew belonged to Hannah. A wine glass etched with sunflowers. She drank the wine gratefully; what would it hurt? Their father had died and a glass of wine seemed ritualistic, a sign that life went on, a token of honor. Rain began to fall. Hard, necessary rain for the end of May. Clouds out the kitchen window bunched up, malevolent, bruisers. The wisteria tossed in the wind, its tendrils flying like a dancer's hair. They talked while the lights flickered. Jack had not been ill, far from it. He'd been talking about retiring. He'd been talking about moving to Naples. For the beach. "He'd gotten into a beach fantasy,"

Vinnie said. Vinnie had been looking forward to remodeling the house when Jack moved to Naples. He had been thinking of skylights, a second bathroom, a wood-fired hot tub under the sycamore tree. Modernization. A house built for a young man's pleasure. Vinnie worked for a contractor who built one-of-a-kind custom homes and he knew what to do. With the weak floor joists and the old chimney and the worn-out plumbing and the austere kitchen with its aluminum cupboards.

Meg said, "We're all more prosperous now, aren't we?"

Vinnie folded his arms and began to cry. The thunder was so loud, Meg didn't notice at first. She'd bent to undo her sandals. When she looked up, Vinnie's face was squeezed into grief. Meg felt a push—do something, comfort him. But she felt stuck to her chair. They had been close on occasion—they'd hugged good-bye, hello, and two-stepped self-consciously in a crowd when he'd visited. But she had not held him, for comfort, since he'd fallen and cut his upper lip on the edge of a coffee table. There had been stitches at the emergency room. And Meg, fifteen, had rocked him to sleep after. Some Sarah Vaughn on the hi-fi.

She touched his arm.

Vinnie took a handkerchief—a folded, tidy square—out of his back pocket and pressed it against his cheeks. "I'm okay," he said.

Meg nodded. "Okay."

Thunder rolled away from them. Meg stood at the kitchen window over the sink. All plants—maple leaves, old lilacs, mock orange, grasses—shimmered in the wind and rain gloss. The green was deep. In Santa Fe you could forget that such tiers of green existed.

The phone rang. Vinnie ran a hand through his hair and answered it.

"Dennis," he said. "She's here. Yeah. We just ate. I'll put her on."

Meg shook her head, No, no. But it was too late. The beige receiver was in her hand, against her ear, and Dennis was saying, "How's tricks? Sorry you had to come back for this. Helluva thing."

"Uncle Dennis. How are you?"

He said, "I jog to keep my ticker tickin'. I'm almost seventy. Did you know that? And I've got a girlfriend—she's nearly eighty-four. She can dance like you wouldn't believe. We go to all the dances."

"That's good," Meg said. She pointed to her wine glass and Vinnie passed it to her. "We'll see you at the funeral home, I guess."

"I called to tell you where Hannah's at."

"Where is she?"

"Someone saw her at the Legion last night. Dressed fit to kill. She's a clothes horse still. Like you. So I've heard." He lowered his voice. "She's got something going with Leroy at the hardware on the 52 bypass."

"I thought you were going to tell me where she is right now."

"I'm getting to that." He chuckled, an old-mannish accompaniment to gossip. Meg realized that gossip had been mostly weeded out of her life. Whatever her faults, she had changed that much.

Meg shoved the phone at Vinnie, her hand over the receiver. "I can't talk to him," she said. "I just can't. Just yet."

And when he hung up, Meg said, "You're too good for this place, Vinnie."

Meg remembered a prowler, a season of fear, when she tried to piece together how Jack and Hannah had separated. This is what Vinnie wanted to hear about in her rental car, driving over to Battle Ground where Hannah had last been seen at RC's, a steakhouse.

"I think it started with that prowler. I was twelve or thirteen."

She'd been doing something she shouldn't have been—primping—when her mother came to her bedroom door and said, "I think there's a prowler outside." Then Hannah had shut off the overhead light in Meg's bedroom. It was nearly eight o'clock on a November night. The nearest neighbor was a quarter mile away. Vinnie was in his crib sound asleep. Jack Ransom was as usual on the road somewhere in central Illinois or Indiana, though by that time of night, Meg imagined, he was standing at a bar. Sometimes while Hannah was in the bathroom, Meg would sneakily read the letters he'd written to her mother. *I believe I'll head down to the hotel bar for a nightcap, Sweetie pie.* She liked the words he used: nightcap, sweetie pie, severe weather, profit, long-range, Democrats. Her mother would never say sweetie pie.

"What should we do?" Meg whispered. She set down her mascara in its little red box, without a sound, as if the prowler could be disturbed by the slightest noise. Mascara seemed trivial then, though when the nuns warned all the seventh grade girls against primping, mascara took on the properties of magic, tool of sinners.

Wind like an old bedsheet wrapped around the house.

She had never before that moment thought that her mother could be afraid in their own home. She thought of Hannah as pretty, bossy, and fearless. The summer before, she had killed a black snake they found in the bathtub, chopped him in two with a hoe.

"Come into the kitchen," Hannah whispered. She wore a chintz kimono and yellow scuffs and her face had been scrubbed pink.

Soundlessly they crept through the dining room; every room was dark; Meg was keenly aware that all of the windows but hers had no curtains. Her breastbone felt pummeled by her heart. Light, we need plenty of light in this old house. Hannah had taken down the curtains the summer before and never put them up again. Meg insisted upon privacy—brown paper blinds, and over those, opaque vinyl drapes from the Woolworth. What you could see outside the other windows of the house, the curtainless windows, what the eye chose to settle on, depended on the season: waves of snow, gray or gleaming; redbud trees in pointillist splendor; black-eyed Susans branching taller and taller; or a maple blazing with turning leaves. Or the dark, country dark, night like a dark broth.

Meg sat down at the kitchen table. She could smell fried potatoes. And scouring powder. Hannah went to the back door and checked the lock, snapping it open and closed. She carried the black telephone from its niche in the wall to the table; the cord just barely reached. She dialed the number of the sheriff's office. It was busy.

They sat there for a quarter hour or more. The silence outside pressed against them and they pressed back, whispering of inconsequential things, shoes polished or not, a hole in one of the baby's mittens, the way Meg's pajamas hit her at the shin. An inordinate amount of time and energy went to the organizing of, the maintaining of, clothing. Hannah was a great proponent of mending. Meg thought that the other girls felt sorry for her because she only had one pair of shoes for school and one pair for Sunday Mass. Saddle oxfords and cream-colored flats. But she had lipsticks galore, greasy ones, handed down from a second cousin in Indianapolis. The same cousin stored her old prom gowns in a cedar closet, gowns Meg hoped to wear someday: velveteen and nylon net, rhinestones and bows.

Meg's teeth chattered. Wavelets of heat slipped through the radiator from the coal furnace in the basement. Hannah dialed up the sheriff's office every few minutes. The line was always busy.

"Times like this," Hannah said, "you need a man around the house."

Stories of men escaping from prison edged into Meg's mind. Stories of demented fellows who'd never been taught the Golden Rule.

"What would a man do?" Meg said.

"He'd open the door and pitch a fit. He'd have a gun, no doubt."

"Like Uncle Dennis."

Hannah made a sour face; Meg could tell that in the dark. "Don't hold your breath," Hannah said.

Truck headlights, like luminous ropes, swung into the driveway. A man was heard whistling—I'm walkin' the floor over you—and a truck door slammed.

Hannah went to the window and stood on tiptoe, peering out. "It's him," she said, a little irritated. Meg let out a big sigh. They heard Uncle Dennis crunching over the snow toward the house.

Hannah let him in and the cold came in with him. He was dressed in a plaid wool coat, boots with thick lug soles, and a hat trimmed in fox fur; Meg had a hard time telling his reddish hair and moustache from the fur.

Uncle Dennis said, "There's a peeping tom about. I came to check on you."

"You needn't've," Hannah said. "We're locked up tight and fine."

When Jack Ransom came home for Thanksgiving, he installed a floodlight over the kitchen door.

Everyone had rules and Meg Ransom learned them quickly, rather than risk getting a slap or the switch. When she'd grown up and left the house on Bicycle Bridge Road, Meg thought her mother's rules quite odd. But you don't know that when you're young; you imagine everyone lives as you do. Finding out that they don't is one of the best or worst discoveries of childhood. Hannah Ransom did not allow Meg to stare out the windows during lightning storms. She did not allow her to walk near people operating gasoline or electric lawn mowers. She did not allow her to watch television. And she did not allow her to cross the railroad tracks into the lanes of Webber, a batch of leaning shotgun houses encircled by a muddy creek, the railroad tracks, and a sea of soybeans. The houses were painted Easter egg colors and trash drifted in the plain dirt yards among the autos up on cinder blocks and the broken iceboxes. There was reputedly what polite people called a sporting house in Webber's inner region, beyond the prying eyes.

Jack Ransom sold sewing and yard goods gadgetry to fabric shops. He drove a black Nash that was nearly always coated with brown mud or dust or a film of road salt. The back seat was a jumble of yardsticks and pincushions shaped like tomatoes and wooden embroidery hoops and measuring meters, black boxes you could attach to a table for measuring out yard goods. His suit was brown worsted wool and too tight across his hips; he was heavier than when he'd bought it in 1955, and he could no longer button the jacket. But his shirts were nice. He had seven white ones and when he came home, every two weeks, Hannah washed them and starched the cuffs and collars and plackets and ironed and hung them on individual hangers in a canvas garment bag. He'd make the shirts last until he came home again.

Hannah had married Jack when she was twenty-three, against her parents' wishes, right after she'd come home from Wright-Patterson where she'd been a WAC until 1946. Her mother and father had not approved of her war effort. They had hoped she'd still be a girl when the war was over, that she'd move back in with them and wait demurely for the right man to come along. But Hannah met Jack on the train that brought her back home from Dayton, Ohio. Him still in his Navy uniform. Once Meg had said, Why did you marry Dad anyway, Mama? And Hannah had said, He blessed me whenever I sneezed.

By the time Vinnie was born Hannah had given up for herself, but she still thought her children might have a better life. She could imagine it, blurrily. On a knick-knack shelf above the kitchen stove Hannah kept a ceramic vase she had made in high school. It was glazed midnight blue and had been built using the coil method. The vase was not handsome, Meg knew that for sure, but her mother could look at it and imagine a flute concerto. The ugly blue vase was Hannah's idol, Meg thought, and her reason for sending her to Catholic school and saving to buy a second-hand upright piano and not allowing her to play in Webber, where the children bathed only once a week. And smoked. And performed other unspoken secret acts that made their eyes glitter in shame and slyness on the school bus.

If there was gossip, Hannah attributed it to the Pentecostals whose house was situated in the middle of a cornfield. She was sure they kept a close watch on her—a married woman left alone, always suspect—and all that happened on their road. Meg rode the school bus with their boy, Glenn, a thin scowling junior who attended the consolidated high school and defiantly slicked his blonde hair into a duck's tail. He worked for Uncle Dennis, tilling and planting and picking. From her own bedroom Meg could see the light in what she thought was his bedroom, a yellow pinprick in the winter night. On the bus she smiled at him suggestively. Later, alone, she'd wonder what made her do it. But she wanted him. Hannah would say, "Stay away from him. He's not what he's cracked up to be."

Meg said to Vinnie, "Whatever happened to him—you know, Glenn—who lived down the road?" Her mouth had dried out from the wine. They crossed a bridge over the muddy Wabash.

Vinnie said, "He's around. He went in the war—Vietnam—and he came back and married a woman who'd never cut her hair. Her Dad gave them a piece of land. I think they grow cut flowers and tomatoes and sell 'em at the farmer's market."

"That can't be all they do."

"He works at Subaru, I think."

"How do you know?"

"Osmosis," Vinnie said.

Dusk had always signaled a calm solitude, a comfort to Meg and Hannah. But after the prowler incident, because his identity had never been ferreted out or revealed, they were watchful and on-edge. Rex Pratchett delivered diapers at just that time of day after the Christmas holidays. He was youngish, tall—tall enough that he hunched over from the neck down like an ungainly bird when he spoke with women and children—and his hair curled on his neck, the necessity of a haircut forgotten. He had the habit of petting his moustache with his thumb and forefinger, as if to make certain he still had it. He carried a key ring of five-inch long safety pins, and twice a week he came to truck away the soiled diapers and bring bundles of snowy clean ones. He took his time with everything, lingering, Hannah said, because he liked the air in the country. On his ring finger he wore a flat gold band. At first he and Hannah would stand in the darkening kitchen, Rex beside the pie safe, leaning on the doorframe, as though to say, I'm really on my way out, and Hannah, with a dishrag in her hand near the sink, the big oak table between them. She did not turn on the light. They would talk for ten or fifteen minutes. He had a kind voice.

As the days lengthened, so too their conversations.

In March, while washing baby bottles at the sink, Hannah said to Meg, "When the diaper man comes, stay in the room, would you, please?"

"What for?" Meg said.

"Just read or whatnot," Hannah said, "but stay in the kitchen with us."

Meg sighed.

"Young lady—"

"Oh, all right," Meg said, gritting her teeth. And she began the habit of reading her library books, or pretending to, when Rex Pratchett and Hannah talked.

Rex would sit at the table, with his chair turned sideways and his hands on his knees. A formal pose. Hannah continued to stand, though before he arrived she would brush her hair—just a quick, jabbing stroke or two—and she would put on a gold cross pendant that slipped perilously between her breasts. You would never notice Hannah's modest neckline of her modest blouse if not for that cross. They would drink wine from Hannah's good glasses.

Meg's interest in their talk would ebb and flow, though she always feigned indifference. Once Hannah showed Rex a photograph of Uncle Dennis in his war uniform. His cheeks had been tinted in an unnatural way. Handsome. Though some might say handsome is as handsome does. He was a prince. When I was a girl. When I was a girl, Meg would repeat to

15

herself. She tried to picture Hannah as a girl. A town girl in white cotton gloves, a proper girl who did not pit herself against her mother—that's how Meg imagined her.

She read and daydreamed while Hannah talked with Rex. She only vaguely recognized the steps they took, confessing bit by bit. They were getting down to something, excavating delicately.

On the first official day of spring—a day windy and cool, with the sun still wintry and pale overhead—Meg held her books on the schoolbus and stared out the window at the greening countryside. Glenn sat down beside her, in a tattersall shirt and a windbreaker. He wore English Leather. They sold it at the Woolworth in Lafayette. Meg wondered what his Pentecostal mother thought of that.

"I'm workin' for your uncle now," he said.

"It's planting time, isn't it?" She thought she sounded like Hannah.

"Not quite. We're gettin' organized. Diggin' in some manure."

She did not think he would say manure to Uncle Dennis. It would be shit plain and simple and she took that as a good sign, a sign of respect. Everyone said it was important for a boy to respect you. He stared straight ahead, up the road.

"I work there after school," he said, "though your uncle ain't home 'til dark."

These words rooted in Meg.

Two days later she said to Hannah, "I'm going for a bike ride."

"In this weather?"

"It's not so bad."

The blustery sky was softly gray, like a mourning dove's chest.

"The diaper man's coming," Hannah said.

Meg waited.

"Don't go today, Meg," she said. "I'm making brownies and I need you here to tend to Vinnie if he wakes up."

Meg sighed. "When can I go?" she said.

"When the weather improves there'll be plenty of time for that."

"I'm not a baby."

Hannah silenced her with a look. There was and always had been a rule about back talk. You did as you were told. The body remembers pain. When Hannah gave Meg that look, Meg could feel a tingling across her face—ghost of Hannah's palm.

She picked up her homework, a list of spelling words to memorize: gender, genre, gelatinous. She sat beside the telephone niche and wrote the words over and over, using a clipboard to keep her paper straight. And Glenn. Glenn. Glenn. She wrote that while Hannah and Rex talked. My brother too. All dressed up with no place to go. Torment. Foxtrots. No, waltzes. There were times like that. Ellen was my high school sweetheart. I never—

"Who's Ellen?" Meg once said, when Rex had gone.

"Ellen's his wife," Hannah said. "His little wife."

When Jack Ransom next came home, Hannah said, "I want to have a Sunday dinner, with company."

"What company?" Jack said. He was sitting at the kitchen table in his undershirt. A ledger was open before him, a glass of whiskey near his hand. It was a warm day. Hannah had opened all the windows and breezes blew throughout the house.

"A couple. Rex and Ellen. They're driving out, looking for a place in the country. We rarely get to do that, Jack. You being gone and all."

"All right," Jack Ransom said. "I'll have to leave in the evening. You mean a mid-day dinner, don't you? After Mass?"

"After Mass. Yes."

And so it was arranged. Rex and Ellen would come to Sunday dinner the next time Jack was home. Hannah went about her preparations. The tile floors were swept and scrubbed, the corners scraped with an old paring knife. Rugs were hung on the clothesline and beaten. The furniture was given a coat of beeswax and oil that smelled like oranges. Linens were mended. The house felt like Christmas. And just as at Christmas, Meg was set free by her mother's preoccupations. Hannah flew about the house, her dark hair pulled into a pony tail, slamming drawers, vacuuming, straightening. The hi-fi would be on: Mendelssohn, music sweet enough to make Hannah cry.

On the Wednesday before the Sunday dinner, after school, Meg said, "Just a short ride, that's all I want."

Hannah looked at the clock. She said, "Rex'll be here soon. You come back—hear? Come back in half an hour."

"Yes, Mother," Meg said, feeling her heart move, like a hand opening.

She wheeled her blue bicycle down to the end of the driveway. It was still cool and a wind blew up from the river. But she did not want to go back for a sweater. She wore blue jeans rolled up at the bottom and bobby socks and saddle oxfords and a white blouse. She pulled a tiny round mirror and a lipstick from her pocket. She stood beside her bicycle and ducked close to the mirror and painted on the lipstick called Sugar 'n Spice. The thought of going to confession entered her mind, but she pushed that thought away. She hid the mirror and lipstick in among a clump of daffodils and took off flying at breakneck speed down the road. Goosebumps rose all over her body.

At her uncle's trailer she let her bicycle fall to the ground. Big clouds brewed above her. Glenn's bicycle was there, outside the greenhouse. She went to the door. He knelt beside a flat of strawberry seedlings. His fingers were muddy.

"Meg," he said, surprised to see her. "What you up to?"

She stepped into the greenhouse and it was warm inside and humid and smelled of dirt and foliage. The opaque glass of the walls made her feel protected.

"Is my Uncle here?" she said.

"He don't come until dark."

Doesn't, she thought. Then she said, "Can I watch you?"

He grinned. "Sure. You c'n help me."

He showed her how to prick out seedlings and plant them from a flat into peat pots, how to hold each seedling from the bottom leaves, the ones that come first from the seed. "Try to not ever touch the roots," he said. "They're fragile." He pronounced it fra-gile. Meg hadn't known he could be gentle.

They stood side by side at the counter. "Why do you have that stuff on your mouth?" Glenn said.

"I like it," she said.

"You look better without it."

She wiped her mouth with her forearm and a rosy smear came off.

He had a practiced hand; he turned her around and kissed her, leaving muddy fingerprints on her blouse. She kissed him back; she hadn't known she knew how.

"Here," he said, turning on the hose at his feet, "let's wash our hands."

She did as he said. Their hands bumped under the silvery stream of water. She wiped her cold wet hands on her blue jeans.

"I know a place we can go. He won't be back for a bit." He lifted a folded tarp from a shelf and took her hand.

Outside the sky darkened with the storm. Wind blew hard and velvety topsoil was swept away from the newly tilled field. The kerosene lamps of Webber were being lit. She had never been so close to Webber at dark. She wondered what the people there were doing. He led her to the steps of the trailer her uncle lived in. Uncle Dennis had set the trailer on a knoll and the steps to the porch were steep. It was underneath the steps he was leading her, through a small opening in the canes of the rambling rose.

He went under and spread the tarp on the ground while she shivered and watched the sky. He said, "Hurry up. It's okay."

Meg crawled under the porch. A rose thorn scratched her arm. Tears sprang into her eyes. Under the porch was dim, cobwebby. He kissed her scratch, to make it better, he said. He pinned her down and lay on top of her. A rock or walnut shell poked into her back. He kissed her face, stickily. He licked her face. Thunder clapped; it sounded as though it came from the river. He pressed the part she had always wondered about against her. He took it out and said, Please, please—

She touched him. She felt as though she were in a scientific experiment. Her fingers icy. That part of him candent. She wondered, Did all of his body heat come from there? She said, "I'm not fourteen."

"I won't hurt you," he said.

"My mother's wondering where I am," she said.

"Your mother has her delivery man," he said.

She jerked her hand away. "What're you talking about?"

He leaned back on his elbows, looked away arrogantly. "My ma says she don't miss a trick." He gripped her wrist. "Please—"

"I've got to go home," she said, scrambling away from him. "Let me out."

She crawled out between the canes. Uncle Dennis' truck pulled into the driveway. He laughed when he saw her. He got out of the truck and clomped up to the porch. Glenn came out from under the porch; he hung his head sheepishly and busied himself with folding the tarp. A wave of hail rattled down on them. The lamp in the greenhouse was on—yellow against the skillet-black night. The trees, the trailer, the drive, the clouds and sky—all were blackening with the storm. Tree limbs whipped around. Rain began to fall in cold needles.

"What a sight you are," Uncle Dennis said. He gave Glenn a shove between his shoulder blades. "Gîte home," he growled. "I'll deal with you tomorrow."

Glenn slid the tarp onto the porch, got on his bicycle and pedaled away.

"Go inside now," Uncle Dennis said. Though he told her what to do, Meg could feel the coax in his voice, something he didn't quite have control over, something almost fine-spoken.

"I want to go home," she said.

"Can't you see it's fixin' to storm bad? There's a tornado warning, girl."

Uncle Dennis held her hand and led her inside the trailer. His hand was big, big as a catcher's mitt, with every fingernail outlined with grease. He turned on a lamp and turned on the electric heat. He took a brown quart bottle of beer from the refrigerator. Sterling Beer. He sat down at the table and poured a glass and rolled a cigarette. But he didn't light it. Meg stood in the tiny trailer kitchen, her arms around herself, staring out the window. She shuddered with the cold. Her bicycle was out in the rain and she did not like that. She spied a stack of movie magazines.

"I saved those for you," Uncle Dennis said. Then, "Call your mother. She'll be worried sick."

Meg picked up the receiver and dialed her own number.

She spoke to Hannah haltingly. Hannah asked to speak to Uncle Dennis.

"I'll take care of her," he said. "Now don't you worry none. Storm's over, I'll bring her home." He met Meg's eyes. She looked away. "Hold your horses, Hannah. I said don't worry."

He hung up. The trailer creaked in the wind. He turned on the radio and the radio announcer was tracking the storm.

He said, "Cat got your tongue?"

She stared at his row of blooming African violets. He was a man with violets. This way of seeing him brought up buffeting half-formed thoughts: embarrassed denials, tender urges. She had never thought of him as a man before. With her back to him she said, "Can I look at those magazines?"

"We better both clean up first."

At the sink he took off his workshirt and scrubbed his hands and arms with Lava soap. His back was winter-white and muscular. He said, "Whyn't you clean up? In there—" He nodded toward the little bathroom. "I guarantee your mama's gone treat you better if you clean up. I know her pretty well."

Meg went into the bathroom and shut the door. His shaving things were on a shelf above the little basin, a silver razor, a brush, an Old Spice lather mug. She held her breath, thinking she did not want to be in her Uncle's bathroom or smell his smells. But when she inhaled, there was no foreign odor. She washed her face and arms and combed her hair with his black pocket comb. Her face looked different. She was certain she was the only girl in her seventh grade class to have been kissed. To have touched a boy's privates. It was all she had been warned against. She took off her blouse and tried to wash out the mud prints. Her cotton brassiere wrinkled where she did not fill it.

Uncle Dennis knocked on the door. She opened it brazenly.

"Next time you're all dressed up with no place to go," he said, "come visit your Uncle Dennis."

There was a hint of gratitude in his voice, an emotional pitch she'd never heard before. Something she realized she might deserve. "Take me home," Meg said.

"After the storm," he said. He touched her shoulder. His fingers felt like sandpaper. Then he shut the door.

At home, Hannah beat her with a wooden spoon. The baby stood up in his playpen and screamed bloody murder. His diaper was falling down. Hannah chased Meg from room to room and beat her with the spoon. She knocked her down on the kitchen floor and Meg tried to protect herself by curling up like a baby, but Hannah did not stop. Hannah's hair was loose and tangled and she squealed and Meg could see into her mouth, her big teeth stained with coffee. Hannah cried and swore. She swore with words Meg had never heard or read in books.

She brayed, "He'll never come back. You left me here, you left me, you left me here. With him. And what were you doing—don't you know he's not to be trusted? Don't you know? What were you up to? I suppose I can't let you out of my sight now. I can't let you out of my sight." She paddled her with it and when the wooden spoon broke, she slapped Meg's face, each cheek.

Meg crouched and sobbed underneath the oak table. Hannah sat down on a chair, her knees splayed wide, hanging her head. The kitchen light shined on her nose where she'd hastily smeared the wrong color face powder and left an orangish streak. She whispered, "Get away from me."

Meg had picked herself up and slipped into her room and slumped down on the bed, dirty as she was. She could be alone there with the dream of pleasure: please, please, the baby skin of it.

Secrets she knew how to keep. Some parts she'd keep from Vinnie. Memory serves us in ways that allow us to go on with a little dignity. She could stand to recall everything. But there was no sense telling everything. At some point what you told became only gossip on yourself, stirring up old trouble. And no good can come from that.

She had known without doubt that, given the chance, she would go back there again and again.

It was dark by the time Vinnie and Meg pulled into Battle Ground and turned down the pocked narrow road that ran along the railroad tracks. RC's parking lot was full. She parked across the road in a stand of fireweed. They sat in the car for a minute, steeling themselves.

"How come you didn't ask me all this before?"

Vinnie said, "Jack didn't want me to. Oh, he didn't come right out with it. But I got the drift."

Meg said, "How often do you see Hannah?"

"Pretty often."

"That's good. I guess," she said.

"I wish I could see you more often."

In a soft voice, Meg said, "Is that so?" Then, "I wonder how they fit so many people in there?"

"Let's check it out." Vinnie got out and opened her door for her. The rain had faded away and killer mosquitos swarmed to their flesh, lighting, biting.

The ceiling was low in RC's, the room smoky blue. A jukebox played: honky-tonk. Diners were crammed at little Formica tables spread with slabs of meat, bowls of slaw, glass pitchers of iced tea and beer. The walls seemed brown with the fumes of grilled steak, the accumulation of decades.

"That smell," Meg said, "makes me hungry."

"That's why we conquered the West," Vinnie said, coming close to her ear to speak, nearly pecking her ear. "Look. At the bar."

At the bar in the back of RC's perched Hannah, a wad of tissue in one fist. Her print dress seemed trendy, definitely too young for her, Meg determined. Not at all the way she had expected to find her. At that moment she realized, a little spitefully, Of course, Hannah would have moved on fashion-wise, that's what Hannah did best. Meg was afraid she might say exactly what she was thinking. Not a good policy. Strangely, she remembered a friend telling her about his trip to New Zealand, how every day he would see people on the street with scars from sun cancer. No more ozone down there, he said. Hannah's hair had been shaped by someone expert: a shiny black-from-a-bottle hood, stacked in the back. Her hair swung cheerily when she turned to them. She punched out her cigarette in an ashtray. She'd been crying.

"Jelly, Jelly," she squeaked. "Look who's here." And Hannah came rushing toward them, nearly colliding with the waitress who had a tray aloft, her midriff bare and sloppy below a spangly bustier.

"Mother." Vinnie spoke first.

Hannah hugged Meg and Hannah smelled good, a capsule of well-groomed female odors in the midst of the stale beer and steak and grease. Hannah reared back and stared into Meg's eyes. The hair on Meg's head prickled in memory of hurt. Music jarred them, a ballad ballooning from the jukebox, and the three of them managed to move haltingly to the bar where Jelly in her big woman's one-size T-shirt and tights, her her voice rough, tried to greet them, tried and managed to express her complicity in their grief about Jack, without Meg really understanding anything that was said. The music was too loud. Jelly pushed a big box of tissues toward Meg.

"I have to find the bathroom," Meg said to Hannah. Hannah pointed her in the right direction.

The bathroom was tiny. In there, no one had scraped the corners with a paring knife for a long time. Maybe never. A chrome condom machine hung on the wall across from the mirror. Meg washed her hands, combed her hair, put on hand lotion. The sun can kill you now. She thought about all the times she had lain in the sun without a care, the way the sun made her flesh iridescent brown so that she herself liked touching it, smoothing on lotion, so that a man might want to do the same. Long touches. Gin days. Beaches without a worry. The glory of all that. She still thought of it as glory. Those were her twenties. Jack would never know the beach. She thought of him in his hotel rooms in all those strange towns. The scant bars of hard soap. The way you had to go out for the merest consolation, a cup of coffee or a newspaper. That's when she cried. Niggardly tears. Sweetie pie. He'd always called her sweetie pie. But there was always so much he didn't know.

Outside, the lightning bugs lit up.

Vinnie and Meg and their mother stood outside RC's while an Amtrak train went by on its way to Chicago. It was the first time they'd stood on the same ground in a long time. Someone had died. Someone connected to them. A black waiter listed on the steps of a dining car, smoking a cigar. Meg slipped her arm through Vinnie's, squeezed his hand. Hannah said something, her mouth open, darker than the dark, but the train was grinding by. When the train had passed, Hannah gingerly leaned toward Meg and said, "Don't be afraid of me, Meg."

Hannah had lived with Jack for three more years after Rex was in their lives. She waited until her parents passed away and left her money. Money can change everything, not only the way you meet your obligations, but the very nature of those obligations. Meg had gone to Aunt Georgia's and Jack hired a housekeeper to come in and care for Vinnie. Hannah moved to town, first to Delphi, then to Lafayette, then to Terre Haute. She kept a post office box in Delphi, but Meg was not so sure where Hannah actually laid down her head most nights. She swore she would never live in the country again. But living like that, taking the Greyhound from town to town, acquaintance to acquaintance, to make the money last, with the clothes she could fit into a big blue Samsonite suitcase— Meg did not know how she stood it. She thought Hannah saw her life as though she were a character in some nineteenth-century novel. Spending a fortnight here or there. Always with lemonade in tall glasses on a sideporch. The orange daylilies in view. Wicker furniture. A game of hearts to lighten the load of a humid summer afternoon.

The morning after Hannah had beat her with the wooden spoon, Glenn did not sit down beside her on the school bus. No one had said a word about the bruises on her arms. Not even Jack Ransom, who came home on Friday night. Hannah told him that the Sunday dinner had been cancelled. He suggested they invite Dennis. Dennis could bring his shotgun over and they could kill the possums in the ravine where they threw their trash.

At Sunday dinner Uncle Dennis sketched out his plans for the truck garden. He told them that Glenn, the Pentecostal boy, would work for him all summer. He trusted him, he said. He wanted to know if Meg would like to sell strawberries for him during the month of June. He thought Glenn could show her how. I'm only a piece up the road, he said to Hannah, you can keep an eye on her.

Jack said, "That'll give the girl some business sense."

Hannah said, "I need her here."

Meg detected in her mother some relenting, some tiredness, and she thought that eventually she would allow her to sell strawberries. But Hannah would search Meg for signs of squalor every time she came home.

Jack Ransom and Uncle Dennis went out to the ravine to kill the possums. It was nearly dark when they returned. Hannah was changing the baby's diaper. Meg sat at the treadle sewing machine, staring out the front window, ready to weep. Hannah had not spoken directly to her all the long weekend. What mysterious grief she and the diaper delivery man had worked over those stolen winter afternoons. Hannah had not gone to communion that morning. But Meg had gone, morosely, with a cloud of doom hanging over her. She had chewed the dry host, though the girls at her school thought it more solicitous of Jesus to let it melt.

"Boo!" Her Uncle Dennis popped up into view, out on the porch. Her father was nowhere around.

She burst into tears.

"Don't cry, Sugar," Uncle Dennis said, through the window. "I didn't mean to scare you that bad." His voice was muffled, an arabesque of seduction and danger and care. Beyond him a row of slim red tulips had tenderly closed for the night.

1997

The Pleasure of Pears

On the deck, after their first cookout of the year, Molly came out of the kitchen with a plastic cutting board, an Opinel knife with a water-bleached wooden handle, and one Bartlett pear from Argentina, knobby and yellow. Cheerfully out-of-season.

"This'll go nice with the white wine," Molly said.

Bax had been thinking of a glass of skim milk and a plate of Oreos for dessert. But what Molly was after was mood. The sky luminous, blue-green at dusk. No mosquitos yet. A little swing music coming from the house next door, which was a good hundred yards away. The psycho dogs down the lane mercifully quiet. Right before dinner they had walked around their acre and checked out the growth, the strawberry blossoms, the pink peonies. They had been together long enough to plant and wait and enjoy growth in their yard: six years in July.

"Looks good," Bax said, about the pear.

Molly sat down on the deck step. With the cutting board glowing on her lap, she delicately sliced the Bartlett into eighths and each eighth she trimmed of core and seeds. Her hands were deft, square, competent, her nails polished with French Buff, almost bare. Bax liked knowing the color of her nail polish and her dress size and the way she organized the glove box in her car, every little thing, surprises, gifts in his hum-drum. He was charmed by her. As she cut up the pear Molly talked and it took Bax a moment to tune in to what she said in such a murmur, an after dinner reverie.

" . . . yes, it was a gift from Stephen, this knife. He'd gone to France without me and that was his way of saying he missed me. . . . "

He felt she'd planned to tell him this. There was a reason she'd chosen the Opinel knife to cut the pear. He thought of all the times he'd used it, how he'd actually favored it over their other knives. He would never look at it again in quite the same way. He had nothing against Stephen. They'd never even met. He usually thought, Better that Molly had been occupied those years with a man who obviously wasn't right for her than if she'd been with the love of her life. That was all in the past. The void. Bax was a nightstand Buddhist and one of the Buddhist teachers he'd been reading had said, "Last year's Superbowl is in the same void with the Civil War." Ditto, other marriages. Bax himself had not been married before. He liked to say, "I saved myself for you, Moll."

"That was before the serious fights," Molly said. She offered him a slice of the pear, grainy and sweet. She chewed hers thoughtfully. "I've been feeling kind of bad about old Stephen."

Bax took another slice. "He's not so old," he said. In truth, he did think of Stephen as getting old. He was nearly sixty to Bax's thirty-seven. Molly was forty-three.

Their neighbor's teenage daughter started up a riding mower and began chugging around her property, cutting grass in the near-dark, the sweatbands on her wrists Dayglo green. Like fireflies. Rascal, Bax's yellow cat, zipped up on the deck from out of nowhere, spooked by the lawn mower. Bax thought again about building a fence, planting a row of Russian olive trees: privacy—he wanted more of it. He said, "So why're you feeling bad about old Stephen?"

Molly ate the last of her share of the pear slices, then she set the cutting board aside and stared toward the mock orange, which bloomed in creamy wild profusion. "Time passes and you forget the worst."

"You do?"

"Almost."

And then she proceeded to tell him that she wanted to contact Stephen to apologize for all she did to him back in the bad old days. Lies she told. Selfish demands she made. Poor judgment all around on her part.

She said, "Would that bother you? In any way?"

"No, it wouldn't," he said. By that he meant that he did not think she would ever do anything deliberately to hurt his feelings. He'd be hard-pressed to think of a time when she had.

"Stephen and I picked pears once," Molly said. "Did I ever tell you about that?"

"I don't believe you did," he said softly.

"We needed to make some extra money. I forget what for."

Fireflies flashed among the burning bushes at the edge of the deck. They were trying to attract responsive females. Molly had told him about fireflies and the pitfalls and hazards inherent in their brief lives. She worked at the vet hospital and knew all about animals and insects and why they do the things they do. The male fireflies search for several nights to find the right mate. A long time by firefly standards. Their flashes are answered only half the time by females of their own species. At other times, very similiar answering flashes come from females of a larger genus—femmes fatales—who are predatory and eat the males who come too close.

"The taste of pears is forever bound up in my memories of him. And that time."

"Forever bound," Bax repeated.

"Once I thought we'd grow old together and share those memories." She took his hand and ran the tip of her index finger over his wedding band. "This doesn't have a damn thing to do with you and me. We have our own memories. You know that, don't you?"

The night ended fantastically, with a fat moon and Molly and Bax in the hot tub. The scent of the mock orange. Rascal keeping watch on a stump near the stream. Mending fences, that was Molly's intent. Bax thought it was probably a stage you go through in your forties.

The next morning before he left for work, he opened a flat white paper bag that lay on the microwave. Molly was in the shower. In the bag was a birthday card with this message: *Since your birthday's coming up, I've been thinking about all the crazy things we've done together. Actually, I was thinking about selling the film rights.* There was a guy on a motorcycle with a woman riding on the back, standing up gleefully. Cartoon people. Appealingly reckless.

It wasn't anywhere near Bax's birthday. Down the hall the hairdryer droned. He slipped the card back into the white paper bag and knocked on the bathroom door. "See you tonight," he said.

"'Bye, hon," Molly hollered.

The card had to be for Stephen. All the way to Winding Woods he tried to remember what Molly had told him before about Stephen. If he could remember, he would know Molly. And if he knew Molly, he couldn't be caught off-guard. He could postpone what he felt creeping up on him: a maelstrom of doubt. And that was the worst thing to have happen on a work day.

Sandra Mosher insisted that he build the playhouse on the old flagstone patio, against the fence. It was an expensive play-house, Bax said, and he thought the walls would be a little out of true if he built it on that patio. But no, she insisted. He was working for her, so the buckled patio it was, right next to a crabapple tree. The girls had chosen a Swiss chalet from Bax's picture album of playhouses he'd built since he'd stopped working for a contractor who built real houses. Those play-houses had paid for three years of pharmaceutical school. So far, so good. In the neighboring backyard, across the low fence, a couple had set up their backpacking tent and they were sealing its seams. The woman—a redhead like Molly— wore a polka-dot bathing suit. The houses in Winding Woods were so close together he could see a tiny pink sickle, a scar, on the woman's calf. The skimpy yard was the size of a coun-try kitchen.

All day, sweating, thinking through the Swiss chalet, his mind worked over the conversation with Molly. He couldn't stop. Who else had she done crazy things with? By the time she and Bax had met, the craziness was finished. It had been the sort people die from or go to jail for or suffer irreparable broken hearts over. Illegal things. All night things. Raunchy things. He didn't know the half of it. And he didn't want to know. But he felt locked in a very small room with Molly's words and that birthday card.

The two little girls came out and perched on a kid-size picnic table not far from where he worked, staple-gunning cedar shakes to the plywood roof. They were twins in overalls, eight years old, with glossy blonde pigtails. He figured they must've just gotten out of school; an entire day had passed without notice.

"Don't bother him now, girls," their mother called. Her voice seemed to tremble.

"We won't," the twins said in unison.

Music burst from inside the big suburban box: Frank Sinatra. He had just died. Somehow Sandra Mosher did not seem like a Sinatra fan. He liked the sound of it, though. Bax wondered if she'd turn it up a little bit. He decided to ask her.

"Be back in a flash," he said to the girls.

One of them said, "Can we go in?"

"You can peek in," Bax said.

He slipped inside the screened porch, knuckles ready to rap on the door. Through the window he saw Sandra Mosher at the ironing board. A man's dress shirt belled out beneath the board. She was crying. The iron in her hand suspended above the shirt.

He tiptoed away. He went out and picked up his staple gun and wondered about her. The girls took their seats again on the picnic table: good girls. Seeing the woman crying brought to mind his grandmother, who lived in a farmhouse near Delphi across from fields of corn that was harvested to make jelly beans. When his grandfather had died in the fall, he and Molly had driven out several weeks in a row to sit on the porch with his grandmother and drink iced tea while she cried. He had not known what to do. But Molly had held her hand and replenished her tissues. One time on the drive home Molly said, "She's crying for what they didn't have together." He hadn't understood that, but seeing Sandra Mosher at the ironing board cut through his perplexity. He thought she cried for something she did not have.

Twenty minutes later Sandra opened the screen door and said, her voice rising, "Would you care for some lemonade, Mr. Baxter?"

"Don't bother him now, Mother," said one of the girls, with a fake-exasperated twist of her lips. The girls giggled.

Bax put down his staple gun and wiped the sweat from his forehead with a blue bandana. "Sure. Sounds good," he said.

He went inside the screened porch and dropped his carpenter's belt. He sat down at the table with the glass top and noticed what you couldn't help noticing about her—she was pretty in a country-singer sort of way. Slightly plump, in modest white shorts and a sleeveless sea green blouse. With curled blonde hair and smooth skin that looked like she always wore sunscreen and a hat. She wasn't worn down. Her husband had a good job at a chemical corporation.

The lemonade had been made with powder, not lemons. Bax was vaguely aware of the twins hovering around the playhouse, peering in the window frames above the empty flower boxes. Sandra Mosher wanted to know if he liked his work, a question he'd been asked before. Some women held their husbands up to the light with the question. He told her about pharmaceutical school and she seemed relieved to know that he was not simply a builder of playhouses. Though sometimes he thought that building playhouses would be a perfectly acceptable life all by itself. There was always that look of unfettered bliss on the faces of the children when they entered the houses for the first time.

The girls came rambunctiously into the porch, thirsty, giggling. Like prizes, their mother pulled them near, kissing their foreheads in a gesture Bax imagined she repeated many times a day. That didn't go into a void. Love like that accreted. For a few more minutes they talked: of the oily smell of tar nearby, the flat of begonias she hadn't planted yet. Mourning doves made their pearly call. The girls wandered away.

Sandra leaned her elbows on the table, involuntarily flexing her muscles, and he saw the smooth white underside of her arms and silky blonde tendrils there. She'd shown her secret self to him, without intending to.

At five-o-five Bax admitted to himself that he would have to come back and finish up the trim, paint the flower boxes, stain the shakes. He packed his tools in the lock box in the bed of his pickup. He saluted Sandra Mosher, who stood just inside the screen door in the afternoon sunlight. Like a fire viewed through mica. He wanted to go back to her and say, How did you meet your husband? Because we arrive where we are by mating. Whether we like it or not. He wanted to see honesty flitter across her face, to feel it on his own, that brief softening.

From the picnic table the girls said, "You're not done yet?"

"Not yet," he said. "I'll be back Monday."

"Can we play inside?"

"If your mother says so."

Driving home, he saw the mallards splashing in the bog behind Ace Hardware. The cab of his pickup smelled a little like Molly, a citrus splash she used in the summertime. He thought about the time they first met. He'd taken Rascal to the vet and they had sat in the waiting room, Rascal on his lap, until a Doberman with a large growth on his belly had come fitfully into the room. Rascal had been shaken and leaped out of his arms. Molly had come around the counter with a bath towel and she had wrapped Rascal tenderly in the towel and handed him to Bax. He knew he could ask Molly anything, if he were willing to hear the answer. And he thought the houses were too close together in Winding Woods. Where could you tell a secret out loud?

He passed a church he always passed when driving out that way: Mary, Mother of God, Joy to All Who Sorrow. He did not know what it meant to sorrow. Not yet. And he thought he might never know. The tiny brick church had a comforting name, even to Bax, who hadn't been to church since he was fifteen years old. He tuned the radio to the classic rock station and thought about the woman, how she had wanted his attention. How he had given it to her.

1997

Worship of the
Common Heart

"Think Provence," Grace said, her elbow hanging out the driver's side window. She drove their father's pickup, a Chevy from the eighties, with extra chrome do-dads on the grill. She'd had her hair cut again, layered against her scalp in gelled half-inch hanks. Brassy. With a split of mouse-brown at the roots. "Think *brocante*."

"I'll pray for you, kiddo," Sister Stephanie said. Grace waved jauntily and gave the truck too much gas, kicking up pea gravel in the circle drive. A life-size granite statue of the Blessed Virgin remained unperturbed.

Not so Sister Stephanie. A secretion of anger, unblinkingly familiar, spilled through her body. For several years they'd had little contact. But after her temporary vows, she'd been allowed more family visits.

Their mother and Aunt Caroline's visits would stretch indolently over an afternoon. In their Sunday best. They brought tins of Toll House cookies and boxes of Aplets and Cotlets—sticky fruit candies they purchased mail order. Old lady candy. Her mother often seemed on the verge of tears. There were no grandchildren to console her and that came as an unrelenting surprise. Stephanie imagined she kept toy catalogs in a bedside drawer, at the ready.

It was Aunt Caroline who had paid for Stephanie to go to art school, and it was Aunt Caroline who had always given her beautiful boxes of oils and pastels, and it was Aunt Caroline who did not try to keep her from entering the convent.

And then there was Grace. Thirty-two years old, an emergency room nurse, divorced, skinny in a red leather bomber jacket, her fingers pink and chapped from going all winter without gloves. Sex on her mind. Stephanie could read that a mile away, in the way Grace squirmed, the way she felt up her own thigh muscles, proud. Stephanie's other half, with whom she'd shared their mother's womb.

Their father was the only one who did not make the greening pastoral drive to the country. He *sent* his love.

Sister Stephanie had a hard time looking any of them in the eye. She had nothing to say. Or was it that they never elicited anything from her? As though they were the ones with real lives; she was the nun.

She went inside—it was a raw afternoon in early May, just after a hailstorm. The hail had accumulated on the windowsills and in the creases of rhubarb leaves. All through cleaning up the art room, a responsibility she had taken on voluntarily, all through evening prayers and the sweet clear girlish voices singing the psalms to and fro across the chapel, all through dinner, and all through the evening of filling out a job application, washing out a cardigan by hand, and watching the Indianapolis news, she thought of France and Grace's offer. Grace had won a trip for two to Europe—airline tickets, a rental car, and cash. She had written a poem for a multinational that manufactured perfume. She'd shown the poem to Stephanie. Something about trains and lavender. Something about the inevitability of passion. The risk of it. What Grace considered herself good at.

Stephanie missed Aunt Caroline. She was a widow living above her liquor store in Speedway. Aunt Caroline and their mother had been educated by the Sisters of Providence and then Aunt Caroline went away to a small liberal arts college in Baltimore. There she met a man whose work took him to foreign soil. This was just after the war, in the fifties. On a sunny narrow road in Provence he'd been hit by a truck as he waited with his bicycle for Caroline. She'd just gone into a shop for a palmier. Her life had been blessed, and then that life had ended. She came back to Indiana, bought the liquor store with the insurance money, and took an interest in her sister's children when they came along, especially Stephanie.

The liquor store, with its lit up Art-Deco façade, had looked like a miniature movie theater to Stephanie when she was a girl. A place of ever-changing escape. The bottles on the wooden shelves gleamed brownly in the store's dim interior. It smelled of bergamot—Earl Gray tea. Aunt Caroline had a back room behind a louver door and in the back room were stacks of library books and magazines, a chintz-covered easy chair, a hassock in the shape of an elephant, a chrome hotplate whereon a battered copper teakettle perpetually simmered, tea things—wire balls and spoons, cream and lemon wedges in

Tupperware containers—and other comforts. Lemon Drops. Baby blue tissues. There, in Aunt Caroline's back room, Stephanie had discovered the world. Reading Denise Levertov and Margaret Mead. Listening to public radio. Stephanie, too, went away to college, and she did not return until she entered the motherhouse and Aunt Caroline had become old, unreasonably so it seemed. Her legs were swollen below the knee and she kept them wrapped in white cotton towels she purchased from a Goodwill. The towels were imprinted with *Emerald Hotel*. She soaked them in an herbal solution that stank to high heaven. Her feet were crippled: bunions and corns signaled stormy weather. Her glasses were heavy and she refused to consider surgery to correct her vision. She'd had a life of promise but Speedway had pulled her back in, like a raveling thread.

Where Stephanie had grown up, with Aunt Caroline nearby, the houses had a muddied, shrunken look, as though time and the elements were beating them into the ground. Gutters dipped and tapped in wind against the aluminum siding. Storm drains clogged with twigs and trash. Whenever her family came to visit the motherhouse, it was as though she were forced to go back. Back to their front yard turned into a parking lot for the Indy 500, her father in a T-shirt, collecting twenty dollars a car. Back to her mother's bottle of tears from a statue of the Virgin Mary. To Grace's filthy ashtrays and her smoke smell. And the television always on. Disjunctive memories. Permanent and substantial. She often thought sinfully, pridefully: how could I have come from there?

She lay in her narrow bed. The moon a scrap in the sky. The last trip she'd taken with Grace was in 1979. Aunt Caroline had treated them to California. In La Jolla, they feigned sleep until Aunt Caroline had left for Mass and then they fled the hotel room and found Black's Beach. All those smooth brown naked bodies under the California sun. She considered the difference between naked and nude. Pale and skinny, Grace had taken off her clothes and strutted naked along the surf, elbows jutting, knobby knees rough with winter, laughing in a high-strung false crescendo. While Stephanie had trailed a few steps behind in madras shorts and a T-shirt. "I can't be here and not," Grace had insisted.

How like Grace. In elementary school at St. John's, they'd had separate playgrounds for boys and girls, but after school, when the nuns no longer patrolled, Grace would shriek around the blacktop with the boys, laughing at their obscene cat-calls, their sly jokes about hot dogs and buns. She would come in at dusk—spent, sweaty, and starved—her homework yet to be done. Their Black's Beach foray had ended abruptly when Stephanie spied a gray-haired man, his balding pate sunburned, handling himself under an upturned Kentucky Fried Chicken bucket. She begged to go back to the hotel; Grace had reluctantly agreed.

The heat in the motherhouse had not been turned off for the summer; radiators detonated somewhere beyond her room. Stephanie got up, slipped her feet into cool sandals, pulled on a robe. The numerals on the clock glowed: after midnight. At the window she could see the cemetery, a wooded plot, its grave markers like old teeth. Beyond was the neighboring campus—a secular college where the sisters attended concerts and took the occasional class. It was there she had applied for a job, assisting an art therapist who worked with outpatients—children—at a clinic in the psych department. The job would begin July 1. She hoped that it might make her want to paint again. On the far side of the cemetery, students traipsed among the graves: swishes of baggy clothing, a flashlight. Though she hadn't picked up a brush for six years, she viewed the students with a painterly eye. Under the leafing maples. *Students Looking for Love.*

Stephanie shut her door without a sound and shuffled silently down to the dim computer room on the first floor. No one was about. The same screen saver scrolled at every terminal: *Lord, make me an instrument of Thy peace.* She sat down and burrowed her way into a Cezanne website: There were his bathers, none of them making eye contact; there was the address of Cezanne's studio in Aix-en-Provence. Someone from Halifax—an art student—had posted a description of the studio: the monk's beads, the bowler, the smell of linseed oil. A religious experience, he wrote.

"What a night owl," Sister Rose said from the doorway, startling Stephanie. She was dressed in pink sweatpants, her plump cheeks pink, as well. Old acne scarred her forehead.

Stephanie's hands hung above the keyboard, guiltily. Sister Rose was her spiritual director. For two years she had turned her heart inside out to Sister Rose, emptied herself like a purse. "I won't be long," she said.

"I'm not being critical," Sister Rose said.

"What're you up to?" Stephanie said.

She grinned. "Stairmaster." Then she disappeared. Another soul afloat in the motherhouse night.

The next morning at five Stephanie rose for meditation. Her head felt heavy from lack of sleep. At a window the blue-black sky wavered behind a grain elevator. She took a zafu from a closet and sat, lotus-style, her knees immobile as bentwood. Across the room, Sister Rose tapped a gong three times, a silky vibration, a bit of beauty in an otherwise lumbering morning. There was about the sisters the smell of wool blankets and shampoo and skin cells exfoliating and menstrual blood. The smell of women emerging from dreams. Eyes closed, Stephanie watched. Her thoughts flew. She had her cherished broken records, as Sister Rose called them. Will they fix the cappuchino machine or will she have to drink the watered-down Folger's? Why doesn't Grace have the strength to quit smoking? What would happen should she ask permission to go to France? Will her vows stick? Or will she make a fool of herself, put her three earrings back in, leave the motherhouse in shame, move back to Speedway and have babies? What were those students really doing in the cemetery? Will she get the job? Each thought was like a package she opened and foraged within, until she caught herself and came back to silence with the sacred word she had been using since her training. The foraging brought up her fears, her pride and righteousness, her irritation. She could spend entire sits being irritated at Grace for things Grace had done decades before. A twin is not like any other sibling. A twin is a part of you.

But she felt cleansed. Nothing had changed, but in the stopping, in the being still, she clarified.

After lunch, at the mailboxes, Stephanie reached gingerly in and took out a blue linen-like envelope from Aunt Caroline. She was aware of Sister Rose in the switchboard room across the narrow hall, observing her. She opened the envelope anyway. A check slipped to the floor and lay there on the carpet for a suspended moment before she scooped it up, folded it twice and tucked it in her skirt pocket. The note from Aunt Caroline said, *You must go!* in wavery fountain-pen script.

"It seems as though you must," Sister Rose said later in Stephanie's room. They drank green tea and a cellist serenaded them on public radio. On the desk, under a marble paperweight, lay the check from Aunt Caroline for five hundred dollars—for extras, Aunt Caroline wrote, for whatever struck her fancy in France: books, paints, a print.

"Not at all," Stephanie said.

"But why not?"

The answer came to Stephanie, a swift arrow: "I don't want to be that close to my sister."

"So it's not about . . . "

"What God wants?" Stephanie sipped her tea, though it burned her tongue. "No. It's not."

"Perhaps you're being called there," Sister Rose said.

"I doubt that," Stephanie said. Called to what? Called to suffer Grace's impetuousness? Her unpredictibility? Called to sample sixteen different cheeses? And the wine; she'd thought about the wine. Or was it Cezanne who called her? Was it that linseed oil she wanted to smell?

After that, they talked of the inconsequential. Sister Rose's workout. The newly planted petunias ruined by the hailstorm. The architectural salvage Grace hoarded in their parents' backyard. How she planned to quit nursing at St. E's Emergency and open a business on the north side of Indy. Grace's Antiques & Artifacts. Sister Stephanie acknowledged later, when she was at last alone, that she must go, that she wanted to go, and yet she could not imagine going.

When the time came, in June, Sister Rose herself drove Stephanie and Grace to Merrillville where they caught the bus to O'Hare. Grace was on her best behavior: no smoking, no cursing. When they were left alone at the doughnut shop to await the bus, Grace smiled conspiratorially, lugging her tight little duffles. She said, "I'm kidnapping you . . . " All the way— on the smoggy bus ride to O'Hare, in the vast terminal, on the plane, with its sleepy-eyed stewards, and over the sea— Stephanie watched herself being with Grace as though through several lenses: scriptural, psychological, historical. She pestered herself with analysis. She couldn't stop.

Grace had chosen the *gîte*. An upstairs apartment in a small village, Puget, within driving distance of castles and St. Remy and Aix. *Brocante* vendors in all directions. Across the dusty town square a Protestant chapel-turned-gallery glowed in sun-light, its stone walls tawny brown. It was late afternoon when they arrived. Grace sat on her bed and counted her francs.

"Antiques here," she said, "are antiques. Ancient. If I can afford something, anything, from the sixteenth century, I'll be happy." Then, "Did you see that guy? At the fruit stand?"

"What guy?"

"Get out of here," Grace said. "You saw him."

"I saw him."

An orchard—pear trees and cherry trees—swelled neatly from the village out to the main road. Produce from the or-chard and the fields was sold at a wooden stand they had to pass by each time they left the village. The man selling produce was burly, blonde, with a farmer's sunburnt face, blue eyes. Stephanie and Grace had stopped there on the way to the village, and as a welcome he had given them a pint crate of baby zukes. He had handed them to Grace, who was driving, and when she took the crate he had not let go for a moment. They would have gone on talking if she had not been there.

That first night they retired early, sharing a room for the first time since high school. One of them could've slept on the foldout sofa in the living room, and Stephanie held that idea in reserve: if Grace drove her to it. They had a history of Grace driving her to extreme measures. Someone knocked on the downstairs door. Grace went to the window in her pajamas—a skimpy top over boxers. The man from the fruit stand shouted up, in French, "I have left melons in a basket for you. For your breakfast."

They introduced themselves, giddily; he was Jean. "Please pick the cherries on the trees," he said. "As many as you like." Grace's voice changed when she spoke to the man. She had taken an intensive language course for only six weeks, but she sounded playful and worldly-wise, making the *oui-oui* French sounds that eluded Stephanie.

"*Merci, merci*," Grace fluttered.

A silent ten minutes later, outside the open window, two girls giggled on the terrace below. Stephanie had seen the two girls earlier, shyly watching them unload their baggage from the rented Renault. One blonde, one brunette. Perfect girls. Their talk was the only sound nearby; out on the main road the rare truck or car spurted along. Then a boy came by as though the girls had cast their sweet girl breath and hair and thighs like nets.

"What're they saying?" Stephanie whispered. Her bed was flat and hard.

"Something about soccer," Grace whispered. "He's a soccer player."

"Is that all?"

"He's bragging. Can't you tell?"

Yes, she could tell. She did not understand his French, but she could hear the brag in his voice. "What else is he saying?"

"He's describing a car he wants to buy when he's older."

"And?"

"A trip to Paris he took when he was twelve."

"Keep on," Stephanie said.

"Look," Grace said, "I'm not going to translate everything for you. It spoils it for me."

When Stephanie did not respond, Grace said, "Get out that gizmo. Start communicating." She meant the electronic translator Sister Rose had purchased at Radio Shack and wrapped in pale tissue paper with a sunshiny ribbon.

Stephanie lay there missing Greencastle. Missing the motherhouse. Missing Sister Rose translating the world. A wind picked up and hurled the limbs of the plane trees surrounding the terrace. Not wishing to consider the implications of what Grace said, Stephanie pretended the lost voices in wind were faraway music, the liturgy of adolescence, a boy and two girls with no place to go but the town square. She thought: the girls are green the way the orchard pears are green.

In three days they developed the routines of a summer or a year, as though they might stay on. Stephanie did dishes and cooked; Grace did laundry and drove. Every day the melon was in the basket on the terrace, though Jean himself was mysteriously absent. Every day they dressed in their travel uniforms, Stephanie in a loose cotton jumper over a T-shirt and practical white sneakers for walking, Grace in a short clingy shift. She had brought three, each one printed with different flowers: calla lilies, daffs, and poppies. Her sandals would skim the sidewalks sensually, announcing her arrival at cafés and shops. She picked a different town each day and they separated upon arrival, Grace to methodically shop the *brocante* vendors and Stephanie to seek out a museum or a gallery or a church. During the drives, along the narrow winding roads, Grace might have said, Nice trees, or, Is that too breezy for you? But not much else. They would shop for dinner, return to Puget and cook, and Grace would show off her treasures. Evening bags from the 1700s, dark velvet, embroidered with silk. A copper sconce. Illustrated menus reminiscent of Dufy. The time before sleep was the most intimate, fearfully so. Stephanie always changed into her nightclothes in the bathroom. Grace shimmied out of her dress in the bedroom's near-dark, dropped her underwear to the floor, and pulled on her pajamas.

Once in bed Grace talked, haltingly, but persistently.

One night she said, "Tell me what it's about for you, being a nun."

Faintly, as though she'd lost her voice, Stephanie said, "When I can, I will."

Then, "Don't you want to know anything about me now?" Grace said.

"Is there something you want to tell me?"

"Don't do that."

"Do what?"

"Answer my question with a question."

Stephanie could not fall so easily into old habits. She remembered the humid nights when they were girls, the way they'd plan babies, swimming pools, china patterns, whole domestic scenarios, the life-dreams thrust upon them by circumstance.

"Did you ever wonder why Jeff and I broke up?" Grace asked her.

"Of course, I wondered."

"It wasn't me."

"Oh?"

"Not me entirely. Of course, I was selfish. What do you know when you're twenty-three?"

"Not much."

They whispered, though there was no one to disturb. An airplane droned overhead. Then, the summer silence subsumed them. For a brief moment, Stephanie felt disoriented, as though she were back in Greencastle, in the hush of the motherhouse.

"You don't know which end is up," Grace said. "But—to tell the truth—he wanted to be with someone else."

"I'm sorry. I didn't know."

And Grace went on to tell her the story, each twist and bend. At last Stephanie said, "Do you still consider yourself Catholic?"

"Not a very good one, but yes."

Stephanie thought she could smell the melons sweetening the air. Her mind was full of the castle she'd trod that day, the dimly lit pentices between chambers and chapel, the wooden bathtub in the garden among the sweet fennel and chamomile, the lavender and mint, far images from what she had painted before. She'd won a few prizes in school for technical drawings; she'd been good at rendering, at precision. After graduating she'd been hired to do three corporate murals in the nostalgic style of the WPA murals of the 1930s. After that, nothing. She had taken a job in a museum putting up shows and caring for the drawings in deep metal drawers. Her paints and equipment had sat untouched for several years until she moved, and when she moved she packed them into boxes and gave them to a high school teacher who said his students could use them. *Finis.*

Grace leaned over the side of her bed, fumbled in her purse, found her cigarettes. "Mind if I smoke? At the window?"

"I don't mind."

Grace scooted to the open window and lit up, leaning on the sill. She whispered, "Wow." She positioned herself slightly to the side of the long window and held the gossamer curtain aside with one thumb.

"What?"

"Come see."

Stephanie got out of bed, her feet cool on the tile floor, and she stood like a mime of Grace on the opposite side of the window. What she saw gave her a start: hidden from the road behind a brick patio wall, the blonde girl and the soccer player on a picnic table. Her with her skirt up. Their tongues raw and muscular and coiling together. Moonlight coating them iridescently.

Stephanie leapt back into her bed. She hid her eyes. "You *knew* I wouldn't want to see that."

"I did not."

"You did."

Grace peeked out again. "Nasty," she crowed softly. "And sweet." It was as though she were alone, unguarded, with her appetites revealed. But she wasn't alone and Stephanie resented being drawn into it. She resented the way Grace assumed an intimacy with her.

Grace shut the window quietly, so as not to disturb the lovers. Back in bed she said, "Don't you ever think about men?"

"I can remember thinking about them, but no, I don't."

"You're thinking about painting, aren't you?"

"No, I'm not." The image flamed in her mind: the girl's desire savage in the way her legs fell open, the boy's gluttonous mouth. It was the worst moment of the trip. There was no dignity in it. A place she could not avoid with Grace.

"I just remember that look you get. That silence."

"I doubt I'll ever paint again." By that she meant she did not know if she had the stamina or the naiveté to begin anew.

"They don't have a rule against that, do they?"

"No." She could not confide in Grace the way Grace confided in her. She couldn't chatter anymore. Chatter required trust.

"Well, that's good," Grace said. And by the abrupt way she pulled the covers over her shoulder, Stephanie saw that even Grace was tired of talking. And it was just as well to end before they touched on things that might be hard, though Stephanie could not entirely imagine what those things might be. She knew only that they were there, little dangers like the scorpions that lay in wait on the paths around the village or in the stairwell. They had been warned to shake out their shoes and keep watch.

The fourth night, turning toward Stephanie's bed, Grace whispered, "Did you know Mom sleeps in our old room?"

"No —"

"She does."

"Since when?"

"I don't know."

Stephanie said nothing. She felt a slight twinge down low, a cramp. What she wanted to talk about was Aix and then Paris: they would be leaving the *gîte* in three more days so that she could tour first Cezanne's studio and then the Parisian museums. Imagining Paris would distract her from the cramps.

Grace said, "You know—of course—about Pop and Aunt Caroline."

"*What* are you talking about?"

"I know you know."

"Grace, come on."

"Pop has always had a thing for Aunt Caroline. He courted her before she met the guy she married. Then he settled for Mom."

"Pop loves Mom."

"Oh, yeah, he loves her. But Aunt Caroline has been there right on the corner all these years. Think about it." She got out of bed and went to the window. "I'm restless."

Stephanie sat on the edge of her bed, bare feet grazing the cool ceramic floor. Disparate moments long buried rose up. Pop coming to Aunt Caroline's to pick her up, his cap in hand, lingering against the door, the light a shaft of autumn sun through the liquor store window. The sun blinding. Pop's head in sunlight, his expression unreadable. Fingering his cap. And Christmases. Significant silences as Aunt Caroline opened her gifts from Mom and Pop. Pop watching.

Moonlight poured into the room, across the paisley sheets. The night was hot and no breeze stirred. Eager footfalls chanted in the dust outside the *gîte*.

Grace said, "Hear that music?"

"Sort of."

"Let's find it."

"Let's not." She wanted secrets. Finally Grace had something to give her.

"Please, Stephanie. Let's see what life is like here."

"This *is* life here. For us."

Grace went to the bathroom and when she came out she begged, "Come on. I'm not asking you to do anything sinful. Just take a walk with me."

It had been a long time since she'd had the chance to please Grace, to go in search of the vitality Grace desired: music, clothes, wine, company. Grace had almost always done the desiring for both of them. The music was not hard to find; an outdoor party was underway. At the school, blinking white lights had been strung in the trees along the perimeter of the stone parking lot and a DJ controlled a turntable. He wore a purple beret and a beaded vest. Rock-and-roll blurted scratchily from the speakers set precariously on sawhorses. A bar had been established on a cafeteria table, the wine bottles glimmering in the merry white light. The women wore summer dresses and the men were in shirt sleeves.

Stephanie and Grace loitered beside a cedar tree. Stephanie wanted to ask her how she knew the things she knew.

A man with slicked back silvery hair sidled up to them. He wore loafers with no socks and Sansabelt slacks. "*Bonsoir*," he said, his voice oily.

"*Bonsoir, Monsieur*," Grace answered, pleased with herself. She picked at a cedar twig, swaying to the music.

He waved one arm, as if to own the village, the festivities. "*Je suis le mairie.*"

"*Mairie?*" Grace said.

The man plucked imaginary six guns from imaginary holsters at his pudgy hips. Bang bang. "*Le mairie*," he insisted.

Jean appeared, smiling broadly. He swept Grace into the dancers. It was a slow dance: The Righteous Brothers. Grace looked back helplessly, happily.

That was the trouble with Grace. She allowed herself to be swept away.

"*Le mairie*," the man said, a little grudge in his voice. He frowned at Stephanie's inability to respond. His eyebrows crept together menacingly.

She put up her hands. "*S'il vous plait, s'il vous plait*," she said, backing off. She could not remain on the spot while Grace whirled away. She could not even communicate. It felt like an alien dream, a place she didn't belong. Once in a while she ached for the loss of the times that went before, the years of dancing, of yearning. But she did not want those times again.

She walked back through the darkened village. Televisions were on in a few of the houses, their garish light like a tinfoil mirror. The sound of cats snarling erupted from a garden. As the music faded, she thought she could hear the rush of the Durance on the other side of the road. That's what she wanted to hear, merely a river, not some seventies rock-and-roll. Creedence Clearwater Revival. Tina Turner. The brutish English sound of it was dissonant among the French—artificial; she realized it had always been false. A substitute for a more fleshly encounter. Or prelude, Grace might say. At the gallery, she saw a light was on. She tried the door but it was locked. She peeked in a window. The walls were hung with metal objects, tools and baskets and implements, all fashioned from wax impressions of vegetable matter she surmised, then cast in bronze. There was a bowl in the shape and texture of a cabbage leaf. Female art. So obviously crafted by a woman of the earth. She wished she could bring Aunt Caroline to the gallery window and let her peek in. Then talk about it after. Aunt Caroline, who always quoted Emerson: "Sincere conversation is worship of the common heart." She hadn't thought of that in years.

Inside the *gîte*, Stephanie sat in the dark and drank a half glass of red wine for her cramps, feeling the brocade of it on her tongue, trying not to think too much, trying not to judge. Not trying. She made mental lists for Grace: burning questions.

Grace came tiptoeing in, humming to herself, her sandals dangling in one hand. It was after one o'clock; Stephanie had lain awake without wanting to. No one spoke. Grace lay down in her clothes, sighing. Minutes went by and they might've drifted to sleep without speaking. They might've begun again the next morning, as though nothing had happened, secure in their routines. But Grace said, in a harsh voice, as though she'd been shouting for hours over the loud music, "Let's go to the beach. His family has an apartment there we can stay in."

"The beach?"

"The Mediterranean."

"What about Paris?"

"We'll go to Paris. This is just for one day, one night."

"Is he going?"

"No, no, no. He's just letting us use it."

"You're so unpredictable."

"Don't start."

"I'm not starting."

"You sound like Mom."

"I don't want to go to the beach."

"Flex a little, Stephie-loo."

Stephie-loo. What they'd called her whenever she'd balked at a shift in plans, at a change. That had always been her place, her role, to maintain order and predictability, to save enough newly baked cookies for tomorrow. She did not want the beach with all its idleness.

"Well?"

"What choice do I have?" She knew she sounded obstinate.

"Please, Steph?"

Time and the night took on a density, a heat. They had reverted.

Grace leaned between the beds and opened her hand, showing her the stubby chrome key to the beach apartment. "I just want to see the Mediterranean. Haven't you ever wanted to see it?"

Stephanie did not answer. She had a reservoir of anger that lay in a hidden place; every time, she came upon it by surprise. Every time, it amazed her with its seductive depth.

Grace had them up and out by seven the next morning. Stephanie's cramps had faded. It was Sunday—she had to find a church at the beach. If there was time for that. Meanwhile, Grace drove gaily, ignoring the heart-snarl as big as a house between them. Nothing got through to Stephanie; nothing soothed her. Not the lavender fields or sunflowers. Not the castles in ruins. Not the French laundry on the clotheslines, fluttering in the sea breeze.

The pastel beach town was a little down on its heels; perhaps a storm had gone through recently. A few roof tiles lay on the sidewalk. Palm leaves were twisted in odd shapes. The main thoroughfare ended at a mile-wide sandy cove crowned with limestone cliffs at the far end. A long distance across the water, refineries or factories emitted gray smoke. Hundreds of people had congregated already; it was not quite eleven o'clock. Children filled their sand pails or dipped their toes into the surf; men smoked; and the women wearing only scraps of bikini bottoms sat or lay on towels, sedate animals in repose. The beach was abobble with breasts.

Grace turned the car around and puttered up a steep hill, as though she'd been going there all her life. She stopped in front of a cream brick building with red geraniums in pots on the steps.

"The women are free," Grace said, defiantly.

"I see that," Stephanie said.

"Are you shocked?"

"No, I'm not. But I want to find a church with a late Mass. Will you come along?"

"Not today," Grace said. "Today I'm a sun-worshipper. That must be the oldest religion, don't you think?"

They went into the second-floor apartment and dropped their duffle bags. The place was one room, stuffy, the smell of old fish emanating from the little refrigerator. Telephone and electric wires criss-crossed the view of a long-needled pine and a triangle of sea. Grace tossed two bathing suits on the double bed, bottoms and tops, saucy and new-looking. One striped. One printed with tropical fruit.

"Pick one," she said.

"You go ahead. Let me have the key, would you?"

Stephanie walked down the precipitous street and back into the town, watching for a church. She found one, a small confection: white and blue and gold leaf. St. Pierre. A Mass was in progress. The priest was wizened, but cheerful, his vestments patched. He spat a little when he spoke.

She sat in the back pew, still aggravated, still talking to herself about Grace. She set the electronic translator on the empty pew in front of her and turned it on. A game called Hangman arose on the tiny screen; she promptly forgot the gizmo was there. In the foyer, a family waited impatiently for a christening. They chattered in whispers. The matriarch—a robust woman in her fifties—was worried about something, as women are at ceremonies. What ardent keepers of the rituals we are, Stephanie thought. She let the memory of her mother enter her, the tears that now seemed somewhat explicable.

How circumscribed their lives were, her mother's at home, Aunt Caroline's at the liquor store. But the longing had been there, she saw that now. She pictured the three of them, Aunt Caroline, Mom and Pop, failing now little by little—their blood pressure up, their hands arthritic—in their gray and black coats and galoshes, kneeling side by side at Mass every Sunday. That was where she had come from, that hardship, that discipline. It had taken so long to catch on.

The priest's gestures brought her back to the little church, and she began translating, not the French, but the gestures. She could do it without struggle. Which is to say, the celebration was in her nerve endings and her cells, embedded there, when she was free to notice. Free to let it work on her.

Grace's note read: *I'm on the beach. Be back soon.* Stephanie had to find her. She wanted to say, "This is what being a nun is about. You have to consent to be transformed." She hoped Grace would laugh and say, "Talk about unpredictability." She hoped she'd see that. Stephanie changed into the extra bathing suit bottom, with its curving ruffles, its tropical fruits. She put on a big white shirt over that. Would she be the only nun on the beach?

The beach lay below a limestone cliff, the sand creamy-tan, the umbrellas like buttons from such a distance. She adjusted the straps on her day pack and went down the quickest route, switchbacks lined with aloe that lovers had carved their names in. She walked among the oiled sun-bathers, watching for Grace. Sunlight glared off the crackling waves. The sand was hot. Would she recognize Grace when she saw her? It was the women who interested her, the decisions they had made with their bodies: nymphs and virgins, hussies, young mothers, menarchs and crones. If she were ever to paint again, she would begin with Black's Beach. Kites in primary colors. Two naked sisters. Small against God's immensity of sky and sea. They would make eye contact.

1998

The Secret of Cartwheels

The winesap trees along the road were skeletal in the early evening light. I stared out the school bus window and cupped like a baby chick the news I looked forward to telling Mother: I'd decided on my confirmation name.

"What's nine times seven?" Jan Mary said.

"Sixty-three," I said. *Joan*. That was Mother's confirmation name, and I wanted it to be mine as well. She'd told me it was a name of strength, a name to carry you into battle.

"I tore my cords," Christopher said. He stood in the aisle, bracing himself with one hand on the chrome pole beside the driver, who wore a baseball cap and a big plaid mackinaw.

The bus driver sang, "Don't sit under the apple tree with anyone else but me." I knew we were nearing our stop, the end of the route, whenever the driver sang this song. We were the last ones on the bus. Although the heater was chuffing hard, frost in the shape of flames curled along the edges of the windows.

"Sweet dreams," the driver said, as we plodded down the slippery steps of the school bus.

Aunt Opal's pale green Cadillac was parked at an odd angle near the woodshed. I knew something was wrong—she never drove out from Wenatchee to visit in the winter. I remembered what our mother had told me the night before. Before bedtime we all lined up to kiss her good night, and when my turn came, she'd said, "There are signs in life. Signs that tell you what you have to do." Her voice had frightened me. I didn't want to hear what she had to say.

Jan Mary said, "Who's that?" Her knit gloves were soggy, her knees chapped above slipping down socks.

"Aunt Opal," Christopher said. His voice was dead and I knew he knew and understood.

Our breath came in blue blossoms in the cold, cutting air, and a light went on in the living room. I didn't want to go in, but I kept trudging through the snow.

Inside, everything was in its place, but our mother was gone, which made the house seem cold and empty. Four-year-old Suzanne stood on the heat register, her grubby chenille blanket a cape around her shoulders. Her hair had been recently brushed, and she wore plastic barrettes, a duck on one side, a bow on the other. When I remember those years at home, this is one of the things I focus on, how nothing ever matched, not sheets, not barrettes, not cups and saucers, not socks. And sometimes I think the sad and petty effort to have matching things has been one of the chief concerns of my adult life. Aunt Opal perched uneasily on a ladder-back chair with the baby, Laura Jean, on her lap. Laura Jean, eyes roving, held her own bottle of milk, and when she saw me, her look latched on to me and she stopped sucking and squirmed and kicked. Her plastic bottle clunked onto the floor. Aunt Opal's white wool pantsuit stretched tightly across her fat thighs. Her teased hair stood hard and swirled. Ill-at-ease, she shifted her weight gingerly as though she might get dirty. I thought I saw pity in her eyes, and I looked away. Christopher and Jan Mary hung back by the kitchen door, Christopher banging his metal lunch box softly against his leg.

"Where's our mother?" I said, scooping Laura Jean away from Aunt Opal.

"Now I hate to have to be the bearer of bad tidings," she began. " I know this will be hard on you children. I don't know what your mother was thinking of." She got up and stalked over to Suzanne, her spike heels dragging on the linoleum.

"Just tell me where she is." The baby stiffened in my arms. This was the first time I'd ever issued a command to a grown-up, and I felt both powerful and worried. Without our mother there, I was suddenly older.

Aunt Opal took a few seconds to adjust one of Suzanne's barrettes. "At the VA hospital," she said. "She's sick. Surely you must have known? She needs a rest. She's gone away and left you."

Christopher and Jan Mary went meek as old dogs into the living room and turned on the television. I snugged the baby into her high chair, wrapped a receiving blanket around her bare legs, and began peeling potatoes for supper. Suzanne sat in her miniature rocker, holding a Dr. Seuss book upside down and mouthing the words she knew by heart. I remember thinking if we could just have an ordinary supper, do our homework, fold the laundry, say our prayers, then it would be all right with Mother away. We might feel as though she'd just gone through the orchard to visit a neighbor, and that she might return at any moment.

"You'll have places to go, of course," Aunt Opal said, lighting the gas under the stale morning coffee. The sulphurous smell of the match lingered.

"Places?"

"Christopher can stay with Grandma and Grandpa. Janice will take the baby."

"We'll stay here together," I said.

"Roxanne," she said, pouring coffee into a flowered teacup. "You can't stay here alone with all these children."

I remember feeling small and powerless then, and I saw that I still needed to be taken care of—in fact, wanted to be taken care of—but I did not think I would be. I had no trust in anyone, and when you are a child feeling this way, every day becomes a swim through whitewater with no life jacket. Many years went by before I allowed myself to wonder where my father was during this time.

"How long will we be gone?" I said.

"It's hard to say," Aunt Opal said sighing. "It's really hard to say."

I was thirteen, Christopher twelve, and Jan Mary eight. We went to St. Martin's and rode the public school bus home, aware of our oddity—Christopher's salt-and-pepper cords instead of jeans, the scratchy scapulars against our chests, the memorization of saints' names and days and deeds. The week before our mother went away, I had stayed home from school twice, missing play auditions and report card day. She had written excuses on foolscap: *Please excuse Roxanne from school yesterday. I needed her at home.*

Our father worked in another state. The house was isolated, out in the country; our nearest neighbor lived a mile away. During the summer I loved where we lived—the ocean of apple blooms, the muted voices of the Spanish-speaking orchard workers, the wild berries, like deep black fleece along the railroad tracks. Winters were another story. We heated with wood, and the fine wood ash smudged our schoolbooks, our clothes and linens, our wrists and necks. The well was running dry, and we children shared our bathwater. By my turn the water was tepid and gray. Our mother fed the fire, waking sometimes twice in the night to keep it going, and her hands and fingers were cracked, swollen. I wanted to cry whenever I looked at them. The loneliness was like a bad smell in the house.

In the evening while the others, the younger ones, watched "I Love Lucy," she sipped Jack Daniel's from a jelly glass and told me her secrets, plucking me from childhood's shore. Very late, when the others had gone to bed, she'd curse our father in a whisper. One night, when she had filled that jelly glass for the third time, and wanted company, she told me about her true love, a woman she'd known in the WACS during the war when they worked together in the motor pool in Dayton, Ohio. You can learn too much too soon about your mother's past. The weight of her concerns made me turn from her and wish that something would save us from the life we shared with her. I couldn't make the wish while watching her split and bleeding hands light a cigarette. But later, lying confused and rigid in the double bed I shared with cuddling Jan Mary and Suzanne, I wished that our mother would go away.

All of the moving took place at night. Aunt Opal drove Suzanne, Jan Mary, and me up the Entiat River to Entiat Home, a place local people called the orphans' home, but in truth the children there were not orphans but children whose parents could not care for them. The frozen river glittered in the moonlight. The fir trees rode in dark procession along the far bank. I sat in the front seat, a privilege of the oldest. The car was vast and luxurious and foreign. Most of the way, no one spoke.

Finally, from the cavernous backseat, Suzanne said, "Where's the baby?"

Don't ask, I thought, don't ask. I tried to send this silent message to Suzanne, but she didn't get it. Blood beat in my head.

"Laura Jean might need us," she said.

"Laura will be fine. Fine, fine," Aunt Opal said. "She's with your cousin Janice, who has another baby for her to play with."

Her jolly voice made me feel as though someone was hugging me too hard, painfully. When we'd left Christopher at Grandma and Grandpa Swanson's I'd felt sick to my stomach, not because I would be separated from him—no—but because I wanted to stay there too. I wanted to cling to Grandma Swanson and say, Take me, keep me. But I was the oldest. I didn't cling and cry.

I would miss Christopher. We had fallen into the habit of sitting in the unfinished knotty-pine pantry, after our baths

and the dishes were done, listening to the high-school basket-
ball games on the staticky radio. We knew the players' names
and numbers. Together we had anticipated the mystery of
going to high school.

Aunt Opal turned slowly into the uphill drive, which was
lined with billows of snow. The dark was my comfort—I didn't
want to see everything at once. We parked in front of a red
brick house with two wrought iron lamps beside the neatly
shoveled steps. Silence leaped at us when Aunt Opal shut off
the engine. The place seemed a last outpost before the black
and convoluted mountains, the Cascades, which, I imagined,
went slanted and ragged to the sea. Then quickly, nimbly, a
man and woman came coatless down the steps and opened the
car doors, greeting us as though we were their own children
returning home. The woman was thin and wore pearls and a
skirt and sweater. The man had hair as black as an eggplant.
Their voices were cheerful, but they kept their hands to themselves, as though they knew we would not want to be touched
by strangers.

One moment we were in the dark, the car, the winter
mountain air; the next, all three of us were ushered into the
blinding white room, which was like a hospital room, with
white metal cupboards, white metal cots, and everything
amazingly clean and shiny under the fluorescent lights,
cleaner even than Grandma Swanson's house.

We sat on the edge of one cot without speaking to one another. Snow dripped in dirty puddles from our saddle oxfords.
The floor was black and white like a checkerboard. In the hallway, out of sight, Aunt Opal spoke with the man and woman—
"Well behaved," I heard her say—and then she departed with

all the speed and indifference of a UPS driver. Through a tall window in the room I watched her headlights sweep across the cinnamon bark of a ponderosa pine. From someplace faraway in the house came Christmas carols, wreathed in pure recorded voices. My body played tricks on me; my head hurt; my stomach knotted in an acid snarl.

Suzanne growled in a baby way she had when she was tired or angry. I pulled her onto my lap and she sucked her thumb. Consoling her was my only source of reassurance.

Jan Mary stamped the dirty puddles with the toe of her shoe. "How will we get to school?" she said.

"We'll go to a different school."

"I don't want to."

"We don't always get to do what we want," I said, shocked at the way I parroted our mother.

The woman in the pearls came into the bright room and leaned over us, one arm around Jan Mary's back.

"I'm Mrs. Thompson," she said. Her words were stout with kindness, which seemed a warning to me, as though she could hurt me, and she smelled good, like flowery cologne. She's someone's perfect mother, I thought.

"You'll need baths before bedtime, girls," she said. She strode to the oak door across the room and opened it, then switched on the bathroom light. "You have your own pajamas?"

"Yes," I said, nodding in the direction of the cardboard *Cream of Wheat* carton, which held my clothes. Each of us had packed a carton with our best things.

"You can help your sisters bathe, Roxanne," she said. "Then I'll check your heads for lice."

"Our mother wouldn't allow that," I said.

"What did you say?"

"Our mother wouldn't allow us to have lice," I said. My voice seemed inordinately loud.

"It's just our policy," she said. "Now get moving. It's late."

We bedded down the first night in that same room, on the single cots made up with coarse cotton sheets and cream-colored wool blankets with a navy stripe around the edge. The light from the hallway bridged the high transom of the closed door, and I didn't sleep for a long time. Our presence there rebuked our mother, and I felt that humiliation as keenly as though I were she. I kept thinking, We'll be better when we go home—we'll work harder, knock down the cobwebs more often, check Jan Mary's homework, throw out the mismatched socks. Keeping domestic order was, inexplicably, bound up with being good, blessed. The fantasies that lulled me to sleep were of cupboards packed with thick folded towels, full cookie jars, an orderly abundance like perpetual fire against the night.

The next morning I lay there, warm but wet, with the covers up to my neck. Suzanne and Jan Mary were still asleep. A cat meowed urgently in the hallway. The windows were long and divided into panes of wavery old glass. Outside it was snowing; the dry, fine net of winter. There was an old cottonwood tree in the yard that had been struck by lightning some time ago. The split in the main trunk had been girdled with an iron band; it had healed, and now the scar tissue bloomed over the edge of the metal ring. I wondered what time it was and what would happen next. The procedure of moving, being dropped off like a litter of kittens, had been bad enough, and now I had to admit I'd wet the bed. I dreaded telling someone, but wanted to get it over with.

I thought of Mary in *The Secret Garden* and the way her spite protected her. I remembered the places I'd read the book: on the school steps at recess in second grade, under the cooling arms of a juniper tree when I was eleven. My own spite and anger could not protect me. They were repulsive thoughts I couldn't bear to admit to myself, because then I'd have to admit them to the priest. I'd told him once that I'd wished our mother would go away. I'd wished it for my birthday, which seemed to magnify the sin. He did not understand the power of wishes, and for penance he gave me a mere five Hail Marys. And now our mother *was* gone and I tried to imagine her inside the VA Hospital, but I could only picture the rusted iron bars, the flaking pink stucco walls. It was down by the Columbia River. The summer I was ten, a male patient people called *a crazy* had deliberately walked into the river and drowned.

The door opened, Mrs. Thompson peeked in, and Jan Mary and Suzanne sat up in their cots, their choppy hair all askew, eyes puffy with sleep.

"Time to get up, ladies," Mrs. Thompson said. She wore a robe of some soft peach fabric.

"Snow," Suzanne announced.

I threw back the covers, and the cool air sliced through my wet pajamas and chilled me. I forced myself to slither across the floor.

"Mrs. Thompson," I said officiously, as though I spoke of someone else, "I've wet the bed."

"Oh?"

"What shall I do?"

She stepped into the room and closed the door. "Does this happen often?" She walked to my cot, with me close behind.

"Roxie wet the bed, Roxie wet the bed," Jan Mary sang.

I flung her a murderous glare, which silenced her at once.

"Sometimes," I said vaguely. By this time I had no feelings in the matter. I'd killed them, the way you track down a mud dauber and squash him.

Mrs. Thompson quickly jerked the sheets from the bed and carried them into the bathroom, holding them at arm's length from her peach robe.

"Please," I said. "Let me."

She dumped the sheets in the tub. "Run cold water on them. Add your pajamas. Rinse them good. Ask your sister to help you wring them out and then hang them over this shower curtain. When they dry, we'll put them in the dirty laundry." I felt I'd depleted whatever good will there'd been between us.

The entire six months at Entiat I followed this routine. I managed to keep from wetting the bed four times in that six months, by what miracle I could not tell. I tried prayers and wishes, not drinking after six in the evening. Nothing worked. I lived in the Little Girls' House, though my age was borderline— they could have assigned me to the Big Girls' House. And every day all the little girls knew what I'd done when they saw my slick and gelid sheets hanging like Halloween ghosts in the bathroom.

Mrs. Hayes, the dorm mother of the Little Girls' House, had two immense tomcats, Springer and Beau, whose claws had been removed. They lived like kings, always indoors. Everyone called the dorm mother Gabby Hayes behind her back. She was in her fifties and smelled of gardenias and cigarette smoke. Her lipstick was thick and cakey, the color of clay flower pots. She prided herself on her hair—it was coppery and resembled scrubbing pads we used in the kitchen. If someone broke the rules, she would announce to the group at large, "That's not allowed here." The chill in her voice always arrested the deviant.

Life in the Little Girls' House was orderly, neat, regulated. Before school in the morning we did our chores, young ones polishing the wooden stairs, older ones carting the laundry in duffle bags to the laundry building. Some were assigned kitchen duty, others bathrooms. Everyone, down to the four-year-olds, had work to do. I was impressed with the efficiency and equanimity with which work was accomplished. I wrote letters to our mother, in my experimental loopy left-hand slant, suggesting job charts on the refrigerator, new systems we could invent to relieve her of her crushing burden.

There were twenty-three of us. Jan Mary and Suzanne naturally gravitated toward others their age. They slept away from the oldest girls, in a drafty long hall near Mrs. Hayes's apartment. Our family ties were frayed, and I was genuinely surprised when I met Jan Mary's musing blue eyes in recognition across the dinner table. She seemed to be saying, How in the world did we arrive here?

The first day at the new school I was issued a faded blue cotton bloomer for PE. At St. Martin's, PE had meant softball on the playground. At the new school the locker room was my personal hell: the body smells, the safety-pinned bras, the stained slips, the hickeys, the pubic hair growing wild down our thighs. Sister Michael had always told us not to look at ourselves when we bathed, to be ashamed and vigilant. In the locker room we girls were elbow to elbow in the narrow aisle beside the dented pink lockers.

"What is your *prob*lem?"

"The F word. That's all he knows these days."

"My mother won't let me."

"Bud's getting a car for his birthday."

Their conversations shimmered around me like a beaded curtain. We couldn't help but see one another—our new breasts, our worn underwear—but the talk kept us on another plane, a place above the locker room, where we could pretend we weren't totally vulnerable, absolutely displayed.

Georgia Cowley, a squat freckled woman, ruled that class with a cruel hand. When I entered the gym for the first time, she waved sharply in my direction and I went over to her.

"Name?"

"Roxanne Miller."

"We're tumbling, Roxanne Miller," she said, writing something on her clipboard. "You ever tumbled?"

"No, ma'am." I looked at the girls casually turning cartwheels, blue blurs, on the hardwood floor. My hope of fading into the wrestling mats for the hour fluttered like a candle in a storm.

"Come out here with me," she said.

I followed her to the sweaty red mat in front of the stage.

"We start with forward rolls. Squat down."

I squatted, glancing desperately around to see if there was someone I could imitate. All motion had wound down, and the girls were gathered in gossip knots, chattering and watching me with slitted eyes. I remember staring at Miss Cowley's gym shoes; there were dried tomato seeds on one toe.

"Tuck your head. Now one foot forward, hands on the mat."

She gave me a little shove to propel me forward. I fell sideways, my pale thigh plopping fishlike on the floor. The girls giggled and hot tears swelled in my head. The seconds on the floor expanded, seemed to go on forever.

"Get up," she said. "Sit over there on the bleachers for a while and watch. You'll get the hang of it." Then she blew her chrome whistle, and the girls lined up to do their forward rolls.

On the bleachers, a Negro girl from Entiat, Nadine, slid next to me, sighing hard. "Got the curse," she said. "I'm sitting out."

"You can sit out?"

"Sure 'nough." She scratched her skinny calf. "You know the secret of cartwheels, Roxanne?"

"No," I said, interested, thinking there might be some secret I could learn from her, some intellectual knowledge that I could translate into body knowledge.

"Catch yourself before you kill yourself," she whispered, as she retied her sneaker. "Catch yo-*self*." And then she leaped up and turned a few, flinging herself into them with a flick of her pink palms.

"Jefferson," Cowley barked. "Sit down and keep quiet."

For the rest of gym period, Nadine and I wrote messages on each other's backs, using our index fingers like pencils through the scratchy blue bloomer blouses.

At Christmas we were farmed out. I do not know how these decisions were made. Certainly I don't remember being asked where I would like to go for Christmas. Suzanne went with Mr. and Mrs. Thompson. Jan Mary was taken by Aunt Opal. I went to stay with the family of Darla Reamer, who had been our neighbor for five years. Darla was two years older than I was. When I'd been in fifth grade and Darla in seventh, we rode the school bus together and wrote love notes to one another using a special language we'd developed, a lispish baby talk in writing. Later that year she chose another girl as her best friend and left me miserable. Going to spend Christmas with her and her family, enduring their charity, was like an arduous school assignment I had to survive to attain the next grade. Her mother gave me a Shetland sweater and a jar of Pacquins hand cream. Her father took me out in the wind-crusted snowy field to see his apiary. We went to church, and those brief moments kneeling in the oak pew and at the altar, with its starlike pointsettias, were the only familiarity and peace I experienced. Darla spent many hours on the telephone with Julia, the one who'd taken my place. I was relieved when Mr. Reamer drove me back to Entiat on Christmas night. Many girls were still away and Mrs. Hayes let me stay up late. I drank hot chocolate alone in the dining room and wrote our mother a letter of false cheer and fantasy about the future.

In the older girls' sleeping quarters, after lights out, under cover of dark, some girls took turns revealing fears, shames, wishes expressed as truth. When this talk began, their voices shifted from the usual shrill razzmatazz repartee about hairstyles, boys at school, and who'd been caught smoking. They spoke in church whispers.

"My mother tore my lip once. I have five stitches."

"My father's coming to get me on my birthday."

I didn't participate in this round-robin, but instead lay on my stomach, my pillow buckled under my chest, watching the occasional gossamer thread of headlights on the river road. It seemed there was so much freedom and purpose—a will at work—in night travel. Their talk was sad and low, and I, in my isolation, dreamed of going away, of having the power, the inestimable power, to say *I'm leaving*. Boys could somehow run away and make it, survive. But everyone knew that a girl's life was over if she ran away from home, or whatever had become home, whatever sheltered her from ruin.

Some nights, if we heard the rush of Mrs. Hayes's shower, we would sing in our thin voices a maudlin song that was popular at the time—"Teen Angel." One night the community of singing gave me courage, and after the song faded, I said, "I saw my mother hit my father with a belt."

As one they sucked in their breath. Then Nadine said, "No *wonder* your mama in the hospital, girl."

And the others laughed, a false, tentative snicker. I hated Nadine at that moment and felt heartbroken in my hate. I'd always tried to be nice to her, because our mother had said they were just like everyone else inside.

On Valentine's Day, we received a crumpled package wrapped in a brown grocery sack and tied with butcher twine. Inside was a cellophane bag of hard candy hearts stamped BE MINE and I LOVE YOU. Our mother had enclosed three penny valentines and on mine she wrote, "I'm home now with Laura Jean and Christopher. See you soon." She was home!

I'd given up on mail from her, but I'd kept writing. I tried to imagine her there with Christopher and the baby, without me to help her, and the thought made me feel invisible, unnecessary in the world. Don't think about it, I said to myself, and I began then the habit of blocking my thoughts with that simple chant. *Don't think about it.*

In April we were allowed to go home for a weekend.

"Your neighbor's here," Mrs. Hayes whispered in my ear, early that Saturday morning. "Help your sisters dress. I'll give him a tour while he's waiting."

I had a great deal to be excited about: seeing Christopher, going to our old church, being with our mother. Our mother. Her life without me was a puzzle, with crucial pieces missing. I had high hopes about going home. Our mother was well; everyone—Mrs. Hayes, Mr. Reamer—said so.

We met him by his pickup truck. His khakis were spattered with pastel paint; he said he'd been painting his bee boxes. We fell into silence on the drive home. The thought surfaced, like the devil's tempting forefinger, that though we were only an hour's drive from our mother, we hadn't seen her since that morning in December when we went to school not knowing life would be irrevocably changed by the time we returned home. Did she know that morning that she wouldn't see us for four months?

Spring was alive down in the valley. The daffodil leaves were up along the driveway, though the flowers were still just pale shadows of memory, curled tightly and green. Mr. Reamer parked his pickup truck and sat hunched, arms folded across the steering wheel, waiting for us to get out.

We were all shy, bashful, and I hung back, urging Jan Mary and Suzanne forward with little pushes on their shoulder blades.

Jan Mary flinched and said meanly, "Don't push."

"Don't spoil it now," I said.

And we three walked forward in a solemn row down the gravel drive toward the house. We wore our next-best dresses. Mine was a taffeta plaid with a smocked bodice and a sash, and I'd worn my cream-colored knee highs, saving my one pair of nylons for Sunday morning. I hadn't wanted to go home in nylons—they were a new addition to my sock drawer and I was afraid our mother would say I was growing up too fast. The house looked the same, sagging at the roof corners, the gray paint blistering along the bottom of the door. It was a sunny day. Darla Reamer's cocker spaniel came yapping out the drive, flipping and bouncing the way cockers do. As we drew near the house, I saw that Darla was sitting with our mother in that small patch of grass in front of the house. Someone had put a wooden cable spool there for a table, and Darla and Mother sat near each other in lawn chairs. Darla was painting Mother's fingernails.

"Here come my girls," Mother said, waving her free hand.

Music was on inside the house and we could hear it through the open window: *you made me love you*. I didn't know what to do with Darla there. I'd imagined our mother embracing us, welcoming us, with significance. My heart shrank in disappointment, a rancid feeling, everything going sour at once. Suzanne, being only four, went right up to our mother and slipped her little arms around her neck and kissed her cheek. Jan Mary said, "Will you do mine, too, Darla?"

Laura Jean started crying from somewhere in the house. Mother, startled, rose partway from her chair and then sank back, waving her wet fingernails and looking helplessly at Darla. There was a raw, clean smell about the yard, like cornsilk when you go outside to shuck corn in the summer dusk. Darla looked older, in a straight linen skirt with a kick pleat in the back. She had on slim flats and tan-tinted nylons. Her hair was in a French roll.

"I'll get her," Darla said, and she went in the house, letting the screen door slam. Suzanne was close on her heels.

Mother pulled me near, her arm around my waist. "How's my big girl?" she asked. She'd had her black hair frizzed in a permanent wave and her nails were painted fire-engine red. With one hand she shook a Lucky from the pack on the table. A glass of whiskey and melting ice was on the ground beside her chair. Her knuckles looked pink, but the cuts and splits were healed.

"Fine," I said.

"Darla's been helping me," she said.

I held my breath to keep from crying.

I felt exhausted, not the clean exhaustion of after-dark softball but a kind of weariness; I was worn out with the knowledge that life would be different, but not in the way I had imagined or hoped. I didn't want to forgive her for being the way she was, but you have to forgive your mother. She searched my eyes and tried to make some long-ago connection, sweet scrutiny, perhaps the way she'd looked at me when I was a new baby, her first baby. I looked away. Jan Mary gnawed delicately at her cuticles. Christopher came around the corner of the house swinging his Mickey Mantle bat, his leather mitt looped on his belt. The new spring leaves were so bright they hurt my eyes.

1986

Lessons in Joy

Beau called collect from Belize City on a sleepy Monday morning. Alice fumbled the receiver, said, yes. Yes.

"Gordie's van's broken down," he said. "We're stuck here for a few days." A pause. Wherever he was, Alice could hear the rackety belch of a truck or bus, muted reggae, and a hawker—selling what, she wondered, wanting to be there herself, on a foreign street. "You said to call collect."

"That's fine."

"Were you sleeping?"

"I'm in a different time zone."

"I'm sorry."

"It's okay." She cleared her throat. "Really. I have to get up soon anyway." A dollar a minute okay, she thought. There was a lag between his spoken words and the transmission of them, so that they were interrupting one another. Still, she half-anticipated that he must have something important to say. Perhaps, When are you coming back?

She said, "Who's that hollering?"

"Some guy with a tub of lobsters."

She tried to picture him: his home-cut curly hair under a red kerchief, his knees. For Christ's sake, she thought, I'm gaga over his knees. They talked about the weather, they talked about the 49ers, they talked about the dog dying at their favorite saloon, Mama Jane's Rum & Poker Paradise. He said they were going out to the beach to play Frisbee. He never went anywhere without his Frisbee.

Then, "I better go. It's expensive."

"It's okay."

"Are you all right?"

"Uh-*huh*," Alice stressed. "I'm over culture shock."

"Gordie's waiting, Alice. It's great to hear your voice."

And that was it. She was left holding the receiver, the night still there outside her window, opaque as their conversation. Long distance was the tease of the century, she thought, the empty calories of romance. Her fingers ached from squeezing the phone so hard.

Alice Waverly's weakness was younger men. She'd learned this phrase from an old rockabilly tune on the jukebox in a Chinese restaurant she'd frequented back in Dillon. Except the singer was an old man who said, with a little leer in his voice, "Young girls is my weakness." That's me, she'd recognized, feeling wicked and ashamed, but incorrigible. She liked their spunk, their vulnerability, their childish delight in all things ordinary, hence, sacred: moonlight, puns, raisins in curry, little kids. She liked the way they shivered when you touched them certain ways. They had thin histories and few regrets; that kept them in the present, full bloom now. She liked, too, that she didn't have to be responsible to them somewhere down the crazy river, as another song went. They weren't inquisitive; they didn't collect your fears and longings and hold you hostage; they were easy to leave.

The last one had been Beau. She'd met him at a Peace Corps party near Mango Creek. They had stayed together one month, a month of late-night talks, beach outings, bike rides, daytime lovemaking—the light always pastel through the tattered curtains, the green smooth coconuts just out of reach on the palm tree. Right before Alice had planned to vagabond north, toward the States, they were gripped with the merest beginning of love, something like the first day of coming down with the flu, in spite of themselves. He'd surprised her with the strength of his affection, though she didn't think that had that much to do with *her*. He was twenty-eight and had love in him waiting to be tapped. Alice had thought she could leave Beau behind. But they'd exchanged a few letters—letters deceptive in their lightness. Much went unsaid, nearly everything. The less he asked, the more she wondered. Mostly she wondered what the letters meant; they were so skeletal; they seemed like the leftover bones of a fine meal.

Now Alice thought of herself as passing through California, though she'd been in Quincy for two months, clerking and baking at a natural foods store. California's not my cup of tea, she'd said to Trina, who owned the store. What scared her were gang wars and toxic yellow smog and earthquakes. But Quincy was small-town, with one cappuccino bar, no *L.A. Times*, no chain stores, and high country hiking nearby. Before that she'd been in San Francisco for two weeks with a roommate from years ago, and before that she'd been in Tucson where Matt, her nineteen-year-old son, was studying engineering. She was on her way home to Dillon, Montana, after eight months traveling on an inheritance too small to use for anything else. In January she'd quit her job and flown to Costa Rica and worked her way back, by bus, from there. This was something she'd always wanted to do, and after her father died—suddenly, of a heart attack, at the dry cleaners, right on the heels of her mother, who'd passed away the summer before—Alice was hounded by a sense of time running out, though she was only forty. Now she felt better, years younger.

She was counting on getting her old job back; it was a hard job, counseling divorced women trying to find work. She'd known their stories; their new boyfriends' names and foibles; their kids' problems—which ones wet the bed, which ones were on the way to being teenage mothers, which ones had trouble reading. It was a job to make you drink to forget, a job that made you cry sometimes, a job that could make you cynical about men, if you were the least bit inclined to be that way. Alice wasn't. She loved men. She'd been married once—to a good man she'd tell you, it just hadn't worked out, she'd been just as bullheaded as he was—and she'd had more affairs of the heart than she cared to remember. Alice had trained the young woman they'd hired to take her place and she didn't think she would last long. She was a greenhorn and had no calluses from rubbing up against life.

Her plan was this: return to Dillon and put her father's house on the market; take her things out of storage, comfort herself with her own things again; apply for jobs; go bird-watching on Red Rock River; wax her skis; enjoy winter coming on; wait it out. Oh, yes, she had a plan; she just wasn't excited about the plan. But there were people in Dillon expecting her: a man who taught logic at the college who had been—and might still be—a little sweet on Alice; Georgia, her friend at the library, with whom she skied and drank coffee nudges; and Mrs. Hopper, her father's next-door neighbor, whose apartment must seem vacant now without Alice's father and his fusty cigar smoke. In memories, she could hear Mrs. Hopper fussing at him, razzing him, calling him a polecat. She could picture her mother's potting shed, with the clay pots and bags of dirt and peat moss. This saddened her, imagining the absence of her parents. She tried not to think about it. She'd bought a sea-green handwoven rug near Lake Atítlan. She could imagine unfolding that rug in a new apartment, doing yoga stretches on the rug, creating her own pleasing space for whatever might happen next in her life. Whatever.

Out the kitchen window of the store, on Wednesday morning, she saw the yellowing cottonwoods—it was mid-September—and Professor Felder, next door at his stone barbecue pit, slopping starter fluid on a Confederate flag windsock.

She went to the screen door, her hands floury with pie dough. "Whatcha doin', Connie?" She called.

"You probably know where this came from," he said, without looking up. "You've probably seen it around. Goddamn rednecks."

Alice *had* seen the windsock. It had appeared one day on the porch of a duplex rental three streets away. She hadn't seen the new people, just the windsock and the plywood windmills they'd planted in a row along the crocus bed.

Professor Felder's white hair shone like river water in the morning sun. He had it cut in an old style that had become new, thick and long on top, short around the ears and neck.

He'd told her it was prematurely white and had been for fifteen years; he was fifty-five. No grass grew under his feet. He wore Birkenstocks with ragg socks, he had an extensive collection of Blue Note jazz CDs (he'd informed her; she hadn't heard them, because she'd steadfastly weaseled out of visiting him at home), and he jogged twelve miles a week. His doctor had told him not to overdo it if he didn't want to ruin his joints. The Professor—that's what she called him to herself, though he had insisted she call him Connie to his face—was retired from parasitology, a widower. His wife, Carla, had taught junior-high English in Davis for twenty-three years.

"Where'd you get it?" she said.

"I filched it, my dear. Liberated it, as we used to say. In the middle of the night."

Alice laughed. "You're asking for trouble," she said, then she turned back to her pies, all berry—blueberry, blackberry, raspberry. Tart and almost sugar-free.

At the window, her hands gently, gently in the dough again, she watched him as he dropped a lit match on the windsock and stepped back, fists on his hips, grinning at Alice, satisfied. The burning windsock lapped into flames like a magic act, and after the first flames died down it glowed blue and orange around the edges, like one of those fake fireplace logs.

From the front of the store Trina said, "Go light on the white death."

"Yes, love," Alice said. She gritted her teeth and chafed under Trina's bossiness. She remembered something Matt's father used to say: The trouble with hippie desserts is that there's never enough sugar in them.

Trina was at the cash register, pricing licorice bars from Finland. She was recovering from hepatitis she'd caught at a blender drink stand in San Miguel, and that's how Alice had come to be there in Quincy, baking pies and carob chip cookies the size of round tarot cards. Trina and she had traveled together in central Mexico. Trina had come down with hepatitis at home and realized she couldn't keep the business open without good help during her recovery. Alice had shown up in Quincy at the right time, and Alice had a charming way of taking over the chores of others and letting them believe they were doing her a favor. She liked cooking good food, with love; there was service in that, something old-fashioned, almost spiritual. She liked the gleam of eggplant piled in lovely curves; the scent of cardamom and cloves; the sizzle of falafel frying. And of course, she liked the little moans of pleasure from people who ate her food, the appreciative glances.

"Addictions are lurking everywhere," Trina said. "And we don't want to contribute to anyone's addiction."

Give me a break, Alice thought. And then, It's time for us to part company while we still respect one another. She thought about how some music is just right for certain times in your life. You think you'll always love the sha-boom of sock hops, a boy's hand trembling on your hip. You hear the music years later and it's laughable, tinny. Places are like that, too, Alice thought, and the time of Quincy might be over soon.

"Just say no's not good enough," Trina prattled on. "We're talking *physical* addiction here. Remember *Sugar Blues*."

Alice sprinkled a shallow layer of tapioca beads on the bottom crusts in the glass pie plates. She tried to picture somewhere else, someplace soothing, a beach, or an eddy on the Red Rock. Joni Mitchell was on the stereo, singing about parking lots. Alice glanced up and saw the Professor in his backyard, his pants pockets pulled out like rabbits' ears, shrugging in her direction and smiling sheepishly. She laughed out loud; experience had taught her what he wanted: a wedge of free hot pie.

After that, they got busy. People from the courthouse came in for mid-morning coffees and baklava; there was a honey delivery; two young mothers, with five children between them, did a month's shopping—buying up bulk rice and couscous like survivalists—while the children flushed the toilet in the bathroom; the pies baked; Alice made the lunch sandwiches, wrapped them in plastic wrap, too efficient and organized to let Trina get under her skin again.

When the mail came, she took a break. With a lemonade and her letters and a slice of pie for the Professor, Alice nudged open the screen door, no-hands, and went out to the picnic table behind the store, under the cottonwood. The table was covered with leaves. She could smell new-cut lumber and fall, a kind of damp and pleasant rotting. Beyond the Professor's backyard, three bow hunters in cammies were target shooting. Insects snapped in the tall dry tansy, a sound like a rubberband being rolled off a newspaper.

The Professor sat down and started in on the pie.

Alice shuffled through the mail. There was Matt's faithful letter—he wrote every three weeks—with a bit of graffiti on the back of the envelope: *Reporter: What do you think of Western*

Civilization? Mr. Gandhi: I think it would be a good idea! An Exxon bill. She kept forgetting to tell them she'd cut up her card after the oil spill. A request from Planned Parenthood for a donation. A postcard from Mrs. Hopper. And a letter from Central America. Alice's heart punched her chest a little harder when she saw the return address on the airmail envelope. She was surprised at the response she felt at recognizing his handwriting, a response at once curious, anxious, aroused. It was a visceral response; she felt momentarily weak with lust. Wasn't imagination a curse and a blessing? She thought she could feel his mouth on her nipples just from looking at his handwriting. She wanted to get on her magic carpet and be there.

"Mail galore," the Professor said, wiping his chin with a cottonwood leaf.

"My cup runneth over," Alice said.

He licked the fork and then said, "I'll leave you to read it. But later—I'm going to look at some houses. Would you like to come?"

Alice didn't look up. She tapped the edge of one letter against the tabletop. "Not today."

The Professor wandered away, whistling. He'd left his cotton sweater draped over the bench. The bow hunters were disagreeing about something; their voices rose and they talked over one another. One of them—a short man with a stubby black pony tail—slung his bow testily into the open back of a station wagon. Another one spread a big map on the hood of the car. That's what she longed for—a map, certainty, directions for contouring around dangerous places. A cloud pushed a bluish shadow over the backyard, then over the alley. She read Matt's letter first; the gist of it was that he wanted to "stop out" of school for a semester. She felt shocked by this—he hadn't given her any hint of his intentions when she was in Tucson. She drank half the lemonade, set Matt's letter aside, unfolded, under the lemonade glass. In Beau's letter, there was no gist. It was as though he existed only in that ten minutes during which he wrote the letter—she was privy to what music he had on the boombox as he wrote, the cat's acrobatics, and that was that. A cinematic letter. She could see him but she couldn't know his heart and mind.

Trina opened the back door and wagged her kinky blonde head. She had a perm, stiff as a wig. "They're lined up at the register, Alice," she shouted. "I'm desperate."

Yes, ma'am, Alice thought, scooping up the mail. She felt pinched from all sides and remembered a motto on newsprint that Mrs. Hopper had under a teddy bear magnet on her fridge: If you think things are going pretty well, watch out—adversity is probably just around the corner.

There was plenty of lore about your forties. Jane Fonda on a talk show telling the host, Honey, this is what forty *looks* like! Ingrid Bergman saying, At forty you get the face you deserve. And Lauren Hutton spelling out your options. After forty you have to choose between your bottom and your face. When asked how it felt to turn forty, Alice would say, It's harder to pretend you're a sweet young thing. She had trained herself to sleep on her back to avoid wrinkling her cheeks and forehead. She lay there long into the night, in her dormer room over the store, with the moon sliding by her cracked window, counting question marks like sheep. She admitted she had been thinking of going back to Belize; Dillon hadn't been looking that good, in spite of all her forced fantasies. But common sense—that strict witch—reminded her that the very things she loved about Beau might break her back in the long run. And now Matt. She had a book of accounts—what she could and could not do in order to be a member in good standing of their family unit, as Matt referred to the two of them. She didn't think she could leave the country if Matt dropped out of school. She'd have to be more responsible in the world—she wasn't sure why. And what would she say to him? She didn't want to be the kind of mother who said, Do as I say, not as I do. Something about the loss of potential passion—and not just Beau, but the person she herself became when she was in Belize, a person at once wise and childlike, willing to risk—imagining that loss made her throat tighten, made her feel, if not exactly old at least ageing.

A small rock pinged against her window.

She went to the window and looked down. A street lamp cast a watery salmon-colored light in the yard; everything looked sharply defined and hyperreal, like the leaves, gravel, hedges, of a model train world. And there was the Professor, in a batter's stance on the picnic table, wearing a periwinkle blue jacket and a plaid cap she'd given him from Panajachel. He rubbernecked up at her and grinned. His skin looked hyperreal, too, sun-roughened, he'd told her, from spending so much time in the Central Valley picking up animal droppings to study.

She lugged open the window, wincing at the metallic screech. "What the hell are you doing?" she said. The night was cool. Alice wore a long cotton nightgown printed with rows of tiny blue and gray fleurs-de-lis.

"You're beautiful," he declared, not the least bit shy.

"Are you drunk?"

"Bet your bottom dollar I'm not," he said. "Why don't you come out to play?"

Alice glanced up and down the alley, hugging herself. The dense covers—down and flannel—were curled back over the bed, beckoning to her. "It's much too late for that, Connie," she said. "Come back tomorrow. Tomorrow's my day off."

The Professor leaped to the ground. "Do you mean it?"

Alice shooed him away. "Yes, yes, I mean it. Now go. It's getting on toward fall, isn't it? Go home and go to bed." She shut the window and watched him meander away. When he turned once to catch her standing at the window, she pressed herself against the wall where he couldn't see. She smiled in the moon-roiled room, stunned at herself for not realizing until now the Professor's intentions. No way can this be more than a corny moonlight encounter, she thought, timeworn, truly timeworn, but she liked the sound of that, *You're beautiful.*

The Professor wanted to buy an old house and start a bed and breakfast out near the Pacific Crest Trail. "Not your run-of-the-mill B & B," he'd told her. "Streamlined. No Little Bo Peeps staring down from the chifforobes. Only teak. Nothing cutesy."

That Thursday afernoon they wheeled over the winding mountain roads in the Professor's mint-green rehabbed VW bug, poking around lodges that'd been boarded up with plywood and let go, a cedar-shingled bungalow, an A-frame with a shiny tin roof, all places that people were getting rid of. Maybe they'd found a more glitzy place for vacations, maybe business was bad, maybe families just petered out. "Nothing's really grabbing me," the Professor said. "How about you?"

Alice shook her head. "Not a fixer-upper in the bunch. Not a one with character."

They stopped now and then to look at trees. The Professor knew all about them. Grand fir, black oak, sugar pine. And Alice thought what a solid, happy thing she found that trait in a man, some esoteric knowledge about one aspect of nature. Matt's father had known the birds by song and sight and habit; she still missed that.

By and by, in the twilight, they found themselves at Buck's Lake, at the lodge tavern. And that is how they happened to go dancing. The band was called Pie Face. The Professor could really dance, no getting around that. Alice had known this—they'd danced together at a barn dance on the Fourth of July—but she'd forgotten it. The barn had been dismantled for the barnboard, but the stone foundation and floor were still there, in the cradle of the wide valley with the burning stars overhead. Tipsy and happy, they'd danced until the roosters crowed. The Professor had won half a pig, freezer-wrapped, in a drawing, and the next day he'd invited Alice over for a loin roast, but she hadn't gone. Dancing, he made *you* look good, led you into steps, slick moves, graceful sways—jitterbug, fox-trot, salsa—you never knew you were capable of.

Later they went laughing out into the foggy night. The roads were inpenetrable with fog, the headlights burrowing back at them.

"It's bad," Alice said, suddenly alert.

The Professor pulled over into the gravel shoulder and stopped. He turned off the headlights and slid the heater lever to high. "Let's wait here a bit," he said.

She stared out the passenger window. "It's a long way to Quincy."

"Patience, my dear, patience. It's a virtue possessed by no men and few women."

"These roads make me nervous. Even in broad daylight."

"Alice. You can't prevent disasters."

Alice did not answer for a minute. She pulled up the cuffs of her white cotton socks and folded them down, almost prissily. Then she said, "You're not talking about the roads, are you?"

"What was in those letters, anyway?"

His aftershave smelled citrusy, orangy. "Nothing," she said. "Nothing I feel like getting into." She dug around in her crocheted purse for hand cream, squeezed a dab from the tube and rubbed it over her hands.

"You're grieving about something."

"Grief's a pretty strong word."

She silenced him with that. He folded his arms and stared out his window. Alice did the same.

Finally he ventured, "How's Matt?"

And then she told him: how Matt wanted to stop out of school; how out of control this made her feel; what retro-rebels his friends were; how they listened to the Doors and Jimi Hendrix and talked about buying land and moving to the country; how she worried that Matt would make the same mistakes she made at his age; that Matt might not listen to her or value what she thought. She didn't mention Beau. She had an inkling that if she talked about him his memory might turn as stale as last week's cornbread.

"What mistakes?"

Alice shrugged. "Dropping out. Breaking rules."

"You haven't turned out so badly."

"You don't know."

As they talked, the fog sailed around the mountain, thinned, grew diaphanous.

"It's better now," Alice said.

The Professor shifted around to face her in the cramped car. The backseat was full of fresh basil he'd picked at an herb farm; he was planning to make his own pesto. The darkness was dense, loaflike. He lifted the hair at her neck, touched her at the nape, his fingers cool and deliberate and gentle.

She hadn't been touched in a while, and she sat there liking it, teetering. For just a few seconds she could have gone either way. Then she thought, This is a real person here; he's courting you or thinking about courting you; you don't want to lead him on; think of the trouble. She gingerly eased away and said, "We should go. I have to work in the morning."

The Professor turned on the headlights and pulled onto the blacktop road. "Cows to milk and chickens to feed," he said. "I see. I see."

Coming down the hill past the junior college, Alice said, out of the blue, "I could change my mind. About anything."

"That's what minds are for," the Professor said.

Alice laughed out loud. Something about what he said gave her pause, lifted her out of her brooding.

And right before she hopped out of the car, the Professor said, "Don't leave yet. I mean, Quincy."

"Professor," she blurted, striking a sour note altogether and knowing it, even as she spoke, aiming for teasing at the wrong time, "why don't you mind your own beeswax?"

He flinched. Then he whispered, surprisingly kindly, "You've got a little killjoy in you, Alice."

She was immediately sorry and irritated; her heart hurt a little from hurting him. But she got out of the car and went inside without setting things right.

In her room, she sat in a wicker chair, staring out the window, with just the seashell night-light glistening low in the room. She was resentful that they'd come far enough to be hurt. That was much too far for safety's sake. *Killjoy.* Was that what she'd become? She could see the teal blue side pocket of her backpack under the bed; she imagined packing. Their last words had made her feel at once inert, weighed down, mapless, yet poised for flight.

Without saying goodby, the Professor went out of town, leaving his yellow porch light burning, his kitchen blinds closed. Mail accumulated in his wooden mailbox. Alice felt a little sadness, like a paper cut that kept getting in the way. She watched for him. Catching herself, startling herself, she realized she knew the purling of a Volkswagen engine and that she was listening, keen for that sound. But then she would remind herself, He's not what you're pining for. She wanted closure, friendly forgiveness.

On Saturday morning Trina said, "Listen to this. Some people never learn." She was standing in front of the community bulletin board, stretching both arms over her head. "'Good company. Non-smoker. Urgently needs ride to Seattle Labor Day weekend. Can drive, share expenses, change tires. It's a matter of love.' Then there's a guy's name and phone number."

Alice was sweeping the wooden floor. She stopped beside the dried fruit bins. "So?"

"So," Trina said, eyeing her. "It's a little corny, don'tcha think? 'It's a matter of love'?"

"I think it's sweet," Alice said meanly.

"Touchy, aren't we?" Trina said.

Later, after the lunch crowd dawdled away, Alice said to Trina, "Next week's my last week." Quitting felt like opening a window on a stuffy room. She'd quit jobs before and the first few weeks were always wonderful, a heady emancipation from routine.

Matt called over the weekend. "It's just for a semester, Mom. I need to switch my major. To what, I'm not sure."

"What're you thinking of?"

"Do you think people'll think I'm an airhead? I've changed my mind three times this week." And Alice knew what to say, encouragingly. "That's what minds are for."

Then Matt asked her how to bake a berry pie; she was happy to tell him everything she knew about it—the tapioca, the fragility of the dough, the way you have to use a hot oven for the first twenty minutes to get a good crust. She hung up feeling as though they'd exchanged unexpected gifts.

The Professor came back on Monday evening. Alice spied on him as he unloaded his belongings. There was a saturated orange sky beyond his car, his pale yellow house. She sipped at two fingers of straight gin diluted with lemon juice and pretended to watch the sunset. A block away, at the Rialto, teenagers were lining up for the six-thirty show. Next to the Professor's house a man and a woman, in matching Day-Glo helmets, swung their legs in arcs over their mountain bikes, springing into the empty street.

She went over and knocked on his door. She'd practiced saying, in a nice way, that she just wanted to tell him she *was* leaving soon. She didn't know what he would say then, but she thought they might have a cup of herbal tea or a glass of wine. She thought it would all work out.

He opened the door and said, "I found it. I found just the place, Alice. Come in, come in. I've got Polaroids."

She entered his kingdom, his territory. His past was abundant in the house, the accretions of a life explored, travel books and poetry books, masks from Latin America on the kitchen wall, shelves of cookbooks—Moroccan, Italian, Alaskan, Thai—a row of burgundy-colored home-canned cherries, cross-country skis and poles in the corner. The place smelled like the basil, which had been abandoned on the kitchen counter before he went away. Alice thought, I'm supposed to learn something here. On the wall were many photographs of the Professor—at the summits of mountains, in a hammock by some tropical sea, in an inner tube on a river with a redheaded woman.

"That's on the Yuba River," he said, watching her intently.

"And the woman—that's Carla?"

"That's her," he said softly.

"She was pretty."

"Yes. Some people think I should get rid of that picture. But it's a comfort to me." Then, "Look." He took her elbow, led her to the teak kitchen table. The snapshots were laid out in a row between a typewriter and a stack of folded paisley napkins.

The house was made of logs, smoky and aged, with a deep front porch and a row of wind chimes glimmering in the sunlight. A big blue spruce slanted to the right of the porch, away from the house. It looked like a place where babies had been born, where people had fallen in love, where, possibly, people had grown old and died. The stone steps swayed down into the yard invitingly.

"Nice tree," Alice said.

"I thought you'd think so."

"How big is the house?"

"Wait'll you see the kitchen. The kitchen'll knock your socks off."

The Professor stood just behind her, his chin grazing her shoulder as they leaned over the snapshots. He smelled like a ponderosa pine. With certainty, he rested his palm on her hip. He was intrepid, willing to try again. Alice thought about Carla dying, then her own death. She strained to imagine the end of everything: Matt's letters, dancing, pie dough, confusion, weather, touch. In a wild leap of mind that made her feel almost as though she'd left her body, she thought, It doesn't really matter who you settle on to love, finally, providing you both deserve it.

Later, she would tell him about her parents dying. And then about Beau. He would whisper, So that's what you're grieving over, and he would read aloud to her a poem that Carla had always liked, a poem about unremembered lads and summer ending. She would want to hear all about Carla, his love for her, what was possible. They would put Stan Turrentine on the CD player and slow dance to saxophone in the living room. He would kiss the vaccination scar on her arm.

But for now, in the very changing of her mind, Alice thought about how they might someday—barring any unforeseen disaster—reminisce about coming this far: the fog at Buck's Lake, shimmying to Pie Face, the barn dance, with the stars like stars you were seeing for the first time, that bright, that extravagant. She saw how you could be longing, yearning, for the woman you were at another place, another time, and still be changing, inexorably, into who you were now. The longing and letting go and becoming weren't separate steps; they happened in the same paradoxical moment.

She turned around and breathed deeply, kissed his cheek.

"No cold shoulder this time?" he bantered.

Smiling, Alice said, "Not if you butter me up."

She wondered what would happen next.

Whatever it was, she thought surely history was in the making.

1990

Aces

"Kit, baby," my mother says, "he's my lover, not my husband."

Red light, I think. Our voices grate against the Montana to Mexico connection. It's like we're talking in a tin can, vacuum-packed. My mother says lover the way she says *Brie*, and husband comes out like *saltine*. She's explaining why she can't ask Dan to front Ruck and me the money to retain a lawyer. I can picture her there in San Miguel, among her geraniums, smoking the Virginia Slims her minister brings her in caseloads from Laredo. She can sit on her patio all day and never see the yoked women hauling well water in molasses cans. I've been to Dan's house, which squats high on a mountainside behind a white-washed wall. She and Dan treated Kevin and me to a trip there when Kevin was just a baby, five years ago. Dan's generosity was more evident when they were first together. Before Ruck. B.R., I've heard my mother say to my brother when she thought I wasn't listening. When she's in a certain mood, time in my life is measured *before Ruck* and *after Ruck*.

"Mother," I start. Then I don't know what to say. I want the money and I'm afraid I'll say the wrong thing and screw up my chances. The pay phone receiver's sticky and dirty. My breath is ashen like the sky. It's twenty below in Bozeman, enemy cold, two days before Thanksgiving. I'm at the phone booth outside the Molly Brown, and smashed paper beer cups litter the gravel parking lot. Chilled rivulets of sweat run under my navy pea jacket. My sneakers have holes in the toes; my pink socks tuft frozen through the holes; my feet ache from the cold.

"This is costing, Katherine."

"Are you getting the drift? We were *busted*."

"How did you get out of jail?"

"This woman. Ruck used to work for her."

"Where's Kevin? Poor thing."

"Kevin's with us." I do not want to tell her the way the local deputy said, "Come on, son," to Kevin and led him away in his pajamas and moon boots in the middle of the night. I do not like to remember the embarrassed half-wave Kevin gave me, ducking his head, as though he'd known all along this might happen. Do you know what you think about when you are suddenly separated from your child by forces beyond your control? I didn't think about the sweet afterbath smell of him or the wilted oxeye daises I find lined in a row in his room or the proud way he recites nursery rhymes. No. I sat on the bed in my cell, the walls of which were painted hysterical orange, and thought of every rotten remark I'd ever made in exhaustion or impatience. I tormented myself and hoped to God Kevin was not remembering what I was remembering. He's out of the foster home now and he sticks like glue to Ruck.

"Did he do it?"

She means, Is he guilty? "No, Mother. You know Ruck. He had the horse barn all set up with his lab, his inventions. Someone—a Jehovah's Witness or the woman who brings the milk—someone just saw all that stuff and misunderstood."

"Metham—what's it called?"

"Methamphetamine. Like diet pills."

"They used to call it speed."

I do not ask her how she knows this, but I remember the Halcion sleeping pills, little blue dream wheels, I once stole from her medicine cabinet. I do not tell her that it doesn't matter to me whether he's guilty or not. Just as it will not matter to the lawyer as long he has his money and Ruck finds a path of even terrain through the truth and never deviates from it.

"They treated us like dangerous people," I say. This seems to strike just the right note, since she knows we are not dangerous people and deserve better treatment. She's bending my way, like a tree under weight of winter snow.

"Are you in Jardine right now?" I hear her blowing smoke away from the phone, a weary sound.

"No, we're in Bozeman. The feds won't let us go back to the trailer yet. They say they're still sifting the evidence."

"Where're you living?"

"In a friend's garage."

"A garage?"

"It's not so bad. Really. It's insulated. There's a wood stove."

"You're not—"

"Not what?"

"You're not sleeping on the floor, are you?"

"Ruck built a loft. Sort of a platform."

She sighs. "What about legal aid? They have that there, don't they?"

"We tried that," I say. "It was no go." Too corrupt for legal aid, I think.

"Give me your number."

"I'm at a pay phone. Ellen can't afford a phone yet."

"Call me again on Thanksgiving," she says. "I'll see what I can do."

"Thank you, Mother," I say. My mooching voice fills me with self-loathing. It's chronic, whenever I speak with her. Thirty-four seems too old to be calling collect, to be asking for money.

"Kit, dear," she says, just before we hang up, "take care."

And for a split second her voice brings tears to my eyes, but that is my response to my own life, not my response to her.

Jardine, Montana, is not a place I ever thought I'd end up.

I went to university at UC-Santa Cruz for two years, had a surfer boyfriend, and took weekend trips with my girlfriends to the Napa Valley, where we'd drink our way from winery to winery in a maroon '65 Impala. We still liked to listen to Motown. This was in 1971, a time when I thought I would—could—be somebody. I wanted to be in advertising or journalism.

But a woman does not find out who she'll be or what life will be like until she has a child. And for most women, having a child is like having all the windows in your house painted shut forever. Liberty is my oldest—thirteen. She lives in

Pocatello with her Dad, who's been through several reincarnations—surfer, computer repairman, snowplow driver. Liberty was pure accident, as I believe so many babies are, even now. When I look back on those times, I do not think I made too many conscious decisions about sex; I was wild and only wanted experience; I did not think ahead.

Liberty is a teenager who knows what she need to know—about condoms, about diaphragms. She and her friends call them 'phragms. We talk about these things when she comes to visit in the summer. She can say blow job with the same ease I might have said ice cream cone when I was her age. So far it's all talk, no action. I hope she stays a girl for a few more years, keeps her life for her very own as long as she can.

That was the time of the Big Split between mother and me—when I was pregnant with Liberty. There was no more school, no more surfer boyfriend. I found a job in a bookstore, sold my car to save for the hospital bills, bicycled all over town, and had some notion about baby and me against the world. There were abortions then, but I couldn't bring myself to make the decision to take control.

I didn't have much money, Liberty was colicky, I had to apply for food stamps, and we lived in a studio apartment where I had to beg the landlord for more heat. The first year of Liberty's life I probably saw the ocean twice; I realized the ocean was not that important to me anymore.

We moved around some after that, to Mendocino, to Klamath Falls, to the Okanogan Valley in central Washington, always looking for a place to be where we could relax, hide out, live cheap. Then Kevin came along when Liberty was seven, conceived in a burst of craziness one weekend when I couldn't stand my four walls anymore. I can't remember his father's name; I had my tubes tied on the delivery table.

Ruck and I met right after that and Ruck babied Kevin like he was his own. I think I loved him for that. There are so many men who won't touch you with a ten foot pole if you have children. I had that handicap—the kids—and Ruck's was an artificial leg. He'd lost his own in a car accident.

We moved to Jardine because Ruck had a friend who'd abandoned this paid-for trailer up there and it sounded good—free rent at the end of the road, with a garden plot, and the mountains like a bulwark against the outside world. We'd given up on getting anywhere, having credit cards, owning anything besides our pickup and chain saw. We wanted to survive with as few hassles as possible. Sometimes I try to remember when it was that I ran out of aces. I think it happened a long time ago, in Santa Cruz, and I just realized it when we were busted.

The next morning Kevin's squirmed down to the bottom of the queen-size futon we're all sleeping on. He's tickling my feet. I'm not very ticklish, but I pretend to be. When I squeal, he giggles. Ruck's breath is warm against my cheek. Sunlight glazes the aluminum strips of insulation between the studs.

"Wuck," Kevin says, suddenly sitting up and shivering, "I want to watch cawtoons." His white-blonde hair is cut in a burr all over except for a six-inch rat tail curling on the nape of his smooth neck.

"Rrrr," Ruck says, his palm on my hip.

"Oh, yeah," Kevin says, "Rrrr . . . Wuck."

Ruck kisses my shoulder and switches on the radio. "Car-toons coming right up." He hops out of bed, his sweatpants loose and floppy below his stump. He slips Kevin's jacket over his PJs. "You stay here," Ruck says to me. "I'll set him up in-side with Darcy and the VCR. Be back pronto." Darcy is Ellen's little girl. We're staying in Ellen's garage.

Ruck puts on his single Sorel, pushes Kevin's moon boots on over his bare feet and lifts him down to the concrete floor. Then they're out the door, Ruck with one crutch, their voices trailing away, while I'm still snuggled under the flannel sheets and blankets, listening to the Top 40 station. I push away the thought of the garage and concentrate on the embroidery on the top quilt, a flowery line of worn feather stitches, somehow more valuable to me, prettier, because they're old.

Within minutes, Ellen's at the door. She sticks her head inside and says, "Rise and shine, girl. Blueberry muffins are in the oven." Ellen's a morning person. She just got off welfare with a graveyard shift at a Minimart. When we're waking up, she's unwinding from her job, but she's still a morning person.

"Ruck was coming back," I say.

"No longer. I seduced him with those muffins." She cackles.

Inside, it's festive. Ellen's current boyfriend, Glen, is light-ing a small marble pipe of hash and its sharp, musty smell hits me first. The kitchen's warm and cozy. A long strand of red chilies hangs over the stove, souvenir of Ellen's summer trip to visit her folks in Socorro. Darcy and Kevin are lounging in front of the television in the living room, separated from the kitchen by only a knee-high bookcase. Ellen's smoking a black cigarette and lip-synching "Cary," which is playing on the radio. She's glossed her lips with shiny magenta. Six people in the house and we're crowded. For a brief inner moment, I'm in California when I hear that song, and my life is still ahead of me, spanning open like a fan you might buy at Pier 1, something foreign and exotic.

Then Kevin says, "Mom, Darcy says Big Bird's a jerk."

We all laugh. That annoys Kevin, but he turns back to the television.

On my way to the bathroom, I squeeze behind Ruck's chair and he reaches out and pats my calf. He and Glen are talking about hash. They remind me of my mother and Dan talking about their wines; after a while in these conversations you realize you've heard it all before. When I come out of the bathroom, the muffins are on the table.

"Real butter, babycakes," Ellen says to me.

Coffee steams in the mugs. Ellen's opened the back door a few inches to get rid of the hash smoke.

Just as I'm breaking open a muffin, there's a knock at the front door. The grown-ups raise their eyes to one another and Kevin runs over to Ruck. Glen opens the back door wide and the frigid breeze sweeps over us. Ellen flaps her hand, signaling him to close it. She goes to the window behind the television and looks out on the front steps.

"Sally Ann," she says to us.

She opens the door and it's a Salvation Army officer carrying a wicker basket of food. His uniform is royal blue, the elbows and knees shiny from being pressed.

"I'm looking for Katherine Ruckerson," he says, rocking back and forth, toe to heel. His face is a pale slab of authority.

"That's me," I say, spilling my coffee.

"What does he want?" Kevin says to Ruck. Glen has disappeared into the bathroom.

The Sally Ann officer steps inside and Ellen closes the door and folds her arms across her chest and waits beside the door, kind of smirky. His entry into the house changes everything. When someone like that—a social worker or police officer, whoever—comes into your home, you all at once see your house, your kids, the way they might. Kevin's bare feet on the cool linoleum, Darcy's hair ratty, the ashtray full of butts, the cracked window repaired with cardboard and duct tape. Certainly whatever vitality the morning might have had gets let like blood.

I go over to the coffee table. "I'm Kit Ruckerson."

"I'm Captain Cripe," he says. "This is your food basket from the Salvation Army."

"Thanks," I say, taking the basket and setting it on the coffee table.

"Is he a policeman?" Kevin says to Ruck.

The Nylons come on the radio.

"This is a food basket for four. My information stated that you have two children. Is that correct?" His watery blue eyes meet mine.

"I have another child, but she lives in Pocatello."

"Oh, dear," he says. I can see him eyeing the food in the basket, trying to decide what to do. Should he take back the canned spinach or the day-old coffeecake?

I look at Ellen and she rolls her eyes. I am grateful for her. Behind me I can hear Ruck hopping to the sink. He turns on the tap.

"Well," Captain Cripe says, "Have a Happy Thanksgiving." This reminds me of the way my brother in New York always signs his letters "Happy Trails," as though he thinks I'm Dale Evans in Montana.

Ellen opens the door and he waddles out. We crack up when she shuts the door.

"At least," Ruck says, plopping back into his chair, "it's not like the old days when you went to them for a meal and they'd make you drag the 'Old Rugged Cross' around before you could eat."

"At least," Glen says, flinging his long gray ponytail over one shoulder. He picks up a wooden match and uses it to scrape the inside of the pipe bowl.

"Paramilitary, aren't they?" Ellen says, patting Ruck's shoulder as she returns to the table.

"It's a turkey, Mom," Kevin says, pawing through the basket.

"A big bird," Darcy shoots at him.

Our muffins are cold, the sun's blocked by a gauzy cloud, and Ruck hasn't shaved in days. He has more gray now than he did a month ago, and there's a frown line between his eyebrows, a groove he must be cultivating. The things that make us happy are like Cracker Jack toys: Ellen's new job, the gram of hash, songs on the radio. I pour my cold coffee back into the pot and turn the gas up and stare out the window. I try to imagine what I'll be doing this time next year if Ruck's in prison. Nothing comes immediately to mind. The holidays all seem like rituals made for other people, people who have some refuge in the world, some margin of safety, who've never seen the inside of a welfare office or the lust in the eyes of an arresting officer.

Ellen laughs. "He sure took the fucking wind right out of our sails."

Speed's not a substance to mess around with. Rumor has it that it makes men impotent and women bitchy. I don't think many people do it anymore. I tried it once and I know what homemade speed looks like before it's crystallized: gooey and gray, the texture of Sterno fuel or peanut butter. I never knew what Ruck was doing in the horse barn. He was home, he was affectionate, he spoke to Kevin with respect. That was enough for me. But speed, sweet Jesus, speed.

The time I ate that speed was with Casey, an old boyfriend of mine, who came to see me one June when I was thinning apples in Brewster, Washington, near the Columbia River. I remember we used to catch carp in that river and cook them up with plenty of curry to cover the trash taste. And I remember Liberty had gone to see her dad, and Kevin wasn't born yet. I can remember all this as though it were yesterday—even the songs on the jukebox at the Bohemian Tavern. I guess you can consider yourself fortunate if some of the events in your life take on the sheen of a movie, that romance sheen, when trees are in bloom, light's gold on the water, and you look in the mirror and know you look the best you ever will. That summer was like that for me.

I had worked for nine days straight, thinning the little green reds and golds from the trees of a man named Cooper, who provided a trailer and some cabins for his workers. Every year I'd ever been there, he offered the women extra money— fifty cents more a tree—if they would work topless. I never did, but it's possible I never did just because the price wasn't high enough. After nine days, I woke up thinking, Today's my day off. I dressed up in an old forties church dress, blue rayon with padded shoulders, painted my toenails a color called Sea-Lily, which shimmered like the inside of a seashell, and thought about hitching into town to the Bo for lunch.

I heard a horn toot and when I looked out the window, there was Casey in a little green sports car with rusty fenders. He doffed his cap and said "Hi, sugarpie," just as though it hadn't been three years since we'd last met. Casey is the kind of man you can have a good time with for a night or two, if you're in the mood to strain your capacity for excess.

We bought a fifth of Cuervo Gold and headed over to Chelan, where he had a connection to buy the speed. We rolled over the river highway, feeling like we owned it, listening to the Dead's "Mars Hotel" and catching up, gossiping about every old hippie we knew between Spokane and Bellingham. Casey was a shameless gossip.

In Chelan, I waited in the car outside a ma-and-pa grocery while Casey went in and made his deal. I could see the long lake, and the carloads of tourists lined up to take the ferry ride into the glacial heart of the Cascades. I remember I imagined what it might be like to live there in Chelan, on the edge of the wilderness. I liked the thought. This was not unusual for me in those days to think of moving. Moving's something you can do a lot of when you're young; you can kiss your friends good-bye and not look back. When you're older moving takes its toll—it's a kind of death to give up all you've known and start all over somewhere else. But then I could daydream, I could picture it. I wanted to go to brunch in the old white clapboard hotel there, on a Sunday morning. I thought that would be the ultimate in elegance.

After Casey came out, we went over to his friend's place, near the lake, and we stayed there late into the night, eating speed with a knife blade from a sheet of aluminum foil, drinking the tequila, and when that ran out, we walked out for beer. We talked and talked. It seemed we could remember every tiny detail of every meal we'd ever eaten, every argument we'd ever had, every relationship we'd ever been in. We shared the most forgettable details of our childhoods, my Dan River dresses with the sashes in back, his obsession with Sherlock Holmes. We told the true stories of the lovers we'd had before one another, including all the parts we'd left out before, out of discretion or fear. And all the while, there in that Chelan apartment, over a paint store, we listened to the country station on the radio, which was so unlike us, but the music seemed to fit that night: Kitty Wells and Bob Wills and Patsy Cline. I remember Casey saying, "She's *so* sexy," when Patsy Cline sang "Crazy." And the next day, I really didn't care that things seemed a little raw around the edges. I was happy in a way, happy to have talked myself out, to someone I could trust, in Lake Chelan, where nobody knew who I was and the very air seemed a precious cold blue from the firs, the deep lake.

The next day we do Thanksgiving: cook and bake and eat and watch the Christmas parade with Kevin and Darcy. Ruck and Glen go out several times, and each time they return they seem a little more wasted. "It's a holiday, baby," Ruck says, when I give him an evil look. In between the sweet potatoes and the parade and the time Ruck and I made love in the bathroom, I keep going out to call my mother. My whole day revolves around making that connection. Each time, a butchy high-tech voice says that all circuits are busy. Around seven that night, snow begins falling in lacy ellipses, and I decided not to go out anymore.

On Friday, it's a piece of cake. The call goes right through.

"Kit," she says, and right away I hear that she's swallowing tears. "We just can't."

We. There's static on the line behind a shadow conversation, a man saying, "I'll meet you in Butte. At Denny's. We'll take it from there." Even at this distance, I recognize the optimism in his voice and I wish I were talking to him, someone upbeat, someone with solutions.

"You can't."

"But, Kit. I have an idea."

No ideas, I think. We need money.

"I could send you that brooch. Grandma's brooch. You could pawn it."

I'm standing at the phone booth behind the Safeway; the heavy grease smell from the deli hangs in the air. There's a man with a bedroll and an army surplus pack, opening the lid to the brown Dumpster. The snow has stopped and the sky is a pale winter blue, like old jeans. I can picture Dan at his roll-top desk writing checks, and I wonder why he can't just write one for me, why he wants to make it difficult for her, why she has to cry and offer me the brooch. Which is probably worth about three hundred dollars anyway.

"Don't do it, Mother," I say.

"Why not?"

"It's not enough anyway."

"It could get you started. You could get it back from the pawn shop when your ship comes in." She giggles.

I want to say, we are marooned on a desert island, there is no fresh water, there are no fucking ships. But in her giggle there is more desperation than I am feeling.

"It would take too long," I say, improvising a response. "To mail it, hock it. We need the money this week."

"What will you do?" she whispers. She's afraid.

"I think we'll sell the truck," I say.

That makes her feel better and, in truth, it makes me feel better, too, knowing that selling the truck is an option, and that if we do, we'll consider ourselves really on the bottom, two people without a vehicle in winter, and that that will probably be the very worst time and improvements are bound to happen after that. I promise to call again in two weeks and we hang up.

I walk down to the courthouse to see the social worker I've been assigned. There's not much traffic; the snow is still pure and untrammeled on the sidewalk. I remember Jardine and wonder if we'll ever call it home again. On a day like this in Jardine, I might have strapped on my beat-up cross-country skis and glided down to town, to Gardiner, where my friend Louisa and I would drink drafts at the Blue Goose and complain about our lives in a good-natured way. Almost always we would go out at dusk, across the potholed street to where the park begins, and we'd listen to the elk cows calling, singing, the way they do. Then she'd have driven me home, five miles into the mountains. I liked going downhill and not having to work my way back up.

At the courthouse there is one receptionist for all the welfare workers. She is young, around twenty-two, I guess, with a polished made-up face—no smiles—and she keeps herself removed, at a distance, as though she might catch a disease from the people who pass through the door asking for help.

"Did you have a good holiday?" I say, just to put her on the spot, force a reply.

"Yes, thank you," she says, her eyes scanning the appointment book. "Have a seat in the waiting room."

The waiting room is a dull place, with old copies of *Family Circle* and *Redbook*, posters about nutrition, and a laundry basket of broken toys, fire trucks without wheels, dolls without eyes. I count the change in the bottom of my purse and consider buying a bag of Bugler and some rolling papers. Smoking's a crutch I pick up in times of crisis.

My worker comes to the door and invites me into her cubbyhole. She's a big woman, with hair the color of old brass doorknobs; she wears papier-mache jewelry in the shape of animals—whales, herons, grizzly bears.

When she asks me if Ruck has found a job, I say, out of the blue, "I wonder why I ended up with a man who's handicapped?"

She looks up from her triplicate forms and says, "They're all handicapped, Kit. His just shows." And I see that she has been crying recently, and for a long time. Her eyes and cheeks are swollen. She's not wearing her fake fingernails and her thumb cuticles are ragged, as though she's bitten them.

I stare out the window and say, "No, not yet. We're both looking."

And I think about what might have happened to her Thanksgiving Day to make her that cynical, that hard. A woman can get hard from hurt if it's repeated often enough, and the hardness can make her say the bitterest things. I haven't been hurt much. It's true I've been in some rough water, but I've never been with a man who called me names or made me cry all night. And even as I tell her about the garage and the food basket from Sally Ann, I am picturing Ruck and Kevin waiting at Ellen's for me, and I can be sure that Ruck is giving Kevin his turkey sandwich for lunch and conning him into drinking a glass of milk. I think of selling the truck, finding the lawyer, going to trial, starting over afterwards, all the slogging months of winter ahead of us as we pick up the pieces. And I think, this is just another one of life's predicaments, worse than some, but not as bad as others. For a few minutes, it's like I'm up on Sacajawea Peak, looking down on all of us, instead of locked in my life like a child in a closet.

1987

Hard Feelings

Caroline walked down through the princess pine and sword fern to the river and beyond, to the spit. The sun was out and this was the time of afternoon when the sun struck the river. The sun was not out often. She fished through the big pockets of her apron and found her Ray-Bans. Through the sunglasses the cedar trees seemed dark and monstrous, the glaze on the riffles like a photographic negative. She considered this hour hers exclusively. She'd cleaned up after lunch, assembled and measured the ingredients for the bouillabaisse, and baked three loaves of herb bread. The last anglers had flown out at dawn. Will was due back soon, from Vancouver, with two new guests who had started their day at O'Hare in Chicago. The spit ran parallel to the bank with a tongue of shallow water lapping in between. Granite stones studded the bank. Two flat-bottomed riverboats—*Tupelo Honey* and *Chinacat Sunflower*—were moored to a stunted cottonwood.

Caroline tried to remember the last time she had listened to Van Morrison. She pictured a moist summer dusk at a commune near Hagerstown, the women in the sloping yard whipping a bedsheet for a tablecloth over a door-and-sawhorse table, the men smoking together near the woodpile. She and Will had been on their way to Canada, to a new life on the edge of the wilderness. It was just a dream that had spread like gossip then among people their age. Birch hadn't been weaned; she'd been born needing a father and Will had, for the most part, been that father. Though he'd changed. Or Birch had changed. Will had come into their lives when she was nine months old. They'd had a microbus loaded down with all their belongings and a cashier's check for five thousand dollars, all the fortune in the world.

She sat down in one of the low canvas camp chairs, which were frayed and bleached with the weather. One of the guests had left a *New Yorker* face down on the beach next to a grizzly track. The track was six inches longer than the magazine. It was old; the claw depressions, little moon sickles, still sharp; the edges around the heel crumbling. She peeled away her apron and rolled her culottes high to take advantage of the sun. Her legs were pale and though it was July she still had what Will used to call her winter coat, fine strawberry blonde hair that grew in an almost invisible layer from her knees down.

Birch was upriver a few hundred yards, sunning her fourteen-year-old body on a flat black boulder. She didn't have her top on. The week before she'd been caught like this by two anglers, who had politely, silently, backed away, but Will had seen it all from a distance. Caroline took off her Ray-Bans to be sure. Birch sat cross-legged and stroked sunscreen on her shoulders and arms. Her breasts were really *there* this year.

Her hair was Caroline's hair: kinky and floating, not quite red. They were both glad of that. The green river pooled behind her boulder and beyond that there was a stretch of white water and above that, dense hemlock and spruce cut the view. She could see only the very highest section of dirty blue glacial ice on one mountain.

Caroline stood up and yelled. "Get dressed. Your Dad'll be here soon." She had the fear that any day now Birch would simply refuse to do what she asked, that she was losing ground as authority.

Birch didn't respond, so she yelled louder. She didn't like yelling, but the river noise was always there, its crash and caterwaul buffering bird and animal sounds, human voices. The only louder noises were motors, the outboards, the plane, the pandemonium of the generator late at night.

Caroline heard the plane long before she saw it, the swooping drone of the engine as Will sparred with the mountains' eccentric air currents. Birch stood up on the boulder and tipped her breasts back into the bathing suit top. Caroline drooped back into the chair and imagined what they were seeing from the air: the green slash of the valley, female, fertile, against the bold snowy coast range mountains. She was relieved, keen for a reunion with Will, but the argument they'd had that morning slinked around in her thoughts like a scolded dog at dinnertime.

Will had leaned over his logbook in the thin milky light of the fluorescent beam. It was five-thirty in the morning, not quite day, and Caroline had sat braiding her hair in the center of the sagging bed. She wore faded blue longjohns and there was an oily stain on one knee. They had been arguing, and then there was a lull in the argument. The radio was tuned to the flight weather: winds and ceilings and visibility.

"She's acting like . . . like a chippy," Will had hissed. He didn't look at Caroline when he said this. He scratched something in the logbook with a mechanical pencil.

Surprised, unable to believe he meant it, Caroline had laughed. She'd thought Birch's behavior was a small thing, easily corrected, not worth name-calling.

"I mean it."

"She's my *daughter*," Caroline said.

One of the departing guests came out on the porch one cabin over. "Zip-a-dee-*doo*-dah." Caroline pictured him: the portly margarine executive from San Jose. He hadn't liked her using real butter.

Then they had talked about the flight breakfast, the left-over coho, the dinner plans.

Finally Will said, "Talk to her, Caroline, or we'll board her down in the village for the rest of the summer. She's a distraction to the guests."

"If she summers down there, so do I."

"What would I do without you?"

"Hire someone."

"Caroline."

"I don't want her down there. The kids're up to no good. The keggers go on all night."

Will shut his logbook and, with military precision, placed his pencil in his chest pocket. He clicked the flashlight and they were in the dawn shadows, softer light, returning Will's face to the way Caroline preferred to see him, still handsome, his hair over his forehead drifting a little silver, the intensity of his nettled eyes hidden by the dark.

"Love," he said. He moved close to her on the bed, conspiratorially. "Speak with her. We're in business here. Can't you do this for me?"

"I'll see," Caroline said. It had been all she could muster.

Chippy. Where had he gotten that? She could imagine some Brits saying it, at a tavern down in the valley over a table gummy with stout. Some shift was taking place, the way eddy lines might change after a bad storm or during spring runoff. What bothered her was that there wasn't a male equivalent for chippy. And deeper than that, she was trying to understand that Will saw Birch as an enemy now. He'd been distant and irritable for a few months.

The plane pounced above the river a few hundred yards away before splashing down, each pontoon spraying a sunny fan of water over the wings. Will would never land so sloppily. Caroline gathered her apron and the magazine and walked down the spit and through the cottonwoods to the trail.

"A ride to write home about," the first man said. He was the older one, the father, and he wore a fishing vest with blonde-colored flies perched on the fly patch. He was ready. His aluminum rod cases clanked as he alighted from the plane. "Hello, hello," he said to Caroline, pumping her hand. "I'm Joe. Joe Regalo." His crusty wedding band pressed into her palm. "This is my son Steve. He's hurt himself already."

Caroline saw the new wood of the crutches through the plane window as Steve struggled with them. He was laughing with Trevor. So Trevor had been piloting; he'd worked for them the summer before.

"What happened?" Caroline said.

"It's nothing," Steve said. "A sprain. I twisted it jogging." He situated the rubber tips of the crutches on a boulder and boosted himself out of the plane.

"No more o'your salty jokes now," Trevor said. "Missus, your good man had to stay in Vancouver." He squatted in the plane and handed Caroline a liter of rye and a long black mesh bag of clean towels. "The provincial office—the licensing office—they wanted him to sign some papers an' the papers weren't ready. He asked me to bring these gentlemen up here and fish with them. A nasty job, for sure," he laughed, "but someone has to do it."

"Welcome, Trevor," Caroline said. "Joe. Steve. Welcome to Silverthorne." She nestled the rye and towels in among the boulders.

"This is Caroline," Trevor said, shoving their tweedy luggage toward her. "She's the best cook west of the Fraser River." He winked at her and when he did the wrinkles around his eye made her think of a child's pinwheel. "Steve here— from the sound of it—is the best cook in Chicago."

"That's quite a claim to fame," Caroline said, settling the wide strap of the carryon over her shoulder.

"This is a paradise," Joe said. With his beefy hands on his wide hips, he surveyed the camp, the river, as though he owned the place, and indeed he does, Caroline thought. He's bought us for the week.

"Help, Mom?"

All eyes turned to Birch on the bank. She wore high-topped Converse sneakers and a long T-shirt over her bathing suit. The T-shirt was printed with the words *The Four Stages of Tequila: you're good-looking, you're rich, you're bullet proof, you're invisible.*

"Yes, of course," Caroline said. "Pick up some of these bags and take them to the guest cabin. To the porch."

Trevor sat back on his haunches, took off his baseball cap, and wiped the top of his bald head. "Growing like a weed, ain't she, missus?"

"That's the way with children, Trevor."

"She's a beauty," Joe said, after Birch was out of earshot.

"Like mother, like daughter," Trevor said. He hung two pair of hip waders over the wing trusses.

Steve hobbled further down the riverbank and gestured with one crutch to an ouzel. His wrapped ankle worried Caroline a little. His father had laid his rod cases against a log, hitched up his khakis, and followed him, with the self-consciousness city people have their first few days in the bush.

Trevor handed her a small cooler that she knew contained her fresh vegetables, and just as the weight of the cooler shifted from his hands to her arms, he said, "Will said to tell you 'no hard feelings,' dearie."

"Look," Steve shouted. "Bald eagles."

"This one's more of a birder than an angler," Trevor said. "Wait'll you show him the heron."

"Is the dearie from him or you?" Caroline said, smirking compliantly, and she turned, loaded down, and followed Birch to the cabins.

Treavor had brought the Sunday *Vancouver Sun* and a *Rolling Stone*. Birch lay on her stomach on the braided rug in the main cabin, plundering the fashion ads in the newspaper. The dining table was set, candles lit. The generator battled with their peace of mind and Joe and Steve sipped rye on the red leather sofa. Trevor and Caroline scuttled about the kitchen, separated from the dining area by a long island. The island served as cutting board, bar, lunch counter, bookcase. Caroline's cookbooks were stacked helter-skelter, clippings and notecards straggling in among the pages. Three brass lamps hung along the kitchen wall, their shine waxing and waning with the generator's clatter. It was eight o'clock and still light outside.

"Did Will say when we might expect him back?" Caroline said. She was cutting dark pink chunks of smoked salmon.

Trevor tore open a packet of stoned-wheat crackers and dumped them into a breadbasket. "He said he'd try to catch a ride up day after tomorrow. With the Dean River crew."

"Where's he staying?"

"With his sister in Kitsilano."

"You go on out and have a drink with them, Trevor. I'll finish up in here."

She watched them from the kitchen, she listened. Steve was brushing dust from the inside of his camera. Joe was the serious one, a salesman. He owned an antique shop and Steve had a bakery above the antique shop. They'd lived in Chicago all their lives, on the thirtieth and forty-fourth floors of the same high-rise. They'd been on the Bow in Alberta last year. "Next year New Zealand," Joe said, raising his drink in toast.

"The Tongariro." "Be here now," Steve said. Caroline couldn't believe he said that; it took her back in memory to another time. "I just like to get my ducks in a row," Joe said. They were an odd pair, Joe, the cagey collector of Chippendale furniture, and Steve, the young Deadhead who'd turned his health habits into a business. He talked about whole grains and fiber and Jerry Garcia. He put Caroline in mind of a satyr, with his round bottom and short legs, his corona of curly blonde hair.

"How's the ankle, lad?" Trevor said.

"I'm not feeling any pain. After this."

"Do you think this'd look good on me?" Birch asked.

Trevor leaned over her newspaper and said, "You'd look fine in anything, Birch. Say, why don't you come fishing with us tomorry? Like you used to do, you know."

Birch curled upright in one fluid motion, drawing in her dignity, her arms around her calves. "I don't go out anymore, Trevor."

She had on washed-out denim jeans, torn in white shreds at the knees and across one thigh. There was something about her fleshy brown knees that made Caroline think of breasts exposed and she supposed that was the idea, to expose herself in some acceptable manner.

"Don't you get lonely?" Steve said. "For kids your own age?"

"My parents prefer to have me here," Birch said.

"That doesn't answer my questions, silly goose. You play backgammon?"

"Sometimes," Birch said.

"Poker's my game tonight," Joe said. "You'll make a fourth, won't you Caroline?"

"What're we betting? Pasta?"

"Pennies, just pennies," Trevor said.

Birch walked over to her mother, behind the island, and slipped the shoulder of her T-shirt down and said, "Am I tanning or burning?"

Caroline cut her eyes across to the men, slicing into them, to see what they were seeing. Only Steve had paid attention.

"Trevor tells me," Joe said, "you've had a bit of a bear problem this year, Caroline."

She put her arms around Birch and kissed her cheek, the way she might have when she was a little girl, protectively. They were the same size now. "We haven't seen her in a few weeks, actually."

"This far north they're afraid of us," Trevor said.

"My father has a bear gun," Birch said. "I've never been afraid of bears." She pushed away from Caroline. "I'm famished. Really famished. When do we eat?"

The winey smell of the olive oil, the garlic, swelled Caroline's appetite too. "Help me, sweetie," she said to Birch. And she kept her there behind the island, among the ovens and clay bowls, safe in a familiar ritual.

"Two sunny days in a row. Can we stand it?"

"Someone's asleep at the wheel," Caroline said.

"I read that sunshine makes you—like—horny," Birch said.

"I don't think we have to worry," Caroline said, "up here in the rain forest."

Birch arranged a sleeping bag, unzipped and inside up, on her flat sunning boulder. Caroline set her waterlogged Keds side by side and slipped out of her flannel shirt. She wore her old two-piece: a worn bikini, once white, now yellowing, without much stretch left. Birch's snappy suit was printed with flamingos and watermelon slices. She could have been a model. Her skin had a luminous quality to it.

Caroline tried to remember if her own skin had ever looked like that. When she was fourteen, sunbathing was not something girls did, not in Baltimore, not in her neighborhood. Caroline had grown up in Baltimore, in a flat over a bridal shop on Eastern Avenue. At that time in her life, what she liked doing most was riding the city bus up York Road to The Senator and basking in its dark Art Deco splendor to see Kim Novak, Elizabeth Taylor, Natalie Wood. Afterward, she'd read her yellowing copies of *Photoplay*. She'd counted herself lucky if her skin had broken out only on her forehead where she could hide it with her bangs. Hiding had been a way of life: acne, tampons, your period, hickeys, other girls' secrets, phone calls, your feelings.

"What's he doing down there?" Birch said. She meant Steve.

"Splashing around in the Kikkboat. I think the cold water's good for his ankle."

Trevor and Joe had left early in the morning, after a breakfast of Finnish bread and fruit. They'd taken *Tupelo Honey*, all the gear the boat would hold, a lunch, and a six-pack of Moosehead. Caroline didn't expect them back until nearly dark. They'd filled an extra can of gas for the outboard and gone upriver. She was counting on a fresh catch for dinner.

"Do you think he's cute?"

"Who?"

Birch wiggled her shoulders against the sleeping bag. "You know, Steve."

"He's way too old for you, love." Caroline slapped away a black fly.

"I *know* that. I'm just asking."

"I guess so. Let me have some of that sun-screen."

"Sun-screen attracts bears," Steve said. "Did you know that?" He stood on one crutch among the thimbleberries. With one hand he picked the dusky berries and popped them into his mouth. His Patagonia shorts were the lavender of sunsets, a phenomenon Caroline missed—in the mountains you never get the bright sunsets. "They're especially fond of good-looking women, dipped in sun-screen, french-fried."

Birch giggled.

"We stand forewarned," Caroline said. "How'd you like the Kikkboat?"

"It was more fun than reading ten-year-old *National Geographics*. But I'm getting bored. I'm not healing fast enough."

"It's a shame," Caroline said. She tried to ignore the fillip of arousal she felt.

"D'you ever make croissants?"

"I don't believe I ever have."

"Would you like to? I feel like baking something."

Caroline came up on her elbows and smiled at him and put on her sunglasses. "What a fine idea. Will loves them. He'll be back tomorrow."

"Those are mergansers," Steve said, pointing to the ducks splattering in an eddy. "Not the prettiest duck in the world."

"Have you ever seen a harlequin?" Birch said, all at once agog.

"Those're beautiful, aren't they?" Steve said. "And wood ducks. Ducks are pretty amazing."

Birch flopped over onto her stomach to face him. "I love birds. For their colors alone. There's so much variety."

Caroline thought, Since when?

Steve stumped into the dining room, his Walkman dangling from one hand, music dribbling from the headphones. He sat on a stool at the counter across from Caroline. She was creaming butter for the chocolate prune cake. It was late afternoon and Birch was showering in the bathhouse next to the kitchen. Caroline had started a good fire in the Monarch to bake the cake and that meant the hot water jacket that fed the shower was blistering. All systems are go, Caroline thought. Food, fire, showers. It had taken them a long time—years—to make Silverthorne function smoothly. Those had been the best times for her and Will—when they were struggling to pull it all together. They'd lost that mutual striving toward the virtue of hard work and good enough luck. It wasn't necessary anymore.

"Listen to this," Steve said. He held one headphone to her ear, reaching across the counter. His T-shirt was dark under the arms with sweat and Caroline had the unnerving urge to sniff him there, the way a kitten might burrow in an underarm.

"Alberta Hunter," Caroline said.

Steve sang along. "I'll be *down* to get you in a taxi, honey."

"Please be ready 'bout half past eight."

He turned up the volume on the Walkman, but all they could hear was a staticky bass.

"We need a Walkman built for Siamese twins," he said, snapping his fingers.

She creamed the butter with gusto. "I want to be there when the band starts playing."

"I saw her in person," Steve said. "Last year. What a woman."

"You have a nice life, don't you? The best of both worlds."

"I can't complain. I kid you not—I can't complain."

"You ever hear of the Fabulous Thunderbirds?" Birch said. She stood outside the screen door, a dewy newborn adolescent swaddled in Caroline's long pink terrycloth robe.

"Stop, stop," Caroline said, clutching her midriff. "I'm media-starved."

Steve said, "You should come to Chicago for a little R and R." The hoopla of his smile seemed like confetti in the kitchen.

After their fine dinner of fish steaks and baked potatoes and stuffed artichoke hearts, after the story of the day's outing—the stately moose spied working his way up a tender green draw of alder, the catch, the party on horseback setting up camp just a few kilometers upstream—after the dishes and the sweeping, after the generator was turned off and the low lamps lit, after Birch settled herself at the table to write her best girlfriend, inviting her up to the camp for a week, after Trevor and Joe opened the backgammon board, Caroline and Steve wandered out to the porch steps and sat down with their brandies. The moon was still behind the mountain, its indirect light wooly across the clouds moving in. Caroline felt a rush of love, an affection, for their place, their isolated life, the balm of it. The river swooshed along and Steve strained to recognize the siffle of some birds near the porch. Sea weather seemed to be insinuating its way up the fjord, up the valley.

They were dressed warmly, Caroline in her culottes and a heavy wool sweater, Steve in a pale blue fleece jacket. He fairly glowed in the night, resting his back against the rough-hewn porch pillar, his drink between his knees. She thought of auras. She thought of drubbing his curly hair with her knuckles and she wondered at its springiness, like a brand-new carpet. She was afraid her thoughts were visible, a tattoo on her forehead.

He was talking about his mother, who was visiting a weight-loss spa in Colorado. She did it every year and every year she lost the same ten pounds. He groaned. His groan had a laugh inside it, at its core, sweet and surprising as the center of a hard candy or a French kiss.

"Catch-and-release," Trevor said, inside the cabin. "That's the best approach with fish *and* women."

"Women can think that way, too," Birch warned him.

"You come fishing with us and show us," Joe said.

"I just might. I just might."

The night was lush around them, moist with the weather change, the trees bending like caftan-dressed nymphs, small creatures rustling in among the bracken fern, the huckleberries.

"You and I, Caroline—"

What was he going to say? How could he possibly see through her, into her, already? *Caroline. Caroline.* She'd forgotten how it felt to hear her name from the mouth of a new man. She felt exposed. She didn't usually sit outside with guests like this, drinking and talking in the dark.

"We're people who always want to sit in the middle. Greedy."

"Doesn't everyone want attention?"

"No. *No, no, no.* Dad, for example—let's take an example at hand—he was furious when we threw a surprise party for his birthday. We had those black balloons. A three-tier carrot cake. He hated it."

"Come to think of it, Will's that way too." What betrayal there was in this simple analysis of her husband. He'd long ago made her swear she'd never talk about him to anyone. She thought he was pathologically private. Though, for the most part she'd kept her promise, not because she didn't need to talk, but because they lived the way they did. In a pumpkin shell, she often thought.

"The same people work too hard. They work at play. At everything."

"Serious. They're so serious."

"I saw you in the kitchen—humming, shuffling to your own hums. Soliciting attention from that old goat Trevor."

"That's the way Trevor and I *are.*"

"Playful. I like that."

Birch came to the screen door, her fuzz of full hair wiry in the lamplight behind her. She seemed tall and imposing.

"Steve," she said. "Are you going out tomorrow?"

"I think I might," he said.

"Me, too."

Caroline's legs firmed over with goosebumps. A wind blew up the river. The moon was rising, like a sliced turnip over Mount Nusatsum. "I'll keep the home fires burning," she said.

The next morning there was a drizzle, fine north coast mist. The cloud ceiling looked as though you could reach up and touch its baffles. Steve's ankle was swollen again and painful. He decided to remain in camp, and after his third cup of coffee he returned to his cabin. Birch went out with Trevor and Joe.

Caroline lingered in the kitchen, leafing through her cookbooks, which was one of her escapes, a path to day-dreaming she could justify. She looked up the recipe for crois-sants and saw that the weather was not right. She did not think that the Dean River crew would be able to fly in today. She drank jasmine tea and tried not to think about how relieved she was that Will would not be able to fly in; she didn't want to face that yet—why she was relieved. She wondered what he was doing down in Kits, in the fever of the city. She remem-bered herself there, two months before, prowling through the second-hand stores, eating dim sum with Birch, giggling, teaching her to use chopsticks, buying flowers on the street. On a drizzly day, she longed to be somewhere else. She was quite conscious of Steve in his cabin. She could read, she could write letters, but what she really wanted was to peer again into that intimacy they'd begun the night before, to see if it was still there. It was an old temptation. She remembered the others, three of them in ten years, their faces, their habits—one had called her Carrie, one had wanted her to scratch his back almost to the point of pain—and she remembered the crazy way she'd felt after: buoyant and sensual and sick at heart. The buoyancy trickled away within days; the heartsickness lasted for months. Still, she didn't have solid lines drawn about sex; it was a kind of energy, unpredictable and feral. She only knew she did it when she needed to and the source of that need was murky.

She heated an enameled dishpan of water and went out to the back porch. The floor slanted. Broken rods and old orange kapok life jackets were strewn across one end of the porch. Beyond, the gentle rain saturated the bush, the woods; there was a silvery light over the fir duff in the yard; nearby, thrushes made tiny buzzing noises.

She shaved her legs with Will's razor, in long silky strokes through lime-scented shaving cream. Then she braided her hair at the crazed mirror hanging beside the back door. She'd bathed the night before and shaving her legs had been an afterthought. She pinched her cheeks, settled a sou'wester on her head, pulled on black rubber irrigators and a yellow slicker. The clean towels in a plastic grocery bag were her excuse.

"I thought you'd never come," Steve said. He had a fire going in the little airtight stove.

"Here're your clean towels." She laid the bag on the armchair.

"Have you ever seen sandhill cranes around here?" He was lying on the bed—in khakis and a long-john shirt—looking at a red field guide. There was one kerosene lamp lit, its globe sooty, in need of a cleaning.

"What do they look like?"

"Look here," he said, and he rolled over on his side and flattened the field guide open on the edge of the bed.

Caroline sat down beside him and resisted the temptation to reach out and touch him. His temple was damp and pink. She flung her sou'wester on the floor.

"They're the ones with the red caps."

She leaned over the book. His field glasses were lying on the nightstand, and a pocket watch, and a pipe and a pouch of Captain Black tobacco, and a book of matches from Thai Town on North Clark. She hadn't known that he smoked. She realized there were many things about him she didn't know.

Their hands brushed one another while turning the pages of the bird book. Caroline got up and sat in the chair. They allowed themselves to look into each other's eyes, to hold that, to smile, to affirm each other, silently, mostly with ease.

They talked. Their talk entranced her. It was about the simplest, ordinary things, the pleasures of baking, cranes, their childhoods. They argued about Baltimore. Steve had been there once for a baseball game and he thought it was a boring city. Caroline defended Baltimore, its ethnic neighborhoods, Fell's Point, Pratt Library, and this sudden rearing up, this protection of her childhood memories, took her by surprise. She hadn't thought fondly of Baltimore in a long time.

The aphrodisiac distilled of conversation grew palpable in the cabin, sweet and treacherous, intensified by the rain sealing them away. Steve got up to put another log on the fire. He stopped in front of her, touched her jaw. She looked up.

"You're nice," he said. "And this is a fine way to spend a rainy day."

She went outside to pee. She knew she was putting herself in harm's way, and she loved it, loved being there in harm's way, and at the same time traces of panic needled her heart; she felt pushed onstage partly by circumstance, a somewhat reluctant player, though exuberant, too. She wondered what it would be like to kiss him, to reveal her self to him; she imagined this was the way Birch mused about him, like an erotic emergency, with untried girlish longing. Thank God, she thought, I'm still capable of feeling this way.

She had left him sitting on the edge of the bed, tamping Captain Black into the bowl of his pipe. In her slicker and boots she stepped out into the rain, into the pale greenish light of what had become a downpour. They had a rule that everyone had to use the latrines, but she felt like such an outlaw already, she didn't see that it mattered. She squatted beside the cabin next to a rusty outboard propeller. Her face to the sky and rain, she laughed out loud.

"Caroline. What—are—you—doing?" It was Birch, her fists balled at her side, stiff-armed, puzzled. Her name, coming from her daughter, broke the spell she'd been under. Birch stood about ten meters from Caroline in her Converse sneakers and a long black slicker, her hair dripping and dark and wet against her head.

Caroline said, "There's a bear behind you. Come here." She stood up, jerked up her rugby pants, and grabbed the rusty propeller. She opened one arm to Birch.

"It's just a stupid black bear," Birch said, stalking over to the porch steps near Caroline. "He's been following me." She allowed Caroline to hug her, to push her toward the porch steps. "He didn't even have the good sense to get out of the brush. I was on the trail."

The bear lumbered around the edge of the woods, like a drunken pup. His coat was dirty and streaked with mud, his dumb eyes struggled to see.

Steve came to the door, smoking, with one suspender dangling. "What's all the commotion?"

Birch looked him up and down, coolly assessing him. "It's just a black bear."

Caroline heaved the propeller toward the bear. "Get out. Get out of here."

"Vamoose," Steve yelled.

"Andale, andale," Birch sang out. She giggled.

The bear kinked up his neck as if to complain about the rain, and then he blundered away into the bush, trampling huckleberries as he went. Steve went back inside and left them there on the porch together.

"You're a very brave girl," Caroline said, "to keep walking with that bear nearby."

"I'm not afraid. I get that from you."

Caroline hugged her close. They were both wet and cool. "Why'd you walk back, sweetie?"

"I'm sick of this weather." She surveyed the sky. "Dad won't be able to fly in today," she said matter-of-factly.

"I think that's safe to say," Caroline whispered. It was late afternoon and the rain would be driving Trevor and Joe back home soon. She thought they would like to have brandy and chocolate prune cake and a warm fire; the evening stretched ahead, delicious and sure, an evening of her own making. She tried not to think of how unfamiliar Will's face would look to her when he came home. She would prepare for that in due time.

She kissed her daughter's forehead. Her return had cheated and protected Caroline, like all varieties of love do, and she wondered if Birch ever felt that way toward her. She sensed herself moving, clumsily, toward lucid questions, toward the arguments that mattered. Then she said, "Do you ever think being here's not enough for us? Now?"

"All the time," Birch said. Then, "That bear hightailed it out of here." She shivered.

The rain was letting up, and they could hear the rough sound of the outboard, like a grouse in the distance. Caroline posed like a bodybuilder and said, "Want to feel my muscle?"

Birch laughed and squeezed her bicep.

1989

The Late Hunt

Some days Blue wants to get PG. She can't decide if she would rather move to Denver or get PG.

"Air's bad in Denver," Randy says.

Blue says, "But they have more snow."

Big Sky Resort—where Randy works in the winter—has closed down due to lack of snow. He put in his UI application the Friday before the late hunt. The clerk at Job Service gave him a hard time and he just squeaked in under the wire with enough weeks of work to make him eligible. "We'll make it through the winter," Blue assures him, at least once a day, until Randy tells her to stop talking to herself. She brings home eighty-eight dollars and thirty-two cents every Friday from her cashiering job at Poor Isaac's, the downtown news-stand. Randy spends his unemployed days tying flies, watching Phil Donahue, and reading *Outside* magazine; he talks about buying a llama for pack trips. When Blue comes home, supper's usually on the table; Randy's specialty is elk loin steaks cooked according to Julia Child in red wine and garlic butter.

Blue doesn't want to go hunting. Randy tried to find someone else, with no luck. He has a doe tag that's good for five days on a ranch east of Livingston. His back bothers him and he needs a partner to help with the lifting, the dragging. Blue zealously guards her Sundays, when nothing is scheduled, when she can read the week-old *Denver Post* she scavenges every Saturday night from Isaac's back room. Randy coaxes her into going; they'll leave late in the morning; he'll give her a foot massage when they get home. She packs a Thermos of Montana Gold tea and a chocolate bar, thinking, Maybe we won't get anything.

The interstate is icy, the sky gray and wrinkled as a mussel shell. Randy drives and Blue scans the sides of the freeway ahead for ditched vehicles, prepared to warn Randy in advance about the slippery spots.

"There's an article in last week's *Post*," Blue says, "about the five stages of love."

Randy says, "Would you pour me some tea?" He hands her a blue Minimart mug he's pulled from under his seat. The mug handle is enameled with dried blood from some other hunt. "The fifth stage is co-creation, where you make something together. A book. Or a business. Or a baby," she says, pouring from the metal Thermos. She spills a little when they slide on the ice. Randy is good at recoveries on ice. "A baby, for example."

"Men don't think about love the way women do," Randy says.

The way he says it—decisively, as though closing a window against a storm—lets Blue know the topic is finished so far as he's concerned. Her inner life's becoming a burden, more than she can carry. Changes wake up in her like sow bears in spring and she doesn't understand them all. Years ago, in some tavern, if she'd heard "Honky Tonk Woman," she would have felt sexy and reckless, like dancing with a stranger and maybe letting him see a little way down her shirt. Now when Randy slips *Get Yer Ya-Yas Out* into the tapedeck, she imagines cruel struggles between Mick Jagger and anonymous women who don't know any better. And they always submit to him. Maybe MTV makes her think this way. The song disgusts her, makes her skin crawl, and who can she tell?

Her best friend, Mona, doesn't seem like a best friend because she's married to Tom, Randy's pal. Anything she says to Mona feels like betrayal. The closest she's come to being honest was one night last winter when Randy and Tom were gone all weekend with Search and Rescue, looking for two skiers who were lost in the Bridgers. Mona had spent the night. They drank Liebfraumilch and listened to old forty-fives, records from 1964 Blue keeps stashed in a pink satin heart-shaped candy box. The songs had brought back memories. Eventually, after midnight, they had told one another about their early sexual experiences, from the age of thirteen on, and the talk had been exhilarating, breaking past the polite barriers. But the next day, and ever after, Blue felt embarrassed and sad and ripped off, as though she'd let a piece of herself go with Mona, a piece she'd never retrieve. It felt like snagging a fishing lure on rocks and having to cut it loose. Just when she thought she was going to catch something, she ended up losing something. That was the trouble with confiding in someone—you gave away too much of yourself, and if you didn't watch out, pretty soon you'd have nothing left. Or so Randy had warned her several times in the three years they'd been married.

"Randy sure is a mystery man," Mona had commented to her on more than one occasion, in the privacy of the kitchen as they mixed margaritas or salad dressing. She had a wistful tone in her voice that made Blue think Mona wished she could penetrate that mystery. That scared Blue and made her come on to Randy later in the night, seeing him as she thought Mona did.

"Mick Jagger and what's-her-name—the model, the blonde one—they have a baby," she says.

"Mick Jagger's a candy-ass."

"What's that got to do with it?"

"You've been talking to your mama again, haven't you?" Randy teases. Ernestine dearly wants to be a grandmother. She's in her third year of the Civil Engineering program at the university and thrilled with the thought of holding her own grandchild in her arms on the day of her university graduation.

"Not really," Blue says, clamming up. She folds her arms and looks out the side window.

"Let's talk about Denver," Randy says.

She averts her eyes and picks small flat seeds out of her wool socks. She'd left the socks stuffed in her hiking boots since a walk up Squaw Creek in October.

He says, "What's new there?"

"Six feet of snow over last weekend."

"Look at these hills around here. Wind's blown what little there was away."

"Some people think we're headed into a long-term drought. The ski areas might close down permanently."

"In Montana? Never happen." He sips from his mug and then lodges it snugly against his crotch. "Listen, let's try to have fun. It's you and me. We know how to have a good time." His voice is persuasive, slippery, disarming.

She makes a choice—to let go for the time being. She thinks of Randy waking up in the morning, his soft long hair swirling on the pillow, his face still boyish from sleep before he's put on the mask of manhood, a kind of aloofness.

"Do you know where we're headed?" she says, pulling two maps from the backseat, from beneath their packs and the rifle.

"Check it out," he says.

They have one small photocopied map, fuzzy and difficult to read, given him by Fish and Game at the tag drawing. She matches it to the larger Forest Service map, which is confusing with all its tiny colored squares. After a few minutes, she says, "I've found it. Go past the Livingston turnoff seven miles. There's an exit that goes due north toward Clyde Park. We just stay on that road for a bit—"

"How far?"

"Quarter of an inch."

"Seriously."

"A few hundred yards, maybe. Not far. Then we turn onto a dirt road that parallels the river for a while and crosses over the ranch. Looks like bottom land, north of the river."

He follows her directions, leaving behind the snow and ice on the pass. The wind swoops up and buffets the truck. She remembers stories she's heard of pioneer women going mad from the wind, letting go of the real world, settling someplace deep inside, like gravel in a creek bed, still and safe. They pass a ranch house set up on a northern hillside, and down near the road a man in leather chaps nods to them as he opens the gate. A malamute stands sentry nearby. There are no other signs of life. The river's partially frozen over, in little riffles near the bank, and she wonders about the way it freezes, in messy chunks, and she tries to imagine the river flowing and then reaching the freezing point, caught in motion, like someone seized in a snapshot with her eyes blinking. Or someone trapped by unexpected events and then staying that way, sculpted and still, never-changing, like Lot's wife, a pillar of salt for looking back. She tries to remember the story but can't. All she can dredge up from summer Bible camp when she was five is the memory of the sticky-sweet taste of grape Kool-Aid mixed with powered sugar icing spread on graham crackers.

"You'd think this place'd be crawling with game," Randy says. "Keep your eyes peeled."

"I am."

There's ragged rimrock to the north, patched with orange and green lichen. To the south, the bottom land is stubbled and brown, falling away into the river.

"Look," she says, pointing to a gully edged in a scrubby juniper. "That looks like the kind of place deer would hang out."

"You're right. Let's go a little farther. If nothing looks better we'll come back."

They drive a mile or so more until they arrive at the remains of a burned homestead, a toppling fieldstone chimney, surrounded by the abandoned everyday things of another era, a rusted wood cookstove, an iron bed frame, dented sections of stovepipe, the wooden handle of a food mill. Randy stops in the middle of the road.

"Someone lived here," he says.

"Wonder what happened to them?" Blue says, and secretly she wonders if there'd been a woman in the house and if she'd been glad to go.

"Hard to tell. They put in a lot of work for nothing."

He does a U-turn at a wide spot in the road and they return to the gully. When Blue gets out of the truck the wind bullies her around. She snaps the grippers on her vest and slips into a mesh orange hunting shirt.

"How far do you think we'll go?" she says.

"Hard to tell," Randy says, the heel of his hand on the rifle bolt's lock.

"I'll take my pack."

"Good plan," he says absently.

They cross the road and then the barbed wire fence. At the head of the gully, about five hundred feet from the truck, Randy says, "You head down there and I'll walk around the rim. Walk slow. Don't be too quiet. You want to scare one up."

The desperate January wind blows hard and can't be ignored. Blue picks her way down the slope and the gully turns into a narrow canyon, much longer and deeper than she had imagined from the road. Her pack feels heavy, the hard edge of the Thermos cutting in her shoulder blade. Once she slips on an icy rock. She waves to him just as he disappears from her sight and then wonders if her pace is okay—too slow or too fast. She worries about being in his line of fire.

There's metamorphosed snow in the gully, crusty and gray. She creeps under some deadfall timber and remembers stealthy games she and her sister used to play as children, with bows and arrows made from green sticks and string. She's in the gully bottom when she sees the doe.

Her eyes are round, opaque brown, dumb and wise. She's lying in the snow, her head alert, staring right at Blue. Blue's heart beats faster and she stands stock-still, fifteen feet away, thinking, "You better get up and run or you're done for." For a brief moment she considers ignoring the doe, doing a little detour around her, and saying nothing to Randy. She backs up the hill, keeping an eye on the deer, until Randy happens into her line of vision again. She waves and he waves back in a friendly way. More insistent, she signals him with crossed arms above her head until he moves in her direction. She stumbles up the last hill separating them, over scab rock and through some tangled low-lying brush. Her felt-pac boots are one size too large and they blunder around on her feet uncomfortably.

"There's one down there," she says.

"Where?"

"At the bottom. She didn't move."

"Go back down and throw a few rocks at her."

Blue goes back into the gully, stooping for rocks and slipping them into her vest pocket. Under her wool cap her hair is wet from sweat, her scalp and forehead itchy. She wants to shed some layers, dispel the wind, sit down and relax, but time seems crucial, urgent. She tosses the rocks at the doe, whispering, "Go on. Let's get it over with."

The doe doesn't move; Blue realizes something's wrong with her. No wild animal would be like that. She trudges up the hill again. The wind is driving her crazy; it's like listening to fusion jazz.

"I think she must be sick or something," she says.

"Must be," Randy says. "Or she'd bolt." He holds the rifle parallel to his body, barrel up, in close to the shoulder, his finger on the trigger. The rifle's grip cap is made of swirling bird's-eye maple and Blue feels mesmerized by its beauty—it's like an agate, an unexpected find at the beach. "I'll go see," he says.

Blue waits at the rim while he goes down, out of sight. In three minutes he's back.

"There's no blood," he says. "But she didn't move."

"Should we kill her?"

"I don't know."

"We don't want to eat her if she's sick."

"No," Randy says. "On the other hand, you don't want to leave her here for some coyote."

"Could we tell if something's wrong? When you gut her?"

"Maybe." He slings the rifle over his shoulder by its leather strap. "Let's walk and think about it."

This time they stay together, plodding through the snow along the rim. The sky is drab, the land empty, as far as Blue can see. Without saying why, at the head of a side canyon, they separate, Randy heading downhill and Blue keeping to the rim. She thinks of the chocolate bar in her pack and what a lot of trouble it would be to dig it out. She's disappointed they found the doe so soon. It feels like picking asparagus from the garden rather than hunting. She wonders if they'll walk as far as the river, and then, startled, near a broad juniper, she spots blood, enough to fill a quarter-cup measure, pale on old snow. She looks over the area and there's more, a few drops, trailing away east in the same direction from which they'd come. Randy's far away. She winds around the rim in his direction until the blood peters out. She crosses deep and crusty snow, breaking through up to her knees with each step. Randy moves in a graceful diagonal up the steep slope to meet her.

"I found blood."

"Where?"

"Up there." She points to the juniper.

"Let's go take a look."

They cross the heavy snow again and go directly to the bloody trail, wordless in the wind.

Randy crouches and sweeps the bloody snow with his fingers, as though picking up crumbs. "Hard to tell how old it is," he says.

"It's from her, I'll bet."

"Could be. Let's follow it."

The blood guides them toward the gully.

"Not much of a hunt," Randy says.

"Are you going to?"

"She's injured. I feel sorry for her."

"What if she's infected?"

"If the meat looks bad we'll leave her here."

"Can we get in trouble for that?"

"If anyone knew. Maybe."

"Maybe it won't be."

"I'm going down."

"I'll wait here." Blue doesn't want to see the death throes, the last hopeless gasping. She's seen it and seen it and she never gets used to it. The blunt burst of the knife against the flesh of the throat returns in her imagination for days after a hunt.

Randy descends the slope and abruptly takes his stance, legs wide, rifle to his shoulder. He fires and scrambles farther down into the gully bottom, out of sight again. Blue inches down, giving the doe time to die. It's windless down in the gully, the snow packed down and stained with urine. The doe's hind legs jerk and Randy stands over her, at close range, and fires again.

"She tried to run this time," he says.

"No kidding."

"It's her leg. One of her hind leg's been shot away at the joint. Look at this."

Blue moves in closer, her hands in her vest pockets, and examines the leg with her eyes only. The lower portion of one hind leg dangles by a few ligaments, a dirty olive green, infected.

"Coyotes would've attacked her," Randy says. "Poor thing. Wonder how long she's been here." He thrusts the butt end of his rifle in the snow, takes off his mesh hunting vest and his wool shirt, and rolls up his sleeves. The doe's head has exploded from the last shot, her prickly tongue lolling from her mouth, one side of her face blown away. The spray of blood under her head is fan-shaped. Blue feels oddly detached, as though she'd spilled a kettle of hot jam on the kitchen floor. It's that kind of major mess. She doesn't want to get bloody, but she does what she can, moves the packs, braces the rear legs apart, while Randy does all the dirty work, down on his knees, his arms inside the doe up to his elbows. Her entrails steam on the snow. Three canny ravens sail above them, croaking and flapping their wings.

Blue looks at the droppings littering the ground and says, "She's been here a while."

"I think she's okay," Randy says, leaning into the concave interior of the rib cage and sniffing.

"No wind down here."

"That's a relief."

He has several skeins of rope and clothesline, which he ties around the doe's neck and forelegs. His knots are precise, tight.

"Bombproof," he says, attaching the ropes by carabiners to wide sky-blue straps of nylon webbing; they wear the webbing like bandoleers.

"Let's come back for the packs," she says.

"And the rifle."

"I'm ready."

"Now we'll have to pull together," he says. "To share the load."

So long as she doesn't look in the doe's eyes, the deer is just meat to Blue. They struggle through the brush, one step at a time, hauling the carcass over deadfall and rocks. Stew and steaks, she thinks, her breathing growing labored.

Before starting up the final slope, they stop and rest. Cheat grass protrudes through the snow at oblique angles, like scarecrow stuffing. Randy grins and teases, "Mush, you husky."

Halfway up they stop again. "You're a good soldier, Blue," he says. "Buy you a kamikazi when we get to Livingston."

She says, "Now we're making something happen." And she wonders if this is what the fifth stage of love feels like and if it could somehow lead to Denver.

1987

Slinkers

"That house has gone to rack and ruin since they moved in," my father said. Then he picked up the *Wall Street Journal* and shook it dismissingly. Aunt Margie freshened his coffee. She had an unobtrusive way of moving around him, serving him, without him ever noticing her. At ten, I was only beginning to observe the behavior of grown-ups with a clinical eye.

Our house was on a small rise and we could see into the Slinkers' back porch from our breakfast nook. Someone had busted their lattice work wall the yellow roses climbed in July. The workbench on the porch was littered with gobs of drying raw wool. Lily's Avon bottle collection snaked along the railing. A tower of nesting clay pots teetered on the steps. Next to the steps there was an old copper washtub they wanted to use to hold firewood in the winter. And two cars rested on cement blocks—a red and white Corvette and a pale blue Malibu. There were bikes and more bikes, at least two for each Slinker, and a dented Mad River canoe. We lived in a subdivision east of Bozeman, within view of Interstate 90. From our redwood deck we could see the Spanish Peaks. The Slinkers' house had been the original farmhouse when the land had been a family farm, before the developer came along. With its gingerbread trim, painted black, their house stood out like a beaded vintage dress among a row of sleek Calvin Kleins.

"Looks lived-in to me," I said.

"*Lived*-in?" Aunt Margie said, her lips set in a grim rectangle. "Becca, where did you pick up that expression?" She said it as though I'd caught a contagious disease.

I shrugged.

I'd learned that expression from Joanne Slinker. There were five of them: the mother, Joanne; the father, Ned; and the children, Jennifer, Lily, and Moonlight, whose given name was Karen. They'd arrived in Bozeman the weekend after Easter, during a bellywomper snowstorm. This was in 1973. Joanne was a weaver and planned to study fine arts at the university and Ned had signed a contract to teach social studies at the high school. They'd come from Arizona and they all had tans; I fell in love with them immediately.

My mother died of leukemia when I was four years old. I do remember certain things. At that time in my life, we lived in town in a little shingled house with an arched entryway and brown squirrels in the backyard trees; sometimes we'd call the squirrels by tapping a wooden clothespin on the sidewalk. I remember sitting on the basement steps while she ran the laundry through the wringer, flattening the corduroy, the oxford-cloth shirts into stiff bundles that made me think of a taffy factory. Sunlight pearled in the empty pitted blue canning jars on the shelf behind her. She'd sing as she worked and the sound of my mother's singing was like a feather bed or hot cocoa crowned with marshmallows, a comfort so palpable that when she sang, nothing else existed for me. *Oh I had someone else before I had you and I'll have someone after you're gone. Streetcars and sweethearts never worry me, there will be another one along.* And I remember her dressing table, kidney-shaped, with a homemade cotton skirt printed with cabbage roses. The skirt was pleated and tacked to the dressing table with upholstery tacks; the upholstery tacks had lions' heads on them. Her dresser was thick with bottles of nail polish and lipsticks: Kiss Me Pink and Deep Deep Red. Once she painted my lips and said, "You're like Snow White," but I didn't know who Snow White was for sure. I confused her with Cinderella. I remember the way her hair fell over her forehead, in a straight blonde swath, when she knelt down to tie my shoes. That's all I remember, though I try sometimes to remember more.

Aunt Margie, my father's sister, had been divorced from Uncle Chick, for reasons I never understood. She came to live with us while my mother was dying, and then she just stayed on. My father is a thin man with a concave chest, fine hair the color of wet newspapers, and a quiet dictatorial manner. This is how he was when I was ten and I'd still describe him that way today. He works for Farmer's Insurance. His pleasures seem to be keeping his accounts, and smoking an occasional cigar on the deck with Uncle Chick, who still comes around. Aunt Margie doesn't allow cigar smoking in the house. After my mother died, Aunt Margie soon organized our house on the principle of hospital corners. Every drawer had its purpose, every piece of linen its peculiar fold. She had a special brush for scrubbing the grooves between the ceramic tiles in the bathroom, and a special brush for cleaning the inside of the toaster. Her dusting rags were whiter and brighter than the Slinkers' tea towels. She'd once been in nurse's training; she spoke of pathogens as though we were about to be mired in them, without hope.

I never knew how deeply my father and Aunt Margie felt anything. An only child, I existed in a stupor of solitude when I wasn't at school, aching and longing for what I did not know. When the Slinkers moved in, I recognized within days that what I had in stability—boredom I called it—they had in intensity.

Ned was political. He had posters and newspaper photos of his heroes taped in odd places throughout the house: Che Guevara inside the pot and pan cupboard, Mao over the tub, Bobby Kennedy on the lid of the stereo turntable. A news junkie, he listened to the radio news throughout the day on the university station, watched Walter Cronkite at night, and on Sundays he made a beeline for Poor Isaac's Newsstand downtown, where he bought the *Billings Gazette*, the *Seattle Post-Intelligencer*, and the *Chicago Tribune*. He'd chide Moonlight and me for going for the comics first. He always brought home donuts too and even now, years later, when I buy the Sunday paper I think of buying donuts. He adored Joanne. Joanne and Ned Slinker were my first encounter with married lust. I'd watch out the corner of my eye as he'd sneak up behind her at the sink or at her loom and nibble her neck until she turned around. And they'd kiss like they really meant it, his hand sledding down the curve of her back, her fingers in his fleecy black hair. They were better than the movies. Ned collected hats, embroidered skullcaps, tams, toques, baseball caps. He had friends all over the world and they sent him hats. Next to worldwide revolution, hats were what he wanted most. Ned was a solitary man in a world of women. We'd sometimes gang up on him for those pursuits of his we considered particularly masculine. He was a hunter. Whenever we'd feign disgust and act squeamish—a performance complete with high-pitched squeals and shivers—Ned would tweak his moustache and say, "Ladies. Let me tell you about the time we were reduced to eating snake in Grand Gulch, Utah." And the very idea would send us into spasms. He'd grown up in northern Michigan where they ate muskrat, or so he said.

Lily and Jennifer were the oldest and lived upstairs in their own studio apartment, with a private entrance and a private phone line. Lily was fourteen, Jennifer fifteen, when they first moved in. They were cyclists and kept a log of distances and speeds per hour. Jennifer swaggered when she walked and worked out with weights at the high school; one of our favorite things was to measure her muscles. She had smooth brown calves like sanded oiled wood. Lily was the beautiful one, with a snug cap of short dark red hair and eyes the green of kiwi fruit. They lived in peaceful coexistence upstairs, arguing over nothing more, that I knew of, than whether to share the Ouija board with Moonlight and me.

Moonlight and I were the same age. During the six years the Slinkers lived next door to me, she and I became blood sisters by pricking our little fingers with the tip of an X-Acto knife, started our periods in the same month, and fell in love with Dore, short for Theodore, a mad poet who was a grade ahead of us, and we decided to share him rather than fight over him. This puzzled Dore and he found another girl with more traditional ideas, but not before he'd made love to Moonlight. We were fifteen. I heard the story in such detail and so many times, I began to feel as though he'd made love to me as well. She didn't like it. She said his penis was like one of Uncle Chick's slim cigars. She said he wasn't as handsome up close as he was from a distance. She said he'd closed his eyes and kept telling her she was just like the girl in one of his skin magazines. We'd thought Dore was sensitive—a poet with a soul. He had long blonde hair. In my moody daydreams of him, I'd confused him with angels. In the letters we wrote after the Slinkers moved away, whenever Moonlight and I would tell one another about our romances, Dore became the symbol of disappointment. "He was another Dore," she'd write in her thick calligraphic script. And I'd know what that meant, another illusion stripped of its glimmer. Moonlight had a canopy bed and Ned helped us find a parachute to hang over it so that we had a haven, all slippery silver-blue nylon, and we'd lounge around under there on fat pillows like harem girls. We wanted tattoos and debated at length the merits of butterflies versus flowers. I tingled with pleasure as we became more bold in suggesting just exactly where on our bodies we should have these tattoos. Though we oohed and aahed over Jennifer's muscles, we thought we were much more feminine than Lily and Jennifer. Ned called Moonlight and me *femmo*— the female equivalent of macho.

Joanne Slinker was the hot-wire, the source of energy in that house, a cross between Janis Joplin and Bette Midler. Her laughter always made you feel good. She was an artist and painted large splashy watercolors of androgynous women emerging from flowers. Once when she and Ned hosted a party for his fellow high-school teachers, everyone admired her paintings, and we heard her say, "Yes, when Ned first met me he just thought I was a good screw. He didn't even know I could paint." Moonlight and I were in the kitchen wrapping oysters with bacon strips and we rolled our eyes. "Wonder if the principal heard that?" I said. "I hope so," Moonlight whispered. "Shake him up a little."

Joanne Slinker was good at the womanly arts. An inveterate shopper, she'd drive us downtown—all four of us—on a snowy Saturday, and we'd fervently plunder Main Street. Joanne had rules and advice about shopping, admonitions I remember to this day. Never shop for a bathing suit until you have a tan; if you have cellulite or bludges—that excess baggage on your thighs—never look at yourself unclothed in the dressing room mirror; if you find a pair of jeans that *really* fit, buy two pair. She believed in intuitive shopping. She'd be irresistibly drawn into a certain store, where she'd find some impossible bargain: a midnight blue leather jacket on a rack of T-shirts, slashed to half price. She'd say, "I had a feeling there was something in that store just waiting for me." She called these things her magic clothes, and she wore them when she needed special power, special attention. She thought you should never look at something you feel obsessively drawn to and then say, "That's way out of my price range." She thought, There's always layaway. There's always an early birthday present. "When you're older you can sell your blood," she'd kid. When we shopped with Joanne we were girls we never knew. We saw the daydreams of who we could be, the dream of multiple possibilities. One of Joanne's primary shopping rules was buy new makeup as often as you can; old makeup makes you feel sleazy. She'd take Moonlight and me to the cosmetic counter at the Bon and say to the clerk, "Becca's blue today. Let's do her face and cheer her up." And I'd be transformed, with exfoliants, color rubs, gels, and powders. Everything came in its own pastel flowered box and there was the promise of discovery in every purchase, like deeds to old silver mines. It's okay to run around without makeup when life's all peaches and sunshine, Joanne would say, but never go out depressed without doing your face.

If Aunt Margie had heard Joanne Slinker's language, that would have been the end of my connection with the Slinker family. I'd been reading novels from the adult shelf in the library for two years—unbeknownst to Aunt Margie. I'd seen *damn* and *hell* and *shit* in print. But Joanne said everything, shocking things. If she burnt a cookie sheet of gingersnaps, she'd say, "I sure fucked those up, didn't I?" And then she'd hoot with laughter. She believed cursing was a form of tyranny adults had over children. *Do as I say and not as I do.*

Joanne thought it was okay to leave the dishes until morning, that children should learn to use a washer and dryer when they're eight years old, that it was a natural human inclination to get high. She quoted some book: Even little children try to change their consciousness by going around and around in playground swings. Whenever she said this, Ned would say, "That's why you go to the hairdresser, to change your consciousness." I smoked my first joint at their house, kissed my first boyfriend, nearly lost my virginity there, ate my first avocado. Joanne Slinker was the person who told me how the sperm gets to the egg; she said it like it was something to look forward to.

The stress of keeping to myself all I had learned and done at the Slinkers made me feel like a water balloon about to burst. I made a point of telling my father and Aunt Margie little tidbits of information I thought they'd approve of, to throw them off the scent. I'd say, "Mrs. Slinker made the dean's list this quarter." Or "Mr. Slinker gives sixteen dollars a month to Save the Children." Or, "Mrs. Slinker's sister is a nun in Florida." All true statements, designed to paint a virtuous portrait of the Slinkers. Whenever I smoked grass at their house, I'd spray my hair with Estee Lauder Youth Dew to veil the smell. Whenever we had boys up to Jennifer and Lily's studio, I'd lie and say of course Mr. and Mrs. Slinker would be home. And Joanne would sometimes talk with Aunt Margie across the greening yards in spring, about Aunt Margie's lobelia, about her cat's cancer, about me. I can remember sitting hunched with Moonlight on the widow's walk, out of sight, glorying in the candy-colored, tie-dyed sunset, and listening to Joanne tell Aunt Margie how much she enjoyed me, what a fine girl I was, such ambition, I'd go far. I imagine this was the kind of talk that made Aunt Margie uncomfortable, but it was neighborly talk, and my father thought it was important to have some sort of communication with the neighbors. At least they'd call the police if they saw burglars creeping in while you were away. I began to think of our house in symbols: white bread, Mr. Clean, the double lock on the bathroom door. The most emotion I ever saw between my father and Aunt Margie was a brief bickering snarl over whether to join the group of subdivision dwellers who were petitioning the county to improve our roads. My father's chief sign of affection for her was driving her to Heeb's Supermarket every Friday night. At Slinkers' there were fits and tirades and swatting and hugging—high drama, characterized by ceremony, convoluted language, conflict, love. The Slinkers loved to talk, usually at high speed and high volume. Their communication was efficient—they often finished one another's sentences. I led a double life. Sometimes I'd stop by the lilac bushes that separated our front yards and stand there between the two worlds, breathing in the cloy of the lilacs, calming myself to move from their house to ours. Alpine glow glazed the mountains. I'd feel like the luckiest twelve-year-old in the world.

Joanne moved out twice during the six years they lived next door. The first time, the summer I was twelve, she moved into a boxy little pre-World War II house on campus, with a woman she thought she'd fallen in love with, another art student. Her name was Shandell Walks-on-Water; she was from a reservation up on the Hi-Line. I saw them together only once before Aunt Margie got wind of the whole scandal at church and forbade me to ride my bike into town to see them. That one time—a sunny day in July, the mountain air finespun—Moonlight and I ate ice cream from pie plates while Shandell and Joanne lay on their backs in chaise lounges, glistening with coconut oil, listening to us retell the story of some horror movie we'd been to see the night before. I remember I felt privileged, inducted into a private female world. She stayed away for a month, and Ned, resigned to her doing what she felt she *had* to, spent the month fishing at Ferry Lake.

166

The second time she moved out, Moonlight and I were fifteen, old enough to figure out how to take full advantage of the situation. Joanne had met a ski instructor at Bridger—a man who didn't talk much, as far as Moonlight and I could tell, and we weren't sure what she saw in him. Moonlight had a theory that it was the adventurer in him Joanne liked. He'd skied on four continents. He wore a silver chain on his wrist he claimed some Gypsies in Spain had given him.

We were all taking skiing lessons that winter, except for Ned, who was embroiled in teachers' union politics. He said he wouldn't have time for skiing until after the revolution. He was at a conference in Helena the first evening Joanne stayed with her ski instructor.

That Sunday night, Moonlight and I rode the ski bus home, as far as McDonald's, and then Lily and her boyfriend picked us up in his station wagon. We'd met some boys on the slopes—they were older than we were, seniors at a private school in Colorado, still on Christmas break, visiting their Bozeman cousins. They were crazy skiers, reckless, and at that time in our lives Moonlight and I were attracted to what we called bad boys. We'd given them Slinkers' address and invited them over. I can still remember standing outside the ski bus at the bottom of the mountain, in the grip of the wind, the darkening sky as blue as my lapis lazuli earrings, my fingers stiff as I wrote out directions on the back of a cash register receipt. The one I liked was Rob. He was tall and hovered over me. There was something raw and new in the pull I felt toward him. Before we parted he kissed me roughly and left my face wet and chapped, and when I got on the bus and saw Moonlight, I grinned an idiot grin.

At the Slinkers' we conferred. Joanne had said she'd be home by the time Ned was home. Ned would be home by ten. We had four hours. Jennifer was at the library—she was a clerk in circulation. Lily and her boyfriend—he'd been president of the Honor Society the year before—went upstairs, giggling at us. "Be good, girls," Lily said, "at whatever you do."

I went home to clean up. The uncertainty of our plans, my fragile state of erotic chaos, made me stealthy. I ever so quietly propped my skis against the garage door. My father was on a late elk hunt up near Yellowstone. I imagined Aunt Margie was watching television. I opened the back door silently and moved soundlessly into the hall. The clock chimed the half hour. Aunt Margie had been cooking with garlic. A dim light from the kitchen looked yellow on the waxy hall tiles. It was possible to get to my room without passing any door but the kitchen. I was in my sneakers. I passed the kitchen and kept on walking, and my brain did not register at first what I'd seen. In my room, I reviewed. Aunt Margie and Uncle Chick had been standing at the sink, kissing. She'd looked soft and limp, her blouse pulled out of her slacks. Uncle Chick wore a maroon velour pullover and his gray beard was neatly trimmed. His big belly had pressed against her insistently. Her hair had been mussed. I kept thinking, *But they're divorced.* I turned on the radio so they would know I was there.

After my shower, when I was dressed and ready to go, I leaned against the door frame between the living room and the dining room and said, "Hi. How's everything?" Tucked in my jeans pocket were two rubbers Moonlight and I had bought at a drugstore in Billings when we went to a Heart concert.

They were watching a black-and-white movie, a TV tray of beer and cashews between them.

"Fine as wine," Uncle Chick said, without looking my way.

"Did you have a good ski lesson, Becca?" Aunt Margie said. She twisted around sprightly in her chair. I tried to remember how old they were.

I said, "I fell down a few times."

"There's leftovers in the oven," Aunt Margie said.

"I want to spend the night at Slinkers'."

"It's Sunday," she said, turning back to the movie.

"We have homework," I said. "We're drilling each other on the periodic table."

"All right, all right," she said. "I suppose you'd wear me down if I kept saying no. Try to get to bed at a decent hour."

And I was gone, feeling crafty, that exhilaration you're pumped full of when you think you're free, free at last. The moon was out as I crossed from our yard to theirs, the old snow frozen in a smooth hard slab that reminded me of suet we put out for the chickadees. My thighs ached from skiing.

Moonlight and I were nearly hysterical with anticipation. We weren't sure they'd come. She sat on the toilet seat while I curled my eyelashes and rolled on inky black mascara. We felt we could do whatever we wanted with them, because they were from Colorado. We wouldn't have to live with the consequences. I showed her the rubbers. When I look back on those times, it is hard for me to imagine that we were the same girls who argued reasonably on the debating team, who ran for student council, who wrote heartfelt political letters to the editor of the school paper. It was as though our minds simply stopped functioning when we felt the rowdy urge to be bad girls, to break every rule ever made.

The doorbell rang and Moonlight went to answer it. I put some music on the stereo. Rob and his friend Jim stepped into the house chanting, "I see London, I see France, I see someone's underpants." They'd been drinking. Moonlight and I looked—perplexed—at one another and laughed. They were dressed in tweed overcoats and brought the cold in with them, and something else, a presence that separated Moonlight and me, diluted our connection. Before they'd arrived, we'd been like lovers, or as I imagine lovers could be, in my more idealistic moments, close enough to be real. When they arrived we picked up a dialogue of pretense like some skit we were auditioning for. I could see we were doing this, but that knowledge was below the surface, the nagging thought that we were being phony like an evanescent fish under a frozen lake.

At first we sat around the kitchen table and talked about our schools. Theirs was all boys. They said for fun they went out to Boulder and tried to get in the bars and drank drinks with names like Slippery Nipple. They skied at Mary Jane on the weekends. They'd both been accepted at three universities. Rob wanted to be an officer in the Air Force.

Moonlight told them she wanted to study cultural anthropology. "Oh, yeah?" Jim said. "My mother's into that. Lots of girls are."

The light in the kitchen had a dimmer switch and in due time I dimmed it, on my way to the fridge for a beer. Someone suggested we dance. Later, when I told Lily about dimming the light, she said, "The rest is history." But the whole experience didn't turn out at all the way I'd expected or hoped.

Rob and I soon maneuvered ourselves privacy, in the greenhouse that jutted out from the kitchen to catch the southern sun. Tomatoes and basil grew in black plastic tubs there. The white pebbles rolled under our feet, and we giggled and leaned against one another. I had on a rayon blouse that I thought felt like nightgown material. When he pulled me by the waist, his hand large and adamant, I thought right then that I'd do anything he wanted to do. There were purple grow lights in the greenhouse and an old dusty red car seat. We sat down on the car seat and started kissing. The place smelled like herbs and dirt. He moved along pretty fast, into my blouse. At first it felt good, pushing my breasts into his hands, then he leaned down and started sucking one of my nipples. That hurt. I tried to urge him back to my face, but he wasn't interested. I looked down at his hair and his scalp was flaky; something about that revolted me.

"Oh my God," I said.

"What's wrong?" he said, not bothering to take his mouth completely away from me. His finger flicked the copper-colored zipper tab on my jeans.

"I just started my period," I said.

His shoulders slumped. "Oh, baby."

"I know. It's awful, isn't it? I'll have to go to the bathroom. Be right back."

I extricated myself from his grasp and half-hopped, half-hobbled out of the greenhouse, out of the Slinkers', across the yard to my house. Yellow light from our kitchen leached into the snow. I stood there without my jacket, buttoning my blouse, letting the cold freeze his spit on my breast. I wanted the comfort of my own room, with its dull corduroy bedspread, the horse pictures on the wall. My jeans were so tight I could feel the seams chafing the insides of my legs.

I sneaked in my bedroom window. I tiptoed to the bathroom and scrubbed my face and chest with Dial soap. I brushed my teeth for about five minutes. Then I brought the phone into my bedroom from the hallway, and called Lily and told her I'd left and that she might want to check on Moonlight. Then I put on a flannel nightgown and climbed into my bed.

I left my door open. I lay there wide awake for a long time, so relieved, just repeating to myself, *He wasn't the right one to be the first one.* After a little while, I turned on the radio very low and listened to the kind of music they play on a Sunday night, some sad country, and I listened to the house sounds too, and thought how fine they were, the clock chiming every half hour, the water filter purring in the aquarium in the living room, the rustle of my own blankets. I thought about my mother and wondered if she could see everything I did. I didn't think so. I'd stopped believing in heaven when I was thirteen. I wondered if she had lived if she'd have been the kind of mother who'd have told me about how the sperm gets to the egg. Then, as I lay there, loving my aloneness, Uncle Chick walked by my door on the way to the bathroom. He had on big white boxer shorts that seemed to incandesce in the dark like the face of an alarm clock. And I thought about how everyone has a secret life of some sort, a private array of lusts and sins and longings and dreams, even Ned at his conference and my father on his elk hunt. Right before I drifted away into sleep, I had this picture in my mind of human beings all over the world, squirming with longing, their arms open to one another, waiting to be touched.

1988

Labrador

Finally, we were moving.

My mother stood in the dirt section of the yard, beside the green pump, holding the rooster Pete in her arms the way you might a kitten. His feet clawed against air. A neighbor woman was there and my mother was readying herself to transfer Pete to her, knowing full well that, with this woman, there was no sentimentality about roosters, and, tough as he was, he'd be in a pot on the stove before nightfall. Pete was the last chicken left of a flock that'd been slaughtered early one morning by an unknown dog in a messy, cruel way. I don't think my mother ever completely recovered from the shock of finding the torn up chickens under the pear tree. I didn't understand this then when I was fifteen, but now I do. It was a violation, like having your face slapped or your pocket picked, and a lifetime of just such seemingly small violations can leave you worn out and sad, nearly depleted of dreams.

Though she was putting on a happy face for the move. We all were. My father had taken a job in the state of Maryland, at the telephone company in Rising Sun. To get there, we would have to cross the states of Ohio, West Virginia, Pennsylvania, all of it unexplored territory. I'd never been farther from home than Indianapolis. I longed to be a traveler and had a book I planned to read on the way, a dog-eared paperback about the Amazon Basin.

"Good luck and all that," the neighbor woman said. My mother handed her the rooster. They'd known each other nine years. I don't think they knew what to say or that it was possible for them to imagine each other's absence.

My mother sidled toward the Rambler, waving over her shoulder. She was wearing new madras Bermuda shorts and a sleeveless white blouse. "Don't forget to write," she said. I thought they would write to each other, but I don't believe they ever did. Like a schoolgirl she added, "Don't do anything I wouldn't do."

We children—all seven of us—and two dogs, one cat, and my father, had been waiting impatiently in the cars. Bingo, the Saint Bernard, didn't like to travel. We'd gotten tranquilizers from the vet and he lay passive as a rug in the back of the blue-and-white Ford station wagon. The plan, elaborated on, refined in detail over many evenings, was this: Mother would drive the Rambler with me, the oldest, and the two youngest, Maureen and Colleen. My father would take the four boys—David, Kevin, Stephen, and Joe—and the animals. Big Bopper, the long-haired black cat; Bingo; and Rummy, an old female beagle who'd had more litters of pups than I could remember. We had headlight signals and signs to communicate between the two cars. We'd picked a place on the map to stop for the night: Zanesville, Ohio. There was much concern and talk about losing one another on the interstate highway. But my father assured us that would not happen and I believed him.

We drove away and I don't think anyone looked back, though perhaps my mother did and I didn't want to notice. I didn't understand then about the pain of moving or what we might be relinquishing to do so. Now I know that my mother had for years fanned a spark—a dream—about that place in the country, and the dream had to do with chickens and pear trees and blackberries and children roaming the woods. Not an unusual dream, naïve and touching when I think of it now. Perhaps my father shared that dream with her, though of that I'm less certain. That ordinary frame farmhouse and seven acres had been given to my parents by my mother's father, who lay dying of emphysema in the front bedroom of his house on South Seventh Street in Terre Haute. My mother loved him dearly, but somehow she was able to leave him, able to give up the predictability of our life in Indiana—for she and my father had both been born there, on the south side of Terre Haute, just blocks from each other—in exchange for the risk of a new turn in the road, a turn none of us had expected. We were going to get on in the world without grandparents and aunts and uncles. Since then, of course, I've wrenched my love away from many places and people, and my heart goes out to my mother for what she must have experienced. I wish I could tell her that now. When parents die young, you become old before your time, living in the past with them, in memory. You think they'll never know how much like them you've become, but it's possible they did know. It's possible she knew what I could become before I did, and I console myself with that.

We followed our plan and arrived three days later at the house my father had rented for us, a big Victorian in the country, with a fireplace, a creek across the property, an empty lot for softball next to a cornfield, a screened-in back porch on the second floor and bedrooms enough for me to have my own. We never knew how old and drafty the house was until winter. My mother would put on an extra sweater and curse the house then, because, by that time, the reason we'd moved had unraveled like cheap goods.

This move took place in the summer of 1963. Before that I hadn't thought of my parents as people who had dreams that might be dashed. I knew that there were difficulties between them and that those difficulties had to do with money and drinking and gambling. There was a shadow of another problem, possibly having to do with other women in my father's life. But that was never mentioned outright in the arguments I overheard. My thinking on that comes from a memory of when I was four years old: my father arriving home late at night in a yellow taxi, my mother meeting him on the street, screaming and striking out at him. She and I had been watching a late movie on television. On the porch, in my pajamas, I could see my breath. My mother's loafers kicked up the ankle-deep sycamore leaves on the sidewalk, a cutting sound. A caved-in pumpkin rotted on the porch next to the white milk box. Now that I have been married twice, and twice divorced, I know the sound of jealous screaming. There's a powerlessness to it, like a wounded animal that cares only for its own hurt. That's how my mother was screaming that night. Still, I never heard her mention it afterwards. The root of the trouble seemed to be that my father worked away from home. In order to be at home with us, my father had to take jobs that were beneath him. At the meat-packing plant or the glass factory, work like that. He had taken those jobs for a year, here and there. Otherwise, he'd worked away from home; he was a telecommunications wizard, a crackerjack. Everyone said so and I imagine that is true, since my brothers have turned out the same. That is, they work as electronics engineers and one of them, the youngest, before the age of thirty, has risen to a position of prominence in one of those long-distance companies that make your phone bill so complicated. My father discovered his genius in the Philippines during World War II. The Army taught him what he knew. When he returned home to Terre Haute and married my mother, who'd also been in the war, telecommunications was still all he knew and loved and he took what opportunity came his way, in spite of babies being born right and left. He went to work on the DEW line in Labrador, and after that, on installations in New York and Pennsylvania and Michigan. My mother was always pregnant and my father was always gone. She used to say he came home just often enough to make a new baby. He used to say my sister Colleen looked suspiciously like the milkman; that was one of his standard jokes. He traveled, leaving in the tang of aftershave, with leather suitcases, and when he came home for visits, we'd meet him at the train station across from the Wabash Cigar Store, and he'd bring home green boxes of pastry and Chicago newspapers. And there was always that trouble between them, and the trouble would flare up at night when he was home for a visit. I would lie awake in my bedroom and wait for it in dread. That dread had become something that was always with me, that I was ashamed of, as much a part of

me as a humiliating middle name might have been, or a birth-
mark I'd want to hide. It had been made clear to me, mostly
through eavesdropping, that in making this move my father
was making a promise to change his ways. He would come
home for supper every night—that's how my mother phrased
it. They envisioned family life in this new place, and listening
to them, I believed it was possible.

That summer, I wanted only to read and be kissed. I did
my chores without being asked, then squirreled away in cool
places, going back and forth between what even then I knew
were junk books—romances, nurse stories—and literature.
Willa Cather. Victor Hugo. I turned sixteen in August and
had been casting about for someone to kiss. My brothers had
made quick friends, softball buddies, but they seemed too
young, sweaty, pimply, their voices still high. Not that I was
any dream girl. There was a scholarly sluggishness about me,
I knew. I wore glasses. And my clothes seemed to fit me
oddly, clumsily. But in ninth grade, I'd been told I had bedroom eyes by a Latin teacher who drove an Austin Healey. I
knew it was out of the ordinary to be told this by a teacher
and that there were probably rules he was breaking to do so.
I hoarded the remark, turning it over and over in the dark of
the night, knowing there was shame in having been told that,
but also pride. In spite of everything that had been drilled
into me—and insinuated—about the difference between
good girls and bad girls, my body was ready, keen as a trained
falcon. I knew from reading that erotic pleasure was a force
to be reckoned with, perhaps the most powerful force. I

thought of it as sudden, transformational, a little like severe, unexpected weather.

Up a long and winding hill, past a dairy farm with violet salt blocks in the pasture, lived another large family, the Karskis. They were Catholic too, and like us, their father had worked away most of their lives. He was in the Navy. They were older than we were, with girls still at home who'd graduated or quit school. Their youngest was ten. Their mother was a jolly-faced portly woman who took for granted that some of the time we would break rules or yearn to be wild. She'd take us to movies at the naval base and keep watch from afar in the outdoor amphitheater as we flirted with the swabbies. They'd let us wear their glowing white caps, but it never went any farther than that with me, even though I thought I wanted it to. Charleen, the oldest Karski, must've been taking it farther somewhere else, because she was married early that fall to a sailor about to ship out for the Mediterranean. It was common knowledge she was pregnant, though we didn't call it that, of course; we only said she'd gotten herself in trouble.

There was to be a party after the ceremony, on a school night, at the Karskis. I thought I would get my kiss at that party, I was determined. My mother would be in attendance for a little while, but she would go home early, to get the little ones ready for bed. Mrs. Karski had already interceded for me and gotten my mother's permission for me to stay on. She'd promised to bring me home herself. I had the idea no one else from the high school would be there. The guests would all be sailors and Charleen's friends who'd graduated the year before. It seemed like the safest place, in terms of reputation, to get a kiss. I gave much thought to locations: behind the latticework on the side porch or in the stairwell, what had once been the servants' staircase, when the house had been a finer house.

I itched for my mother to leave. She had two piece of wedding cake and had asked Mrs. Karski for an extra sugar rose. This mortified me, though I'd thought of asking for an extra sugar rose myself. She wanted to see the newlyweds—everyone called them that—open their presents.

Charleen and Bobby were in the kitchen and it was clear that's where the real party was, with loud music playing—the Supremes—and drinking. They'd made something called artillery punch. I'd passed in and out of the kitchen a couple of times, afraid to join them, longing to. Sailors were lounging in a row against the counter and seeing them there, in that small room, with their starchy summer uniforms tight across their hips, I realized they were men, all grown up in a way I certainly was not. Charleen's girlfriends were there, too, smoking Swisher Sweets, whispering in the ears of the sailors. The room felt freighted with sexual tension. Weddings are like that sometimes; I know that now, but then I thought all that desire was knotted in me and emanated from me.

My mother and Mrs. Karski and a few children and the old women neighbors sat in the living room drinking tea, or sherry in little blue glasses that still had oval POLAND stickers on the bottoms. They passed the time with talk of squash reaped and winter's prospects. I sat falsely dutiful near my mother on a hassock.

"It's dark," I said once, thinking to remind her of her own departure.

"Yes, the nights are coming on sooner now," she said.

"I wonder if Dad's home yet?"

"Well, I wouldn't worry," she said. "David's there. He's nearly fourteen now. You shouldn't have to do it all." She meant all the baby-sitting. She swept my bangs to one side of my forehead in what I knew was an affectionate gesture, but I hated it. I jerked away, more abruptly than I'd intended.

She sniffed and shrugged, to cover her hurt feelings. She hadn't dressed for the party and I was ashamed to see her there in bobby socks and blue jeans, with a kids' barrette in her hair. I felt bad about hurting her feelings and being ashamed, but they seemed like responses I couldn't resist or control. These were venial sins I often confessed of a Saturday so that I could take communion on Sunday.

"No rest for the wicked," she said, to no one in particular. She got up to go and I felt it was a fragile moment, that she might change her mind.

"I'll walk out with you," I said.

At her car, she said, "Don't drink yet, Kate."

"What makes you think I will?"

"Don't swell up like a toad now," she said. "I'm telling you this for your own good."

She got in then and I turned and went back to the house before a real argument happened, one that might make her take me home. I watched from just inside the front door until her taillights disappeared.

The kitchen was dim and blue with smoke. There was dancing and loud laughter. Someone grabbed me as soon as I walked in the door.

"Here's a gal might be able to cowboy jitterbug," he said, shoving me into the middle of the kitchen. He was short and drunk.

181

It was a kind of dancing I'd never done before, where you hold hands and the man leads you, swirls you. It would've been hard enough to do sober, but he tripped on his own black shoes.

Someone shouted, "Hank is from Wyoming, honey. You got to have a cowboy hat to learn to dance like that."

I pulled away and went over to Charleen, as though I had an important message for her. "He's weird," I whispered. I stared at a holy card of the Virgin Mary on the windowsill next to a packet of carrot seeds.

She rolled her eyes. "I'm having morning sickness at night," she said. "So soon." Charleen had a big, puffy face in which I could already see her mother. A smear of yellow cake frosting had dried on her chin. She tipped her beer can up for the last swallow. Then she said, "Have a drink, kid. Relax." She pushed me toward the counter. "Robbie, give Kate a drink."

I must've looked taken aback, because Robbie put his arm gently around my shoulder and said, "What's a nice girl like you doin' at a party like this?" We both knew it was a joke. "I'm Robbie. You're Kate. Let's be friends."

The tile floor was gummy with spilled beer and my flats stuck to it. Robbie was drunk too, but he wasn't rough, and I wanted to linger there with him, pliantly, with his arm around my shoulder. Mrs. Karski came to the kitchen door and shook her head and laughed.

Robbie said, "Here, honey, drink up," and he handed me a blue aluminum tumbler, the kind I'd drunk Kool-Aid from for as long as I could remember. There was whiskey in it.

I took a sip.

"One more," he coaxed.

He squeezed my waist. "'Atta girl," he said. "You little bohemian, you." I'd never heard that word before, but it sounded like what I wanted to be. When he smiled, I saw that all of his back teeth were filled with gold. "Little more and you'll be flying high."

I'd lost my head. It tasted terrible, and the burning made me think of fireworks for some reason, those little snakes you light on the sidewalk, but the lure of experience and the desire to defy my mother pushed me on until I'd drunk about a half-tumbler of whiskey in a short time.

The party ended for me then. I had to lurch outside to the edge of the herb garden, among the chives and borage, and throw up wedding cake. I could smell the honeysuckle tangled on the latticework. Inside, Robbie was laughing, and I heard Charleen yelling at him, calling him a creep. For months afterwards my face would turn hot and red when I remembered how I squandered my desire on him. Mrs. Karski drove me home with the windows rolled down.

My mother saw the whole story, in one knowing glance. She said, "What a sorry case you are."

I stood at the bottom of the stairs for a minute, shamefaced, my hand on the newel post for support. I knew I deserved her scorn, or even worse. I fixed my eyes on the mud I'd gotten on my stockings and shoes when I went out to throw up. The little ones were lined up on the sofa in pastel pajamas, watching television, and their innocence made me sad. I wanted to be among them again.

My mother sat in a rocking chair in her house slippers, rocking angrily, her mouth a stern straight gash. "Your father didn't come home tonight," she said.

At the time I was too drunk to understand the significance of that, and I went upstairs and tried to read *Henry Esmond* for English the next day, tried to push the foolish thing I'd done out of my mind.

My father didn't come home for the next three nights. At the same time, word had gotten around school about what I'd done at the party. I was left alone to eat my lunch in the cafeteria, by girls I'd been cultivating as friends. At home I was on my best behavior, helping out without being asked. For punishment, my mother was distant and spoke to me only when necessary. As the three days wore on, though, and my father still did not come home and there was no word from him, she weakened, needing me, and found small ways of letting me know I was back in her good graces. Asking about the debating team; offering me a lipstick sample given her by the Avon lady. When no one else was around, my mother would say, not directly to me, but to the space around me, "He's gone to play the ponies, no doubt. To Delaware. Or Baltimore." She knew him, she knew his patterns, she knew his weaknesses.

When he did come home, nothing was the same.

It was late on an Indian summer morning, a Sunday, after Mass. My mother had taken off her earrings and plunked them in a glass salad bowl on the buffet in the dining room. She said I could make a Chef Boyardee pizza for lunch, and that she'd fry a chicken for supper.

My father drove into the driveway, came into the house in an ordinary way, slinging his navy cardigan on the sofa, as though he'd been away for an hour running an errand. He could, once in a while, seem a happy man, energetic and up-beat. My brothers and sisters gathered around him, hungry to see him, and he let that siphon away his attention. He picked up the baby, Colleen, and held her over his head and with his lips made sounds she thought were funny against her stomach. Joe hit his leg with his little square fist, and my father knelt down and roughhoused with him for a few minutes, trading phony punches. I went in the kitchen to start the pizza, posted myself near the door so I would hear whatever they might say. My mother sat at the round oak table in her church dress, her arms bare on the table, fiddling with an unlit cigarette.

"You kids go play now," he said. " I need to talk with your mother."

He sat down across from her, just as they'd been on so many evenings, discussing the war or some old movie or the Depression, things from their past they liked to remember. He borrowed her lighter and lit a cigarette.

He tossed some money on the table. "I won two-fifty," he said.

"How much did you lose?" she said bitterly.

"That's none of your damn business."

His tone frightened me. He was not by nature a harsh man, but he could be driven to harshness by my mother in quick spurts that surprised me.

"I'm going on the road again," he said. "It's not working out at the phone company."

"I figured as much," she said, her voice hard. And when I think of that, I wonder how much that hardness cost her. He'd moved her there with such high hopes. And now she'd be by herself, responsible for all of us, but she didn't say that. She kept that to herself.

And him, what did it cost him to give up what he'd moved there for? We children sided with our mother, and it was many years before I could think of him and his life on the road, a life that I imagine as lacking in joy and sometimes mean. The motels; the meals in taverns; the interminable evenings.

He did spend the night. My mother did fry the chicken and he whipped the mashed potatoes and we sat down to supper together. Later they watched television, and I saw in my father a kind of leaden passivity. He wasn't forty yet and had seven children. My mother used to say the house could burn down around him and he wouldn't budge. The next morning, before we left for school, we kissed him good-bye at the bathroom door. He was bare-chested, wrapped at the waist in a towel, and half his face was lathered with shaving cream. That was the last time I saw my father for a year and a half.

My mother began changing then, but I didn't want to notice the changes.

At school I worked hard at ingratiating myself to the right people, girls who ran the yearbook, the newspaper. At my old school in Indiana, I'd been in line for responsibility and limelight. Now I had to start all over again. The gossip of my drunkenness faded as other, more serious, scandal arose, an attempted suicide in the tenth grade, vandalism of the principal's office. And then, President Kennedy was killed. We were awestruck and unified in our mourning. For months, I mooned around over the chemistry teacher, a crush shared by a boy named Seth, my first gay friend, though *gay* was not a word we used or had even heard of. What thrill there was in trading confidences with Seth. We felt we were destined to live beyond the boundaries, in regions of experience few but us would ever know.

I took a weekend waitress job at a Christian camp not far from home. By this time I'd stopped going to Mass and was—I told anyone who would listen—seeking a spiritual experience more satisfying. I lived at the camp on weekends, in the dorm, and listened with an open mind to the evangelical preachers, who were lean men with visionary eyes, never without their Bibles right at hand. At the same time, the staff—the waitresses and cooks and dishwashers—had their own private world at the camp, staying up in the lounge until two in the morning, with a good fire in the fireplace and the cook's little television on the hearth. We were all smart and quick of tongue and irreverence was required of us in order to belong. We were lewd in the kitchen, even while the blessing was being said in the dining room. The cook would crack eggs with one hand—plop, plop, plop—a skill I greatly admired, and he'd say, "These are my birth control glasses. Guys in black glasses never get laid." What esprit and exuberance there was in all our free talk. We thought we were daring, subversive. I still hadn't been kissed, but beyond home I had this rich life, discovering my own eccentricities, my intensity. As a daily signature, I wore a red velvet beret.

Warning signs did arise now and then to bring me back to what was happening at home. One spring evening I was reading a children's story to Maureen and Colleen. This was nearly eight months after my father had gone. We were on the front porch steps, near a rick of fragrant stacked firewood. The boys had a softball game going in the field not far from us. We could hear them egging one another on, hear the thwunk of the bat against the ball. My mother was at the dining room table—I could picture her there and hear the music she and her friend listened to: show tunes from the fifties. She'd found a woman friend who liked to drink and the two of them sat there murmuring of an evening, smoking and drinking, either beer from a sweaty quart bottle or sometimes, if they were in the money, they'd have gin and tonics. When the tonic was gone, they'd drink the gin neat from jelly glasses. It was evening, as I said, and almost too dark to be reading, but I loved the fecund smell of spring and the sense of life going on all around us as I read aloud.

"Kitty has an owie," Colleen interrupted me.

"Oh, no," I said, just being polite to her. She was three years old.

"No, he *does*," Maureen insisted. "Momma says Big Bopper has a mikaphone in his paw." She was five and much more savvy than Colleen.

"A what?" I said.

"A secret mikaphone. Someone's listening to her secrets."

"Uh-*huh*," Colleen said.

"Momma's only kidding," I said.

I took them into the bathroom then and bathed them and put them to bed. I did not give any more thought to what they'd said, not for months, and I don't know if anything would have turned out differently if I had paid attention to them. I wanted to continue with my discovery of myself out in the world. Now when I remember Maureen's words, though, I see that my mother's grip was loosening months before I faced that fact. Doctors have labels for what she felt. She was suffering, at war with herself, fearful, and I didn't want to notice. Noticing was sure to make me feel powerless, unable to change what needed to be changed. If my mother could read my mind now, thinking this, she'd be fatalistic and dismissive. She'd say, Hindsight's always better than foresight. Still, I think we always have to wonder, in families, what would happen if we paid attention early on.

The last week of school, in June, our grandfather died.

My mother heard the news over the telephone, early one morning, as we sat around the table eating cereal. The radio was on. Our brown lunch bags were on the table, the tops still not folded down, with milk money beside each bag. Her face turned dark red. She squeezed shut her eyes and began crying.

Stephen said, "What's wrong, Momma?"

When she hung up the receiver, she picked up her cigarettes and went in the kitchen. We all looked at one another uneasily, questioningly. She moaned, a cry that hurt my heart to listen to. She banged on the cupboard door above the counter. Then she came back to us and we were stunned and openmouthed around the table.

"Your grandpa's dead now," she said, still crying. Her face puckered with sorrow and shock.

Maureen went over to her and took her hand. None of the rest of us knew what to do; we were old enough to be embarrassed by death. We knew it was a solemn moment, but, ignorant of the right thing to do, we only wanted to get away.

"Bus's coming," Joe called from the front room window. He'd slipped away from the table as soon as he saw her tears.

That was our cue and my brothers and I left her there alone with the two little girls. She had no one with whom to share that grief, and I imagine she felt lonely then, more lonely than she ever had, since marriage, if it serves us at all, serves us during those times of loss.

In the late afternoon, at the end of study hall, my name was called out over the loudspeaker. My mother met me near the principal's office, next to the trophy case. The floor was waxed brightly all around her, and amid that shine and order, she looked all the more downcast, beyond comfort. She hadn't combed her hair and she wore a pair of muddy irrigators. They were David's. He worked at the dairy farm on Saturdays. It had been raining all morning and I thought she must have been out walking in the rain. Her face seemed swollen from crying.

"Kate, I want you to go to Grandpa's funeral," she said.

I was surprised and I'm certain my face revealed that.

"You're going on an airplane. You've never been on an airplane before."

"Who's paying for it?" I said. I couldn't imagine we had money for airplanes.

"Never you mind," she said. "Money's been set aside."

"It's the last week of school."

"The principal says it's okay."

While we were talking, she pushed me out the double glass doors. I think she felt uneasy at school; she rarely went there.

In the car I said, "Why don't *you* go?"

She started crying and put her arms around the steering wheel. "I just can't," she said, through her tears. Then she straightened up and wiped her eyes on her flannel sleeve. She rummaged in her tooled leather purse for a handkerchief. "I'm just treading water, Kate. I can't push myself."

I believe she couldn't bear to know the truth, to see the dead, to be owned again by what she'd left behind. I don't know if she ever went back there, to Terre Haute, until she was buried there herself. Though it's possible she and my father passed through there years later, the years when I was out of touch with them, and she had gone on the road with him.

"Okay, I'll go, I guess."

"That's my big girl, Kate. Look," she said, feigning cheeriness, "I've packed a bag for you." She put the flat of her hand on a plaid suitcase in the backseat. "I'm driving you to Friendship Airport right now. You're as good as in the air."

And that is what we did. We drove to Baltimore in the light rain, with "The Buddy Dean Show" on the radio. She did not mention my grandfather or give me any messages for anyone at the funeral. Her silence roared at me. She did not speak at all, except to say, "You can stay a couple weeks if you want. Would you like that?"

I stayed there, with one of my aunts, for ten days. The summer humidity had closed upon the Midwest like a vise and the funeral was held on a sweltering day. The women wore white cotton gloves and cooled themselves with papers fans printed with Bible verses. They were Protestant, the funeral service economical and plain, though my grandfather had owned his own business—the Dixie Bee Garage—and half the block it stood on. My grandmother was unapproachable; she cried in a terrifying way at odd times. Still, I liked being away from home. I'd seldom been a guest anywhere. People took care of me and that was a novelty. There were picnics and trips to the new shopping center and evenings of iced tea and layer cakes and television. I was allowed to read in bed each morning as long as I wanted. It did not seem such an unbearable thing that my grandfather had died. Being there, listening to people talk about him—exalting his virtues, forgetting his faults—it seemed only a part of life I'd never experienced before. I could almost forget home, forget mother. Almost.

The very night my mother called me home, I was kissed for the first time, on my aunt's sun porch by her stepson, Lannie. Lannie had been a greaser and a roughneck in high school, cocky with talk of cars and fistfights, and there'd been a brush or two with the law, again, having to do with cars and driving, and he had spent at least one night in jail, though he had straightened himself out by this time. He was twenty-four. He worked at an auto parts store and had a canoe and went canoeing on Sugar Creek on the weekends. He still lived at home with my aunt. His father had died of a brain tumor, leaving my aunt a widow for the second time.

This particular evening, she had gone to my grandmother's house. Strawberries were coming in and my aunt was afraid my grandmother, sick with grief, would let them go to waste. Lannie and I were in the house alone. The temperature had been in the nineties and the house seemed to pulse with the heat. I'd been reading in my room, the front bedroom, with the window fan turned on high. I had my hair done up in sponge rollers. When I went to the kitchen for a drink of ice water, I heard music from the sun porch and went out there to investigate.

The wooden venetian blind slats were shut against the evening sun. Lannie sprawled in an easy chair of red cracked leather, eyes closed, with his ear next to the big radio, the Roosevelt radio my aunt always called it, since she associated that radio with listening to Roosevelt during the war. The walls were knotty pine, the light a dim gold in the room.

I had never heard music like that before and I felt irresistibly drawn to it. Now I know it's called delta blues. Lightnin' Hopkins. Bessie Smith. But that was my first exposure to the blues, to the physical clutch of it, that sensual gift.

Lannie squinted, and when he saw me there, enthralled, he mutely patted the chair arm, motioning me to sit down. I went to sit beside him on the arm of the chair, though there were other places to sit on the sun porch. It seemed most natural—and dangerous—to be perched there beside him. He had on the cleanest blue jeans and a white shirt, the sleeves rolled up on his forearms. By that time, the forearms of men had begun to intrigue me; I liked the sunny pattern of blonde hair growing on his arm near the wrist, the way the veins intruded softy on the underside. He wore sandals and his feet were tanned. My aunt had always said he'd be a heartbreaker when he grew up, be able to wrap women around his little finger. He had dark, coppery curls and his eyelashes were sunbleached on the tips. In one hand he held a harmonica, gently kept time with it against his thigh. The other hand, within minutes, he had placed against the small of my back and he left it there, warm and firm, while we listened to the music.

The program ended at eight o'clock and I thought the spell was broken. But Lannie reached over and turned off the radio. He said, "When you were a little girl you used to come in my room and listen to Elvis. Do you remember that?"

"'Heartbreak Hotel,'" I said. He'd had a ukulele hanging on the wall and live turtles in an aquarium.

"How old're you now?"

"Seventeen," I lied. His hand brushed my back.

"Would you do something for me, Kate? Would you take off your glasses."

I took off my glasses, carefully folded them at the temples, and set them beside a stack of cork coasters on the wagon wheel coffee table in front of us.

He stood up, smiling, and took both my hands in his. My knees trembled. With the sponge rollers in my hair, I wanted to hide. I was thankful it was nearly dark in the room.

He said, "Boy oh boy."

"What?"

"You look nice without your glasses."

"Well," I said, "I can't *see* without them."

He laughed and pulled me near and kissed me. This kiss was no peck on the mouth, certainly not a peck. Neither was it voracious or insistent. It was a kiss I yielded into and felt all over my body and I know he felt it, too. For a first kiss, it was just right.

Then there was the rattle of the back door, my aunt coming home. We sprung apart. Lannie nearly leaped to the light switch, turned it on. She came to the door of the sun porch.

"Kate," she said, "I've got news for you. Come sit down in the kitchen with me."

Lannie and I looked at one another, perplexed. I followed my aunt into the kitchen. There was a quart bucket of just-picked strawberries on the table. I sat down. She opened the refrigerator and got out the ice water and poured herself a glass.

"Your mother called Mom tonight."

I had trouble hearing her. In spirit, I was still on the sun porch.

"Are you listening to me, Kate?"

"Yes, ma'am," I said.

"She needs you to come home." My aunt drank her ice water, almost a glassful before she went on. She sat down wearily across from me. She looked very much like my mother at that moment, plumper, more rested, but they had the same frown lines, the same graying cowlicks.

"Is something wrong?" I said.

"She doesn't sound good, Kate. Do you know how to get a hold of your father?"

"No, I don't," I said, ashamed that that was the case.

She sat there mulling over something, but didn't say a word. In a distracted manner, she pulled a grocery coupon from her blouse pocket, tucked the coupon under the sugar bowl.

"Lordy, Lordy," she said. And then finally, "Be that as it may. I've changed your reservation. She wants you to come home in the morning."

She woke me up at five in the morning. I'd had a restless night. I was afraid of what I'd find at home and I felt cheated of the feelings—the sensations, really—that had begun on the sun porch. In retrospect, I think it was probably for the best that my aunt had come home when she had. Though I wondered always about Lannie's intentions, I knew more about my own, and we might have found ourselves in deep trouble if she'd come home a half hour later. While I was eating breakfast, with my aunt sipping her Irish breakfast tea, Lannie slouched to the kitchen door in his terrycloth bathrobe, sleepy-eyed, and with a salute and a wink, he said, "Bon voyage, cousin Kate."

At home, my mother had taken to her bed. I'd been met at Friendship by a neighbor, a twaddling, bossy woman who offered no word of what I should expect and I didn't want to ask. The first words out of her mouth were, "Well, guess your gallivantin's over with." Her face was rodent-like, shrewd and sly. She had a crucifix glued to her dashboard, and her car smelled cowy. She made butter and cheese at home and delivered it door to door to customers in the surrounding hills. On the hour-long drive from the airport, she told me about some people on her route who'd lost a lot of money playing bingo, money they could ill afford to lose, she said. There were others she ran down. A male elementary teacher who'd moved away for some mysterious reason having to do with a senior girl; a woman whose trash was filled with empty sloe gin pints; another who kept her good furniture protected in plastic. I wondered how much she knew about my family, what she might say to our neighbors. I minded my manners, though, and thanked her profusely. She let me out at the end of the driveway, warning only, "Don't slam the door." I felt irritated at my mother for sending her to fetch me. My heart beat wildly as I approached the house, out of anger I told myself, but more likely it was apprehension.

It was full summer, with the mustard high along the edges of the cornfield, nubbins of green apples clustered on the fruit trees. Joe was up in the treehouse, an encyclopedia open on his lap. He was becoming a bookworm just like me. Maureen and Colleen had mapped out rooms in colored chalk on the front porch, their playhouse, and Maureen was spanking a baby doll while Colleen stared into a hand mirror, painting her lips in a greasy curve with an old poppy red lipstick. She had on a straw beach hat. They still wore their summer nighties, flowered, ruffled affairs.

When the girls saw me, they dropped what they were doing and ran up to me, for hugs. This made me happy to be home.

"Where're the big boys?" I said to them.

"Riding their bikes," Maureen said.

"David's all gone," Colleen said. Her corn-colored hair had been brushed, but Maureen's had not.

Then I remembered David was away at Student Council Leadership Camp. I realized how trying the week must have been for my mother with David and me away.

"How's Momma?" I said. We were sitting on the stone steps, my arms around them. Bingo lay in a sweaty, panting heap nearby.

Maureen frowned, shook her head. "She's sleeping."

I left my suitcase there on the porch and went in the house. It was cool and quiet inside. In the dining room, no one had cleared after lunch—peanut butter and jam jars were open, bread crusts and raisins littered the table. Dead irises, like tiny gray rags, dried in a milk bottle of cloudy water. Someone had been looking at a photo album, the kind with the snapshots stuck in little black corners. There was a picture of my mother coming out of the water at a lake, smiling in a careless way, a way I'd never seen her.

"I'm home," I called.

"I'm here," she called back, her voice croupy and frail. "In the bedroom."

She was propped in bed against pillows, wearing a frayed dress shirt of my father's. Her eyes were bloodshot. The curtains were drawn. A week's worth of newspapers lay at the foot of the bed. Six empty waxed milk shake containers were lined up on the blonde headboard of the bed, and a Gideon Bible lay open beside her.

She patted the bed. "Come sit here, Kate," she crooned.

I sat down. "How're you feeling?" I said.

"Not so good," she said. "Was Grandpa okay?"

I hesitated to answer her. There was a stale smell in the room, like soiled laundry left too long in the hamper. "Everything *went* okay," I said.

She frowned at the door. "Close that, would you?"

I closed the door, and then she said, "Your father was after me all night."

"Is he here?" I said.

"He was in the basement all night," she whispered. "He's after me."

"Momma—he's not here, is he?" I hadn't called her Momma in a long time. I believe at that moment I wanted to be the child again, but I sensed I was being jimmied out of childhood and that she needed me to be the grown-up.

"I don't *know*, Kate." She started weeping then. "Sometimes I can't *tell*."

"You're just tired," I answered. I wanted to believe this. "Tired and worn out."

She took hold of my hand, placed her palm against mine, as if to measure me. Our hands were the same size. Pensively she said, "Truer words were never spoken."

"That's it," I said. "You need to rest." I squeezed her hand. "And not worry."

She lay back on the pillows and stared at the ceiling.

"I'm going to make it nice in here for you," I said. "You don't mind, do you? If I straighten up a bit?"

She rolled her head side to side, touched my knee. "I don't mind."

"How about some music?" I said.

"No. No music," she said, a trace panic-stricken. "I remember too much."

I was filled with a largess of energy. I thought by the weight of that, my energy, I could make it all better. I'd flown in an airplane and I'd been kissed. There was a generosity I felt, and a certainty, that if I worked hard enough and loved her enough, she would change. I did not know the places in her mind she could go where I would never go. Or where I hoped I'd never go. And when that happened, there was no retrieving her. Coming back was something she had to do for herself. But I didn't want to know about it. I thought I could salvage what was happening. I cleaned her room, and then the dining room and kitchen. I fed my brothers and sisters, ordered them to bathe and shine their shoes for Mass the next morning. I put Maureen's hair up with bobby pins and setting lotion. Kevin wanted to iron his own shirt and I showed him how. I locked the doors at dusk. And I brought my mother pot after pot of tea, held her hand, listened to her ramblings.

The next morning, I brought her breakfast in on a metal Coca-Cola tray she usually kept hung on the kitchen wall. "It's a beautiful day," I said.

She said, "Kate. I've something important to tell you. Sit down."

Her voice was conspiritorial, low. I slipped the tray onto her lap, and I sat down on a bright blue kitchen chair she used for a nightstand. The sun lay in a warm lozenge on the afghan at the foot of her bed, and Rummy slept there in the sun. I thought she must've pulled Rummy up there, for the company.

"What is it, Mom?"

"I've been thinking," she said. She folded and smoothed, over and over, the edge of the topsheet. She'd begun to have liver spots on her hands. "I've been thinking someone needs to be sacrificed."

"What?"

She set the tray on my father's side of the bed. "Sacrifices are called for. In the Bible." She was wistful, slow-spoken.

"Those're just stories."

"Kate, I know what I'm talking about."

"What *are* you talking about?"

"David."

"What about him?"

"He'll be sacrificed."

And this is when I knew that it would be a mistake for me to care for her alone. In families like ours, boundaries blur, and some of the time you cannot distinguish between truth and lying, sanity and madness, right and wrong. You can go on having a life together, pretending. But this was the point at which I was sure she'd gone beyond a boundary. It took this long to be sure.

She frightened me. I'd heard of stories like this before, on the late news, or in crime magazines on the newsstand, a home suddenly turned violent. Something still protected us, though. She'd chosen David and David wasn't here. I couldn't believe she would hurt one of us.

"Here's an egg in an egg cup," I said. "Just the way you like it." I'd given her a red-and-white cloth napkin and rye toast.

"I'm not crazy, Kate," she said. "And I'm not a child."

"No one said that," I said.

"I know what you're thinking."

I did not believe her. I was thinking that I never wanted to be where she was. I said, "What'm I thinking?"

"That mothers shouldn't be like this."

"The kids're getting ready for Mass," I answered. "The priest's stopping by for them. At the main road."

"You better walk them out," she said, driftily, turning to her breakfast.

Before that day was over, my mother had signed herself in to a psychiatric hospital. Kevin was an altar boy and I'd given him a note to give to the priest. After Mass, he came to the house. He knew many things about us, as is often the case with troubled families. People who make it their business—priests and teachers and social workers—know the details of your trouble though you've never breathed a word of it yourself.

He spoke with her in the bedroom. I stayed away in the kitchen, scrubbing a cast iron skillet with salt.

He took me out in the yard and said, "She needs help she can't get at home." He was an old priest, with yellowed white hair, sloped shoulders, and a kind manner. He wore gold-rimmed glasses he'd repaired with electrical tape.

"What should I do?" I said, unimaginably relieved that I had someone to ask.

"I think she'll do what's best. I think she knows that," he answered. "I'll drive her myself to the hospital."

Within ten minutes she had packed a small suitcase and said good-bye to those of us who were around the house. She went peacefully, in low spirits. Instead of shoes she wore scuffed pea-green corduroy house slippers. Kissing my cheek good-bye, she said, "Do what makes you happy, Kate. I left out so many things." Her words seemed final, as though she were going away to die rather than to recuperate.

Arrangements were made. A social worker came calling. The powers that be decided we children could stay together in our home if an adult relative came to stay with us. Spinsterish, afflicted with a near martyr's sense of family obligation, my father's great aunt rode the Greyhound from Evansville to be with us, though she was very old, and hard of hearing, and she shook from Parkinson's disease. She was the only one who would join us, and I was set against her from the beginning because I'd once heard my mother say that this particular aunt blamed her for my father's comedowns. We did not know her well and she did not know us. Moreover, she did not know how to contact my father. She believed in prayer and that is what she spent her time doing. She owned three rosaries, blue glass, wood, and pearl, and she made herself feel more at home by fixing up a shrine to the Virgin on top of the television. A votive candle burned there, above the evening news, above "American Bandstand." She held to all sorts of superstitions and old wives' tales, about evil eyes and blood in eggs. Good things she credited to God's will; bad things were our fault. Rock and roll offended her deeply, handiwork of the devil, she said. I had no patience with any of this. We argued. I said that when I had children—*if* I ever did—I'd tell them only the truth. They would know nothing of the Easter Bunny or Santa Claus or God or the Tooth Fairy. She persisted in believing I was a good Catholic girl, though I hadn't been to Mass in six months. On and on it went. When I think of the ways I baited her, I am ashamed. Truth be known, I didn't want her there. I made the lunches and suppers, delegated chores. I was in charge and felt invincible and had no faith whatsoever in grown-ups or authorities. As often happens, my empathy comes much too late; how feckless, how green, how burdensome, all this progeny must have seemed to her.

Summer rolled by, my senior year began. We got on surprisingly well; the weekly visits with the social workers went smoothly. Maureen learned to read, Joe won spelling bees, Kevin kept on serving as an altar boy. Stephen and David took a paper route, and on the night they collected, they'd buy loads of penny candy to share around at home. We pretended we were all right without our mother; any mention of her would bring tears to our eyes, especially late in the evening; we avoided talking about her.

At school, I won awards, performed in plays, wrote articles for the school paper. I had a boyfriend who liked me. We never pretended to be in love; we were pals. Our mutual interests were theater arts, World War II, and what I thought of

as making out, though we never put words to what we were
doing in his mother's car in the depths of an apple orchard
after dark. Before going out to the orchard, more often than
not, he'd give me a tour of his father's study, the war memo-
rabilia stashed there, Nazi helmets, insignia patches. Japanese
buttons and knives. I knew my mother wouldn't approve of
what I did with him, the whisker-burned cheeks I returned
home with, the chapped lips, but I felt free of that, as though
her sanctions weren't important anymore and I were no
longer her child. Other times I'd dwell on the blank hole of
her absence, and long for what I'd rarely had, someone to rely
on, counsel, consistency. If I didn't think about my mother,
didn't allow myself to get in a stew about her, the pieces of my
existence fit together like a children's puzzle, so long as I had
stamina for it all, and when you are that age, energy seems
abundant. I was nagged close to the bone only by the thought
of college—how would I be able to afford it?

On Sundays, we were taken to visit our mother, and
though she would come out to the shady grounds of the hospital, among the birches and conifers, and we would show
her our schoolwork and the little ones would tell her of their
triumphs and concerns—I myself was secretive, watchdog of
my exploits—it always felt as though we were talking
through a glass wall. Her medication buffered her from us.
Sometimes David and Kevin and I would rove away and peek
with curiosity at the other patients, placated, bovine women,
sharing sticks of gum and cigarettes, waiting for visitors. Her
life there was a mystery to me; she never spoke of it. We were
witness to change in her, though—she'd begun to wear her
hair differently, in what we called a "pixie," and she'd had a

manicure. Eventually, as winter came on, she talked of coming home.

On Pearl Harbor day we had our first real snow. It accumulated in elegant peaks in the porch corners, covered all manner of junk piles around the houses, making new and bundled shapes that pleased me. Mother had come home that day, and she was there when I arrived from play rehearsal. It was nearly dark outside. David grunted over a snow shovel, paving a path from the front door to the driveway. Inside, there was a fire in the fireplace, a clove smell from the kitchen. Colleen and Maureen sat cross-legged in front of the television, eating warm molasses cookies. My father's great aunt had left the night before, on the bus heading west. She'd given me a book for Catholic girls, about love. She'd said I should think about starting a hope chest.

I ranged into the kitchen, without taking off my car coat. Mother was browning a pot roast in a black Dutch Oven.

"Things're moving a little slow here," she said. "I'm not used to being in the kitchen." She seemed optimistic, a touch awkward. She had an apron on.

"I thought we'd have pork chops tonight," I said. "Didn't you see them thawing?"

"That's a fine greeting," she said.

We looked at one another as though we could hardly recognize ourselves. The kitchen was steamy, the hair on her forehead in damp fringy curls. Overlapping cookies, row after row, cooled on waxed paper laid out on the butcher block.

"They might spoil," I said, self-righteously.

"What're you all in a huff about?" she said. "Why don't you take off your coat and stay awhile? You could peel the spuds."

I did as she told me; I didn't want us to get off on the wrong foot, as she might've said. But I felt none of what I'd expected to feel when she returned home. The welcome; the affection; the relief; the praise. *The praise.* More than anything, I'd expected her to tell me what a fine job I'd done, how selfless I'd been. I'd done for myself, so my life would go on uninterrupted, but I hankered after her approval, felt cheated of it. She treated me like any other child.

"You'll do dishes, David," my mother said, after supper.

"David doesn't do dishes anymore," I chimed in. "He only does laundry."

"Since when?" my mother said.

"There's a chart on the fridge," I said.

"I don't give a tinker's damn about your charts," my mother said, in a mock lighthearted voice. She lit a cigarette, nervously tapped her lighter on the table.

"It works," I said, incredulous.

"I'm home now, Kate." She blew her smoke toward the ceiling.

I hated her—no, it was more complicated than that, I felt stripped of any glory or authority or value—and I pushed my plate, a little too insistently, until it collided with the lazy susan in the middle of the table. David got up and began slapping silverware against the plates, mixing the scraps for the dogs into a bowl. We exchanged smart–alecky shrugs.

"Don't get on your high horses," she said.

I lived at home as a near stranger after that, working at the camp on the weekends, staying late after school, keeping up my guard to everyone but my little sisters. I found constant fault with my mother, her way of doing things, but I held my tongue. She served the same monotonous vegetables over and over, creamed corn and green beans with bread crumbs. She allowed sweets before supper. Her drinking picked up again. She encouraged Joe to fight back when he was bullied on the playground. To my way of thinking, she could do nothing right. How unfeeling I was, how arrogant and smug; how much I stored up to regret, enough to last for years.

We had one night of truce, in April. I came home laughing, dancing, jumping up and down.

"I won," I shrieked into the dining room. "I won a scholarship."

She took the letter from me; it was on heavy watermarked bond paper, an important-feeling letter. My brothers and sisters gathered around and she read the letter aloud to them.

"A full scholarship," she said. "That's the finest thing, Kate." She cupped my cheek in her palm. "That's really fine."

I felt shy, embarrassed by her touch, it'd been so long. I turned away, knelt down, and said to Maureen, "I'm going away to college."

"I don't want you to," she said, pouting.

"I'll miss you," I said. "Oh God, I can't believe it."

"I believe drinks are in order," my mother said. She went to the buffet and opened a bottle of sherry. She poured it into two shot glasses; we didn't have the proper ones. The television was on in the front room, big-band music on a cartoon show. My brothers and sisters bashfully clustered around us, diffidently leaning with their elbows on the table. The long window was open and birds were trilling, nesting for the night. The world seemed luxuriant with possibility. My mother toasted my future, we sipped the sherry, and after a few minutes my brothers and sisters wandered away, and I petted Rummy as we drank, to avoid my mother's eyes. We sat there talking cautiously. She smoked and I fingered a cigarette without lighting it. We had second sherries, this time in the jelly glasses.

"You'll do it all, Kate," she said. "You're my bright and shining light."

I cried then, but I don't believe she saw me crying. The dining room was dredged in a slate blue dusk. In her Baltimore Colts sweatshirt, her cigarette at a jaunty angle, my mother looked to me like a grainy photograph of some other time in my life, a time I thought I was breaking free of, a time I would try in vain to forget.

My father came home for a visit, the night before prom night. No one mentioned our mother's hospitalization or the months we'd lived there with his great aunt. Perhaps my mother and father had kept in touch all along. I know nothing of that. I only remember the welcome we gave him, festive and cheerful.

After supper, only the three of us were left at the table, my parents and I, drinking coffee with evaporated milk from thick china mugs.

"Kate's won a scholarship," my mother said.

"Good for you, kiddo," my father said. He looked much older than I remembered, his hair nearly white, in a crew cut. He wore baggy green work slacks and a V-neck sweater over a T-shirt. His sight was failing and he'd had to get glasses.

"She's going to need some help, though," she said.

"How much help?"

"I'm not sure," my mother said. "She'll need clothes. And books." Almost as an afterthought, she added, "I don't know how I'll get along without her."

"I've got a job there already," I said. "In the library." It gave me great pleasure to lie awake at night, imagining myself stamping due dates inside the covers of books.

"She'll still need money," my mother insisted.

"We'll have to see about that," my father said.

His tone, the inconclusiveness of his words, stirred up uneasiness in me. I excused myself and went out to the porch. No one was about. The grass was deep in the yard, and hadn't been cut yet for the first time that year. I took a yellow canvas camp chair out into the grass and sat down not far from a stand of irises. To calm myself I thought of the prom, the library job, my graduation dress, swatches of dream I handled over and over in my mind, for comfort.

Ten minutes later my father came up behind me, touched my hair, his hand gentle, tentative. Even now, after all this time, if a man touches my hair I am moved to tears, and I will, more often than not, find myself falling in love with that man.

"You mother still needs you, Kate," he said.

"I-won-a-scholarship," I whispered deliberately.

He took his hand away. "You don't know how strapped we are."

I stood up, faced him, my arms folded across my chest. The men in my family are short and stocky, and I had grown—I was nearly as tall as he was.

"I can't help that."

"Your mother still needs some help." He said this is a voice intended to be appealing, his hand on my arm, pressuring.

I yanked away. "You can't stop me."

"Why not put it off a year? She wants you to think about that." A pickup truck went by, switched on its tallowy headlights. His eyes were trained on the road, not on me.

"She *doesn't*."

"She asked me to ask you."

I raised my arms and clenched my fists. "I'm going," I pitched at him, screaming. "*You* went to Labrador."

He looked surprised, bilked in some way. Then he slapped my face hard, hard enough to make my sight go reddish black for a brief moment. He'd never done that before.

The shock of it fired through my body, and not just the slap, but what I'd done to provoke it. *Honor thy father and thy mother* popped into my mind. I planted myself there, stoic and confused and crying, my shoulders hunched and hands stuffed in my pockets. My nose ran, but pride kept me from wiping it.

He pinched my chin and said, "Look at me, damn it."

I silently refused to open my eyes.

He booted away the camp chair, then hustled quickly into the house, swearing under his breath, the keys on his belt loop clinking. He slammed the front door.

It was a warm spring night and if I try to imagine it, I think the Japanese maple leaves were probably just beginning to unfurl, like little brick-colored boats, and my brothers might have been playing catch. But I saw none of that. My senses were shut down and I felt only that slap and its ineluctable wake, a conviction that I *must* leave. I told myself he had no claim on me. When you are seventeen you have no idea what people and places will claim you, own you, forever. And though I didn't go away to college until after Labor Day, my connection with my parents was severed at that moment, not to be healed for many years. My father went on the road again two mornings later, and I lived at home that summer, working nights at a soda fountain, sleeping late, reading in bed, hard feelings, sad ones, lodged in every corner of the house, every place I turned.

Since then, I have always wanted to be the one to leave. Sometimes I think there must be tricks to leaving, to keep the hurt at bay. But my father never told me if there were, and I have spent a lifetime trying to find out.

1988

Love You Can't Imagine

In small towns you never know who will appear from out of your past. You give up being vigilant about it, you just expect to have to confront mistakes you made, dead-end roads you drove down way too long. Sandra thinks this—*there's a living, breathing, dead-end road right before your very eyes*—when she sees Tom Crib in the light of a pink Japanese lantern, on the veranda of the cabin where the cast party is getting underway. He's in a rocking chair, drinking Moosehead beer, snuggling a little boy in his arms. The boy looks to be about two years old, with Tom's whitish-blonde hair, but curly, cherubic.

"You were fantastic, Mom!" Desiree squeals.

Sandra had the female lead in *Take Me Along*, the community theater's major summer production, and this was the end of the run, a Saturday night in late July, Chelan, Washington. She arrives, contented, modestly proud, exhausted but wired, trailed by a devoted melange of supporters. Kelly Ford, a trail crew supervisor, whom Sandra thinks and speaks of, a little self-mockingly but lovingly, as her beau; her seventeen-year-old daughter, Desiree, and three of Desiree's friends, all of whom are dressed in tony vintage clothes, shorty lamb jackets, petite hats with black veils, print silk dresses, big pearl and rhinestone clip-on earrings, kid gloves; her sister Pat and her ten-year-old son, Roger, who sat through the entire performance listening to Bob Marley and the Wailers on his Walkman; and Easy Whip, Kelly's rotund lumbering malamute, with his sleet-colored eyes. He didn't name the dog; his ex-wife did. They are tramping up the gravel drive toward the friendly lights of the cabin, the aluminum beer keg in a tub of ice, the members of the cast and families and friends already gathered there, the slapping of the lake water against the shore, where it's promised, later, they'll have a bonfire. They had to park the van near the county road and the drive is lined with cars and pick-ups. In wind blowing off the lake, the rotting lodgepole pines creak like old bones.

"Thank you, sweetheart," Sandra says to Desiree, reaching for her, curling her hand around Desiree's. Their fingers feel chilled in the mountain night air.

Pat swats her affectionately on the fanny. "The theater in you's finally coming out," she says. "You were terrific."

Once Sandra had thought about becoming a clown. She imagined starting her own small business—Clowning Around she'd have called it—to entertain children at birthday parties. She knew she had theater in her. She'd been in one-act plays in high school, *The Lottery* and *The Open Window*, but those were cloying with heaviness, with meaning. Clowning Around would've been light and breezy and the laughter of children would have followed her like hummingbirds after honeysuckle.

Now she has a job she likes, GS6, Secretary, Forest Service District Office.

She hides her face behind the quilted lapel of her ski jacket. "I don't know if I can take any more attention," she says.

Kelly says, "Buck up. You deserve it. You *were* terrific." He draws Desiree and Sandra in close for a hug, says, "Listen, girls, I spied T.G. out back. I'll be there helping him with the fire. If you need me." Easy Whip trots behind him, around the frost-tinged poppies, the flowering butterfly bush. On uneven terrain in the dark, Kelly has the walk of an arthritic dancer. He's paying for all the times he carried murderous sixty-five-pound packs into the backcountry. A worn hip joint causes him increasing pain as he grows older—he's forty-two—yet still he walks with grace.

Desiree squeezes her hand and offers Sandra a secret womanly smile, meant to convey how much she understands that Kelly loves Sandra. Desiree is pro-Kelly all the way. She brainstorms wedding plans. Not a week goes by without her saying, "He's truly a nice guy, Mom. Look at the way he treats you." Usually Sandra will answer, "You don't have to convince me."

At the veranda they go their separate ways, Roger to the side steps where he sits down and picks through the stock of cassette tapes he's brought along, Pat to the knot of people around the keg at the far end of the veranda near the hammock (her husband's on a canoe trip in the Yukon and she misses him, but she's determined to have a good time without him), the girls inside to the stereo where they will jockey for control of the music. Sandra feels momentarily abandoned.

"Here she is—queen of the hop," Jerry—the play's director—says, saluting her with a red plastic cup of beer. It's his cabin. She thinks of Jerry as an older man; he took early retirement from teaching high-school speech and drama in Seattle.

She kisses his cheek. "You brought it out in me."

Then she meets Tom's eyes.

He says, "You hid your light under a bushel for a long time."

She feels defeated and put down by his first remark. How does he know she hasn't starred in every play of the past decade? "I'm surprised to see you, Tom," she says.

He rubs the sleeping boy's head. "We're just passing through. On our way home from Spokane."

Inside the girls have put on Tracy Chapman. They seem to be moving into a social awareness stage—watching the news on PBS, saving money to go to a Farm-Aid concert— and Sandra's pleased by that. At the keg someone is singing, slightly off-key, not quite sober.

Oh the women
are all fat in the ankle
and they all
kind of droop in the can.

Jerry says, "How do you two know each other?" He takes off his glasses, eases one side of his shirttail out of his khakis, and wipes the lenses with the shirttail.

"You first," Sandra says, skittish, suddenly tongue-tied. "How do you two know one another?"

"Tom's wife, Debbie, was a student of mine." Jerry explains. "It's funny how these things happen. I was in the Nickel

Ad office a few days ago, trying to compose an ad for a boat I'm selling—that Fiberglas canoe—the blue one—and lo and behold, in they come. Debbie, Tom, and Lance here. You know Rick. At the Nickel Ad. He's Tom's brother."

"Small world, as they say," Tom says. "This's my boy, Lance."

"He looks like a real sugarpie," Sandra says.

"Are those girls your girls?"

"Just one," Sandra laughs, and she sounds phony to herself thinking, Don't you remember anything? "Just Desiree. When it comes to plants and pets and kids, one of each seems about right to me."

And she casts about for ways to extricate herself—a friend, or even an acquaintance, will do. She keeps thinking, What's wrong with this picture? People change, just like Pat always insists. It's possible, they do. The miracle of human adaptation never ceases to amaze her. There was no mistaking his love for the boy and she feels glad of that. For the boy; for his wife; for Tom himself. Though she feels cheated too, infected with a selfish streak of wondering why he couldn't have been that way with her. With Desiree. When they needed it.

She squats down and says to Roger, pressing her finger to his chest, "Aren't you freezing with just that T-shirt on?" She can smell the watermelon gum he's chewing.

He can't hear her; under a reggae spell, he has his headphones on. "Batman," he says.

Kelly peeks between the dowels of the veranda rails. "Sandra. Sugar. Why don't you come on around here and help us out?"

She figures they are smoking a joint. "I'm on my way," she says, relieved.

"Whoa," Jerry says. "Not so fast, young lady. Come again. How do you two know each other?"

"From the old days," Tom says.

That about covers it, Sandra thinks, the bad old days. She steps off the veranda onto the path, zips up her jacket. "We met there too, didn't we? At the Nickel Ad office." She's aiming for a devil-may-care tone, but she's not sure it comes across.

"Sure enough," Tom says. And just before she turns the corner, he catches her eye. "Let's talk. Okay? In a while?"

"Let's talk, Tom. Fine."

Her high heels sink into the pine duff on the path. She wonders what they will say, what they can possibly say after all these years. Pat would say, A lot of muddy water passes under the bridge in twelve years.

Around the corner Kelly and T.G. are between the cold frame and the compost pile, huddled over a joint, trying to light it. Kelly circles her in a bear hug from behind, lifts her off the ground, snacks on the nape of her neck. He says, "Here's my partner in crime."

She twists in his arms, kisses him on the mouth. His nose is cool, his skin smells like the woods.

"You guys are great," T.G. says, then, parenthetically, passing her the joint, "Special occasion." Getting stoned has become a once-in-a-while treat for T.G. and Kelly, and usually she turns down their offer to join them. Sandra has even given up her nightly Watneys Red Barrel in favor of a clear head every morning. But not tonight; tonight she'll have a ritual toke. T.G. is drummer in a country band, president of the local Sierra Club, kindergarten teacher, and Kelly's younger brother. He's after them to find him a woman. He says he wants what they have. "How do you do it? How do you *maintain?*"

"True love," Kelly says. "True love, my man."

And Sandra feels that same physical stirring, quickening delicate as a fern's shadow, a gleam throughout her pelvis she always feels whenever Kelly speaks of his feelings for her. He is a man who knows the aphrodisiac women can't resist: free-wheeling conversation about feelings, dreams, desires. One of Kelly's dreams stands in the way of them moving farther into their lives together. Kelly wants a baby and Sandra is sterile. "You knew that from the get-go," she always says to him whenever he talks about his confusion, his inability to relinquish the option of being a father. "Indeed I did," Kelly will answer. "I shook every apple off your tree anyway." It's true; he'd shaken her to her roots.

Sandra's love for Kelly is not the sort you hear about in songs on the jukebox. It's not desperate or crazy. They met three years ago and it was one year before they made love. Kelly said he wanted to get to know her first and Sandra thought that was a novel idea. When she remembers that year going by, she imagines ranging in the high country on a long hike, when it's tough-going at first and you don't know what to expect. Maybe you slip and fall when the trail crosses a creek bed, maybe the first lake is small, disappointing, but you push yourself, you glory in the little things along the way, the shooting stars and glacier lilies, the marmot whistling, and before long, just as you are simply traveling, putting one boot in front of the other for the bliss of it, you come upon grand peaks and a string of alpine lakes so rare and peaceful that you imagine no one else has ever been there before you. It's where you belong. That's what being with Kelly is like. Easy, once you reach cruising altitude. Paradise, kind of. And ordinary. Common pleasures renew them. Razzing one another; watching a video in their bathrobes; dividing the foxglove in the fall; lying awake in one another's arms at midnight, waiting for Desiree to come in from some breakneck double date. Love you can't imagine when you're young, when you think that love is you winning him over, a treadmill of pursuit and chicanery.

Sandra's linen skirt was soft, worn, a Jonathan Logan she'd bought at a church rummage sale for seventy-five cents. She ironed it on the kitchen table, sprinkling it with water from the tap, then steaming out the wrinkles. The pleasant hot earthy smell of the linen—like grasses in sunlight—rose around her as she ironed. The people in the next apartment were listening to "60 Minutes." She'd taken two Advil for the menstrual cramps that'd begun right after the car broke down.

Tom Crib would be back any minute and they were going to see *Annie Hall* at the dollar theater on Main Street. This was their first night in the studio they'd rented; new town; new apartment with a pepper tree in the courtyard; new landscape. No one knew where they were or how to get a hold of them, and they liked the freedom of that. They'd driven from Bishop all night on two white crosses a hitchhiker'd given them. Tom said they shouldn't take them, you can't trust hitchhikers. Sandra said she trusted this one, he was A-OK, she liked the way he shared his six-pack and he didn't throw the empties out the window. They'd eaten the white crosses and the talk had picked up, accelerating through their memories. The Volvo was jam-packed with their belongings and had out-of-date '77 Colorado tags. Sandra and Tom had been picking apples in Washington, near Brewster, and when that ran out they decided to "check out California," drive the length of it to see if they might like to settle there, in some small town in the Sierra foothills or the Owens Valley. Tom knew bookbinding, and a little about photo-offset. He wasn't afraid of heights and knew how to trim trees. He was confident he could find work, enough to get by on. Sandra talked about starting a business. Maybe she'd be a clown for children's birthday parties.

"You need wealthy people for that," Tom had said. From a café in Lone Pine he called a buddy of his in Palm Springs—someone from the old days in Seattle—who said he was thinking about starting a small press to publish guidebooks. He said, Come on down, the weather's fine.

When the car lost compression and died, about four in the morning, they'd pushed it onto the sandy shoulder near Yucca Valley and hitchhiked into Desert Hot Springs, figuring it would be a cheaper place to live than Palm Springs. It was a Sunday, and there was not much they could do about the car on a Sunday. They took the first apartment they looked at, unloaded the few things they'd brought from the car in rucksacks, and settled in, more or less. The studio was one small room, with a kitchenette and brown shag carpeting and brown nylon furniture. In the cupboard there were Teflon pots and a skillet—the Teflon crosshatched with scratches—an iron, three plastic coffee mugs, and an open box of roach poison. The table where they ate was next to the double bed. Someone had left a Baptist Church calendar from two years back nailed to the wall. There was no phone, but the landlord had pointed out a pay phone just across the road, near a coffee shop whose windows were boarded up with warped plywood. It hadn't taken long to hang their clothes in the closet, stack their books on the orange plastic Parsons table.

Sandra was reading a book about starting your own business, Tom was reading *Black Elk Speaks*. They'd met some people in the Okanogan Valley who lived year-round in a tipi and sometimes they talked about doing that. It seemed a hard road to turn down, surprisingly complicated and pricey and fraught with tough luck. You were always at the mercy of the weather, and living in a tipi was one strike against you from the beginning with most people, people who thought you were just plain lazy to want to do such a thing. Still it was a dream they toyed with, a way of whiling away otherwise dead time.

She wondered if her ex-husband, Ranny, would let their daughter visit her if she lived in a tipi. Desiree was five years old. She lived with Ranny in Chelan, where he was foreman at a big peach and cherry orchard. With a steady job, legally he had the upper hand. All that stability—the job and a new wife with two children of her own—couldn't be argued with. Almost everyone—Sandra's mother, Ranny, Sandra and Tom—conspired to believe that this was the reason Sandra did not have her daughter. Only her sister, Pat, guessed that there was more to it than that, but Sandra wouldn't talk about it. She felt black-hearted, paralyzed with self-inflicted hurt, when the other reasons danced mockingly before her in the dark late at night. When that happened, she'd get up and drink hot milk and rye to bring on sleep.

As she ironed, she fiddled with the dial on the radio. All the stations carried a grisly story of two women who'd been killed during the making of a snuff film on some beach near L.A.

Tom walked in with two brown bags of groceries.

"I'm not sure southern California's my idea of California," she said. She thought of northern California, the soft shapes of ocean fog, the land's nooks and crannies. She thought she might prefer that to this blonde desert, these infertile hills.

Tom squeezed by to set the groceries on the counter. "I bought a barbecued chicken," he said.

"It's hollow-feeling out here, Tom. It's like an empty gym." She held the skirt up by the waist and eyed it critically for wrinkles.

With a paring knife, Tom slit open the cellophane package of chicken. "It's what you make it," he said.

She though it could be an argument about to happen and she didn't want that. She was dependent on him now and it's much easier to have arguments when you have friends and family nearby to salve your hurt, to take your side. Here she knew no one. They'd had some bad fights. And usually she would pick up and leave for a while, hitch a ride from Brewster down to Chelan and visit Pat, or take Desiree on the boat ride up the lake just to calm down.

"You're right," she said. "I'm just adjusting."

They ate the chicken and Sandra worked at ignoring the cramps.

Tom said, "I tried to call Bill. His phone's been disconnected."

"He was your only lead here?"

"Pretty much. I'll just start making the rounds tomorrow. After I get the car back."

"How'll we get the car?"

"I guess we'll have to pay a wrecker to bring it down here."

Sandra thought of the four-hundred-thirty-two dollars remaining in their kitty and the strange landscape—the Joshua trees like mannequins among the scurfy blocks of quartz monzonite. Reading the free brochures from the tourist office, knowing the names of plants and rocks and radio stations and streets—all that helped. It was the amorphous unknown that left you floating face-down in anxiety. She wondered if she'd made a mistake, if she'd known Tom long enough to move more than a thousand miles away from home. They'd been together sixteen months. He was thirty-six and still a wanderer. She'd had a job selling classifieds when he'd sashayed into the office to visit his brother, who owned the Nickel Ad tabloid she worked for. Maybe moving in itself was a mistake, no matter who you do it with. She catalogued the moves she'd already made in her life—always they were moves *from* someone or something, never *to* something. She'd moved away from home to escape her mother's carping; to shed a rough reputation, she'd moved away from Ellensburg, where she'd studied accounting for a year; and she'd moved away from Chelan because that was too close to Desiree. Tom withdrew whenever Desiree was around, and when Tom withdrew she went crazy with wanting him with her again, and that became the thing she needed and craved most, Tom's presence, his touch, his hard body, the sex, him coming into her, distant as he was. Men were like that, she told herself—most men were, anyway. She could still depend on him. He hadn't said she had to choose between him and Desiree, but he didn't want any family responsibilities. He'd been frank about that, he always reminded her. She thought he might change. She had the idea that they were going to settle down together. It's easy to quit your job in the summer, when the days are long and hot and there are river parties and potlucks and you can hitchhike easily anywhere. But now it was almost winter, their second winter together, and this hand-to-mouth life was no life for a little girl she told herself. She looked forward to going to the movie, she wanted that escape from the confusing ricochet of her thoughts.

Against her skin, the linen skirt, the rose silk blouse, felt good. When they left the apartment Tom took her arm in a courtly gesture. The cool desert wind flung sand against their legs. Halfway to the theater, a squat fiftyish woman in sunglasses, lugging two bright yellow shopping bags, stopped and sharply wrenched her face up at them—like a bird—as they passed her on the narrow sidewalk. "Healthy, healthy, healthy," the woman clucked.

They sat on the aisle near the front. Tom draped his arm over her shoulder and secretly, softly, brushed her nipple. That irritated her. Her cramps were reaching into her now, like a hand grasping. And lately, whenever he touched her there, she remembered her recurring nightmare: her breasts sliced away, gone, gone.

The lobster got away from Woody Allen. A biting pain fixed Sandra—pinned her in wonder—and she could no longer call it a cramp. "I'll be back," she said.

In the restroom she leaned on the sink, quivering, pressing the heels of her hands against the cold porcelain. A Planned Parenthood decal peeled away from the mirror. Her face in the mirror was bloodless, greenish in the fluorescent light. She'd never faced anything this wrong before. It was taking her over and felt like the end of something.

She walked down the aisle to Tom, each step deliberate, measured. She eased into her seat. "I'm sick," she said.

"What?"

"Let's get out of here," she said. "Please."

She leaned on him as they made their way to the back of the shadowy, nearly vacant theater. The light from the movie glazed the faces of the people in the back rows. The popcorn in he lobby smelled almost rancid.

Outside, the sidewalk seemed to draw her down to its gritty surface. Tom held her up. "This is bad," he said.

"I need a hospital," she said. "I want to lie down. Right here."

"Jesus. We don't have the car." He scouted up and down the street. "There's a cop. Betcha he'll help us."

Sandra crumpled to the curb and leaned against the cool steel of a parking meter. Peacock blue streaked the sky, the wispy clouds like tail feathers. There was no traffic. The harsh lights from the marquee cast deep shadows of the palm trees beyond the theater. As though he were under fire, Tom ran in a crouch to the black police car.

The pain cracked through her now. She doubled over and wanted to lie down. Some sense of decorum kept her from it. She hadn't let go of all that yet and maybe that meant it wasn't so bad, whatever was happening.

Tom walked back in long strides, his arms open to her all the way across the street. "Let's go," he said. "He's taking us home. An ambulance'll meet us there."

The police car seemed to move in slow motion the five blocks to their apartment, the radio spitting broken messages.

"If anything bad goes wrong," she whispered, "would you do something for me?"

"What's that?" he whispered.

"Tell Desiree I do love her. Even if she doubts it."

"Don't think the worst."

"You will, won't you?"

"It's okay," Tom said. He had his arm around her.

At the apartment they waited three or four more minutes until the ambulance arrived in a wave of white and red noise and light. The ambulance attendants took over her body. The dry palmetto leaves rubbed in the wind like insects burring, and the wind slipped into the ambulance with her. They slammed the door.

Tom was in the front seat. She could see the back of his head, his pale hair. She was flat on her back and rocked in the swerves of the ambulance turning. One attendant knelt beside her and took her blood pressure, and then said, "This is Demerol." He wiped her inner arm with alcohol.

She culled a joke from the whole deal. "Hit me." The dark-skinned attendant smiled beneath his sparse moustache.

Streetlights rushed by, like hot apples. She couldn't pick them. She could never pick enough apples to make a living, to make do. He covered her with a wool blanket and the Demerol leached through her.

In the emergency room they rolled her onto a high hard examination table. Tom had disappeared, though she could hear his voice nearby, just around the corner it seemed, answering questions. She knew they'd be asking him about money, about paying for things. She curled into a fetal position. That seemed to diffuse the pain just a little. The pain crackled like lit gasoline in line with an explosive core just above her pubic bone. She was cold. The walls were cold blue and they made her cold.

"She's shivering," someone said. It seemed to be the same woman who whipped the green curtain around the rods above the table. "Roll over on your back, honey." The nurse nudged her over and covered her first with a stiff sheet and then a wool blanket. She lifted one of Sandra's arms from under the blanket and laid it in a straight line along her side, the inside of the elbow up and exposed. "Leave that there," the nurse said. "Someone'll come along soon with an IV."

Every time the nurse came near, Sandra smelled the faintest film of soap on the nurse's skin, like a spice. The bluish tubes of light above her hurt her eyes. She was afraid of closing her eyes, afraid of going under. People seemed to be milling about beyond the curtain and she heard the low murmur of decisions being made. She could hear the voices but not the words. An infant cried out in a keen squeal. A new nurse—a man with gray-blonde hair and rough blotches on his cheeks—rolled the IV beside the table. The Demerol was doing its work well. Sandra didn't feel the punch of the needle in her vein. The soft place on her inner arm where the needle went in, like the underbelly of a kitten, looked puffy and torn. It was a big needle.

She drifted, not awake and not asleep. She had the idea that Tom had left her there, that he'd gone to fetch the car. They needed the car. She felt a hand on her forehead and opened her eyes. Tom towered over her, still in his 60-40 parka. His belt buckle was a brass elk head. His gaze flickered up and down the length of her and she tried to make eye contact with him. He looked frightened.

"What's wrong with me?" she said.

He put his hands in his pockets. "They don't know yet. The doctor's coming."

"I want my mother to be here."

"We're out of control here, aren't we?"

"It'll be all right, I think," she said. Later she would remember that, the way she wanted to help him out, to make it easier for him to deal with the hospital. She could've died from the infection, but when she saw his addled innocence, his fear, the way his eyes were glazed and empty, as though he might just neatly break away from what he couldn't control, she rose up with reassurance. That scared her more than anything—the idea of Tom breaking away.

The moon is a few nights past new, a sliver, shining on the black and moiling lake in an iridescent waver. They have the fire going now, a big one, a Billy Blazer Kelly calls it, and he launches into tales of his Boy Scout days, the jokes they played on one another, the blistering ill-equipped hikes. He and T.G. can entertain one another for hours like this and Sandra enjoys it—she's warmed by their rough and tender affection. The party's noisy behind them, fifty yards away. T.G. sits on a log across the fire from Sandra and Kelly, poking at the coals with a rusty branding iron, rearranging a chunk of wood here, a twig there.

"So I'm changing the subject," T.G. says. "Mom and Dad were here when you were building trail last time. They rented an RV. A mo-ho Mom called it. They were headed out to the Olympic Peninsula for three weeks. Dad's stomach is giving him fits."

"Stress?" Sandra says.

"He sounded stressed out on the phone last time," Kelly says.

He slips his arm around Sandra, kisses her cheek, a habit of his. Then he reaches into T.G.'s cooler for a beer. "Sandra?"

"No thanks," she says. She imagines T.G. and Kelly's father—his seriousness, his bluff, his surface talk.

T.G. gets up and rummages in the woodpile for a particular size log, returns to the fire and seeks out just the right place for it. Orange blossoms of sparks fly.

"What do you guys think about this? Give me your honest opinion now. It'd be easy to scoff at this, I know—more hippie-skippie New Age rationalization—but in my men's group someone said that when we get sick you can think of it like a metaphor. For something else in your life."

"A metaphor?" Kelly says.

"Yeah. A metaphor." T.G. is warming to the subject now. He's wearing melon pink climbing pants with a drawstring waist and he hitches them up determinedly and reports, "It's like this. It's simple. Dad's stomach is bothering him, right? That means—it's possible now, it's not out of the realm of possibility— that it means there's something in his life he *can't stomach*."

Kelly pats his own thickening waist. "Like if you eat too much it means you're hungry for something else? Your spirit's hungry?"

"*Exactamente*," T.G. says.

Sandra thinks that later she'll ask him what it is he's hungry for. She pulls out her mittens and puts them on. She hears footsteps and turns to see who's coming.

"What do you think Dad can't stomach, T.G.?"

"I'm working on that one," T.G. says.

Tom and his wife, Debbie, step into the firelight. Tom keeps one hand at her elbow, and under his other arm he's carrying a lumpy cotton sleeping bag. She's pregnant and her due date must be near. She's wearing a flowered shift and knee highs and a black denim jacket. Her shift pulls up high in the front, inches higher than the back hem. Tom and Sandra do the introductions all they way around. No need—right now— for Kelly to know who Tom is in relation to her. She's given him a crash course in all that transpired in her life before she met him, but she's never mentioned Tom by name. He'd become ancient history by the time she met Kelly. Tom shakes hands with T.G. and Kelly, then he unrolls the sleeping bag on the sand and helps Debbie settle down. She's young and still has a sprinkling of acne on her sunny round face.

"So where's the little one?" Sandra says.

"He crashed out," Debbie says. "Dead to the world." She has the distracted look of women about to deliver, as though she inhabits a supercharged inner world of such change and subtlety and potential intoxication that the mundane holds little allure.

T.G. has turned away, looking for wood ostensibly, but Sandra knows him well enough to know he feels their private family talk has been interrupted and he doesn't like it. She can sense Kelly's eyes on Debbie—no, not on *her*, on her pregnancy. Then he fools with the fire, intuition at work; he doesn't want to hurt Sandra with his musing. She can see all this in the silence that ensues. She's been connected to these boys too long not to understand.

At last Tom asks Kelly a question and they begin talking about trails. It's trails versus roads. And they move on from that to conservation in general, and from that to hunting season and Fish and Game regulations, a predictable conversation. Sandra thinks there's a certain security in listening to their talk, and she's allowed to simply drift, to measure metaphors against memories.

The nurse yanked open the curtain and the doctor entered. He was a big Indian man, with straight black hair and a smooth hairless face. He reminded her of someone she'd seen at a powwow at the Sheraton in Spokane.

"When we finish here, prep that baby for the meningitis tests," he said to the nurse. He picked up Sandra's chart and squared back his shoulders, rolled them, as though trying to shuck off tiredness or tension, Sandra imagined. He'd spilled something brown, coppery, on his white jacket.

"You'll have to leave," the nurse said to Tom, and Tom disappeared. She closed the curtain and said, "Pull your knees up and scoot your bottom to the edge of the table."

Sandra did as she was told, though moving was slow, clumsy. She tucked her heels in the stirrups at the corners of the table. The blanket piled up on her stomach and the cool air made goose bumps on her inner thighs. The doctor touched her thigh with something chilled and metallic.

"That's the speculum," he said.

Her muscles involuntarily tightened, clenched, at the foreign touch.

"Let go," he said. "Try breathing deeply. Relax."

The speculum was inside her now. Under his breath, almost inaudibly, the doctor said, "Christ on a crutch."

The nurse stood beside the doctor, staring over Sandra's knees into her eyes, chewing the inside of her lip. Her flamered lipstick was almost worn away and she had the lines of a long-time smoker around her mouth. Sandra thought, She knows what it's like.

"We've got to get that IUD out of there." He rose from his stool far enough to lock eyes with Sandra and say, "You've got a dangerous infection. I'm going to pull the IUD right now."

"All right," Sandra said. And she did feel something, just a tug, something sharp, and liquid running from her, blood she imagined. She tried to picture the IUD: a dark red rag. Then there was the sound of some small thing—like a trinket or a charm from a charm bracelet—being dropped into a metal container.

The doctor was by her side. "I'm going to start you on antibiotics," he said. "We'll do some tests in the lab to make sure—but it looks like PID. Pelvic inflammatory disease."

Then he too was gone. The nurse covered her up again and slipped through the curtain. Sandra wished Tom would come back and be there with her. She wanted comfort, she wanted someone to take care of her.

At four in the morning they went home in a taxi. The doctor had given her instructions to take the antibiotics, the pain killers, to drink liquids, to rest.

"I thought they'd keep you there," Tom said, supporting her as she undressed and sank into the bed.

"We didn't have any insurance," she said.

For Sandra, the next three days passed without structure, without domestic rhythm, with no definite demarcation between sleep and wakefulness. She stayed in bed, did not have the strength to get out of bed, and she wandered, drugged, on the outskirts of consciousness, of making sense. The meds blurred her vision and she could not read. She could not make it to the bathroom on her own. She depended on Tom to carry her there, to support her there while she tried to urinate. She knew it was night when Tom came home from looking for a job. She knew it was morning when he left. Before he left he always said, "You sure you'll be all right by yourself?" And she always said, "Sure. Go. I'll be all right." Though she did not really have a sense that she would be all right. She knew she was still in the part of the sickness where she could go either way. She drank quarts of fruit juice over ice and none of it was coming out of her. When she tried to urinate, there was only a trickle. Her abdomen swelled and she was frightened. She had waking dreams, hallucinations: standing with Tom under an arbor of bones, a black train bearing down on the Volvo; searching for Desiree in a place where children had been found in an abandoned icebox.

The third afternoon he hauled in all their belongings from the car. He brought in his .22 and stood it in the corner. It was a Remington his grandfather had given him and the receiver had been specially engraved somewhere along the line with curlicues and his grandfather's name. Sandra was awake enough to pay a kind of oozy attention when Tom carried in all her things she liked and had forgotten she'd brought with her: the tape player and the Kate Wolf tapes, the wooden Asian tea box she kept her correspondence in, her calligraphy pens, her velvet cape, her hiking boots.

She watched him make a tuna sandwich and sit at the Formica table, eating and reading the want ads. The news was on the radio. Her sheets were damp with sweat and she wanted clean sheets, but she didn't want to ask for anything. Her skin felt hot and abraded by fever.

Once Tom went over to the door and opened it and just stood there, staring out. "I'm glad we're on the edge of town," he said. "We can see the sun set."

"Is it a good one?" Sandra said. Her abdomen was rounded, tight as a drumhead, and she stroked it, wincing, as they talked.

"It's a very good one." Tom pressed his hands high against the door frame and leaned there, one knee cocked. His leather printer's apron lay beside him on the floor. "Dates grow all around here," he said. "I'd like to get some." There was the sound of singing from a nearby apartment: "What a Friend we Have in Jesus." "The landlord's a Bible thumper," Tom said, closing the door.

"Help me, Tom," Sandra said.

He carried her to the toilet and she felt her life depended on whether she could go.

"The poison's trapped inside me."

Tom had his hand on her shoulder.

"I'm afraid it'll kill me. If I can't go."

He stood beside her and waited. She hated for him to see her the way she was, sour and infected and weak. She knew she shouldn't think of that right now, there would be time for that. She focused all her attention on ridding herself of the infection and at last, she was able to urinate, for a long, long time.

"Thank God," she said.

"Do you think you can sit at the table?" Tom said. "I'll change your sheets."

She sat at the table and drank a cup of tea and then he helped her into the fragrant bed. She felt lighter, stronger, more clear-headed. She realized how much getting well depended on her taking responsibility for it herself. No one could do it for her. She thought about the word *responsibility*. Responsible. Responsive. Respond. Respond to yourself. Tom went in the bathroom and she could hear him shaving, the squirt of the shaving cream, the scrape of the razor. The singing next door had ended, and the wind blew the swaying pepper tree.

Tom came out of the bathroom and sat on the edge of the bed. He lit a cigarette. He had on clean jeans and a pale blue plaid Pendleton shirt. His face was a handsome one she never tired of. His hooked hose had been broken twice in wrestling injuries in high school. His lips were full—good kissers, she always thought.

"I'm going out for a while," he said.

"Where to?"

"Just out. I need to get out."

"I'm better."

"I can see that," he said. "I wouldn't leave you if I didn't think you were better."

"Put on a tape for me before you go," she said.

Sandra knew she'd passed over into healing. Her fever was down and she worry warted about Tom. That was a luxury she couldn't afford a day earlier. Tom was a track in her mind she could get on and travel without ever getting anywhere. She was lonely without him. Even sick, she could work herself into arousal thinking of the raw shiver of her skin when they'd had sex for hours, remembering making certain sounds, pretending until pretending made it so, until she would do anything he asked, try anything, say anything. To him, she called it making love, wanting him to hear the word *love* from her, wanting to think it would actually make him love her. Between them they had private words for it. To herself, she was more blunt, she called it having sex. She missed doing it; that was the only time she felt close to him. There was something shameful about that, she thought. She'd never admitted that before; it's possible the meds had cut her defenses, let light into her interior monologue. And then, after an hour or so, she surprised herself by thinking that she might be lonely if he were there. Maybe it was something in herself she was lonely for, some way she had an inkling she was capable of being, but that she couldn't be with him. She wished she could talk to Pat, who was always good company, even if she was probing and plainspoken, too tactless sometimes. They'd always been able to commiserate together, against parents whose wrangling took all the emotional energy they could muster, against adolescent boredom, against harsh weather.

Tom had left the tape player near the bed and she could change the tapes herself. She thought of better times when she heard the music, and almost any time in her life could be considered a better time than this. Careless wild road trips she'd taken; the way the light hits the forest at dusk in the Cascades—green-black and mysterious; and Desiree, how much trust there was in her yet, how serious her voice sounded as she learned her numbers. With a little prompting, she could count to one hundred. The thought of her daughter, the sweet and perfect line of her jaw, her breath like sour warm flowers when she'd crawl in bed with Sandra in the morning—that thought bloomed into a physical longing and fear, fear that she'd never have that again. She was a mother who'd left, and that made her an outlaw of sorts. And outlaws have to run hardest from themselves.

Tom came in around eleven, his key quiet in the door. She'd left the bedside lamp on and she'd been drifting after taking a Tylox at ten o'clock. He hung his parka in the closet, went to the refrigerator and opened a beer. Sandra sat up against the pillow. Rain pelted the flat roof. He came over and sat on the edge of the bed again and patted his pockets until he found his cigarettes. He held the pack to his mouth and drew out the cigarette with his lips.

"You're back."

He lit the cigarette. "How're you doing?"

"Okay."

"You're going to wear out those Kate Wolf tapes."

"They're a consolation to me."

"I went to a bar." He took a long slug of the beer. Then he drummed two fingers on the side of the can.

"Was there music?"

"Yeah. Some band from L.A. The Whitewalls, or something like that."

"Did you dance?" Sandra said. And she knew as soon as the words were out of her mouth that that was a question she didn't really want to know the answer to. She ran a finger along the double side seam on his jeans.

"As a matter of fact, I did."

He cut the ground out from under her with that. For a minute, she felt as though someone were pressing hard on her chest. She felt invisible and weak. It was stupid—overreacting—to feel jealous or envious—whatever it was—over such a small event. She pitched down the feeling. When she was stronger, she'd pick it up again, try to take an honest look.

Tom said, "I just went out and did what I wanted to do."

She had to assume that if he'd done what he wanted then, that he was home now, doing what he wanted.

"At least we're not pretending," she said.

"That's right."

Last year, after Pat'd been divorced and changed jobs twice in three months, she had been in counseling. Sunbathing in her backyard, eating corn chips and cottage cheese, with Desiree splashing in a plastic pool, they would often pick over these counseling sessions, on the lookout for choice morsels of wisdom. And her sister had said that pretending was one way of being in the world that could cause you plenty trouble in the long run. That made sense to Sandra at the time, but she'd forgotten it until now. You could pretend for only so long, and then you split open with the truth. That kind of truth—the kind you've sat on for months, maybe years— hurt everyone too much. She thought of moving back to Chelan. It was possible there were chances in the world you could take that might bring good luck, moves that could bring you closer to yourself.

"Are you sleepy?" Tom said.

"Not really."

"Maybe I'll read to you. Would you like that?"

"Yes, I would."

Tom sat in the overstuffed chair next to the bed and sipped his beer and read to her from *Black Elk Speaks*. He had a good reading voice and she could picture all the things he read about. At the end of the chapter his voice cracked and she looked up to see that he had tears in his eyes.

"It's not the life I bargained for," he said.

Sandra murmured, "That makes two of us."

She'd never seen him cry. He closed the book and sat there, sadder than she'd ever seen him.

"Why don't you come to bed?" she said. "You've had a long day." They had news to break to one another, but all that would keep until tomorrow.

The next morning, before dawn, Tom got up and went out with his .22. While he was out, Sandra was able to go to the bathroom, able to brew a pot of coffee. She looked in the mirror at her lank and greasy hair and resolved to take a shower first thing. She opened the venetian blinds and peeked through the slats. She thought she might be able to make it to the pay phone later in the day. The date trees were gray blue and huge against the lustrous pink sunrise. Presently Tom came into view, his gun at a angle to the ground, a rabbit for their supper dangling in one hand.

She could call collect. It would be better to call collect than not to call at all. She could start with her sister, who'd be cheerful, theatrical, who'd say, You ninny, where on God's green earth *are* you?

It's late. Debbie has laid her head on Tom's lap, a signal, Sandra reads, that she's ready to leave. Sandra thinks she and Tom probably will not talk, and she is neither glad nor sorry. She tries to imagine what they might say, what phrases they might grab to sum up that time, to excuse it, to tuck it away in memory where it wouldn't cause too much havoc in the day to day. Cliches of that era come to mind, for it does seem another era: we were too young (not true); we didn't know what we really wanted as individuals; words they might have already said that next morning to begin the breakup. She doesn't want to say these things; they seem off-center from the truth, not quite congruent with what she feels. What she feels is that everything that happened back then—leaving Desiree, amputating herself from the past—was no one's fault but her own, and that she has nothing of value to say to him, nothing. That doesn't seem right somehow—as though they should have things to say—but it's true. It's herself she has to answer to every livelong day; that's enough.

More people are around the fire now, talking hushedly, some of them holding hands, some of them drinking beer. Near the quaking aspen, two dogs tussle over a weathered coyote skull. Kelly and T.G. are out at the lake's edge, with T.G.'s arm over Kelly's shoulder. Kelly's pointing out a constellation to him. His shiny down vest glistens in the moonlight.

Sandra remembers what the doctor said when she returned to Washington State. "You have to have a hysterectomy. We'll do it vaginally. There'll be no scars. No visible scars." That was in the spring; there was still snow in dirty patches on the doctor's lawn. She sat down there anyway and cried, waiting for Pat to drive up and take her home.

And later still, years later, she brought suit against the company that made the IUD, and it's still pending, tied up in the courts with thousand of others. Kelly made her do it, not for the money—there wasn't a chance of being awarded big money—but for the principle involved. She'd told him, "I'm not sure I want more babies anyway." And he'd said, "That should be up to you to decide. Up to us."

She wants to be the first to leave the party, and she doesn't want to make the rounds saying good-bye.

At the lake's edge she says to Kelly, "Could we go soon? I'm about to turn into a pumpkin."

"It's past this scout's bedtime too," T.G. says. She kisses his forehead.

"Getcher crew together, babycakes," Kelly says. "I'll meet you out front."

On the veranda Sandra's slipped out of her heels—they'd been killing her—and she and Desiree are sprawled on the glider, waiting for the others. Roger's gone—crankily—to collect his mother and Desiree's friends. His cassettes are scattered all over the steps. Paper plates of leftovers—celery stubs and cracker crumbs—are piled on a wooden table. Desiree's make-up is smeared; her daubed-on fake mole streaks like a comet tail across her cheek.

"I've been here so long, Mom—all my life," Desiree says. "Do you ever think I'll ever leave?"

"You might. It's hard to tell. What wayward wind might blow you somewhere else."

"I think I'd always come back. It's my security blanket."

"That's one way of looking at it. A good way."

Kelly comes upon them, whistling for Easy Whip, limping a little, his face broad and serene and ruddy. He jumps up on the veranda, boots thumping.

"Just think about this, Sandra," he says. "Don't say anything yet. Just put this in your pot and stir it. What about a Mexican baby. Or Romanian?"

"What about it?" she says.

"We-could-get-one," he explains, smiling. Then he shouts, roars happily, "We've got goddamned government jobs."

Sandra laughs. "You'll have to talk me into it," she says. She closes her eyes, sighs deeply, and with her bare sore toes pushes off, nudging the glider a little harder.

Desiree abruptly hunches forward, brakes the glider's swing, her eyes glinting with excitement. "No, no, wait," she says, alert and eager, one hand on Sandra's thigh, the other waving Kelly in, the way you direct someone maneuvering to park in a difficult spot. "I'll work on her, Kelly," she promises. "I'll really really work on her. You'll see."

Kelly says, "Good girl."

Sandra feels the shock of blood ties, like standing with them, hands linked, under a waterfall. Bracing, joyous rush, O heady love.

1988

Cargo

Soft spikes of hollyhocks grew along the side of the raft company boathouse. I sat on a flat stone just up the rocky slope, thinking about my mother dying and reading a biography of Katherine Anne Porter. The book would absorb my attention for a few paragraphs; then my thoughts would wander away. Whenever I thought of Mother I remembered a time when I was eleven and the wood delivery truck could not make the slick and treacherous hill to our house. My brother Christopher and I hauled that wood in red-wagon loads and wheelbarrow loads. I remember that we were cheerful about the work at the beginning, but as evening came on and the driveway iced over, we could not be cheerful or glean whatever virtuous feeling we got from being helpful. When I thought of Mother, I felt eleven years old again, and that saddled, that played out.

I'd spent the evening before in helpless long distance conversation with my mother and my sister in Wenatchee. My mother had said, "I'm just waiting to die." I'd heard this from her before, but this time the facts were laid out like quilt pieces, cut already, beyond redesign: the heart attack, the two weeks in intensive care, the emphysema, her fingers stained yellow with nicotine. My sister said she had started smoking again as soon as the hospital attendant removed the oxygen tent. The will to die was strong in her, inevitable as winter, and none of us had ever been able to coax her from death's promise. Suzanne was on her way from the Olympic Peninsula, Jan Mary was already there, Christopher would fly in from Portland on Labor Day, and Laura Jean still lived at home.

"Will you come?" Jan Mary had said, without hope or despair.

I felt nitpicky, asking, but I said, "Is this it?"

"Not necessarily," she said. "We just want everyone together one last time."

"Where's Dad?"

"He had to go to Spokane. With a friend. He'll be back tomorrow night."

She sounded protective, making it sound as though he had business there. I right away assumed he'd gone to play the ponies.

"I have to see," I said. "I'll be in touch." It was the best I could do.

Mo was my friend, a boatman, and he squatted on the boathouse porch, patching a Havasu. A few of the white letters had peeled away from the raft: BIG SKY WHITEW—R. Near the porch steps, peeling red oars were laid in a row across two sawhorses. The radio rippled soul music from Jackson Hole. Wiley sanded the oars. Wiley's been around since before my time and Mo's time; he'd been the one to show us the ropes that first winter Mo and I were snow-coach drivers in the Park. He'd been the one to lead us on our first illicit after-dark visit to the hot pots. Mo and Wiley had been my buddies, but I was no longer in their daily lives. I'd become the break in their routine whenever I passed through. Clouds like garlic bulbs swelled over Electric Peak; rabbitbrush was brightly staggered on the hills. I had a view of the arch at the Yellowstone Park entrance and a lone antelope grazing there, her markings ancient and striking and incongruous against the buy-me clutter of Gardiner, Montana. I waited to have dinner with Mo.

The deputy, whose office was at the opposite end of the boathouse building, stepped outside and righted a trash barrel that two dogs had rummaged in. I imagined the blind eye the deputy must have had to turn to cohabit with raft company personnel. Mo's baggy purple shorts caught my attention as he jumped down from the porch and discreetly visited the latrine area, a strip of grass between the building and a blue-and-white school bus.

Mo and I had met as young and eager poets in grad school in Missoula. Halfway through the first year, he dropped out and moved to Gardiner and he had lived there ever since, river guiding, working the winter season for the park, never writing another poem, though he would read my poems and give me a tough response.

He picked his way up the slope, evading cactus.

"Que pasa, Roxie?" His hair was the palest red, shiny as embroidery floss, and he was beginning to bald. His arms were powdered with fine sawdust, and his hands smelled like the solvent he'd used to clean the abrasion on the boat.

"Just waiting for you, Morrison."

"Louisa's invited us for dinner." Louisa was Mo's mother-in-law from his marriage to Sharon, who had died in a car accident in the Gallatin Canyon. Sharon and Mo's daughter, Celestial—Cee-Cee—lived with Louisa.

"I can't stay long," I said.

"You'll stay the night, won't you? I want to play with Cee-Cee awhile," Mo said, crouching down until our eyes were level. He rocked my knee with one hand. "How're you doing?"

"I'm okay."

"I know this's not what you had in mind. But I haven't gotten together with Cee-Cee all day. We'll go to my place after."

"It's okay."

"I'll just be here tonight," I said, shrugging. I couldn't stay in Gardiner more than a night or two. My welcome there was long worn out because of things I'd done that winter, the winter we were snow-coach drivers, things I was ashamed of now. If I stayed too long, word got around and people showed up and reminded me of pieces of myself I wanted to forget.

"Porter, huh?" He picked up the book and skimmed the blurbs on the back. "What's her story?"

"She lied about a lot of things." He handed me the book. I said, "How *is* Louisa?"

Mo stood up and reared back, flinging his arms as though about to break into song. "Louisa. Louisa's a wonder."

"How so?"

"She's become a Keeper of the Flame."

"What's that?"

He quoted officiously, "Keepers of the Flame is an international organization. They use affirmations and meditation to change what they don't like about the world situation."

"What don't they like?"

"Nuclear weapons. For example."

"What can I say, Mo? You've got a crazy family. Your mother-in-law meditates. Your daughter plays with trucks."

"Safeway let you off?" He was referring to my half-time produce job in Bozeman.

"For ten days."

"Ya-hoo."

"Ya-hoo, you yayhoo." I felt tender toward him at that moment, for the way he feels for other people. He always finds something to celebrate. I said, "I'm hungry. How long do we have to be here?"

"Let me put some tools away. Come on down. Shoot the shit with Wiley. He misses you."

"Where's Sally?" I asked. Sally was Mo's sweetheart, a bareback rider in the Wild West Show in West Yellowstone. She wore turquoise leather hot pants trimmed in white feathers. Before each show she slathered her legs and arms and face with pancake makeup the color of cloves—the show's producer, an ex-carny barker, wanted her to look native. Once when he was a little drunk on whisky ditches, Mo confided that the color turned him on.

"She's working," he said. "Last show of the season."

I gathered up my things, relieved to know Sally was in West and I'd have Mo to myself, once we negotiated dinner with Celestial and Louisa. I had nothing against Sally. It was just that Mo had been my friend for over ten years, whereas she had been his lover for two. It was a question of shared history—we had it, she didn't.

Mo went on down and shouted to a woman standing in the door of the boathouse. She gave him a thumbs-up signal. Wiley boogalooed in tight choreography to Gladys Knight and the Pips. The deputy came out again, hitched up his brown trousers at the pleats, and got in his pickup. I felt as much an outsider as the antelope, though she could trot away into the back country, free of the obligation to be civil and free of the past. I envied her that.

I waited in the passenger seat of Mo's van, with the door hanging open. A scroll of charcoal smoke breezed our way from a nearby house, and the scent hinted at childhood parties, blistered hot dogs, sticky s'mores, the marshmallows crisp and black. Two girls walked by, about twelve years old, one of them skinny and one of them dumpy already. I'd seen her type too often at Safeway: old at twenty-three, pushing a cart filled with babies and beer. They both wore outsized flannel shirts cinched with wide patent leather belts, their new school clothes I imagined. The skinny one said, "*He* knows I'm alive." Wiley looked up and waved to me. I waved back and thought, That's about how much he misses me.

Louisa's house was a collector's item, with a sculpted gate of rusted scrap iron, the porch pillar carved in a totem pole of cats' faces, a mass of fuchsias in hanging baskets, and a blue enamel Home Comfort stove like a shrine to warmth in the kitchen. What was once the living room had been divided into shelf after wooden shelf of stock for her mail-order business, The Unicorn's Horn. She sold metaphysical books, crystals for healing, tarot cards.

"Make yourself at home," Mo said. "I'm going over to the Conoco for a bottle of wine."

I went in the kitchen, stood at the sink, and watched Louisa and Celestial through the screen window, in the garden on their knees, digging up carrots. The kitchen smelled like brown rice steaming and overripe vegetables. Near the phone there was a framed black-and-white photo of Sharon, pregnant, in a Panama hat, drinking a St. Pauli Girl. Sharon had been the best of Mo's women. She didn't let marriage slow her down. Three years after her death and I still half-expected her to walk in at any moment and charm me into going out dancing.

Four-year-old Celestial had on pink-and-lavender overalls and a Yellowstone Raft Company cap. She sang, "I'm a little teapot, short and stout," over and over in a squeaky thin voice while Louisa gave her instructions: "Dig down deep or you'll cut them in half. Shake off the dirt." A small black goat nibbled nearby on red cabbage leaves.

"We planted enough for Choo-Choo, didn't we, Louey?" Celestial said. Choo-Choo was the goat.

When Celestial looked my way, I waved. She stared through me, ignoring me. I felt hurt—she'd known me all her short life. I wondered if she was beginning to see me as an intruder. There was an invisible connection among Celestial and Mo and Louisa, some faith created, simply by living in proximity for so long. I saw what I'd given up by leaving and I'd left so my places, thinking to begin my life again, forgetting every time that the things you hate the most are the things that travel with you.

"I'll tell Daddy about the bear," Celestial said, confidentially to Louisa.

"Wonder if that rice is done?" Louisa said.

"I'll check it," I called, and Louisa acknowledged me with a wave and a nod over her shoulder. Her coarse hair had begun to look more gray than black.

Mo walked in and said, "*Pinot Noir.* This place goes all out for the tourist trade."

On the way to Mo's from Louisa's, he recited from *All my Pretty Ones:* "The town is silent. The night boils with eleven stars./Oh, starry, starry night! This is how/I want to die."

I felt cynical and said, "There's a storm moving in."

Mo's apartment was over a laundromat. Until eleven at night you heard the slosh of the washers, the hum of the dryers. We poured more wine and sat in the dark at the kitchen table, the bathroom light angling around our feet. There were three ragged marigolds in a fruit jar on the dresser. Soon after we came in, the rain began and lightning cast flashes on the creamy curtains.

"Tell me about Anne Sexton," he said. "When you heard her read."

These were our favorite stories.

"It was in Baltimore—"

"Once upon a time in Baltimore."

"People were like leeches at that reading. Everyone wanted a piece of her. She was fragile—in a red dress—she'd have called it a sheath."

"Tell me again what she said."

"She said, 'Writers should be forgiven their bad books.'"

"Sad," Mo said, kneading his earlobe.

This seemed an appropriate time to tell him. "I have some bad news, Mo."

"What's that?"

"My mother's dying."

He reached across the table and sheltered my hand with his. "I'm sorry, Roxie. This's been coming, hasn't it?"

His words—or perhaps his touch—primed my tears. My chest felt hot, heavy with burning cargo. I went to the counter, tore off a paper towel, and wiped my eyes.

"I can't decide whether to go. I can't stand to see her the way she is."

"What way?"

"You know—I've told you. All tanked up on Thorazine and bourbon. Shut down."

"She's had a hard life, Rox."

He spoke the truth. I folded my arms and didn't say anything.

"Have you thought about how you'll feel—years from now—if you don't go?"

I sat back down. "Tell me how it was when your mother died."

He sucked in his breath, then sighed. "I've told you before."

"Tell me again."

Mo got up, turned off the bathroom light, and lit a candle. When he took his seat again he said, "She knew she was going. She insisted on being at home. The doctor agreed." He poured himself another glass of wine. "I just went home for the summer. With Cee-Cee."

"What did you do there all summer?"

"I read to her. Listened to her when she meandered. Went hiking with the baby—Cee-Cee was just a baby then. I need the connection with both of them."

We didn't talk for a few minutes. I scanned the titles on his bookshelf above the table, which was weighted with the West: Snyder, Hugo, Hammill. I picked up *Petroglyphs* and read the poem about the midwife in the tavern. I imagined her at the Town Tavern in Port Townsend, at the wide shiny tress of a wooden bar, fog bleeding under the door.

"She wrestled with dying," he finally said.

"My mother's wanted to die as long as I can remember."

"She might still need you," he said, tentative, his whisper silky against the wooly thunder.

"She's lost to me, Mo," I said, more surely than I felt it. For years I'd thought of my mother and myself inhabiting a range of labyrinthine mountains, creatures whose paths never crossed. Perhaps we wandered by the same boulder or lake, the same memory, but not at the same time.

"Write about it. Isn't that what you always used to say?"

"I'm not there yet."

"You'll get there," he said.

We were quiet. There was no noise but the thud and muffle of the washers spinning. Then he said, "Hey—I bought a second hand copy of *The Bell Jar* last week. I bought it for the dust jacket. Remember that picture?"

I shook my head.

"It was taken when she was a guest editor—whatever they call it—at *Mademoiselle*. The photographer said, 'Show me how happy it makes you to write a poem.' And she smiled then. A lovely smile."

"We all smile then."

"Sure-fire smiles."

We could hear a laundry cart being whizzed around the floor downstairs, the dryer doors slamming.

"You'll write again, won't you, Mo?"

"It's a spiritual quest, Rox. I'm not on it."

"You've set some limits."

"*Rec*ognized my limits. I just want to see my daughter grow up in a place where she doesn't have to be afraid. Ski. Bring Sally coffee in bed. Read the *Times* now and then. To keep from becoming a total barbarian."

"I want to go to Ketchum."

"What for?"

"To see Hemingway's grave."

Mo laughed. "It's much easier to go see the dead than the dying." He swallowed a mouthful of wine and pursed his lips. His raspy laughter had broken the tension of the talk about writing.

"Come with me to Ketchum."

"Sally's coming over for Labor Day."

I pouted, half-faking, half-meaning it.

Mo stood up and came over beside me and hugged my head against his belly. He belt buckle pressed my shoulder.

He said, "Let's camp out on the floor. We'll roll out two sleeping bags like puritans and hold hands."

"Twist my arm," I said, looking up at the candle flicker on his face. He smelled like river water and sun and wine. "Do you have any cigarettes?"

"That bad, huh?" He weaned away and browsed in a basket on the counter. "Here's a few Camels." He tossed the crumpled pack on the table in front of me. Someone had slipped a book of matches from Harrah's inside the cellophane. "Some guy left those here. The bullwhip expert from the Wild West Show. He whips them out of Sally's mouth."

I lit the nasty cigarette and smoked it without inhaling.

"That's what's killing your mother, right?"

I nodded and tried to blow smoke rings. "Let's not talk about it anymore."

At one-thirty in the morning, Mo watered his house-plants, shuffling in his stocking feet from clay pot to clay pot with a half-gallon Almaden bottle. I lay down on the floor, on his swirling antique carpet. It made me think of Willa Cather's house. Mo and I had once driven nonstop to Red Cloud, Nebraska, during a drought summer, in temperatures above one hundred, just to see her house. We were good pilgrims then.

"I have an idea," he said, blowing out the candle. "Let's put on Santana. Very low. And drift away." The care in his voice almost made me cry again.

We laid out the sleeping bags side by side. He put on *Moonflower*. The storm had stopped and the wet cool smell of the rain and sagebrush rolled in the open window. When we lay down he took my hand; hard oar calluses padded his palm and fingers.

I said, "Do you remember the time we tried to make love?"

"You betcha."

"Your tongue felt as impersonal in my mouth as a doctor with a tongue depressor."

"You really know how to hurt a guy."

"We're not meant to be lovers. In the strictest sense of the word."

"Some love's like that. It doesn't engage your lust."

"When's Sally coming?"

"In the morning."

"I want to be out of her before she comes."

"Sally likes you, Rox."

"Her kindness kills me."

"You should let her like you."

"I should be on my way to Ketchum."

When I was a girl there had been an old woman names Mrs. Higginbottom who lived down the road from us. She lived alone in a dirty house with her hunting dogs; she was a bird hunter and would go out, wearing a shapeless housedress and her apron, in the early morning mist along the creek with her shotgun. She hunted grouse. I did not like drinking water or lemonade from her greasy tumblers; I would pretend to sip from them. She had a big black-and-white rooster who charged me if he caught me lolly-gagging in the yard. Nevertheless, I visited her at least once a week. Growing up the way we did, not knowing from one day to the next what to expect at home, we learned to get what we needed—attention or sameness—from our neighbors. Mrs. Higginbottom played her 78 RPM records for me, those heavy ones: "Pistol-packin' Mama" and "The Old Lamplighter." She sat smoking Lucky Strikes in an overstuffed chair whose nap had long been slicked down. The smell in her house was an accretion of sweat, old paperbacks, wet dog, and chicken feed. She talked to me about her life as a young woman. She did not seem unhappy to be in her seventies and alone. I understood that there were choices to be made about the way you lived and what you thought about the way you lived. This lesson kept meeting me in a new disguise. It was the central lesson in my life and I the dunce and fool of the heart who could not get it straight.

I imagined the journey, first to Ketchum, then to Wenatchee, the frugal western towns along the way—Rexbur, Boise, LaGrande—wild with autumn leaves. I would give my mother Mo's comfort, a gift like carried fire, protected over the miles. If she wouldn't take it, my brother and sisters could have it. We would be together one last time, not children anymore, no longer yoked to anyone or anything, no longer shackled except to whatever sore memory we hoarded like misers.

"You won't like it there," Mo said. "This isn't nineteen-fifty-nine. There are too many Beamers."

"Beamers?"

"BMWs." His voice sounded dreamy; he was falling asleep.

I squeezed his hand. Like a bad habit I said, "Don't worry. I'll expect the worst."

1988

Same Old Big Magic

He kept the maps. They'd had a cardboard Kahlua box of maps, forest service maps, topo maps, road maps, some of them from the early sixties when his parents had taken him and his brothers on road trips in the summers. She had to admit they were mostly his maps, though she'd grown to love them, their gift of anticipation, their memory of blind stabs at settling down, of wilderness euphoria. After thirteen years the Kahlua box was soft as dish towels along the corners.

"That's my favorite boulder in the Cascades," she told her sister. They were both on the wagon, drinking cranberry tea and talking early marriages. "We camped under it in February one year and walked up into the mountains and hugged trees." Her sister said, "You were stoned, right?" "Yeah," she said, smiling and shaking her head yes and flipping the photo album page. "And we lived to tell the tale."

Hitchhiking can make you hate one another or forge a link between you that can't be broken. They had taken two major trips by thumb: one from Oregon to Arizona in the middle of winter and one from Lumby, British Columbia, to Seattle, also in the winter. During these trips, life went on. They made love in the A-frame North Face mountain tent; she complained about how cramped she was on top. She sometimes cried at night, missing her sisters. They fed fragile, hopeful camp fires, drinking brandy and talking, weaving the toughest cloth of their fears and desires, finding out what they believed in. They fought over whether to eat in a restaurant or cook over a camp fire. They never had any money to speak of, but there was a stamina to their love. They prided themselves on having endured. Seventeen below; Nevada; camping in an arroyo among cages of snowy sagebrush. That's love of a different color, her girlfriends said. Hard-core. They did it to see Monument Valley in the winter, rime like crystal sugar everywhere. They did it because they thought they were both born to the road.

Once they had a cabin with a big black Monarch cookstove. This was in the beginning. Lightning pinwheeled into their bedroom and he leaped from the bed and found a book of poems and read her a poem in the storm. They carried water from the creek and shared a zinc tub of steaming bathwater. She scrubbed his back with a loofah. They made love in the parsnip patch in broad daylight. At night there were always the stars and he knew them by name. At a garage sale, they bought a cast-iron skillet and an Oriental rug. From secondhand hardbacks, they read short stories aloud to one another. There were always pileated woodpeckers, red whips of willows, evening sunlight only a gold band above the mountain; there were always animal tracks, lichened stones, creeks, applewood, fir, wild plums; there were always, always, the stars, and his arm around her as he named them: Irion, Cygnus, Sirius. He smelled like Balkan Sobranie tobacco and wool Woolrich shirts, and his arms were archetypal arms, arms of the woodsman who'd saved her from the wolf within.

The day they moved away from the cabin they stood on the porch and cried in one another's arms. That was the first loss they'd ever shared, shocked at its sweetness.

In town, the first town, the elementary school blazed white as sand in the winter sun. He was a student at the college and she taught at the elementary school. Kites tattered from the cottonwoods beside the playground. Their wantonness required practice. "Talk to me," she said. "You have to have a bit of the ham, the rake, in you to do this. Coax me. Be sly. You know how easy I am." Beyond the shutters an evening snowstorm muffled streets; all the cars had forgotten how to travel; they moved as though forced awry by enchantment, into berms and woodpiles. "The words," she said, "can be about how much you know I'll like it." "How does it feel for you to come?" he said. "It's like stealing something." "Stealing home," he said. She was a marauder, slip of a woman in the flying night, stealing whatever she could, fingers tender and blind, grafting bliss to truancy, crazed absence of self. It was something like an old blues song; that bad, winsome, visceral. She knew how it worked. They found them—the very words— and they became his charm and code, his mojo, sweetbone totem, the rib and thorn in their fenny winter bed.

They each had private dreams and these were difficult to realize together. The first time she talked about moving away, she cried into a brakeman's bandana until her eyes were puffy. Finally he said, "Maybe it's a good idea. Maybe I need to be on my own too." She said no. She said she'd figure out some other way to make her dreams come true. That was in the second year and they had eleven more years to go.

For a long time they took turns moving for each other; the one who followed always felt cheated.

Even now, when she peruses certain maps, she imagines all the places they slept outdoors together. Beside rivers, with that rushing, that glassy green blooming of the waves: Clark Fork, Gallatin, Yellowstone, Lochsa, Columbia, Methow, Okanogan, Entiat, Wenatchee, Skagit, Rogue, Klamath, Williamson, Santiam, Umpqua, Bella Coola, Fraser, Thompson, Quesnel, Chilcotin. Too numerous to mention were the creeks and lakes. And the mountains they ranged: the Cascades, the Rainbows, the Monashees, the Purcells, the Selkirks, the Tobacco Roots, the Big Belts. Field mice; blackened pots; wood-smoked sleeping bags zipping together; their breath visible in the mornings; aspens shimmering; cutthroat winds. They were caught in the bite of the mother's moon tooth.

At Shi-Shi beach near Neah Bay, they slept together outdoors for the last time. To the Indians, *shi-shi* meant "big magic." The unrestrained Pacific dumped rain on them four days running. Deer cavorted in the surf. They visited a man in a nearby cabin and drank mescal and traded life stories and waited out the weather. He was drunk enough to eat the worm. She has a crescent-shaped scar—petite petroglyph—on the back of her right hand, from falling into a rocky rain-swollen creek on the walk out. She thinks it's a scar that won't fade and that pleases her, to have the mark of shi-shi.

Before that particular July, for several years, they practiced moving away from each other. They were getting used to the idea. First there were separate pleasure trips. Then they began going away to work, a month here, two months there, a summer. Finally she took a job in another state, seventeen hundred miles away. They thought they could manage; they were good at reunions.

They broke the rules like pottery, with that little regret. Their letters of breakup crossed in the mail, one of many blessings that befell them over the years. When next they met—after the divorce was final—they were rife with happy grief, a blessing in itself they realized. He lived in a small wooden house beside a gang of McIntosh trees. The apples were nearly ripe. The whole tiny house smelled of fresh pocket bread; he baked bread so often that the muslin curtains gave off the odor of yeast and sugar. They cried, made love, slept. They had left an open bottle of Polish vodka on the kitchen table. Once, in the middle of the night, she went out to the screened-in porch. An inverted yellow kayak glowed under the clothesline. She couldn't deny feeling free, a kind of joy in the soles of her feet. The night had grown frost on the dull grass; smudge pots tilted under the trees. Stars stirred above them like fading fires, trying to focus through mottled clouds. This is how she thought of the stars: blurry, a little drunk, still there.

1988

Let Me
Call You Sweetheart

I was weeding the strawberry patch when Sunbow walked by the garden singing something bluesy in her whiskey-scoured voice. She was on her way to the loomhouse.

"Hello, Virginia," she called. She squinted and did not seem to care that the sun had cut two indelible lines in the middle of her frown. Her graying black hair was twisted like a pastry into a knot. She wore a dress worthy of a summer day: a wrinkled silk she had found in the rag pile in town. The dress was printed with orange poppies and stained under the arms. I could see through it.

I sat back on my heels, glad for the reprieve from the lambsquarter and dandelions choking the berries. "Hello, Sunbow. When did you get back?"

"Late last night." She stepped into the shade of the nearest pine tree. "I'm going to visit Roger," she said. "Is he still mad at me?"

From the loomhouse came the wooden slap-slap of the beater as Roger worked on his current rug.

"He's worked the whole time since you left," I said. I knew this would assure her. Even though she had gone away and left him, she was still afraid he might take up with someone in her absence.

Her eyes smiled. "See you later, Ginny," she said, and picked her barefoot way among the basalt stones protruding from the path. I watched her go. She is a lovely woman.

Sunbow and I are the same age, forty-six. We have been neighbors for eight years and each year we celebrate the day she moved here and began building the A-frame next to the creek. We were friends right away, talking of our mothers and adolescence and betrayals, laughing as though these things had happened to others, had not left scars. We had similar scars, Sunbow and I. Around three years ago, the stream branched through the geography of our friendship: I chose to be celibate and Sunbow, well, Sunbow did not. Men are as necessary to her survival as water, or so she thinks.

I took off my chambray shirt, draped it over the splintered fence post, and returned to the strawberries. I thought about dying and being buried in the mealy soil I dug in. The wooden slap from the loomhouse suddenly ceased.

Sunbow's daughter came to visit in July and Roger wanted to take her to bed. Christine is nineteen and ran away from the farm two years ago. She didn't go far, just to the nearest big city. She bought thirty dollars' worth of make-up and platform shoes and found a job painting sets for the Children's Theatre. Now she has a car, a battered red Volkswagen she calls *The Gypsy Moth*. She drives out once in awhile to let us know she is not like us. Christine is a well-formed child, but dyes her hair the color of rust or dried blood.

Crazy Heart built a sauna fire about dusk. Christine wore her underpants in the sauna and that is what started the trouble. The rest of us were naked and we are aging and showing our ages. Even Roger, who is only forty, is growing slightly thick in the waist. When Christine undressed, we all watched since it is a natural thing to be drawn to that youthful beauty, the clean lines, the smooth belly. But she immodestly left her underpants on, giving her the air of someone special.

After the sauna, around the fire, Crazy Heart made music on his dulcimer, and the fire gilded our bodies. There was a gallon of cheap wine passed around and around. Sunbow stood up with her tambourine and shook it against her naked thigh and swayed to the music. I saw Roger begin to touch Christine's back, lightly, lightly, just fingers on her spine in the shadows. And I knew why he did it. I'd seen it so many times before: a situation ripe as a pear presents itself: candlelight or firelight, clean bodies warm with summer, music like a narcotic in the blood, heartbeats, bloodbeats, moonlight and wine, wine to wash you into touching.

Sunbow saw it, too, and she threw down the tambourine, pulled on a pale caftan, and stormed away into the night like a whirl of smoke. A tactical error. Without her there, Roger felt free to pursue Christine.

I left the fire shortly thereafter. I don't know what happened. Sunbow never told me and Christine hasn't been down since.

Near the winter solstice Roger went away in his step-van to sell his rugs. He was heading south for warmer weather. He didn't invite Sunbow to go along. He told her he wanted to be alone. Before he left, Sunbow painted a small sign on the side of his step-van: *Any woman who sleeps with this man will be cursed with perpetual menstrual flow.*

The days were short; we lit the lamps at four in the afternoon. Going to the outhouse after dark took on the proportions of an expedition. Snow fell for days on end. We were snowed in for a week and almost ran out of tobacco. Smoking was one of our pleasures.

Sunbow would come over in the afternoon and bring her work. She created earrings and other ornaments from feathers and stones and beads. She made them all winter and sold them in the spring. She sat at the kitchen table and worked while I made tea or poured home-brew and read to her aloud from books of poetry. When I ready Gary Snyder's poem "To the Children," she said, "Raoul would have liked that." Raoul was her first husband, a mountain climber and vagabond. She licked the tip of white thread and held the needle's eye to the dying sunlight. "He believed in going light."

Poems and songs reminded her of the men in her life. No matter what turns and bends the conversation took, it always returned, like a lost river meandering in the same square mile to Roger, to Roger's last letter, or finally and usually to Sunbow's problem, as she saw it, her inability to find and keep a mate.

At these times I listened. That was really all she asked. Her thoughts were like poison; spewing them into air dispelled their power for awhile.

It was during this time, during the clean pure winter, that Crazy Heart came to visit in the evening. He lives in a dugout across the road. We had once been man and wife, lovers, friends. Seeing him sitting there, after so long an absence from my dwelling, I felt as though I was returning to the source of memory, so melded were our early years.

One night as a storm blew outside we drank hibiscus tea and he never budged to go home. At last I said, "Would you like to spend the night?"

He did.

It was good. We were under down quilts in lamplight and his body was the color of dried pine needles in autumn. Afterwards, he nested against my back as though it were habit.

Roger returned during the muddy season. Late one night I heard dogs barking and saw headlights and the white step-van grinding down the road in moonlight.

Sunbow came over early the next morning. Her face was swollen, her eyes red. Her sneakers were caked with mud and she didn't bother to tie them.

"What happened to you?" I said, pouring black coffee.

She sat at the table and held her head in her hands. I rolled a cigarette for each of us. A raw wind blew outside and I could hear the scrape of tin against wood from the cowbarn.

"He's back," she said. She tilted her head and lit the cigarette.

"I saw," I told her.

"He's got a girl with him, Ginny."

"I'm not surprised."

She took offense. "What do you mean?"

I shrugged and sipped my coffee.

"She can spin wool. She knows natural dyes. He wants to work with her."

I waited. The feather was missing from her left earring. She pulled a wadded handkerchief from inside her sweater sleeve and blew her nose.

"Well, it's not what you think, Ginny. He's not throwing me over. He wants us both."

"And?" I said.

"I don't know if I can handle it."

"Do you want to?"

At that moment Sunbow's face looked innocent as a young animal's. Her eyes were soft with idealism.

"It might work out," she said.

The school bus went by on the road and someone walked near the house rattling the milk pail and strainer.

I remembered a rainy night years ago when Sunbow had first been my neighbor. Raoul—the first husband—had written from Guatemala promising if he ever returned he would play his trumpet at the crest of the ridge above her house. Months went by. That spring night the rain fell in black icy sheets. I was sitting in the rocker by the woodstove sorting vegetable seeds. I heard the song, the strained notes, and could hardly believe my ears. Someone, a mad man, was playing "Let Me Call You Sweetheart" on a horn far away. I put on my raincoat and went to the porch. There was no moon.

Sunbow walked by my house swinging a kerosene lantern, deep in the mud. She wound around my house and up the canyon, over slippery scree and through manzanita brush.

After everything, she went to him.

1979

The Birthing

One shot and the killing was over, quickly as trimming a thumbnail. Morgan walked away from the alfalfa field toward the dead goat. It was early evening and the sun had long ago loosened its hold on the canyon.

Angel came running from behind the house. She wore a loose white shirt and was barefooted and soil crept up her ankles like socks. Her braids flew behind her.

"Why the hell did you do that?" she said.

Morgan stood near the dead gray nanny goat and with one hand he absently thinned green apples from the dwarf tree. He held the .22 in the other hand, the barrel at an angle to the ground.

"Told her I would if she didn't keep her penned," he said. "Here. You take this back to the house." He handed her the rifle and lifted the goat in his arms and began walking toward the county road, toward the goat woman herself who had heard the shot and was waiting in the middle of the gravel road, but near her house, a quarter mile farther toward the lake. Morgan could see her waiting, arms akimbo, in a long skirt and a big picture hat. The pine woods behind her were blackening and the goat was still warm in his arms.

It was their custom to hold meeting to resolve disputes among their kind. The authorities had never been called in. At the meeting Morgan showed no remorse. He had changed his shirt, wet his head under the garden hose, and slicked back his wavy blonde hair. He sat nudging loose tobacco into the careful crease of a rolling paper, his feet propped on an applewood stool next to the cold woodstove.

Angel stood up first thing and defended him. "Morgan was forced to this. He didn't want to do it." She sat down then on the sagging sofa and pulled the nearest young child into her lap, murmuring to his neck and smoothing his forehead.

The schoolhouse was lit by kerosene lamps with sootblack globes and the light was a little skittish, like a feline creature among them.

Georgia, the goatherd, sat in an overstuffed chair surrounded by her four children. She tapped her boots on the linoleum floor and, head bent, stared at Morgan through slitted eyes. Theirs was a longstanding feud. When the little one name Banjo whimpered, she put him to the breast to quiet him.

After Angel spoke, no one said anything for a long time. A coyote howled from the rimrock and two dogs wrangled on the schoolhouse porch, their growls low and menacing. At last a tall woman in an old band uniform jacket stood and spoke. "We've got to think about what we're trying to do. We can't be shooting one another's animals." Her hands were grimy with garden soil and she ran them through her frizzy red hair. "What do we believe in?" she asked.

Everyone started talking at once and no one was accorded attention. Morgan said nothing and Angel didn't look at him. She didn't like to think the father of her unborn child would kill a neighbor's goat just for eating apples.

"Hold it. JUST HOLD IT, PEOPLE," Sam hollered, his arms high, gesturing for their attention. The jabbering subsided, like air seeping out of a balloon.

Sam was respected, a leader, a hard worker, a strong wiry man people rarely challenged.

"I can't sit here all night listening to this," he said. "I've got chores. I'll wager most of you do, too." He wiped his face with a blue bandana. There were murmurs of assent.

"Okay," Sam said. "I'm going to ask Morgan to relinquish his .22 for three months. All we can do is let him know we disapprove." No one disputed him.

"What about the goats?" Morgan asked.

"And we will put pressure on Georgia to pen up the goats. I will help you build a pen," Sam said directly to the goatherd before she could say one word in defense of animals running free. She slumped in her chair, defeated. The lines were deep around her mouth and eyes.

"Meeting adjourned," Sam said. The people filed out of the schoolhouse, resuming conversations and laughing, drifting home in the cool night, quick to forget the conflict. Angel and Morgan were last. They stood on the porch and looked at the stars while the others dispersed. The cloying smell of the lilac bush was thick in the night air.

"Want to feel the baby moving, Morgan?" Angel said. She reached for his calloused hand.

"Sure, Sugar," Morgan answered, dutifully placing his hand on her abdomen. He kept it there until the baby kicked. Then he hugged her with the baby like a bundling board between them.

"Are you scared about the baby?" Morgan said.

"Scared?" Angel loved for Morgan to ask her how she was feeling. He didn't ask her often since they had quit courting and settled down to have a baby. She was nineteen. He was twenty-four. They had met a year ago at a healing gathering in British Columbia, linking hands in a circle of two hundred people dancing and not letting go.

"I mean scared of the delivery," he said.

"No," Angel said. "So many ladies have done it before me. It must be almost foolproof."

"Let's go home," Morgan said, and he took her hand to guide her in the shadows to the red house beside the rushing creek.

The holy folks came the first of July when the sun was relentless and the people sometimes gathered in the afternoon to soak in the deepest part of the creek, watching the water striders skim across the water and the nightshade curling around the cottonwood roots. They drove into the canyon in a rattletrap Ford stationwagon, circa 1956, blue and white beneath Arizona and California dust, and overloaded. The tailpipe scraped the first real bump the car came to off the blacktop and the tailpipe was lost, so that the holy folks made quite an entrance, a noisy entrance disturbing the quiet rising of the heat waves.

Morgan watched from the grove of aspens shielding the creek pool. They stopped by the mailbox and all three piled out of the car, two women and one man, dressed in graying, once-white clothing. Morgan stepped from the shade and waved them in his direction.

The three strangers walked abreast down the lane, kicking up small dust clouds. They stepped into the shade where they had seen Morgan. Morgan, Angel, and Sam soaked in the creek.

"Come on in here," Morgan said. He had settled on a sub-merged log, thigh deep in the cool water, the lingering branches of a willow trailing around him. Angel's freckled breasts bobbed in the water like some lush riparian fruit.

The three strangers sat down beside the creek, but didn't get in. The women pulled their skirts above their knees and hung their legs over the bank so that their feet splashed in the water. The man sat a little away from them and took off his raggedy straw hat and fanned himself. He was young, younger than the women, perhaps Morgan's age, and slender and white-skinned, as if he ate too many vegetables and not enough meat. His shirt was open to the waist and a brass fish hung on a thin chain around his neck. His chest was hairless and white as wax. The faces of the women were lined and creased. Morgan reckoned they were in their thirties, though one seemed older than the other. They looked alike, slightly plump, with the same dull black hair in braids. There were rings of dirt around their necks and wrists, as though they hadn't been able to bathe in a long time.

"My name's Adam and this here is my family, these women," he said, and he gestured with an open palm toward the women who lowered their eyes in a modest way. "Greta and Gail." He had a slur of an accent.

"Where'd you come from?" Morgan said. He was curious, but not wary. They were used to strangers passing through.

"We been on the road awhile. Started in east Texas. Tennessee before that," Adam said. "We're lookin' for a place to camp for a bit."

Morgan and Sam exchanged glances and Sam shrugged and nodded his head. The milk cow mooed long and loud close to the barbed wire fence on the other side of the creek.

"We got a spot not far over there—across the road—where we allow folks to camp for a few days," Morgan offered. "It's right by the creek and off in the woods so you can have a little privacy."

"We'd appreciate it," Adam said.

"I'll take you over there if you like," Sam said.

"That's mighty friendly of you," the older woman said, her voice thick and sweet.

The holy folks set up a tipi before dark, a bright canvas structure like a temple in the juniper woods. That night they had a campfire and the people heard the rhythm of a tambourine and singing, a strange high wail and syllabic chanting in a language they could not decipher.

Angel went to visit them the next morning and took a pint of pickles as a gift. When she came home, Morgan was watering the rhubarb, wearing only cut-offs and sandals.

"How was it?" he said.

"How was what?" Angel said.

"The visitors," Morgan answered. He held his thumb over the end of the hose so the water sprayed and made a fine prism.

"They're okay. They deliver babies, Morgan." She knelt beside the first row of onions and pulled some pigweed.

"Deliver babies?"

"One of 'em's a midwife," Angel said.

"Do they all sleep together?" Morgan said.

"How should I know? They call one another 'brother' and 'sister'."

Morgan absorbed this information in silence.

"Morgan," Angel said, still squatting, "we're going to need a midwife soon."

"Maybe they came here for that reason," Morgan said.

Angel stood up satisfied and went into the house. "Maybe so," she said.

That night Angel baked a rhubarb-strawberry pie and presented it to Morgan. He insisted they whip the last bit of cream. The sun gave way to evening and they ate supper on the narrow deck of the red house. The cool air soothed them. Morgan talked enthusiastically about planting more fruit trees and maybe raising turkeys next year. Angel liked it when he talked about the future.

Nighthawks swooped and rose like rags on the grassy slope before the alfalfa field began. From away high on the canyon wall they heard the coyote cries of children at play. Angel felt the baby flutter inside her. An owl sang from the shadows and Angel held her breath and listened for the holy folks. They were so far away, a quarter mile at least, and she couldn't tell if she heard them or just imagined she heard them.

Morgan went into the house and returned with a sweater for each of them. "Here," he said, "it's chilly already."

Angel draped the sweater around her shoulders.

"He's a man of the Lord, Morgan," she said.

"Who?"

"Adam. You know," Angel said.

"Oh yeah?"

"He talks about the Lord's will and the Lord's love all the time."

"Talk's cheap, Angel," Morgan said.

Angel seethed inside. "You don't believe in anything, Morgan Riley."

Morgan didn't respond and after a minute Angel went into the house. Morgan followed her and in the loft under the blanket he said, "I do believe in you and me and our land, Angel." He put his arms around her and cradled her head in his hand.

The holy folks stayed into August and became almost a part of the community. Greta and Gail offered to help with the barn repairs. They didn't seek out a winter dwelling, so no one figured they would stay past the first frost, if that long.

One rare rainy day Angel went to make the final arrangements to have Greta, the older of Adam's women, deliver her baby. Her time was near and she needed assurance. She found the holy people inside the tipi with a small fire crackling in the center fire ring. The younger woman, the quiet one, was working yarn around two sticks, weaving a rainbow god's eye. Greta stirred a blackened pot near the edge of the fire while Adam sat, back straight, legs crossed, with fingertips resting on his knees.

"May I come in?" Angel said.

"Come in before you soak to death," Greta said.

Angel settled beside Adam on a rag rug. He placed his white hand on her belly. "You'll be delivering soon," he said. His touch was warm through her thin shirt and Angel was uncomfortable with the touch. He was the only man besides Morgan to touch her like that.

"Yes," Angel said, and he took his hand away. "I need someone to help me."

"I'll help you. I already told you that," Greta said. She had a cocoon-like voice, enveloping Angel, making her feel safe. She was motherly, with soft large breasts free under her dress and a body that looked as though she had given birth herself.

"Morgan says to find out what you want for helping me."

"Not a thing. Just a healthy baby."

"Well, we'll give you something," Angel said.

"Whatever," Greta said, and she began to hum some Bible song, as if to end the discussion.

On the way home Angel looked in the give-away box in the schoolhouse and found a pink dress. She took it home and bleached it in a bucket for three days. Scrubbed and pressed, it was near white with just a wash of color left in the seams like the petals of a rose down close to the stem. She bathed and plaited her hair and wore the dress to the tipi one evening. The holy folks welcomed her as one of their own and together they shared tea and made their plaintive music long into the night. Near ten o'clock, as the moon was setting, they were joined by Georgia, the goatherd. It seemed it was her habit to join them, and Angel felt a tug of loyalty to Morgan, as though she should leave the gathering when Georgia arrived, but she could not bring herself to leave. She felt ecstatic whirling in her cotton dress as the fire danced on her bare legs.

When she went home in the dark, she felt her way along the lane with her bare feet and knew the pleasure of her familiarity with each rock and ridge. The baby was kicking up a storm and Angel suddenly realized Morgan might be lying awake in the loft waiting for her.

She closed the screen door, cushioning its slam with her hand. She pulled the white dress over her head and laid it on the sofa before she climbed the loft ladder to the bed. It was black in the loft, but she knew the way by heart and lifted the blanket on her side and crept under. Morgan rolled over and nested against her back and said, "Let's get to sleep. We got plenty work to do tomorrow, Angel."

Another evening when Angel returned from the tipi she found Morgan under the truck in the day's last light.

"What are you doing under there, Morgan?" she asked. Her voice sounded dreamy, even to herself. She just stood beside the left front wheel, since squatting and rising had become strenuous.

Morgan stuck his head out from under the truck. "Fixin' the brakes, 'case we have to take you to town," he said. His hands and bearded face were streaked with grease.

"Sure is a nice night tonight," Angel said. She sighed and looked toward the creek, keeping her hands folded on her belly. "I saw the heron that lives back there."

Morgan disappeared under the truck again. Angel heard the gravelly sound of him scooting in the dirt on his back. The sky and the horizon seemed to meld in a blue wash and she thought she saw the silhouette of a deer in the alfalfa field.

"Adam plays a silver flute, Morgan," she said.

"Is that right," Morgan said. His voice was faint, disinterested.

"He says he can heal the sky after rain with his flute."

"You got a package today, Angel," Morgan said. "From your mother."

Angel's eyes opened wide. "Where is it?"

"In the house by the radio. Sam brought it from town."

Angel walked to the house and Morgan worked on the brakes until dark.

It was the end of August and the grass was brown as palominos. The people were beginning to journey into the fir woods to gather firewood. Each day Angel and the other women laid out sliced apricots and peaches and pears to dry in the sun. Against the coming barrenness they stored great glass jars full to the brim with the leathery fruit. Batches of wine were begun in clay crocks and the smell attracted insects to the sweet rot. Tomatoes were bending their mother stems and even melons ripened despite the short growing season. There was a sense of accomplishment among the people. They had worked the land and the land had yielded a good harvest. Weather had been with them.

Angel's water broke at high noon while she gathered small green eggs from her chickens. The wetness spilled down her left leg and she remembered wetting her pants as a child and feeling ashamed.

"Morgan. Morgan," she shouted from the fenced-in chicken yard. Morgan looked up from the black plastic pipe emerging from the shower tank he was repairing. The hens chattered around Angel and she waved like someone arriving home.

"My water broke," she said. Then she shooed the chickens and slipped through the gate and locked it.

Morgan met her on the path and put one arm around her shoulders.

"I feel a tightening down there," she said. She held one hand on the underside of her belly.

"Does it hurt?" Morgan said, squinting in the sun.

"No, it doesn't hurt," she said. "I'll take the eggs to the house. You go tell Greta."

"You want me to go the house with you first?"

"No, I'm okay," Angel said. She lifted the egg basket and then said, "Morgan, I want to have it here. No hospital."

"We will, Angel," Morgan said and he walked down the path toward the county road. He didn't look back. His worn workshirt was the same color as the bachelor buttons bordering the path.

Angel carefully placed the eggs in a cardboard carton and set them in the cooler in the shade of the back porch. The creek curved behind the house, silver from the sun, gurgling incessantly in a comforting way. Rude Steller jays hawked at Angel and she knew a small sadness, an awareness that she would never be the same again, that time was passing, that something irrevocable was about to occur. She went in the house ravenously hungry and ate two banana muffins with butter. Then she sat rocking and rocking next to an open window with the pocket watch on the cedar chest beside her.

"I'm coming, Angel," Greta said, as she slammed the screen door.

"No hurry," Angel said.

Greta unloaded a woven shopping bag on the kitchen counter, then turned to Angel with her hands on her hips. She wore a pale shirtwaist that nearly trailed the floor. Her hair was braided and pinned like a helmet against her head. She was sunburned, the skin at her neck fleshy and wrinkled.

"Are you timing the contractions?" she asked.

"Uh-huh," Angel said. "They're not real regular yet."

"Well, keep timing. They'll most likely get regular as they get closer."

"Where's Morgan?" Angel said. She glanced at the open window.

"Checking something on the truck," Greta said. "Where are the sterile linens?"

"Up there," Angel said, and she nodded toward the high shelf of the pantry, above the canned peaches and cherries and pickles.

Greta reached high and brought down the brown grocery bag which Angel had stapled shut and baked in a slow oven. It contained two white sheets and several towels.

"What about the floss and scissors?" Greta asked.

"Right here on the cedar chest," Angel answered. "We got plenty of time." She smiled at Greta in a shy way, then lowered her eyes and folded and unfolded the hem of her smock. It barely reached her knees and she wore nothing underneath.

"Did you buy the shepherd's purse?" Greta said.

"Yes. It's in that little brown crock."

"I'll make a tea of it just in case we need it. Won't hurt to let it boil and boil. You'll need a strong brew if there's much bleeding." And Greta set to work building a fire in the cookstove.

The two rooms were joined by a step up and a double open doorway and Angel could see Greta as she bustled around the kitchen, crumpling newspaper for firestarter, poking around for kindling. It felt good to have someone there to build a fire, make tea, and keep her company. Angel gathered a bundle of yellow yarn from the floor and began crocheting, the shiny silver hook slipping in and out of the yarn like a cat. She was making a bootie the length of a matchstick.

After a while Morgan came in with an armload of split wood. He stacked the wood, then came and stood between the kitchen and the main room. Angel stopped rocking.

"How are you?" he said. He seemed far away.

"Okay. Twenty minutes apart," she said. "Maybe it's a false alarm."

"Do you think so?"

"No, not really, Morgan. This is it."

"Do you need me yet? I thought since Greta was here I could finish fixing the shower and maybe do some other chores."

"I guess I don't need you yet."

"Okay. Just holler, Greta, if she gets close," Morgan said, and he was gone, out the front door into the sun's glare. Angel watched him until he walked out of sight past the garden's tall corn stalks.

"He'll be back." Greta said from the kitchen. "You got a ways to go yet."

"I know," Angel said, and she commenced rocking again and was comforted by the rocker's squeak.

Greta made a cool hibiscus tea with raw honey and the two women sat suspended in the afternoon, in the shade of the main room, gossiping and sharing a secret now and then, a shard of the past. It might have been any lazy afternoon, two women drinking tea and talking, but for the pocket watch ticking away Angel's innocence. The contractions grew closer and more intense so that when one came Angel's speech was slow and distant and she would still be telling her story but it was as if another person spoke and she, Angel, had gone way inside, concentrating on the force certain as moontide, the force that would wash the child into the world.

When evening came and the nighthawks began their ritual swing across the yard, Angel had reached a plateau and her contractions grew no closer.

"I should fix Morgan's supper," she said.

"Don't you worry 'bout his supper," Greta said. "He'll eat somewhere, no doubt. Or I'll fix him something when he comes home."

"Where is he, I wonder?" Angel said.

"I'm home," Morgan shouted, a grin on his face. "Thought I'd never get through at Sam's. They fed me, then I felt obliged to help with the milking."

Angel met him at the door and hugged him hard.

"I'm glad you're here," she said. In the back of her throat her voice flinched in fear.

"I figured Greta would call if you needed me," he said.

"I would have," Greta said. She dealt herself a hand of solitaire on the kitchen table.

"Why, you haven't even made the bed yet," Morgan said. He had built a plywood platform for a single mattress because he didn't want her climbing the loft ladder.

"We don't do that until it's real close," Angel said. "To keep the sheets sterile." She held his large, stained hand. The light around them dimmed and Angel danced into her next contraction.

Greta silently picked up the watch and noted the time.

"Does it hurt?" Morgan said.

"Yes. Yes, it hurts," Angel said. "But maybe that means it'll be over soon."

"Let me clean up a bit, Sugar. Then I'll sit with you," he said, and he untangled her hands from his arm.

Morgan went into the kitchen and Angel lit a lamp beside the single bed. She sat on the bed for a moment, but then moved to the rocker. She liked to think of rocking the baby to sleep in her arms. And she would sing.

Greta finished her cards and sat shuffling the deck.

"How long could this go on?" Angel asked.

"First babies generally take their time," Greta said. "We might as well settle in for the night."

The night was a long one. At first Morgan and Angel and Greta tried to play hearts, but Angel could not concentrate and Morgan's presence disturbed the intimacy the two women had earlier established, so the talk was dull and desultory.

Morgan grew restless and often went to the porch to watch the stars in the sky. Angel sweated and her hair grew tangled and she was alternately subdued and fretful. Once when Morgan was outside fetching kindling—they had let the fire die out—he heard a sharp cry and he ran to the door, but only looked in and saw Angel was still in the rocker and the bed still unmade, so he returned to his task.

In the dark hour before dawn, Greta made the bed with the sterile sheets and Angel, spent and trying to breathe in the proper way, but often crying out, went into the bed and bathed herself with wheat germ oil to lessen the chance of tearing. Her contractions were two minutes apart. They waited and her screams reverberated around the small house, shaking the salvaged barn-board walls and Morgan's heart.

Roosters fiddled at the skywash and Venus pinned the pink shell above the canyon. It was a cool morning, portending autumn. Morgan had dozed fitfully, unable to stay awake during the last hour. Angel longed for sleep and release from the pain. And still the baby would not be born. Greta had held her hand all night and once said, "You've got the hands of a child." The words stuck in Angel's mind.

When the morning grew light enough to see, Greta stirred from Angel's side and blew out the lamp.

"Greta," Morgan said, "don't you think she needs a doctor?"

"Not yet," Greta answered. "It's just hard work, Morgan."

Angel looked as though she had worked hard, her eyes puffy, her face pale. She lay on the bed with her legs bent and apart, the sheet covering her like a tent. The tent was open at her feet and Greta reached under now and then and measured her dilation.

"Four fingers," Greta announced. "Morgan, she needs you now. You stay by her. I must go out for a moment." And she left the house in a hurry, her skirts switching.

"Morgan, it hurts so bad. I can't believe how much it hurts," Angel said. She spoke quickly, desperately.

Morgan took her hand but didn't answer. When her body clenched, she clenched his hand, but it was limp and his eyes avoided hers.

"I want Greta," Angel said.

"She'll be back."

"Morgan." She screamed his name. "Mor-GAN!" And her body tensed, her back and legs arching in the pain and she could not believe it hurt the way it did. She wished to die.

When Greta returned, she had Adam with her. He walked in as though he belonged there and he was fresh and clean in white pants and a white shirt. He was like a vision to Angel. He went to her side.

"You're having a hard time, Angel?"

"Yes, God, yes, it's awful," Angel said, and she cried.

"When did this labor begin?" Adam asked.

"Yesterday noon," Morgan said.

"We've got to help her have this baby. She's wearing herself down," Adam said.

"Listen, Adam, I want to take her to the hospital," Morgan said. His hands shook like aspen leaves.

"No. NO," Angel screamed.

"We can do it here," Adam said.

Then Morgan saw the other man's eyes lock with Angel's and his heart spoiled within, ripe with bitterness.

"Adam, I'm afraid," Angel said. She groped for his hand.

"There's nothing to be afraid of," Adam said. "Be strong."

"I said I'm taking her to town," Morgan blurted. He spread his feet in a defensive stance.

"She needs a coach, someone to help her through. It won't take long," Adam said. "I can do it."

Morgan felt as though he were invisible.

"Yes. Yes," Angel said, breathless and panting and up on her elbows. "Adam, stay with me."

Then she cried in longing, a cry so raw with want and need that Morgan turned away.

"Son-of-a-bitch," he whispered, beating his fist into his palm.

His face was flushed and contorted. He slammed the door hard and rode the morning like a man in a foreign country, a man with no home, working to obliterate the sound of Angel screaming.

And even as she held the waxy child, so new, with sky and clouds in each pale eye, Angel could hear the dull thud of Morgan splitting sugar pine as he had split her.

1980

Victory

Mary Ruth woke up as her father shuffled in his slippers down the linoleum hallway, down the stairs, to the front door. He was home from Vietnam and she was unaccustomed to his presence in the house. There was no privacy; her bedroom and her parents' bedroom were directly across the hall from one another. Her room had no door. Her parents' room had a curtain of off-white monk's cloth, gathered and held aside during the day with a macramé belt Mary Ruth had made in fifth grade.

The cat darted into her room and leaped upon the bed, meowing. Haines, her father, stood at the doorway, a dark stone in the liquid night.

"Don't come in here," Mary Ruth said. She hadn't slept well. She was waiting for the first real light, the blue bars of dawn on her floor, then she was planning to go to work, to escape. Mary Ruth was fourteen and worked in an orchard packing house, packing pears.

"I just let the cat in," Haines said.

"You make me sick," Mary Ruth said, each word a razor's cut.

The furniture in her room emerged from the darkness like gray building blocks. Mary Ruth slipped from the bed and in quick, silky movements dressed in jeans, a flannel shirt, and sneakers. She rummaged in a daypack for cigarettes and a hairbrush, then braided her blonde hair in a loose, thick braid down her back. Over this she tied a paisley scarf. She looked in the mirror, satisfied.

Six steps to the end of the hallway and she was outdoors, breathing the sweet morning, and down the steps no one used but her. She liked to think it was her private entrance. Perhaps she lived in a boarding house where no one knew her, where she could come and go at all hours, drop out of school, take lovers, and drink sloe gin. She knew about life. She had worked in the packing house all summer, with older women. Listening, she had learned quite a bit, and now she felt she knew all there was to know in the mind.

Behind the house there was one row of apple trees, then behind that, a waist-high stone fence, and beyond that, the river. She climbed on the fence and walked the stones for a mile. She knew the fence by heart, never tripping. The sky was lightening, with a few clouds tinged brassy bright. A neighbor's Jersey milk cow licked a salt block with her pale tongue. The salt block pleased Mary Ruth. She walked by it nearly every morning and noted its demise, the depression from the licking growing deeper every day. It reminded her of the worn floor boards at school under the drinking fountain.

The stone fence ended at the river highway. The sun splayed over the hills, spilling on the river, a metallic flow. She walked across the ugly green bridge, ignoring the cars and trucks inches away. On the town side of the bridge there was a store, La Tienda del Pobre, housed in a pink stucco building with a corrugated tin roof. The words, *Tortillas, Beer, Cigarettes*, were painted on the side of the store facing the bridge, so that anyone driving in from the country could see them a half-mile away. Mary Ruth went in for a cream soda.

La Tienda del Pobre was owned and operated by Maggie, a dark, fertile-looking woman, squat and round, with breasts like overripe squash and eyes that some called bedroom eyes, knowing one moment, innocent the next. She wore ropes and ropes of jewelry around her neck and arms. All summer she wore a silver bracelet high on her upper left arm, a snake coiled, its tiny forked tongue flicking. Maggie had a moustache of black down, like the softest baby hair.

She kept the store open from five in the morning until eleven at night. Inside there was a potbellied stove where the men gathered on apple crates to gossip in the fall and winter months. House plants flourished in plastic pots and rusted honey cans. There was an old pool table, with latticed leather pockets. Maggie charged a dime a game, no betting.

"A soda is not a good breakfast for such a pretty girl," Maggie said.

"I'm not hungry," Mary Ruth said. She shoved a quarter across the counter. She went over to the woodstove and stood with her back to the morning fire, drinking the soda, her pack

over one shoulder. A portable television was on in a corner behind the counter, rolling with the horizontal out of control, a
man's authoritative voice recounting the news.

Maggie played solitaire on the counter. Her fingernails
were long and painted the color of winesaps. She flipped the
cards with an indifference and patience Mary Ruth admired,
as though she would play solitaire all her life and not mind.
The fly-speckled Pepsi clock above the door read six forty-
five.

"What time you have to be at work?" Maggie said.

"Seven," Mary Ruth answered.

"Come here. I'll tell your fortune."

"I don't need my fortune told," Mary Ruth said.

Maggie shrugged, her eyelids heavy, creased with shiny
green eyeshadow. She gathered the cards, mechanically shuffling and splitting the deck. Mary Ruth lit a cigarette.

"I do not need the cards. I can read your fortune in the
way you braid your hair," Maggie said. Mary Ruth puffed
hard, holding the filterless cigarette between her thumb and
forefinger. "Oh yeah?" She turned around, her back to Maggie, and removed the paisley scarf.

The television flickered, a greasy gray light in the room.

"There is a misunderstanding in your life," Maggie
said.

"Ha," Mary Ruth said, crushing the cigarette butt into a
beanbag ashtray on the edge of the pool table. "Everyone is
misunderstood."

Maggie turned to a sink and filled a watering can with
tepid water. "Do not take it seriously," she shrugged. "Smoke
cigarettes and drink cream soda."

Mary Ruth tied her scarf with a jerk. Her lips were drawn down at the corners and she felt a hot, sour feeling, a tightening in her throat. "I'm going. See you, Mags." She slipped to the door and slammed outside, rattling the loose panes of glass in the door.

One block from the store, she took a short cut down an alley that ran along a canal. The canal smelled fishy and styrofoam cups floated in its murky waters. A car crept up behind her. She knew without looking it was Franny in his '53 Chevy. He worked at the packing house, loading trucks. Only women sorted and packed.

"Hey, Sugar," he said, slowing to a crawl beside her, hanging out the window, one hand on the knob of the steering wheel. Mary Ruth knew that knob had a picture on it of a woman wearing a bit of gauzy curtain. She had examined it closely once when Franny went into the store for something. Now, with his hand on the knob, and his voice on her, she felt excited, but she ignored him. She didn't want to get into that car. Then it would be all over.

"Let me give you a ride to work," he said. His hair was slicked back, his face ruddy and scrubbed.

"I can walk," she said. "It's just two more blocks."

Two dogs, hound mongrels, knocked over a garbage can behind a brick building and growled over the contents. Franny reached for Mary Ruth, but she had expected that and ducked away. He gunned the engine and splashed through the mud puddles, tooting his horn and watching her in the rearview mirror.

The rest of the way to work she thought of the smooth, lethal sound of the word *sugar* when Franny said it. Sometimes he came by and said, *gimme some sugar,* and she thought she knew exactly what he meant.

That night over supper Lydia said, "Brother MacDowell is preaching tonight. It's Family Night." She saw that Haines's plate was nearly empty and automatically passed him the macaroni and cheese.

No one said anything.

Mary Ruth hated the way her mother said, "*Mac*Dowell," like a hick. She pushed the food around on her plate. The cat scratched at the back door and Mary Ruth went to let her in, then she sat back down, her ankles hooked around the chair legs.

"Cat's going to have kittens," Haines said.

"Yes, she is," Lydia answered. "In another week or so."

"Can't keep 'em all," Haines said.

Mary Ruth excused herself, cleared her plate and silverware from the table, and wandered into the living room. There was a picture of Jesus over the sofa and the eyes seemed to follow her around the room. She knew she would go to Family Night with her mother, but she wanted to let her worry about it.

She turned on the television to conceal the sounds she was making. She opened the wooden box and looked at the teeth. Her father had returned home two weeks ago, bringing with him the carved wooden box of human teeth, some brown with nicotine and worn, others small and perfect. There were two gold teeth, molars, glinting in the harsh light of the pole lamp beside the television. The inside of the box was lined with thin felt, the color of cheap lipstick, the kind her mother had worn before she became a Christian.

She had avoided Haines since he showed them the teeth. Avoiding him had been easy. She was at work all day. He stayed home all day, repairing locks, glazing windows—the house had been neglected in his absence—and making phone calls about work. He was retired from the army, but he was still a young man—thirty-eight—and wanted to work.

The war was on television. She was glad it was black and white and not color.

"Mary Ruth, I'll be ready to go in ten minutes," Lydia hollered from the kitchen.

Mary Ruth did not answer. She knew her mother still wondered if she would put up a fight. She went upstairs and changed into a skirt and blouse. She took down her braid and brushed her hair. She could just not answer and there would be no retaliation. Her father did the same thing to her mother. Half the time, conversations were begun and dropped by one person, for lack of answer. No one ever mentioned it.

Mary Ruth went downstairs and said, "I'm going outside to wait in the car."

Her father said, "I'll tell your mother. She's in the bathroom." He was watching the news, sitting in the rocker in his stocking feet, his blonde hair in a fluffy fringe around his bald spot. He didn't look up.

Victory Temple was across the river and east of town, a concrete block building always in some stage of construction.

It was situated on a hill free of trees and studded with scab rock and rabbitbrush. The main room, the worship hall, was bathed in fluorescent lighting, lighting that left no softness, no ambiguity, no shadow but cleancut shadow. The ceiling made a curving arch, paneled in wainscotting. When she was younger, Mary Ruth had imagined it was the inside of Noah's ark, the belly of some salvation ship. She and Lydia scurried into a wooden pew halfway up the aisle.

The regular members of the church greeted one another with *Brother!* and *Sister!* Their hands lingered long in vigorous handshaking and the men thumped one another on the back. Many people carried Bibles, the men black ones, the women white. There were children, playing sly games when their parents' backs were turned, sticking out their tongues and pinching one another. Across the aisle and several rows ahead, Mary Ruth saw Franny squeezed between his sister Roseann and his mother, a chubby woman in a purple dress.

The service began with singing, the voices loud, accompanied by a woman playing the out-of-tune piano, a woman whose body entered into the act of making music, her shoulders rolling and dipping, her thighs bouncing on the piano stool. This was the part Mary Ruth liked best, singing the old songs, "What a Friend We Have in Jesus" and "This World Is Not My Home." Then one of the brothers, a man in a black suit, made a few announcements and asked for the offering. Wicker baskets were passed along the rows. Lydia laid a dollar bill in the basket, all the while keeping her eyes on the hymnal and singing, the knuckles of one hand white against the pew in front of her. During the offering, Brother McDowell sat a little to the side, up front, on a folding metal chair, scraping splinters from his thumb with a pocketknife.

Mary Ruth eased into a daydream of Franny's voice saying, *Sugar.* When she came away from the dream, Brother McDowell was preaching, speaking in a low voice, leaning on the podium, just like teachers in school. He might have been a teacher. He was good-looking, his brow clear and the hair at his temples graying in waves. He wore a suit of a material that looked dull in some lights and shiny with a slight turn of his shoulder, like copper feathers on a pintail duck. He held a Bible in his hand and offered it to the crowd once in a while, to make a point.

He was talking about living in the world and how hard it is to live in the world as a Christian. He was talking about indecency and Mary Ruth tugged at her short skirt. He specifically mentioned short skirts. He was talking about young people and freedom.

He pulled a clipping from his coat jacket pocket, and here, with a sense of the drama unfolding, Brother McDowell took the time to remove his coat jacket, slinging it over the folding chair. He gave the crowd a moment to stir and wonder. He came around in front of the podium, closer to them, and rolled up the sleeves of his white shirt.

Then he read the clipping to the crowd, a clipping about thirteen high school students in a neighboring town being arrested for skinny-dipping at the gravel pit. He read it with anguish, his voice growing louder and louder, blossoming into an embrace. His shirt was wet in half moons under the arms. His face was red, perspiring. He opened the Bible and read from it, a long passage, and when he finished, he said in a coaxing soft voice, "Come to Jesus. Rest in the arms of the Lord. Come right up here"—he spread his arms wide—"and He'll take care of you. Open your heart."

Mary Ruth started crying, not the kind of crying she could check, but tears she felt she'd saved for years. They flooded and rolled down her cheeks and she knew she had to go up front.

The pianist banged out "Washed in the Blood of the Lamb" and the congregation sang while Mary Ruth made her way, stumbling through the tears, to the front of the worship hall. A few others straggled up behind her. They knelt in a confused knot and Brother McDowell walked along, spreading his fingers on their scalps in a fervent touch.

"These people have come to the Lord. You can come, too. Open your heart to Jesus."

They sang "Amazing Grace" and Mary Ruth knew the service was over. Her mother came to her side and when she stood up her mother hugged her. She hated that hug more than anything. Her mother smelled like Lysol and the inside of closets in winter.

Afterwards, in her bed at home, she knew the feeling she had felt kneeling up front was the same one she expected to feel if Franny ever touched her. It was giving in, letting go. The preacher had said to her as she left the Victory Temple, "Jesus will walk with you."

It was Franny who walked with her, leaning protectively toward her, every day that first week of school. He would

stand beside her locker and wait for her between classes.
Sometimes the crowd in the hallway surged and pushed,
throwing them close, close enough for kissing, but she always
kept her arms curled around her books between them.

He asked her to go to the dance Friday night. She refused. Lydia would never let her go. Dancing was a sin. He
asked her to go to the Victory Temple Sunday night and she
accepted.

Lydia said all right, since it was church.

Sunday after supper he picked her up and drove to a dirt
lane down the middle of a peach orchard. All the peach trees
were growing in one direction, bound by the wind, despite the
winter pruning. The wind off the river was stronger than all
of them. The trees were black fingers in the blue night sky.
There was a moon, slightly more than half full, like a tipped
bowl. He didn't ask her if it was all right to drive there.

"I thought we were going to church," she said. Inside, she
liked the feeling of being alone with him in the car, the radio
playing, the upholstery cool against her arms.

"We'll get there," Franny said. "It's still forty-five minutes
away."

He slid next to her, drawing her near. He was sucking on
a mint she could smell. He had cut his neck shaving and the
tiny flake of toilet paper he had placed over the cut was white
bright in the dim car. She lay in his arms and let him hold her,
the buttons on his shirt pressing into her cheek.

Haines started working as the foreman of an apple orchard, four hundred acres of trees owned by a corporation in

Yakima. He was seldom at home. Lydia went to the Victory Temple nearly every night. Sometimes Mary Ruth begged off, saying she had homework, and sometimes she went along and prayed and sang.

The nights she was left alone in the house were good. She began to keep a journal. She wrote down every exchange she had with her father.

> *He asked me how's school?*
> *I shrugged my shoulders.*
> *He came home drunk while she was at church.*
> *He said me and Lydia used to have fun.*
> *He asked me do you want to keep one of the new kittens?*
> *The gray one I said.*

While she wrote in the journal, sitting in the dining room near the gas heater, she listened to the FM station and smoked cigarettes.

One night, on the way to the Victory Temple, Lydia said, "Run in the store and get me a box of baking soda, Mary Ruth." She pulled over to the curb and dug in her purse for some change.

Mary Ruth ran inside, hair flying, and came to a dead standstill when she saw her father, his back to the door, his arm around Maggie, his meaty hand resting on her hip. Franny was there, shooting pool with a skinny boy in overalls. The woodstove gave off a powerful heat and the houseplants were like a jungle. There was a record playing, more static than music, an old Elvis Presley song. Franny sank the eight ball and crowed, his open mouth a circle of darkness. He moved swiftly to rack the balls again, saying without looking at her, "Hey, Mary Ruth. On your way to church?"

Her father turned, giving Maggie a quiet pat as he drew his arm away.

Mary Ruth could not look at him. "I'd like a box of soda, Maggie, please."

Maggie went behind the counter and took down the orange box and said, "Thirty-two cents." Her voice was soft as the light from the kerosene lantern hanging over the candy counter.

Mary Ruth skimmed across the floorboards toward the door. "I'll take you on again," she heard her father say.

That night she wrote in her journal: *His hand burns her. They have something.*

The next night she stayed home. She watched Lydia's tail-lights bounce down the driveway and down the lane until she turned onto the county road. She waited five minutes by the clock. Then she called Franny's house. She told his sister Roseann, who answered the phone, that she needed to ask him about a homework assignment. That was feeble, since they had no classes together, but maybe Roseann didn't know. She had been out of school for several years.

"Want to come over?" she said.

"What's up?" Franny said.

"Lydia's gone. I'm here alone."

"Sure," he whispered. "I'll be over."

They hung up and she took down the picture of Jesus and laid it face-down on the sofa. There was a clean rectangle of wall where the picture had been. She wrote in her journal: *He's coming over.* She wrote his name several times in a row. *Franny. Franny. Franny. Francis.*

It seemed his car crunched down the gravel driveway in a slow, cautious way. She watched through the crocheted curtains at the front window. He shut the car door, with only a quiet click of the lock, and walked to the house. She opened the door before he could knock.

"Come in," she said, giggling.

"You sure your ma's gone?" Franny said, looking around.

Mary Ruth danced around the room, feeling silly. "Sure, I'm sure," she said.

Franny sat down on the sofa, pushing the picture aside. "Look what I've got," he said, opening a plastic bag and offering it to her to sniff.

"What is it?"

"Dope, dummy."

He rolled a joint and they got stoned. Mary Ruth felt the music from the radio reaching into her ears. She sang along, forgetting she was at home, breaking rules. They ate a bag of gingersnaps.

She went to the bathroom and forgot to come back. After ten minutes, Franny knocked on the flimsy door, then entered the dark room, shadows from the light in the hallway cutting deep into the room. Mary Ruth stood in front of the mirror, the heels of her hands pressing on the rim of the basin. Franny walked behind her and crossed his arms in front of her, his hands resting, palms flat, on her stomach.

P a t r i c i a   H e n l e y

They stood like that for a few minutes. The new kittens meowed from a liquor box in the closet across the hallway. Franny unbuttoned her flannel shirt. Their eyes touched in the mirror. She began to shiver and buttoned her shirt, matter-of-factly.

"Did you see my father?" she said, leading him by the hand to the living room.

"He's at the store," Franny said, "telling war stories." They sat side-by-side on the sofa, kissing in their usual fashion. Franny chewing on her neck and earlobes, their tongues learning.

At nine o'clock Franny left. Mary Ruth went back to the mirror and turned on the bathroom light. Her cheeks were raw from whisker burn, her neck streaked with a long purplish bruise.

The next morning she smeared liquid make-up over the hickey. It was a bottle of make-up she had bought in sixth grade and never worn, a sticky liquid the color of twine. She put on a green turtleneck and a trench coat. The trench coat had a Coke stain on the sleeve and she wondered if Lydia would insist she wear something else. Haines's pickup swerved in the gravel; he was on his way to work.

"Mary Ruth?" Lydia's voice was high-pitched, almost a squeal from the kitchen.

Mary Ruth didn't answer. She looked out the window, chewing her thumbnail. It had rained during the night and the stone wall was slick. The pecan tree had lost its leaves in the wind. She was sick of hiding.

At last she went down to the kitchen. She hated its whiteness, its sterility. It reminded her of the dentist's office. There was an open green bottle on the back of the sink, its wick saturated with pine scent. She poured a cup of coffee from the percolator on the gas stove. She sat on a stool beside the window, pretending she was alone.

"Brother McDowell asked after you last night," Lydia said. She was unwrapping a package of frozen venison steaks.

"When I came home, the picture of Our Lord was on the sofa. Why is that?"

"I don't know," Mary Ruth said. She saw her reflection in the coffee pot on the stove. She pulled her turtleneck down an inch and tilted her head back, staring at the hickey.

Lydia turned from the sink. "Where did you get that?"

"What?"

"I know what you've been doing," Lydia said. Her voice was like a mallet in the room. Her face turned white, all the crow's feet and frown lines gray. She rushed at the girl, arms stiff, hands skeletal, and pinched her neck hard, screeching something unintelligible. She took Mary Ruth by the shoulder, bunching the trench coat around her face, and shook her until her head banged against the wall. Lydia was crying over and over, "What have you done to yourself? What have you done?"

Mary Ruth was limp and did not answer. She sat stock-still until Lydia slumped into a straightback chair next to the sink and laid her head down on the porcelain. Her hair was thinning on top and Mary Ruth could see her scalp at the part, pink as the inside of a rabbit's ear. Lydia took a flowered handkerchief from under her sweater sleeve and blew her nose and whimpered. Mary Ruth walked out.

She would never be like Lydia. She went down the hallway to the closet where the kittens lay curled with their mother.

Their shiny eyes blinked when she opened the closet door and the light shone in the carton. The kittens meowed, a small noise, and wiggled closer to the mother cat.

Mary Ruth plucked the kittens from the mother cat's teats and put them one by one into a shoe box. They were awkward, bumping into one another and the sides of the cardboard box. Their meowing grew more urgent. She carried them outside to the stone fence. It was a chilly autumn morning, with the smell of juniper smoke in the air. Someone had raked the birch leaves into a wet, browning pile.

At the stone fence, she got rid of the kittens. She was very precise about it, using only enough force, a short controlled jerk of her wrist, to break the neck or back of each kitten against the stone fence. She killed them all, even the gray one.

1981

Picking Time

Rein measured sesame oil and vinegar into a pint canning jar, lifting the jar to the light to watch the oil separate from the red vinegar. Diane, his mother, made the salad, alternately tearing lettuce leaves and sipping mulled wine from a mug. Now and then she glanced at herself in the bamboo-framed mirror over the sink. The electric lights dimmed in collaboration with the wind.

"Your father wants it to be over," she said.

"So what else is new?"

"Rein," she scolded.

This kind of talk always depressed him, left him feeling disenfranchised. He regretted his smart-aleck tone, a remnant of his younger days. He was almost nineteen and learning to hold his tongue when necessary.

Diane let the cat outside. The weather stripping tacked to the bottom of the door scraped the linoleum and a small wind chilled the room. Rein shoved another quarter-log into the cookstove firebox.

"We're going to file for a legal separation," she said, matter-of-factly, and she faced him, arms folded, a lean woman in a caftan batiked with tiny blue threads of dye criss-crossing white hearts.

"I've heard that before," he said. He perched on the counter, wiping his glasses with a clean tea towel, his long, pale hair bound at the nape of his neck with a leather strip.

"This time we mean it," she said with a little laugh.

"I don't understand all this."

Diane lit the kerosene lamp on the warming oven, her back-up in case of power failure. "You can't call this a marriage," she said. "He's hardly ever here. He has a new life."

"I know. I know."

"Rein. Have you thought of what you might do?"

"Do?"

"I mean now that summer's over."

"You're talking goals, right?"

"You have Grandma's money. If you want to go to school."

"I don't know what I want to do."

"I feel like we made a mistake, bringing you here when you were so young."

"Mom, lay off the guilt. I might be just as confused if we'd stayed in California. I might be punked up on the street."

"I can see you in purple hair."

"What are you going to do? Stay here?"

"I like it here. If my work keeps selling, I'll be all right here."

There was a knock at the door and Diane threw up her arms in mock helplessness. As she was on her way to the door, Margo sashayed in, carrying a Coleman lantern.

"It's me," she said, slamming the door. "I'm leaving."

"You just got here," Diane said.

She was his mother's friend and Rein didn't know much about her, having relegated her to that nether-region of people who had close connections with Diane the nature of which he did not fully comprehend.

"I just decided to go apple-picking," Margo said, in a hoarse rush. "I know it's kind of late, late in the season, but I need the money and—" she paused and pushed her crinkly, wild hair away from her eyes, "—and I just want to get away. You know?"

She was the only woman Rein knew with a tattoo: a small blue cornflower next to the dimple on her shoulder. He'd seen it during the summer when she wore a ribbed white undershirt.

"When are you leaving?" he asked. Both women looked at him as though they had forgotten his presence.

"Tomorrow. I'm leaving tomorrow," Margo said. Her eyes were sooty-looking and she rolled her head around like a marionette.

"What can I do to help you on your way?" Diane asked, returning to the sink and the salad.

"Feed the chickens and hold my mail," Margo said, twisting a brown curl into a corkscrew with her forefinger as she talked.

"Sure thing. Is your pickup running okay?"

"Good enough," Margo said. "I still need two cords of wood."

"No rest for the wicked," Diane said.

"Goodnight, Diane," Rein said. He pulled on a stained down vest and headed for the door, his boots thumping on the floor.

"What about dinner?"

"It's okay. I need to think." He kissed her cheek and escaped the steamy kitchen.

The rickety porch creaked and the cat rubbed against his calf, arching her back, meowing. The night was clear and frosty, with stars pulsing in the sky. A half moon illuminated the footpath.

Rein followed the path down the slope to the creek, then crossed the sunken bridge and cut a diagonal through the alfalfa field. He liked to walk in the dark. At his house, a renovated woodshed, he stood on the porch for a few minutes and surveyed the sky and land, noting the dwellings across the canyon where lights flickered. He felt good, returning to the house he had made for himself, to his own private brand of domesticity.

Cold as a witch's tit. There hadn't been a fire since morning. He stumbled over something in the dark: hiking boots he had oiled earlier in the day. He lit a kerosene lamp and built a quick fire in the small airtight stove. His dry kindling started with a satisfying crackle. As the place warmed up, he stood at the window looking out and eating smoked fish and saltines and dried bing cherries. He considered going through his meager cache of skin magazines, but he'd been through them so many times, and they were only exciting the first time. He'd left his Ed Abbey book at Diane's and didn't want to go back for it.

He brushed his teeth on the front porch, spitting into the asparagus bed. Inside, he undressed and, in a whisper, cursed the oncoming winter. He gingerly crawled into the slick nylon sleeping bag, a bed which had been with him a long time and smelled of woodsmoke and insect repellent.

He lay in his bunk and his breath made quick pearls of warmth on the windowpane. The corn stalks were ragged, bleached in the moonlight. Feathery clouds drifted above the rimrock. The land, the light, the clouds seemed like a dream. He imagined he saw colors in the wind, and, almost imperceptibly, the golden autumn wind had changed to blue, the blue wind like a hungry coyote's cry, the blue wind glistening on snow. Who could he tell? Almost all of the people Rein knew had known him since he was ten years old. He was a kid to them. He never told them: *I built this house with my heart and hands, but now I have to leave it. I cannot sleep at night and lie awake waiting for something I cannot name.*

His parents were divorcing at last. He was the only remaining symbol of their twenty years together. His mother's wedding band, worn gold, was already lying at the bottom of a reed basket, along with her porcelain thimble and a few African trading beads. He didn't understand.

He felt adrift, without anchor. He'd finished his schooling by correspondence and that left him free, with a freedom that sometimes tasted like too much candy. He wanted to feel connected, to speak his truth to someone. He worked his way backward through a catalog of memories: summers when evenings stretched limitless before him, fishing at the lake, drinking home-brew with his neighbors, building campfires, sleeping late and washing in the creek in the mornings. He measured time by the summers, ripe and abundant. Ardent at last in the arms of sleep, he thought of going picking. There would be people there he knew, people his own age from other communities. He would hitch a ride with Margo.

"That everything?" Margo asked, just before she slammed the tailgate.

"That's it," Rein said. "Sure this truck will make it, Margo?"

"Just get in," she said. "You have to get in the driver's side. The passenger door doesn't open."

Rein slid across the torn seat and Amber, Margo's two-year-old daughter, was jounced in next to him. She was a round, chubby girl in faded overalls and a blue sweatshirt, with a deep hood tied snugly around her face. In one hand she grasped a plastic bag of dried pears. Rein didn't speak to her; it didn't seem necessary.

"Okay," Margo shouted, "say your prayers to St. Christopher. We're on our way."

The truck was twenty years old and used a quart of oil every two hundred miles. The original paint was worn to a dull barn red, the roof interior stripped of much of its padding. The ride out of the canyon was shuddering and noisy, on gravel roads, but once on the pavement the truck settled into a rhythmic bounce. Amber offered him a dried pear and the sun was smoke-white in the sky. He began looking forward to the trip. They passed neat farmhouses and fields of barley stubble and Appaloosa horses.

"Want to smoke a joint?" Margo asked.

"After the crossroads," he said.

At the crossroads they stopped for gas at the U-Serve, U-Save. Margo pumped the gas. Rein checked the oil. Amber yelled, "I have to pee!" The woman in the motor home at the next gas pump—a woman with hair in tiny purple-white ringlets and pink cheeks in perfect clown circles—shot them a look of disgust, the lines above her upper lip deepening like scars.

On the road again, Margo slipped him a joint to light and pushed a cassette tape into the tape player. He didn't recognize the female vocalist competing with the truck's rattle. They shared the skinny joint as Amber watched them pass it back and forth across the cab.

When the tape ended they were passing through a flat town: two cafes, a dry goods store, a church and two taverns. Dust devils whirled among the sagebrush. Amber had fallen asleep, her head on Margo's thigh, her bare feet on Rein's. She made a connection between them. The miles rolled away and soon they were on the river highway, heading for the irrigated valley where orchards lay waiting, the dream site of fruit tramps tracking the mythical good picking.

"Why did you name her Amber?" he asked.

"My grandmother's name. I grew up with her," Margo said. "She was a tough old bird. With a heart of gold. A good woman."

He wondered at the expression, *a good woman*. What exactly did it mean? His father had said, when he left the canyon a year ago, Your mother is a good woman. It had something to do with being virtuous, with not wanting to cause pain.

"Where was that? Where you grew up?" he asked.

"Miles City, Montana. Grandma owned a drinking establishment there."

"My grandma never touched a drop."

"Mine hardly ever did either. She sold it."

He shifted his weight and Amber stirred.

"Look at her toes," Margo said. "Like little sausages." She put on another tape: Pure Prairie League. "Tomorrow's my birthday," she went on. "I'll be twenty-seven."

"Happy birthday," Rein said.

"Wait until tomorrow," she chided. "I had a tarot reading done at the barter fair. Treated myself to it since my birthday was coming up. Did you see the man who was doing the readings?"

Rein shook his head.

"Strangest man. He had long fingernails and hair in a pigtail down his back. Charged me five dollars. We sat right in the dirt and he laid out a silk scarf for the cards. The scarf had a dragon on it."

"So what was his verdict?"

"He told me I needed to seek a balance in my life." She cocked an eye, gray as pepper, in his direction.

"Does that fit?"

"I told him my motto has always been anything worth doing is worth doing in excess."

Rein rolled down the window and breathed in the smell of sage. With one hand, Margo twirled her hair into corkscrews and drove on.

They found work right away at Red Cheek Apple Orchard. There was a crooked row of plywood cabins, all occupied but one, and Margo and Amber moved in there. Rein erected a two-man tent on the hill above the cabins, a site sheltered on one side by aspen trees, with a view of the river and nearby town. They began picking apples at seven-thirty in the morning, had a half hour for lunch, and picked until five-thirty or six at night. Rein was averaging nine bins a day at six dollars a bin. The foreman, a thin man named Shuey with a gold front tooth, liked him and joked with him. The sun shone every day. As soon as he could he checked out the occupants of the other plywood cabins and was disappointed to find three families, another single man around thirty, and two weather-beaten fruit tramps in their fortieth season in the orchards. Old geezers, he called them privately. And then he spent several panic-stricken hours one night wondering if he would be an old geezer himself someday, with a hacking cough and shaking hands, the fingers cracked and swollen and split from some nutritional deficiency. The thought left him drowning in choices and he knew he was spending his last season picking. When he was younger, high school age, it had seemed okay, as though there was little else he could do for spending money. Now it hit him: he was here through choice or the inability to make a choice.

His days developed a pattern, familiar and comforting. Every morning he ate his buttered oatmeal standing beside a sage fire, elated by the rosy sunrise, the occasional wedge of geese in the sky. He wore wool gloves, a wool hat, and danced around the fire to stay warm. He pushed himself all day, piling up apples like money in the bank, beginning seedling dreams of what he might do after picking: hitchhike to a warm sunny place in the southwest, or apply for a job in his favorite bookstore in Spokane, or visit his cousin Glynis is Seattle, a court stenographer who liked wild parties. Some days he was delirious with the idea that he could do anything, go anywhere, and this was a change from the sadness he'd felt at home, a feeling of homesickness before he'd even left.

His evenings were restless. He was hungry for something. He'd heard there was a large camp of young people called the

Rainbow Family at the next orchard. Two nights in a row he walked the three-mile rutted lane, a tractor path, that would take him there most quickly. He hung around their campfires and watched the girls, all hippie girls, that's how he thought of them, in their heavy skirts and ribbed socks and bracelets made of leather and seeds. They had long hair and their breasts were loose beneath their sweaters. A few of the girls had babies and they nursed them openly. Rein watched, ravenous and a little ashamed, but not enough to stop watching. There was an easy kind of touching at this camp, hugs and swats and hand-holding. He wanted to be touched. But the circle did not open for him. He did not have the words to make it open. There was some trick to relating to people, some talisman he had not found, and he felt outside, invisible, and after the second night he did not return to their camp.

One night, by accident, he saw a girl bathing behind the cabins. He had looked out of his tent to check the progress of the full moon above the east horizon. She was standing in a zinc washtub, soaping all over, her short hair like a bud, the petals of a black flower curling on her scalp. Her body was slight but sturdy, and she soaped herself roughly. Her wet pubic hair looked silky in the moonlight.

He watched, entranced and hard, as the girl rapped on the back window of the cabin.

"Margo," she called urgently, "I'm ready."

Margo came around the corner of the cabin, dragging the garden hose provided by the owner for their bathing.

"Hurry. I'm freezing," the girl said.

"Here goes," Margo said, and she sprayed the girl all over with the cold water, rinsing her clean. A truck gunned by on the dirt road, headlights flashing, and Rein had the urge to protect the naked girl from the harsh light.

"I can see my breath," she said, huddling in a bulky robe and darting around the corner with Margo close behind. Her words came to him clear and true like bird sounds in the cold night.

He didn't sleep well after that, aching for the girl. The image of her bending over, soaping her thighs, stayed with him, returning over and over unbidden like a hologram in the moonlit tent.

"Rein? That you, boy?"

Rein looked down from the top step of his aluminum ladder, and through the leafy branches saw his father's face, brown as a walnut.

"How'd you know where to find me?"

"Margo wrote Diane."

Rein hung his canvas picking bag over a branch and climbed down the ladder. He and his father hugged each other, as they always had after long absences.

"How the hell are you?" his father said. And then, without waiting for an answer, he held one arm toward a woman who had been standing around the other side of the tree. She came toward them.

"This is my new lady, Rein." His father took the woman's hand. "Jocelyn. We're on our way back to Mendocino."

"Hello, Rein," she said, and she was shy, holding his father's hand as though it would keep her from floating away.

"Hi," Rein said, hands in his jeans pockets. He wished he had seen them coming from a distance, to look them over, to prepare space for their existence in his mind. She was pretty, with straight blonde hair and green eyes, and young, maybe twenty-four. "Would you like some lemonade?"

"Sure," his father said, relieved, and they sank into the deep grasses and wild asparagus gone to seed in a smear of sunlight.

Rein poured lemonade into the thermos cap and offered it to Jocelyn. "Sorry I only have one cup."

"That's okay," she said, smiling. "We don't have anything contagious."

"How's the picking?" his father said.

"Not bad."

"Know what you're doing after?"

Rein shrugged. "Go back to the farm, I guess."

"We're building a restaurant," his father said.

"Natural foods," Jocelyn said. "You're welcome to come and work with us if you like."

They had talked it over.

"We'd like to have you," his father said.

Rein didn't say anything for a full minute. They each took a swig of lemonade. Finally he answered, "I might just do that." He knew he wouldn't. He didn't know exactly why, but he knew he wouldn't. "I'll think about it."

A tractor chugged down the row, noisy and smelly with exhaust fumes.

"I better get back to work," Rein said, standing.

His father stood up and gave Jocelyn his hand as she rose. She spanked her bottom with both hands, as though she'd gotten dirty.

"Come and see us, Rein," she said. "Anytime."

"Here's our address and phone number," his father said, handing him a green business card.

The tractor lumbered around them. His father shook his hand and said, "Take care. Keep in touch."

"You too," Rein said.

He watched them walk away, ducking branches as they went. His father had reverted to a former style, with neater clothes and shorter hair. *What goes around comes around*, Margo said. Now he understood the expression and he wondered if people aren't trapped forever in themselves, stamped to be a certain way no matter how much they want to change. His father had been a fervent back-to-the-lander, in denim and manure-caked boots. The business card was the color of green apples. It read, *Bean Sprout Cafe and Pickin' Parlor. Eric and Jocelyn, Proprietors.*

"I thought I saw your dad's station wagon today," Margo said. She began talking even before she reached his camp. He was sitting outside against a rock, reading in the day's last light.

He placed a finger in the book to save his place. "You did. He was passing through."

"To where?" She sat down on a flat black stone and set a juice jar of tea between them.

"Mendocino." Rein drew a long swallow from the juice jar.

"Did he see Diane?"

"Margo, you already know the answers to these questions."

"I've got to get back to Amber. She's playing with the girl next door. Would you have dinner with us?"

"What're you having?" Rein said, grinning.

"Look. I'd like some company. There's this guy—Hemp. He's been after me sort of. If he comes around and you're there, he'll back off."

"Can I borrow your truck after?"

"Help me make the salad."

"Deal," he said, and he laughed and was surprised at the sound, he heard it so seldom these days.

After dinner Margo said, "I think I pulled a muscle today. Would you give it a rub?"

"Okay," Rein said. He piled the dirty dishes in the blue-enameled canner Margo used as a wash pan. Amber was asleep on an air mattress, snuggled in a sleeping bag printed with red and green cowboy scenes. It was windy and dark outside. From the next cabin they could hear the bluff and laughter of a card game. A television was on somewhere.

Margo sat in a faded canvas lawn chair, one hand on the muscle to the right of her blue tattoo. The yellow light of a sand candle wavered in the room. Rein used his thumbs as pressure points—a therapy his mother had taught him—and Margo squealed in pain.

"Too much?" he said.

"No, don't stop. If it hurts, it's good."

"Margo?"

"Yeah?"

"Who was that girl here the other night?"

"What girl?"

"The one who took the bath out back."

"Harder, Rein. She's from Appleland Orchard. Her name is Max."

He stopped working her muscle and pulled the light string. A glare flooded the room. "What kind of name is that for a girl?"

"Hey, I hate that light," Margo said.

He pulled the string again and the room was a cave of shadow. Margo stood up and did something she had never done before. She put her arms around his waist, slipped them surely around him and leaned toward him so that her crazy hair tickled his chin and cheek. She was short. He could distinctly feet one of her breasts against his ribcage.

"Margo, I have to go."

"If you gotta go, you gotta go," she said. She sat down in the lawn chair. "The keys are in the truck."

At the tavern he ordered a beer and no one asked for his identification. He sat at the bar and watched himself in the mirror and read the signs: *Sunday Masses, Immaculate Conception Chapel, 7:30 and 9 A.M.* and *All Deadly Weapons Forbidden.* The bartender kept an old potato chip can behind the bar and the men checked their knives as they came in. Longhairs shot pool, while their women watched and gossiped and drank at the tiny Formica tables lining the walls. There was a booth of Indians, seven crammed into the wooden seats that reminded Rein of church pews. The jukebox blared songs like "Ramblin' Man" and "Back on the Road Again."

Rein let the beer flow through him, ordered another quickly, and tried not to think about his father's hand on his new lady. It bothered him.

"Hey, Buddy, the next one's on me." It was an old fruit tramp who lived in one of the Red Cheek cabins. His face was misshapen and red, with rheumy blue eyes, a map of all the taverns he had rested in. He wore a shirt with pearl buttons and a string tie. His leathery neck was cross-hatched with deep lines, his hands knobby and scratched and nicotine-stained. When he talked his teeth protruded from his mouth, yellow as a horse's.

"Sure enough," Rein said.

The fruit tramp sat down on the next stool and raised his hand to the bartender. "You have a good day?" he said, his voice cracking like a trunk lid unopened for years.

"Nine bins," Rein said.

"I got ten." The old man cackled and the cackle turned into a ragged cough as he slapped his thigh. A cloud of dust erupted from his jeans. Then he hunched toward Rein in a confidential way. The can of snoose in his chest pocket bumped against the wooden bar. "I got ten bins and now I need to find myself a gal. To make my day complete. Know where a man can find a gal?"

"Sure don't," Rein said.

The bartender set two beers in front of them. While the old man paid, Rein watched as Max swaggered in with another woman. They sat in the last empty booth, leaning across the table toward one another, lost in their conversation. Rein swung around on his stool, glass in hand, and pretended to watch the pool game.

"Had myself a woman once," the old man said. "We was married in Montana during cherries. Stayed together a long time. A long time." He took the snoose from his pocket, opened the can, and secreted a pinch inside his lower lip.

"What happened?" Rein said. Now Max was leaning on the jukebox, making selections, and tapping one foot in time to the music.

"What happened was this. She ran off with a foreman at a peach orchard down in California. Said she wanted to settle down and live out her days in sunshine. Left me a note."

Rein felt his bones softening and the rock and roll penetrating his brain like a drug. He bought a pack of cigarettes and lit one.

Max was greeting a lanky man, bear-hugging him. "Hemp," she said. "I haven't seen you in ages." They sat down together and Hemp put his felt cowboy hat with the curled brim on Max's head and teased her. Rein didn't want to watch, but he watched, drinking the beer the old man had bought him.

"That foreman had a Buick. Had a dent in the rear fender, but the push-button windows still worked," the old man said.

Max's woman friend joined a pudgy man in overalls at the pool table. Hemp's hand was on Max's hip. She kissed him on the cheek. A Mexican, his khakis torn at one knee, walked back to his booth from the jukebox, singing along with Linda Ronstadt.

"He had a trailer, too. A pink trailer with them Jap'nese maples in a row out front. A woman wants a house to call her own." The fruit tramp shook his head.

"See you around, old timer," Rein said. "Thanks for the beer." He pocketed the cigarettes, bought a quart of beer to go, buttoned up his wool plaid shirt, and left.

In the truck, he shivered and his hands shook as he started the engine. He had a little trouble getting the key in the ignition. The inside light didn't work and he fumbled with the headlight switch. His skin felt raw with cold and drunkenness.

He drove slowly and carefully out of town and down the river highway. He turned right at the Red Cheek sign and the truck fishtailed for a moment in the gravel.

He parked the truck, put the cold keys in his pocket, and stood outside for half a minute watching the stars roll in the sky. The cabins looked like dead jack-o'-lanterns in the night. The owner's house was a stone fortress farther up the road.

He knocked gently on Margo's door. In the blue moonlight, through the curtainless window, he could see her in her narrow bunk.

"Who's there?" she said, with a flicker of fright in her voice.

"It's me. Rein. Can I come in?"

He watched her get out of her sleeping bag and run her hands through her hair. She didn't have any clothes on. She opened the door and spied the quart of beer he carried.

"Brought me a peace offering, did you?" she said, ushering him in with a frantic wave.

When he stepped in his glasses fogged. She shut the door and slid the bolt lock over. He put one arm around her, pulling her near. She relaxed and pressed closer, kissing his chin.

"You smell like winter coming on," she said.

1981

Friday Night at Silver Star

"I had my breasts enlarged last year," Elinor said, flipping down her rainbow tube top. Her hard, gleaming breasts popped out, like hood ornaments.

"They're nice," Jude said, politely.

Elinor sighed and flipped the tube top back up and huddled more snugly into her poncho. "They were good for a while. We had a lot of fun at first."

"Don't you now?" Jude said.

"Sometimes. I still like for Harvey to massage me with Abolene—that's the *preferred* lubricant of the cathouses in Nevada—did you know that?"

Jude shook her head.

"Harvey likes that. He talks to 'em, too." At this she grinned and her gold eye tooth gleamed in the moony darkness.

"That's kinda sweet."

"But it's like he's talking to *them*, not me," Elinor said. "He's talking to a couple of friggin' saline implants."

"How much did it cost?" Jude asked. She was finding herself more and more fascinated with how much things cost. Before she had any money, she couldn't have cared less.

"Twenty-five hundred. More or less." Elinor sighed again and took a short sip from the bottle of apricot brandy. "I'd of rather gone to Florida."

"Why Florida?"

"For the warm weather." She dragged out the word weather, exhaling, jutting her chin forward on the first syllable. "We could've laid on the white beaches at Port St. Joe and drank tequila sunrises. We could've visited my sister Pam in Little Rock on the way. Might have been just as much fun as new tits."

It was the first full moon in May and the cold light frosted the main lodge, the sheds, the gazebos housing the hot pools, the cars and trucks lining the muddy driveway. Jude could read some of the license plates—Foxy Lady, Warhead, Hyalite—from where she sat in the pickup, which was parked in its own personal ruts next to the sagging horse barn. She and Elinor had met a few hours ago, while poking through the potluck's remains, and now they were drinking apricot brandy, which was forbidden on Friday nights, and using up all Mason's gas keeping the heater running. On the tapedeck Bonnie Rait was singing "Ain't Nobody Home." Up the road, in the crossroads town of Silver Star, there were no lights. There was something sneaky and adolescent and wonderful about sitting in the cab of the truck, drinking and talking in the middle of the night.

"This is your first time, isn't it?" Jude asked.

"Here," Elinor said. "It's our first time here. But we've been at it for a couple of years."

"How'd you get started?"

"We always did like to experiment. One thing led to another."

They sat in silence for a few minutes, and Jude wondered if she would plunge on ahead into talking or let it go. She felt like talking, like all the words, the disclosures, the secrets were waiting to spill over the dam of her inhibitions, her censor.

"How'd you get started?" Elinor said, just as the tape ended with a soft click.

The only sounds were the dry hum of the heater and the creek's metallic burbling just the other side of the horse barn. A man in running shorts came out the side door and took a leak right on Jude's daffodil bed. He pulled his elastic waistband down, just like a little boy, and whistled some school song Jude could hardly remember. "When Johnny Comes Marching Home Again" it was. It came to her just as the whistling stopped. He shook himself and went back inside, letting the screen door slam like a shot.

"Out of desperation," Jude finally said. "Mason bought this old hot-springs hotel thinking we could make a go of it. We're neither one of us business types, but we'd always had this dream about living in the country. Which is not all it's cracked up to be, by the way. This is a back road, case you hadn't noticed. There's hardly enough traffic to warrant plowing it in the winter, let alone support a business like ours. So Mason got the idea of having these Friday night potlucks. He calls it our low-overhead night. Our customers even supply the food." Jude laughed, shortly, abruptly. She drank from the fifth and felt the easy burn of the brandy going down.

"But how'd you get started participating?"

"It was a turn-on."

"Simple," Elinor said, giggling.

"A powerful turn-on."

"It's a good setting. The hot pools. The homey hospitality. Harvey and I have been to three other party places," Elinor said, authoritatively, "and none compared to this. It's worth the drive."

"You could write our advertising."

"Word of mouth, Honey. I'll advertise word of mouth."

"It was all those naked bodies did it for me," Jude said.

"I know," Elinor said. "Harvey and I used to be into skin flicks, but now, after the real thing, they bore me to death."

"So that's how we got started. That was ten weeks ago." Jude calculated: thirty couples a night times fifty dollars a couple times ten weeks. Fifteen thousand dollars. Not bad for an ex-horticulture student and a ski bum. She fantasized the hand-tooled maroon suede boots she was planning to buy on her next shopping spree.

"So why aren't you in there tonight?" Elinor ventured.

"I'm not sure," Jude said. "Maybe I just want to see if Mason misses me. How about you?"

Elinor shrugged and lit a cigarette. "Harvey wanted me to get into a three-way with a woman I don't like."

"Which one?"

"The tiny blonde."

"Oh, her."

"You know the one I mean?"

"Julie. Of the Squeaky Cleans."

"That's the one."

"I don't like her, either."

"Why?"

"She's too cute."

"And stuck on herself."

"So you just said no?"

"I said 'Knock yourself out, Sweetheart, but I'll take a raincheck.'"

"It doesn't bother you? To think of him—"

"Oh, yeah, sure, it bothers me. On some level. but not enough to stop him." She puffed two quick puffs on her cigarette. "When we first started we were into one-room encounters."

"Why'd you change?"

"It was too limiting."

"Mason used to say, 'It doesn't matter where you get your appetite, so long as you eat at home.' Looks like those days are gone."

"Harvey'll bring her home, too. Mentally. Miss Squeaky-Clean, I mean."

"That's one thing that bothers me," Jude said. "The rest of the week, it's like all these other people are in bed with us. Ghosts."

"Fantasies. That's what you're selling. Fantasies."

"So it's never just the two of us anymore."

"That's why we don't do parties very often."

"What's your zodiac sign, Elinor?"

"Scorpio. But I don't believe in it."

"Me neither, really."

From up in the foothills, a coyote yodeled. Jude handed Elinor the bottle and switched on the low-watt overhead light. She rummaged through the box of cassette tapes and selected one: *John Denver's Greatest Hits.* She slid the tape into the slot and it was in the middle of a song, "Take Me Home, Country Roads."

"How long have you and Harvey been together?" Jude asked, nudging off the light switch and settling herself again behind the steering wheel.

"Thirteen years," Elinor said, spunkily. "Harvey and I met in Las Vegas. He was a cab driver—that was before his brother offered him the partnership in the steel shelving business. I was a blackjack dealer. One night when I was on my break Harvey was there playing the slots and the money just came *pouring* out and Harvey started hollering, This thing's got the silver shits, and I got the giggles and laughed with him. We laughed until our sides ached. He was stoned on hash. And I thought he was the funniest guy. I took him home that very night and that was that. We got two beautiful girls. Sharleen and Dawn Beverly. Twelve and nine."

"When did you move to Missoula?"

"When Harvey went into business with his brother."

"You can't be a blackjack dealer in Missoula."

"I'm a part-time travel agent."

"You get to travel?"

"Mostly I work the office. But sometimes I get to go on fam trips."

"Fam?"

"Familiarization. So we can know where we're sending our clients."

"Where have you been?"

"Lake Tahoe. Hawaii. Once Harvey went with me on a ski trip to Sundance."

"How was it?"

"It snowed the whole dang time we were there. We sat in the lounge drinking rusty nails. Harvey tried to pick up this other couple, but it was no go."

"I met Mason at a ski lodge."

Jude helped herself to one of Elinor's cigarettes. They were the extra-long skinny kind. Elinor handed Jude the smoldering butt of hers to light up with.

"Finished?" Jude said.

"Ditch it," Elinor said.

Jude rolled down the window and flicked the red-tipped butt into the mud.

"Once I knew this guy named Skip," Jude said. "Dumb name, huh? Anyway, I knew him when I was just a kid. Nineteen. In college. He liked to go cross-country skiing. Once I went on an overnight trip with him. Into the mountains. The stars were so bright. We slept in a tent and had to melt snow for drinking water. We had to melt snow for drinking water," Jude repeated, amazed.

"Was he good? In bed, I mean."

"He was real nice. He played the harmonica." Jude hadn't thought of Skip in years and she wondered where he was now. Was he still out in the pure mountains, naming the stars for some new lady?

"Sometimes I think I'd like to fall in love again," Elinor said.

"Yeah. I know."

Elinor leaned her head back against the seat and Jude said nothing more for a few minutes. She thought maybe Elinor was going to drift away—it was hard to tell in the semi-darkness. Someone turned off the front porch light and the kitchen light. The sky was paling just a bit and a few clouds streamed by over the mountains to the east. The wind must have been blowing hard up there. A snow plume rose and fell on the highest peak.

"Do you ever think of quitting?" Jude said.

"It'd be hard," Elinor said. "This is our lifestyle. I'd be afraid to quit."

"Afraid of what?"

"That it wouldn't be enough," Elinor said softly, her words as whispery as molted chicken feathers falling to the ground. "You know." She paused. "Just me and Harvey."

Jude had the impulse to reach out and hold Elinor's hand but she couldn't quite bring herself to make the move. Somehow comfort was called for, but Jude felt inadequate to the moment. She thought Elinor might be insulted. So she handed her the bottle instead, saying, "Good to the last drop. Go ahead. It's yours."

Elinor tilted back her curly head and drank the last slug of brandy.

"What time is it, Jude?"

"Three-forty."

"Guess I better go check on Harvey. I need some sleep, too. Before the drive back."

"Will you come back?"

"More than likely." Elinor picked up her cigarettes and lighter, opened the door, slipped out and slammed it. "It's muddy out here," she said, but her words were muffled through the cab window and it seemed to Jude she was speaking from under water.

Elinor picked her way around the puddles toward the side door of the lodge. Jude switched on the dash lights and checked the gas. There was still a quarter of a tank. She crouched on the passenger side, pulled the back of the seat forward, and hid the empty brandy bottle behind there, with the oil rags and the tow rope. She decided to drive over to Three Forks to the all-night Grizzly Truck Stop on I-90. Her friend Lolly would be waiting tables the graveyard shift and she could have a slice of lemon meringue pie for breakfast and Lolly's fresh coffee. She and Lolly liked to throw the I-Ching when business was slow. Maybe later in the day Mason would take her into Butte to buy those boots. But she had to pass the time till then. The sky was a cottony gray now, but on the drive home from Three Forks the sun would warm things. The sun would wrap its sweet arms around everything. Maybe the trucker from Kansas City, Bobby Lee, would be at the Grizzly. Lolly had introduced them two Saturdays ago. Bobby Lee had called her Judith, because it's so feminine, he said.

1984

As Luck
Would Have It

Sunbow never knew what hit her. Kelsey rode over from the cattle ranch bordering our land, rode over on a white horse named Shasta, and Sunbow was in love. We laughed about that later—a regular knight on a white horse, Kelsey.

His full name was Obadiah T Kelsey. There was no period after the T because it didn't stand for anything. It was just an initial he had given himself when he was partners with a hunting guide near Woodpecker. He let it be known he was just biding his hard times until he could return to the good life farther up north. Cattle ranching was too civilized and settled for him. Kelsey was six-foot-four, a strapping man, with a face as eroded as the draws during spring flood. His hair was white and thick, his eyes blue as glacial ice.

I was there, in the garden, when Kelsey rode over on a sunny day toward the first of June. Sunbow, Little Egypt, and I were planting corn in long crooked rows near the road. We were barefooted and bare-breasted.

"Scuse me, ladies," Kelsey said, touching his stained felt hat in an abbreviated gentlemanly gesture, "where can I find Virginia?"

"I'm Virginia," I said, wiping my hand on my skirt and reaching to shake his hand.

"My name's Kelsey," he said. His voice was sure and slow, a baritone, and made me think of malt syrup pouring into a batch of beer. "I'm working for Mr. Giles. He asked me to tell you we'll be runnin' cattle through here tomorrow." He did his best to keep his eyes riveted to our faces. His horse was a sleepy, placid fellow, his forelegs muddy. Shasta had been the hired man's horse as long as I could remember, fourteen years or so.

Little Egypt turned her back, picked up a rusty rake, and moved to another section of the garden. I threw on a chambray shirt.

"Tell Mr. Giles I said thank you for warning us," I said.

Without another word, Kelsey reined his horse around and rode away down the gravel road. Sunbow stood there, watching him until he was a white blur against the mud and pine trees. I could see the winter alone had been hard on her. She had a hungry look in her eyes.

The sun came out again. I planted half a row of corn and covered it before Sunbow returned to work. She bent over the row next to me, her braids and breasts swaying, and nudged the seed corn into the damp earth, following the shallow trough Little Egypt had made with the handle of the rake.

"Who was he?" she said.

"I'm heading home," Little Egypt hollered. Her baby, Jade, was due to wake up from her nap. She waved from the old squash bed. We waved back. Little Egypt was young, only twenty-seven, and suspicious of men. She was beautiful was why, with skin brown as bracken fern in autumn and eyes the color of early peas.

"New hired man, looks like," I said.

"I liked him," Sunbow said. She patted dirt over the row.

"I could tell," I said.

"What do you think he was thinking?"

"I think he thought he was in hog-heaven."

Sunbow was over Roger. He left for good summer before last. Out here, most folks find a mate for the winter, someone to share the chores, the wood chopping and water hauling, someone to warm the bed during the long nights. After Roger left, Sunbow was too crushed to make the effort. She spent the winter alone in her A-frame, sleeping by the fire and waking during the night to write down her dreams in a leather note-book. She grieved and her hair grew a little gray and she went to town only once to buy supplies for her jewelry-making.

And then, Kelsey and Sunbow began to keep company, two independent spirits sparking like matches on rock in the magic of the weather, the lengthening daylight. It wasn't long before Kelsey was spending the night. If Gabe Giles minded his hired man staying the night at our place, he kept it to him-self. He knows good help in these distant parts is hard to come by and harder to keep.

Sunbow began the habit of rising with him and cooking his breakfast over a firepit near her front porch. She didn't want to heat the house with the cookstove. I would see her, on my way to the cow barn, squatting in the yard dirt, her hair disheveled and eyes puffy with sleep, in a washed-out nightgown of an exotic Indian print, long worn thin enough to read a newspaper through, and she was lovely, feeding small strips of kindling to the fire. After she got it going a little, she walked around the yard, grasping her gown in one hand to form a bowl, and gathered pine cones and chips of wood and dry grasses, like some peasant woman. Sometimes if Kelsey was still in the house I stopped and talked with Sunbow while she made the coffee. Her pot was ash-black and she made the coffee strong. The light in her eyes was new and not new. I'd seen her fall in love before.

On my way home from milking I gave them a quart of milk. Kelsey loved the cream. They had an old overstuffed chair in the yard, a chair that looked as though it had sprouted there like a mushroom. Kelsey sat there eating while Sunbow perched on the arm of the chair. When he'd finished his eggs and hash browns and a second cup of coffee, then Kelsey braided Sunbow's hair. I saw all this from my kitchen window.

She sat between his knees like a child. He brushed her long black hair with a boar bristle brush he had given her. His hands were large and hammy against her scalp, but Kelsey braided hair as though he had done it all his life, gently and evenly. They made quite a picture, two lovers in the pearly curve of early sunlight, the fire smoking beside them.

Summer went on like this, days and days of the purest sunshine and cloudless skies. We harvested the early peas and rhubarb.

"I want to go on a fast," Sunbow told me. We were sitting on her porch, in the shade, cutting stalks of rhubarb into chunks for wine. My bare legs hung over the edge of the porch and a dampness from the crawl space under the house cooled me. Sunbow wore a ragged straw hat with a cheesecloth veil to keep the flies and mosquitoes away.

"When's this take place?" I said.

"I'd like to go into the woods tomorrow. Would you take me?"

Now it is Sunbow's ritual to have a friend take her to the woods once in the summer, confiscate her shoes, and leave her there to fast and weep and sit by the fire. For three days and nights.

"Why not let Kelsey ride you up there on Shasta?" I said.

"Kelsey won't do it," she said. "He thinks I'm crazy."

"Oh?"

"He's just never heard of such a thing," she said. Then she put down her paring knife and with both hands curled back the cheesecloth veil. "We're starting to spar," she said.

I jumped down from the porch and hoisted up another wicker basket of rhubarb. "That's inevitable," I said. "The fall from grace."

The next morning, early in the clinging fog, we trudged the dusty trail that switchbacked up the canyon wall and into a small wood of birch and larch and aspen. A flicker of a stream ran through there, but the water was not good, contaminated by cattle farther up. Sunbow had brought only two quarts of water to last the three days. I left her in a grassy clearing dimpled with the beds of deer. She was moving stones to build a fire ring, singing some chant as she worked, her voice low and clear.

Much to my surprise, Kelsey came to see me that evening. He looked a little down in the mouth and twisted the brim of his felt hat in his hands, an unlikely gesture for a man so big and imposing. I had to smile to myself to see him that way over Sunbow, but my heart went out to him.

"Why don't we sit here in the kitchen," I said. "I'll bring us up a bottle of tomato wine."

Kelsey settled himself in the rocker, his hat still in hand. He seemed out of place indoors. I sat at the table, now and then replenishing our glasses.

We talked about the weather at first, then Gabe Giles's cattle, their number and value, but I'm not one to waste good tomato wine on such topics, so I asked him to tell me about his life in the north country. As the wine was depleted, he warmed to his subject, stretched out his long legs and relaxed. He had a wealth of bear stories and gestures to go with them as grand as his voice. I could see why Sunbow loved him. We heard a cat's meow at the door and I let in Sugar-Tit, Sunbow's cat, a gray, long-haired beauty who recognized Kelsey at once and curled into his lap. He petted her as he talked.

It took three-quarters of the wine and a cushion of darkness for Kelsey to mention Sunbow. There had been a comfortable silence for a few minutes—comfortable for me, but now I see that he was mustering courage to ask me questions.

"Just where is this place in the woods?" he said. Sugar-Tit jumped from his lap like she knew a betrayal might be in the works. I got up and lit the lamp on the cedar chest.

"She asked me not to tell," I said. I fiddled with the wick, my back to Kelsey. He started rocking and the rocker crunched on the floorboards. Back at the table, I said, "Have some more, Kelsey. We might as well finish it off."

He held his tongue, though I could see that he was mad. I gave him credit for that. Like a lot of big men, he knew how to keep his temper.

"How long have you known her?" he asked.

"Ten years," I said. "Ten years this spring."

"How did you come to be on this land?"

"It's mine," I said. "My father gave it to me."

"And the others?" Kelsey asked.

"Friends, just friends," I said.

Kelsey shook his head. His white hair seemed golden in the lamplight.

I decided to embellish just a bit. "Right now, of course, it's just the six of us on the land," I said. "Rachel lives in the tipi, Laremy doesn't come out of the woods often, and you've seen Crazy Heart around, haven't you? He lives in the dugout."

Kelsey nodded. "He's the one with the steam engine?"

"Right," I said. "And there's Little Egypt and Jade. Jade makes seven. But one summer we had fifty people here. That field below Little Egypt's place—the one that's gone to weeds—it was all planted in corn that year."

"We're so different," he said. It was as though he spoke to himself. I knew he meant himself and Sunbow, but in a large sense, he meant all of us. No getting around it, Kelsey had lived a different life.

He tipped his glass for the last time that night, picked up his hat, and made his good-byes, which were brief. He wasn't the kind of man to linger at the door for half an hour saying nothing. When he was gone I had a moment in bed to wonder what would happen, but sleep came fast and deep.

Two days later Sunbow returned. She looked a little peaked and I thought she had lost weight. Secretly, I thought that's why she did the fast each year—to keep her weight down. I had a barley-and-black-bean soup waiting for her and we had a good time that evening, talking in my kitchen over several pots of orange spice tea. She kept one ear cocked for the sound of Shasta's hooves or Kelsey's jeep. He didn't come, and finally around ten, she went back to her A-frame. I stood on the porch, watching the beam of her flashlight grow dim on the trail. This was the middle of July, but the wind was a cool wind. I spotted Cassiopeia in the northern sky.

I wasn't surprised that Kelsey didn't come right over. A man has his pride. I had the feeling he was mulling over the differences, whether he could stand them. We'd talked about it for months, so the next day Sunbow and I left for Hawk Island to visit friends. We left the animals and garden in the care of our neighbors.

We drove my car, a 1963 Volkswagen. We drove by sawmills and through orchard country, where they were picking cherries. The hills were browning already from the heat. All the while Sunbow and I reminisced about times gone by and she never mentioned Kelsey once.

Hawk Island is in the middle of a lake. Three women, Harmony, Lillian, and Sue-Sue, live there. They once lived in the canyon with us until Sue-Sue inherited the Island from her grandmother, who had built a fishing lodge there in the forties—just a run-down cedar shake house surrounded by ponderosa pines. The three of them had a fantasy about living together and two years ago they moved from the canyon. We manage to keep in touch.

It was early evening when we arrived at the dirt parking strip where the raft was moored. Our clothes stuck to us from the heat and the cool air off the lake was welcome relief. We locked the car and secured our packs, sleeping bags, and a box of groceries—treats like cream cheese and avocados—to the raft. Sue-Sue, the handy one, had built the raft herself. It was six feet long, made of stout pine logs, and there were two splintery wooden gray paddles. They use a canoe to go back and forth and leave the raft for unexpected guests.

The lake was smooth, the trees along the shore reflected in clear lines. We paddled kneeling and within twenty minutes we were in sight of the house and Lillian, waving frantically from the front door. We paddled next to the rickety dock and tied the raft.

Lillian's white mongrel dog came wagging up to us, his tail full of burrs. He had one bad eye, milky-blue, that rolled off to one side and gave him a maimed look. I never could see what she saw in him. But he was a good dog and never slobbered on me, so I could stand him. His name is Haiku.

I shouldered my pack and gathered a rolled sleeping bag in each arm. Lillian came down the path and tried to hug me, in spite of my load.

"You came to rescue me," she said. "The solitude is driving me crazy."

She hugged Sunbow, too. They had once been on the verge of becoming lovers and now it struck me that Sunbow wanted especially to see Lillian after being with Kelsey.

"Where is everyone?" Sunbow said.

"Picking cherries," Lillian said. She lifted the box of groceries. "They've been gone a week." Lillian is a teacher and it is her income which supports them primarily. Each morning all winter she goes to school in the nearby town. When summer comes, there is no orchard work for her. She stays home and keeps the chickens from scratching in the garden.

We followed her toward the house. Statuesque Leghorns strutted in the dirt near the split-rail fence. Lillian walked with a real swing to her stride, athletic in spite of a limpy ankle that had never quite healed. She had had a skiing accident years before. She was tall and tanned, wearing a ragged plaid smock over white painter's pants, cut off and rolled snug above her thighs. Summer was always good to Lillian.

The porch sprawled into the yard from all sides of the house, a welcoming. We set our loads down. It was a wide veranda, the floor boards worn smooth and gray. There were wooden chairs with bright, woven cushions and a chaise lounge with a yellow pillow in the shape of a sun like a child would draw, with floppy tubular rays. Plants hung in baskets from the ceiling.

"Just let me get us a drink," Lillian said. "We'll celebrate." She slammed through the screen door and Sunbow and I sat down. Over the door, someone had carved a motto: *Work, Love, Suffer.* From far away came the sound of a motor boat, probably from shore, anglers coming out for the evening catch.

"This is great," Sunbow said. "I needed this." She fanned herself with a magazine she had picked up from the floor.

It was not like Sunbow to be so still about Kelsey. Usually, when she was in love, she talked and talked, dissecting the experience, trying to understand, wanting to know all the possible angles. What could happen. What he might have meant. I tried to imagine Kelsey riding to Sunbow's house and discovering her absence. I felt a moment of empathy for him.

Lillian returned with three gin-and-tonics on a wicker tray. She bumped the screen door open with her hip. "Ice! We have ice now," she said. "Sue-Sue got her refrigerator working."

We relaxed into the cushions and the drinks. The chickens clucked around the porch and the dog sat there grinning like he was having a private joke on us all. A breeze whipped across the lake and cooled us. The mainland shore was just a curling green blur on the horizon.

"Now tell me what's new and exciting," Lillian said. I noticed a silvery streak in her short brown hair. She was thirty-seven. It always amazes me when I see that we are aging.

"I'm in love," Sunbow said. She and Lillian laughed together.

"He rides a white horse," I said.

"Wouldn't you know," Lillian said. "Now be serious. Tell me all about him."

There ensued a lengthy discussion of Kelsey. After a few minutes I slipped away for a walk.

The Island was a lush green place, not like the coastal islands, of course, but still more wet than our territory at the farm. A trail circumnavigated its perimeter, winding through the deep, razor-edged grasses, over gravel beaches, and within a grove of cottonwoods and pine. In the trees, pinemat covered the earth on either side of the path. Exposed weather-polished tree roots, like the bones of last season's deer, molded step-downs of packed dirt. I was on the Island but I could not be there completely. My mind always wandered back home, wondering about the animals, the garden. I sat down on a flat rock on the southern shore. A cormorant landed on a boulder out in the lake. Ground squirrels scurried among the rocks, inspecting me, waiting to see if I would leave any crumbs.

I sat there for a long time. I thought of Crazy Heart, the way it is with us. He is my neighbor and brother more than my husband. He cares for the animals when I'm gone. I share venison with him, he gives me a grouse now and then. We go for days on end without seeing one another, even though he lives in the dugout just across the road and down the lane a ways. Yet we lean on one another, on the presence of an old friend.

"No thinking," Sunbow said, startling me. She handed me a sweater.

"You should talk," I said. The light was growing golden, a summer dusk.

"Lilly's making a salad. We put the wine in the fridge to chill."

I put on the sweater and there were three sunflower seeds in one pocket. I left them there for the ground squirrels. We started walking, Sunbow in front since the path was wide enough for only one.

"Doesn't it surprise you that we're all getting older?" I said.

"Sort of," Sunbow said over her shoulder. "I think of us as young still."

"The gray hair and the personalities don't go together," I said.

"I'm old enough to be a grandmother," she said.

"A young grandmother."

We walked for awhile without talking until we came to a clearing of vetch and thistle where someone had piled clean new lumber.

"What's this?" I said.

"You won't believe it," Sunbow said. "Lilly has a friend, a man. He's building a little house here."

"A lover?" I said.

"What else?" Sunbow said. "She says this is it."

"Everybody's settling down."

"About time," she said. We kept walking, around the lumber and the dirt heaps.

Haiku barked a token bark as we approached the house. The windows were soft yellow squares of kerosene lamplight. Foxglove glowed along the side of the house.

On the porch, before we went in, I said, "Do you miss Kelsey?" There was a flash of heat lightning in the western sky.

"I miss him. Yeah," she said. "Do you think we have a chance?"

"I really don't know," I said. And we went inside for supper.

We stayed one more night. Though it was plain to see the attraction between Sunbow and Lillian, I don't think they did more than hold one another in a sisterly way. From their talk, it seemed they were each too much in love with the men to be in love with one another. I thought this was good. Sunbow didn't need to complicate her life.

We drove back to the farm, eager to can the cherries we picked in the orchards on the way home. We sped down the canyon, leaving a wake of dust, and who did we see but Kelsey, first thing, riding Shasta with Jade in the saddle with him. She was laughing and having a good time and Kelsey looked like he was, too.

We stopped the green Volkswagen beside him. He was on Sunbow's side.

"Hello, Kelsey," Sunbow said.

"Hello, Sunbow," he said. They were so formal, but they were glad to see one another, that was obvious—they were straining at the bit. They forgot me entirely.

"Stop by and visit on your way home," Sunbow said, by way of invitation.

"I might do that," Kelsey said.

They forgave one another. He spent the night. And after that it seemed things might work out between them. They returned to their habits, the early morning breakfast, Kelsey braiding her hair.

In looking back, I mark our trip to Hawk Island as the middle of summer. After that, time flew. The garden came in and it was nothing but work, day into night. We had so many green beans we sold them at the co-op in the city. The zucchini were thick and we had a zucchini war one evening, slap-happy with the exhaustion of harvesting.

Our third cutting of alfalfa was a good one and we were blessed with sunshine as it lay in windrows. We waited until evening to pitch the hay onto the flatbed and take it to the barn.

Sunbow came by for me on her way to the alfalfa field. She wore a faded pair of gym shorts and work boots with gray socks stretched out around the ankles. Her braids were pinned against her head, out of the way. The sun crested the canyon wall as we walked to the field, our pitchforks over our shoulders. The heat had been heavy during the day. We were still warm enough to work without our shirts.

This was our practice: Little Egypt, with Jade beside her strapped into a car seat, drove Crazy Heart's truck, an old brown Dodge, with the flatbed hitched to the back bumper. One of us—this time is was Laremy who came out of the woods for the occasion—stood on the flatbed, accepting the forkloads of alfalfa the rest of us sent his way. Laremy liked the work and he received his share of milk for it.

The land grew tawny with evening as Crazy Heart, Sunbow, Rachel, and I loaded the flatbed, walking around and around the field. It was a big job for so few people and I remembered a time when the work went faster, when life was richer with personalities.

We worked for hours until the dark lay over us like a blue scarf. At the barn, someone brought a quart of home-brew. We filled the barn, beginning to shiver in our sweat, itching with the hay, and the smell of the hay, the barn, the milky odor, warmed my heart. This was home. I was feeling all these generous thoughts, right with the world, when Kelsey appeared on Shasta.

Sunbow sat on a chopping block, legs out straight, her shirt open to the waist and vibrant, the way some women look after working hard. I was rolling a cigarette and the others were quiet, just settling into the good feeling after a job well done.

"You're going to catch your death of cold out here without your clothes," Kelsey said. His voice was hard as nails. It was plain what he meant.

Shasta looked blue in the darkness, like the snowberries dripping in the brush along the barbed-wire fence. He stomped his front hooves a bit and seemed tense, as tense as the rest of us. I removed a flake of tobacco from my tongue and then lit the cigarette, glad for something to do.

"It's summertime, Kelsey," Sunbow said. Her voice was a whisper, but it seemed she was shouting inside. Even as she spoke she pulled the work shirt together in front. I hated to see her feel ashamed.

"Come on," Kelsey said. "I'll ride you home."

"No thanks," Sunbow said.

"Have it your way," he said, and he reined Shasta around and went away.

"Damn right," Sunbow snapped. But Kelsey didn't hear her. She didn't intend for him to. Their disagreement cast a pall on our gathering and folks began to drift away after a few minutes until only Sunbow and I were left.

"Can I roll one?" she said.

I passed her the cloth bag and the rolling papers.

"What do you think of our chances now?" she said, squinting, sprinkling tobacco into the crease of the rolling paper.

"That depends on how much you're willing to change," I said. And we sat there smoking in the dark for awhile before we went our separate ways. I thought it was over.

Kelsey didn't come around and Sunbow began making plans to go apple-picking. Her birthday came and went near the end of September and we hardly mentioned it.

She went picking in October. In the orchards, she came down with a sickness. I was busy getting my wood in for the winter, spending each day alone with the saw and ax, seeking out dead fir to haul home. I hadn't even checked the mail for a few days. I didn't know she was sick until Kelsey brought her home in his jeep, two weeks to the day after she had left. She had called Gabe Giles and asked for Kelsey and said she needed him and he went to her. This seemed a most positive event if you can call a bacterial infection from drinking water a positive event. There was hope for them yet.

He nursed her back to health. We had our first hard frost and still Kelsey and Sunbow could not make up their minds. One day they would be seen laughing and sawing wood together, each on one end of a misery whip, under the bare tamaracks, and the next day she would come over with a tale of woe and he would be leaving for Woodpecker, a hard way to be heading into winter.

"There are some things I'm willing to change," Sunbow said, "and others I'm not." We were churning apples through the cider press, near Sunbow's wood shed. The juice from the apple pulp trickled down our sleeves and we were a mess, our hands and cheeks chapped, but proud of the twenty quarts we had pressed so far.

"Like what?" I said.

"Like I'd learn to clean his birds. He thinks it's ridiculous that I've never learned to clean chickens and birds. Fish. I *can* clean fish," she said. I heard a chainsaw in the distance.

"What else?" I said.

"What else?" she said.

"What else are you willing to change?"

"Look at the geese," Sunbow said, pointing to the honking wedge above the southern rimrock. "I don't know if he really wants to go back north," she said. "My turn. You toss the apples." She took over for me at the wheel.

The next morning was overcast. About noon, Kelsey drove to my place in his jeep. He was dressed in a sheepskin coat, a hat that covered his ears, and mittens. His jeep was packed tight with duffel bags, saddle bags, and suitcases. It was hard for me to imagine him carrying a suitcase.

I asked him to lunch.

We drank some Earl Grey tea and waited for the leftovers—venison chili—to warm on the cookstove.

"I'm leaving, Virginia. I quit Gabe today," he said.

"Have a little honey in your tea," I said. "Where you headed?"

"Back to where I came from," he said. I didn't press him further for the details. I'd heard it all from her.

We had a cozy lunch and, as luck would have it, the snow began falling as we sat there afterwards. He polished off his milk, scraped his chair back, and wiped his mouth on the checkered napkin.

"I've got to be going," he said. "I'll stop and say good-bye to her, too."